Mia yelled. She moved out onto the ice towards the hole, striking at the shapes in the
churning water. A long thin hand reached like a
tentacle out of the water and grabbed her pole.
It was dead white, the skin wrinkled and sloughing off the wet bones. Mia pulled back, but it
was too strong. She was losing her balance.

The hole in the pond was getting wider; brown
patches appeared in the snow-covered ice and
sank away into open water. There were more
things trying to get out.

TALES BY MOONLIGHT

TALES BY MOONLIGHT

EDITED BY
JESSICA
AMANDA SALMONSON

TOR

A TOM DOHERTY ASSOCIATES BOOK

This is a work of fiction. All the characters and events portrayed
in this book are fictional, and any resemblance to real people
or incidents is purely coincidental.

A TOR Book

Published by Tom Doherty Associates
8-10 West 36 Street
New York, N.Y. 10018

Cover art by Mark E. Rogers

First TOR printing, January 1985

ISBN: 0-812-52552-3
CAN. ED.: 0-812-52553-1

Printed in the United States of America

DEDICATION
to
Dale C. Donaldson
who sits behind the moon

Contents

Foreword

by Jessica Amanda Salmonson

This anthology, more than most, exists as a labor of love. The publisher of the first limited edition, Bob Garcia, entered into the project hoping for the best of course; but he entered knowing that most publishers, small and large, have little use for anthologies in today's "bottom line dollar" way of thinking. My own time and efforts, with much assistance from Wendy Adrian Wees in story selection and editing, was given in full awareness that it could be my first of four anthologies *not* to help me pay the rent.

Stephen King and his agent, Kirby McCauley, graciously provided an introduction and assistance without regard for the fact that this project is on a different level than a New York or Hollywood million-dollar-deal, to which they are accustomed. The authors are here on a straight pro-rata share of royalty agreement, knowing that the royalties might be small and slow to arrive. Many of these contributors are new voices in the field. Others—like Jody Scott, Phyllis Ann Karr, and George Guthridge—are already well-established writers. They all had the same level of commitment to the *book* and not the dollar.

This is not to say everyone is in it for philanthropic reasons alone! A sillier notion could not be had. There's a possibility of Susan Cohen, my agent, pulling together a paperback deal, after the limited edition appears. In that event, everyone's gamble will pay off in royalties, for there'll be more readers than any collectors' edition can reach.

So: a little love, a little calculated risk. But, mostly I dare say love, since no one is going to be distraught if all we have is a gorgeous book that collectors of horror fiction will be grateful to discover.

This is my first major involvement with the small press in some while. Commitments for anthologies, novels, and short stories for DAW, Ace, Tor, and Berkley have freed me from my previous secretarial position, but also forced me to be somewhat mercenary, since otherwise I must starve to death.

Yet, I started out as a small press publisher, writer, editor, and I hope always to keep some connection with this arena. There are professionally thought-out reasons for this, as well as emotional appeal. I have definite ideas about the role of the small press in the future of publishing. I have twice seen small press items hit the New York or national best seller lists, and on numerous occasions seen them hit more specialized best seller lists. This is indicative of something.

Already publishers like Donald Grant, Phantasia, and Underwood/Miller are beginning to fill a void left by the conglomerate-publishers who take fewer and fewer chances peddling well-made books or books with artier intentions. Major publishers nowadays are more likely to pump out badly glued paperbacks that'll sell a million copies overnight then vanish forever. There is so little pride in book quality inside New York that most writers, editors, and publishers believe the hardback will soon be a thing of memory alone. A few gleeful doomsayers even look to the day when a computer in your home will give you a read-out or video image of the new books which exist nowhere but in memory banks and micro-chips.

My own feeling on the subject is that people will always

love the feel and texture of a *book*, the better made the better the feeling. There'll always be a number of readers experiencing something between nirvana and orgasm, just by sitting back comfortably and turning a crisp page.

Now it may be that the vast majority of the population will soon become totally vegetated before their televisions and video screens. And the conglomerate publishers will cater to this trend. But there'll be thousands of us left over, outcasts in a kitsch society, who will continue to seek out and find real books. If major publishing trends don't make a quick, severe turn-around, then the day will come when small press publishers will have the market for quality editions completely to themselves. And it will be profitable, for I'm convinced there'll be no lack of readership. It won't be an audience to support Gulf-Western, but it'll sure as hell take care of the people who are close to the creation of the books themselves, which is how it should be.

Book publishing in America and Great Britain has been, historically, somewhat philanthropic. It is only recently that bottom-line dollar has ruled everything. The future of book publishing will again be philanthropic, as nasty conglomerates move further and further from what book lovers need and want to feel, smell, and read. The quality small press is going to play the key role in this future. It's already starting. I intend to stick around to be part of it, not to get so sucked up into conglomerate-land that I lose sight of where innovation and excellence might occur.

That particular horror story we've all seen—about the future where there is only one reader left, or one writer—is not a very likely premise. There'll always be Robert Garcias and Donald Grants. And there'll always be writers, editors and readers to support the sincere adventure.

Jessica Amanda Salmonson
May 1982

Introduction

by Stephen King

It gets harder each year—not just publishing short stories, but getting anyone to notice them, anyone at all.

But everyone pisses and moans about everything these days, right? Right. Everybody's got a bitch, right? Right. Interest rates are high; the government goes right on spending billions of tax dollars to create new and better warheads while folks in Bedford-Stuyvesant, West Virginia, and East Los Angeles starve to death; it's hard to find work.

So you may be having a hard time finding any sympathy in your heart for the depressed short story market. Well, look: I'm going to say something cheerful in a few minutes, so give me a chance to get this other thing off my chest first.

It isn't just the short story, y'see; in the twentieth century we have seen the entire ocean of popular literature withdrawing in a long and melancholy roar (to paraphrase Matthew Arnold, who was no bundle of cheer himself). Those of you in your sixties can remember when poetry was not the sole property of college eggheads and groaning, discontented high school students; they can remember when it was read on front porches in the evening, sometimes aloud, not because it was an assignment, but because it was fun.

Imagine *that*, friends and neighbors! Reading *Miniver Cheevy* or *The Hollow Men* just for fun! Imagine *that!*

Those of you in your forties can remember the golden age of the pulps, when any given month brought forth a great buffet of fiction to the corner newsstand; you could sit down to a meal for a dime, and for a dollar you could indulge in wild gluttony. Name your genre, and you could choose among at least a dozen magazines, with an average of ten stories per magazine—love stories, horror stories, science fiction, mystery, western, war, more.

Those of you in your thirties may not remember the pulps very well, but you'll probably remember the "slicks"—magazines like *The Saturday Evening Post, Liberty*, and *American Mercury*—that made fiction a routine staple.

Gone, son. Gone my dear daughter. Almost all of them. Gone.

And now it is the novel that is under siege—bestseller lists are populated by junky *roman a clefs* intended for readers whose imaginations are so deprived that they are incapable of following a story they have not already read in *The National Enquirer*. More ominous still is the invasion of the non-books which now choke the paperback racks: books about Rubik's Cube, Rubik's Snake, Garfield the cat, and how to dress in some asshole three piece suit or a pair of designer jeans so you can get a better job or find somebody in a singles bar who'll take you home for the night. Publishers call them "non-books." They don't like them, but they pay the rent.

That sound you hear, that long and melancholy roar, is the sea of literature ebbing from the coastline of popular consciousness. Put your feet up on the porch rail and watch Hollywood Squares on the battery-powered Sony, right? Right. What's books? Something you read in college for a grade, right? Right.

So where's the something cheerful I promised you?

You're holding it, sir or madam. You're holding it in your hand. It is a book (just in case you haven't checked the spine) called TALES BY MOONLIGHT, edited by Jessica Amanda Salmonson. And what should cheer you up is the fact that it exists at all.

Necessity is the mother of invention, we're told (I think Frank Zappa said that), and both writers and editors find a way to get the word out. The audience may shrink steadily and remorselessly from generation to generation, the numbers of the marching morons may increase (at a writing seminar recently, I was trying to ascertain how much grounding my would-be writers had in classical literature—a necessity, I think, if you want to write even break-even stories—one bozo nodded sagely when I mentioned Samuel Pepys and volunteered the information that Pepys had been on the Today program the week before), but writers continue to find that audience, and editors such as the priceless Ms. Salmonson continue to create pipelines by which the audience may be reached.

One of the ways is by means of original anthologies such as this one. In the forties, the fifties, and sixties—even in the early seventies—such anthologies were few and far between, because of the generally accessible magazine market. But as the markets closed up, one by one, there have been more and more anthologies of short stories which have never been published before—in a sense, they are like one-issue magazines (and Jessica Salmonson would probably agree, the rates available are woefully similar . . . which is why some of the contributors herein represented are probably spending far too much time doing numbfuck jobs when God made them to write wonderful stories). Charles Grant has done several anthologies of this type (the SHADOWS series comes highly recommended); Kirby McCauley has edited two (FRIGHTS and DARK FORCES), Frank Coffey has done one.

Young poets publish chapbooks. There's an informal mystery writer's workshop around Boston. Fans publish magazines which spring up, flourish, die . . . and magically reseed the ground. These magazines are usually full of shit, but shit's fine fertilizer. There are ways of surviving, if you can dig it.

TALES BY MOONLIGHT is a particularly exciting case in point, because, unlike most of the books cited above, all of the contributors to MOONLIGHT are relative unknowns outside their own fan-writer circles (Steve Rasnic Tem is one exception). Sitting down with the manuscript was like sitting down to inventory the contents of a large suitcase purchased at a sealed-trunk auction.

How are the stories? Well, I thought several of them were most exquisitely awful—I'll not embarrass either you, me, or the writers of these tales by singling them out. If you have read widely in the field of fantasy and horror, you will spot the clunkers almost immediately. If you have not, you may like them just fine (but your liking for these poorly conceived and poorly constructed things will not speak well for your sophistication—there is the story of the anthropologist who gave a New Guinea native a battery-powered cassette recorder; the native listened to the music of the Boston Philharmonic briefly and with no interest and then used the recorder to mash yams).

But the bad stories lend their own undeniable authenticity to the volume—like the abysmal performance of the rock-blues group Canned Heat at Woodstock, they form a rough-textured background which may be unlovely but which is nonetheless absolutely real and completely felt. And the bad stories are more than outweighed by the good ones . . . and the best of them are better than anything I or any of my so-called "heavyweight contemporaries" have done in a long time. Oh, maybe not in terms of style, and certainly not in terms of polish, but the energy displayed in this book approaches megaton levels.

There is, for instance, the perfectly realized horror of

Eileen Gunn's *Spring Conditions*, with its atmospheric depiction of winter's death lending an eerie credence to the appearance of a number of dead bodies in a pond where the ice has begun to decay (dead bodies and perhaps something else, infinitely worse).

There is Steve Rasnic Tem's terrible fable of a child parting company with reality . . . or perhaps destroying the world itself with the untutored power of his imagination; no one has written so well of the inward spirit of the unwanted child since Shirley Jackson.

If there was any story I approached with undisguised dread, it was *A Wine of Heart's Desire*, by Ron Nance. Sword and sorcery, as delicate a hybrid in its own way as the bonsai tree, has become the home and haven of the worst publishing writers in the fantasy genre, and perhaps in the whole country. The worst of them make Rosemary Rogers look like Shakespeare and Danielle Steele like Francis Bacon. Their untutored lungings besmirch the memory of the great Robert Howard, who was a terrible writer but an *imaginer* of fantastic power, and becloud the achievements of Fritz Leiber, whose Fafhrd/Grey Mouser stories are the sword and sorcery subgenre's finest achievement.

So there I am, looking at the title page of a novella which runs 12,000 words, about two fellows (Edwin the thief and Motley the jester) who sound suspiciously like Fafhrd and the Mouser. *This is going to be terrible*, I think. *This baby is gonna suck like a vacuum cleaner*.

But when you open a locked trunk, you can't tell *anything* by appearances. Nance's story is a perfect delight, working on many levels: as a straight sword and sorcery tale, as a gentle satire of the subgenre, as fairy tale, as morality tale. Nance's good nature and sense of humor make John Jakes' Brak stories look almost dour by comparison. And there is one priceless moment . . . well it wouldn't be fair to tell you, but watch for the guy that bounces.

So here's this guy Nance, bucketing straight out of left field (and if Ardmore, Oklahoma isn't left field, where the hell *is* it?). Here's a guy named John D. Berry who writes clear, elegant prose . . . and then blasts you with one of the strangest deaths in the history of time travel. There's a good were-beast story by N.K. Hoffman just when you thought there were no teeth (heh-heh) left in such elderly creatures; there's a universe inside an egg, courtesy Richard Lee-Fulgham; there's a jazzman who plays the greatest drum solo of all time in Gordon Linzner's *Jaborandi Jazz*, a story that reads like a cross between Fredrick Brown and Henry S. Whitehead.

You getting the idea? The book works; in places, such a Nance's *A Wine of Heart's Desire*, or Janet Fox's *Witches*, with its gorgeous, smoothly sculpted prose, it damn near sings.

The greatest thing about a book such as this, I think, is simply that the explosion can come from anywhere, at any time. The names are not familiar; there's nothing to expect. I found myself thinking repeatedly of the punk-rock groups. Like those groups, the writers assembled in TALES BY MOONLIGHT have got little to lose and nothing to prove. They don't want to put you on Cloud 9; they just want to put a hole in yer head.

In several cases, they damn near succeed—it's been a long, long time since I've read a story as nakedly frightening as *The Inhabitant of the Pond*, by Linda Thornton. Ms. Thornton is not yet completely in control of her prose voice, and at times the note warbles. There are lapses into awkwardness, but these never embarrass, because the tale rivets us, and we sense (at least I did) a voice which is still growing in power, a strong and confident talent in the refining.

I don't want to tell you the story—that is for Ms. Thornton—but I will tell you that there is a small boy in it, and a very large bug, and I'll tell you that when this small boy turns calmly to his older sister and says calmly, "He's going to rip father now. Soon as he finds him", you're going to know that the genre is alive and well. Publishers may cut their lists or just go under (as Fawcett/Gold Medal did during the writing of this introduction), that tide will continue to go out, but the genre, I think, will survive where it has always survived best: in the bush, and along the jungle networks—and some of those jungles are urban in character.

This is not to patronize. I can hear some of the folks saying, "Sounds good, Steve. Tell us about the joys of the small presses and limited run editions while you drive around in your Mercedes." But everything good in this outlaw genre comes from the jungle, and no one understood better than our parents when they ripped the horror comics and the screaming paperbacks by A. Merritt and Richard Matheson and H.P. Lovecraft out of our hands. They didn't want us in the jungle, and serious critics acknowledge that jungle only reluctantly, but it is there, in all its ripe-rotten mystery. These stories explore that jungle, and some of these writers will certainly come out of it rich ("There are diamonds in there! Diamonds!" as one of the characters in KING SOLOMON'S MINES whispers in a voice hoarse with wonder).

One only hopes they will bring some of the jungle with them.

This is a flawed, uneven book, but it compensates with wonder; I hope we will see a sequel soon.

Stephen King

Bangor, Maine
1982

The Nocturnal Visitor

Dale C. Donaldson

Dale C. Donaldson remains, years after his death from cancer, a culture hero to writers of the macabre. He published a low-budget meathook horror magazine called MOONBROTH *which specialized in giving new and often not-very-subtle writers their first shot at publication. My own first sale appeared in a 1973 issue of* MOONBROTH. *As was often Dale's wont, he added a trite, ghoulish ending to my story, without my permission, and this prompted me to withdraw about ten more yarns he'd stockpiled for future issues! Despite our clash on that score, there was never anger between us. We were good friends and his death was a loss which affected me deeply.*

He was a comical occultist, a libertine in his unique approach, and very much into confusing the gullible. He purported to be more than a century old (if he was over fifty when I met him, he was young for the age); he claimed to remember numerous past lives. He admitted to having run a scam before tackling MOONBROTH, *selling very imaginative outlines of other people's past lives. A young ex-drug addict who Dale took under his wing while working at Goodwill Industries (a nice fellow, too, who stole a gold watch and gave it to me as a present) was convinced Dale was a supernatural being. His motivation seemed to be one of making his own life, and the lives of those around him, sort of fun.*

MOONBROTH *was his obsession in the early 70s. He felt he was helping the great writers of the next decade. Unfortunately, a list of his contributors does not look like the Horror Fiction's Who's Who for the 80s. Yet a few of his contributors did go on to bigger things—which really isn't the point. The point is that he loved these writers, and many of them came to look to Dale as a kind of guru or father. Ultimately he sacrificed his own writing in order to nurture others. His short story* Pia *is considered by some to be a classic werewolf yarn; it first appeared in the lamented* COVEN 13 *pulp and has been reprinted in a British anthology of werewolf stories. He published numerous other yarns under pseudonyms which may be impossible ever to trace back to him. He never did get down to pursuing his writing in a professional manner.*

To my knowledge, Nocturnal Visitor *is Dale's last story, written originally for* FANTASY & TERROR, *which saw its last issue before it saw publication of Dale's novelet. The story is proof of the great talent which was put aside to help others—a story of such quality and effectiveness that it merits the opening slot of* TALES BY MOONLIGHT.

It's my hope that the spirit of Dale C. Donaldson's life is reflected in this anthology; for it is to his memory the entire book is dedicated.

Barbs and I found the farm last year, just after I had been discharged from the Service. Although neither of us is a farmer at heart, we had always wanted a place out of the city so that we could grub in the dirt and make things grow. We each had our respective professions; Barbs, a schoolteacher in the nearby town of Sandy, and I, a fraternal salesman of insurance. Home Offices in Portland. We had the country living in our blood, but little expected the horror that would come out of it.

The three and one-half acres, with starter house and

open barn, was sixteen miles straight out Stark Street from Portland's city center. Two acres were wooded, and the third partially cleared. A bubbling stream wound its way across the property, and a forty-foot steel pole gathered our electric wires from the highway. The greatest drawback was the lack of plumbing. We walked fifty feet to the outside rest room, and drew our water from an ancient, mouldering well. Our nearest neighbors, the Barrettsons, were half a mile away.

We had taken the farm in early April, and for three months we spent an idyllic second honeymoon. Barbs would drive with me to the city limits of Portland, we'd have breakfast at a special little restaurant, and then I would take the bus on into town while she drove back to her school. In the evenings she'd meet me at the end of the bus line, the back seat of the car laden with groceries. It was a fifteen-minute drive to our farm, and after a solid, home-cooked meal, we would both don our grubbing clothes and go out to take care of the crops.

As the weeks passed, we became lonely. We accumulated two mongrel dogs, named them Sam and Paul after two of our friends, and when an auction presented the opportunity to buy a horse at a ridiculously low figure, we found ourselves the owners of a stable.

We still had the problem of the outhouse. In June, I succeeded in getting our property attached to the city sewer system, and in July, our first water was piped to the house. This was when the terror began.

The well had been dug long before the place was cleared. Why, and for whom, was anyone's guess. It was all of forty years old, and when constructed must have been far out in the country, away from both farm and road. At the time of its digging, Portland couldn't have been more than a five-church town with only an outpost on the east side of the river. Barbs and I had often puzzled over the well's ancient purpose.

The iron pump was rusted to a point of uselessness, and the well boards were decayed and sagging. With the advent of running water into our house, I thought it best to do something about covering the well. It would be a potential source of danger should we have "little farmers" in the future.

On a warm, lazy Saturday evening I tackled the well with hammer and crowbar. The rotted, dry wood came up easily, and I threw huge chunks of the stuff in a pile for later burning. When I reached the bed of the wood flooring I found a cast iron sheet stretched across the mouth of the well, leaving only the necessary apertures for the pump. This made it evident that someone in the past had also feared falling into the hole, and had eliminated the danger.

Having no knowledge of how secure this well covering was, I picked up the crowbar and pried around the edges to test the strength of the plate. I found that it was bolted to the actual natural stone wall of the well. This piqued my curiosity, and I went to the house for a wrench. Returning, I grunted and swore at the rusty bolts until they gave way to my pull. Then I used the crowbar to slide the iron plate from the mouth of the well.

I lay flat on my belly, and peered into the silent depths. There was the usual dank, sour odor normally found, but to my nostrils also came an odd, meaty flavor, a freshness, and a rawness. My fingers scrabbled around for a pebble, and finding one, I dropped it into the blackness. I turned my head, waiting for the distant splash. Seconds passed, and I heard nothing. I raised myself to my knees, found a larger stone and dropped it into the well. Again there was no sound, even though I waited a full minute.

Puzzled, I rose to my feet. I picked up a five-pound rock and threw it in. No splash. Nothing.

I shrugged my shoulders in irritation. It was growing dark, and further experimentation would have to wait until morning. I left the tools where they were, and returned to the house.

"What did you find in the well?" asked Barbs, folding back the covers of our bed. "A bogey?"

I growled. I considered telling her of the lack of the splash, but decided against it, knowing too well her schoolmarmish sarcasm. After all, the water had to come from somewhere, we'd been pulling it up with the pump for the last three months. I mumbled something about the falling darkness, and went into our sparkling new bathroom.

Minutes later I crawled into bed and found Barbs on the verge of sandland. "Lemme sleep in tomorrow morning, ummmmm?" she murmured, and was fast asleep. I tossed a little while, pondering the well situation, then dropped off myself.

I was abruptly awakened by the dogs, Sam and Paul. They were making an outlandish racket, yepping furiously over some unknown disturbance. I glanced at my luminous watch dial and found that it was four o'clock in the morning. I made a half-hearted attempt to crawl out of bed, giving up when the barking wore off into an occasional yap. I yawned, shook my head groggily, and went back to sleep.

I was up again at five-thirty. I washed my face and went outside to take care of the animals. The dogs seemed particularly happy to see me, and leaping and cavorting, interfered with my way to the stable.

Champ neighed lustily at my appearance. He lunged against the bars, ignoring the first fork full of feed. He stomped and whinnied, refusing to settle down until I had comforted him by several playful slaps at his muzzle and flanks.

Returning to the house to begin breakfast, I noticed Sam

worriedly nosing out the area near the well. Paul joined him, and they both circled and criss-crossed the grounds. Remembering the uproar in the night, I walked over to the well expecting to find signs of rabbit or deer. I had nothing to prepare me for what I saw.

Impressed in the soft loam and leading toward the well I found the bare footprints of a man. But what a man! The prints were nearly eighteen inches in length and over five inches wide. In addition to being oversize, the toe marks were extended about two inches, and ended in a deeper, sharp impression, reminiscent of a spur, or claw. From the depths of the marks I judged that the fellow must have weighed a good three hundred pounds.

The tracks led to the well and then away again. I approached the rim of the hole, ignoring the raised hackles of the dogs, and found that the visitor had scraped his feet on the edge of the iron plate. He had then proceeded in the direction of the house. Frowning, I followed his trail. I didn't like unidentified visitors, especially window-peekers.

The footprints led in the direction of the house for about twenty feet, then turned again to the well. I looked closer. The marks made a small circle. From the well, back to the well. There were no prints leading off the property. Just the one track, beginning and ending at the well opening.

This was ridiculous. It gave rise to the belief that the thing had come out of the well and then returned to subterranean chambers. Poof! Peering over my shoulder to be certain that Barbs was not watching from the window, I carefully scuffed out all signs of the footprints. No need to worry her. I would seal the well after breakfast.

I prepared a tasty meal of crisp bacon, fried eggs, buttered toast, and hot, steaming coffee. Carrying it to the bed, I gazed with affection at the sleeping form of my wife. Bright yellow tresses framed a piquant, oval face, and a smooth arm flung unconcernedly over my pillow exposed the firm, lovely lines of her bosom. Her lithe body was sleek and contented, and a warm, sweet woman-smell emanated from the bed clothing.

"Barbs." I touched her soft shoulder. "Breakfast is ready."

She smiled and rolled over. Her eyes expressed appreciation as I placed the tray on the bed. "Morning, Joe," she yawned. "Get the animals fed?" She stretched lazily, yawned again, sat up, and attacked the bacon.

"Yep." I watched the small white teeth crunch the crispness. She took a huge gulp of the coffee, and squirmed ecstatically. "Ummmmm. Good." She went after the toast and eggs.

"Barbs . . ." I began hesitantly, "I think we . . ." I broke off, shaking my head.

"Hummmm? You think what?" She licked her red lips and looked up at me.

"No. Nothing." I sat down beside her. "Finish your breakfast."

She raised her eyebrows quizzically, shrugged, and devoured the last of her bacon. I watched a few minutes as she finished the meal. She ate greedily but daintily, her full attention on her food. She had always attacked her food like an arithmetic problem, concentrating furiously until the job was done.

At last she regretfully pushed the tray aside, and lay back with a comfortable sigh. She put both hands above her head and stretched mightily, her body writhing in enjoyment of the movement.

"Barbs, what do we have planned for today?" I asked. "I'd like to cover the well."

"Oh, Joe, I'm sorry." She sat up in bed and pushed back her heavy, bright hair. "I promised Mary and Les that we would be over about nine. We sort of half-planned a picnic at Multnomah Falls for this afternoon, and dancing at Jantzen beach tonight.''

I nodded resignedly. Barbs always planned our Sundays. I made arrangements for the entire week, grubbing in the ground, or reading a book, but on Sundays we partook of social life.

"Couldn't we put it off?" I made a disparaging effort to change the plans. "I'd like to get that well covered before someone falls in."

"Silly boy." She touched my lips with her finger. "There's no one around here to fall in. Champ is fenced, and the dogs can take care of themselves. Now let's say no more about it. Move. I have to dress." She scrambled out of bed, revealing smooth, gleaming thighs, and pulled her gown over her head. "Where did I put that red halter?" she murmured. "I'll bet there isn't a clean pair of shorts in the house." She went mumbling off to the closet, and I sighed as I reached for my shaving brush.

Well, we danced at Jantzen, and pulled into our pint-sized ranch in the wee hours of the morning. Both of us had a full schedule for the following day, so I didn't give a thought to the mysterious footprints.

When we approached the front door we found the dog, Sam, hunched and shivering on the wooden steps. Barbs playfully put a silken ankle against his side, pushed him out of the way, and went blithely into the house.

Sam quivered and whined imploringly. I knelt to comfort him. He was trembling in terror, and with a misgiving glance in the direction of the well, I opened the screen door, letting him into the living room. He spent that night on the foot of our bed, snarling and groaning in his sleep.

As usual, I was first up in the morning. On my way to feed Champ, I looked in the direction of the well. A limp, furry bundle lay near the opening. I paused, then encouraged by Sam's whining, walked over to the supposed dead

rabbit, noticing on the way that there were no fresh footprints of a nocturnal visitor.

I looked down at the mound of lifeless fur, then, startled,
dropped to one knee. It was the ripped body of Paul, our
number two dog. He appeared as if he had been slashed by
a heavy rake, the prongs tearing from head to haunches.

I glanced quickly at the well and at the ground around it.
No, there was no evidence of footprints. Then, unbelieving,
I saw that the ground had been freshly swept. Swept with a
large, leafy branch which now lay near the mouth of the
well.

Cursing, I lifted Paul's body and carried it to the rear-
most part of our farm. Tonight I would have to bury it. I
would also have to get the iron plate bolted back on the
well mouth. Slowly the conviction grew in my mind that
there *was* something coming *out* of the well, something
intelligent enough to cover its own tracks. From the size of
the prints the thing must be enormous, and it had just
given proof that it might be dangerous. Yes, I had to get
that well covered.

Another idea formed. We could wait up all night, hoping that the thing would make another appearance. We
could lay concealed in the bushes, rifle loaded and ready.
If it proved to be deadly, we could kill it. If not, perhaps
we could capture the creature. We could . . . We? Who's
we?

I couldn't expect Barbs to be a part of this. Who, then,
would sit all night in the dark with me? If I opened my
mouth down at work, told tales of ten-foot monsters living
in wells, coming out at night to kill, I'd be laughed out of
the office. No, it had to be a close friend. What friend
would sit all night in the bushes? The idea was suggestive
of "snipe-hunting." Nope. The best thing to do was to
cover the well and forget all about it.

I fed the stock, and returned to the house. From my

shower I told Barbs about how the horse had broken free and trampled on poor Paul during the night, crushing his skull. She was both sorrowful and indignant.

"Joe, why don't we sell the horse? We never ride him, and his feed bill is more than his worth. And if he's going to be a danger to the rest of the animals . . ." She was working herself up to a rage, so I chucked her under the chin and reminded her of the good time we had had the previous evening.

"You goof! I know that you're trying to change the subject." She kissed me lightly. "O.K. But he'd better not touch Sam!"

We drove away to work, Barbs singing a silly grade-school ditty. We had our morning meal at Flanagan's and Barbs sped back to Sandy while I took the lurching Foster bus townwards.

There is one magnetic feature about fraternal insurance. When you hit the office doors you are busy, without let-up, until past closing time. One must be a good sales-man to be in this business, but it's also necessary to be a mother, a big brother, and a father confessor. The subject of the well didn't enter my mind until I received a phone call in the late afternoon from my branch manager in Salem. He requested that I drive down immediately to talk to a family who had put in a death claim. A big one. They were refusing to talk to anyone but top brass. The appoint-ment was set for nine p.m., and with luck, I could be home by midnight.

Midnight! Would the thing in the well be out by that time?

I called long distance to the principal of Barb's school, and asked him to tell her to go directly to Mary's house at the end of the school day. I was afraid to place any emphasis on the request, for if Barbs knew that I definitely wanted her to stay away from home, she would flaunt my request to show her independence.

It was two in the morning before I got back to Portland. There was a deep dread inside me as I drove by Mary's house and found our car not there. I hit eighty miles an hour on the way out Stark Street, and pulled the company car into our driveway with rubber burning. Our Olds was in the drive, and lights were burning in the house. I sprinted for the door.

Barbs met me, eyes flashing. "That damned horse!" she flared. "He killed Sam! Look!" She pointed a furious finger at the mangled heap on the floor. "Joe, you get rid of that horse or I'll shoot him!"

I dropped beside Sam, but rose immediately when I saw the unnatural position of his head. Something had snapped his neck.

"But—Barbs—didn't you go to Mary's?" I asked. "Where did you find Sam? What time did you get home? Why didn't you stay . . . Did you get my message? You shouldn't be . . ."

"Wait a minute. *Wait a minute!*" she hollered, interrupting my tumbling words. "Yes. I went to Mary's. We all went to the show. I got home about a half hour ago."

"Where did you find Sam?"

"Out by the well." She clenched her fist and glared in the direction of the stable.

"Out by—the well?"

"Yes. I heard Champ tromping around, and went out to be sure that he was all right. On my way back, I stumbled over him!" She pointed at Sam, and tears spilled from beneath her lashes. "That damned horse."

"But did you see—anything?"

"See anything? No." She raised her eyebrows questioningly. "Was I supposed to see anything? I wasn't carrying a flashlight, you know." She flung herself across the bed.

"You get rid of that horse right now!" she exclaimed and burst into tears.

Grimly, I took the rifle down from the wall and checked the mechanism. I pulled a handful of slugs from the bureau drawer, and picked up the flashlight.

Barbs raised her head. Her face was tear-streaked, and her hair was mussed. "Don't be silly," she sniffed, "I don't mean right this minute. Take him into Sandy tomorrow night and sell him."

"I'm not going after the horse," I retorted. "Sit tight until I get back."

I slipped a shell into the chamber, and approached the well cautiously. The beam from the flashlight showed me that the thing had again covered its tracks by brushing the ground with a branch. This time the discarded limb lay on the other side of the well.

Hesitantly, I shined the light down into the dismal hole. As far as the beam reached, I could see nothing. No bottom, no light reflection. Nothing. I lay on my stomach, and craned my neck to examine the inside walls.

Along one side, running vertically into the depths, were the expected marks. The corrosion and slime of the stone had been disturbed by what appeared to be claw marks, and I could see where a heavy body had been dragged up the side of the well wall. The claw marks led downward, down out of sight into utter blackness. The thing could be looking upward at me at this very moment.

I suddenly felt a cold spot on the back of my neck, a chill feeling that one gets when he feels he is being watched from behind. My blood froze, and I found that my hand would not reach out to grab the rifle. Very, so very slowly, I turned my head. Towering over me was a huge, gray shape, motionless and silent.

With a tremendous effort, I rolled to my side and grappled with the rifle, believing I had no chance to raise it before the monster would strike.

"What do you think you are doing?" It was Barbs, clad in an old flannel wrapper.

Blood rushed back into my fright-drained body as I rose to my feet. I swallowed several times. Hard. I was drenched with perspiration.

"I thought I told you to stay in the house," I began. Then, seeing her independent chin harden belligerently, I changed my tone. "Never mind. Here. Hold the flashlight." I thrust it into her groping hand, pointing the beam toward the well.

She said nothing. Just watched in simulated martyrdom as I wrestled the heavy iron plate over the well mouth. As the plate clanged into position, I thought I heard a long, mournful howl. For sanity's sake, I ignored the sound. I fumbled around in the dirt for the bolts. "More light here," I panted.

I found the wrench, and tugged and grunted until the bolts were all secure. Then I stood upright and wiped the sweat from my relieved brow. "O.K. Let's go in."

"Joe, what's this all about?" Barbs asked, as we stumbled toward the house. "You act as if you're off your rocker."

I refused to answer until we were in the house under the blessed electric lights. Even then I didn't tell her the truth. If I were to admit that there was a monster in the well; if I were to tell the story as I believed it happened; if I were to lay bare all the facts, then, certainly then, I would have to have some sort of proof. I couldn't even show the footprints. No, this would be one time when prevarication would be more readily believed than the actual facts.

"Barbs," I tried to explain, "I'll sell the horse to Mr. Barrettson. He offered me a pretty good price for him last week. Tomorrow night . . ."

"O.K. about the horse," she interrupted. "But that doesn't explain why you loaded the rifle and went tearing out to the well hole. The last few days you've been nutty over that well. Did you discover gold? Oil? Uranium?"

I opened my mouth to answer, but she gave me no chance to speak. "Since Saturday night you've been playing 'Boy Commando' and 'I've Got a Secret,' " she continued. "You've been moping around here like a thundercloud. You've been telling me what to do and what not to do without ever a reason! Why won't you tell me what's going on?" She was working herself up to a high point of emotional disturbance, and her eyes flashed with indignation. *"Why did you have to cover that well tonight?"*

I slipped my arms around her angry body and held her close, smoothing her hair. "There, there, baby," I murmured, "there's no secret about it." As the trembling subsided. I turned her around and began unbuttoning the back of her satin blouse. "I just wanted to get the well covered. If I'm going to sell Champ tomorrow, I don't want him wandering around, falling in, and breaking a leg. Can't sell a horse with a broken leg." I chuckled thinly, hoping my story would hold enough water to satisfy her curiosity.

It didn't. She shrugged out of the blouse, throwing it on the chair with the flannel wrapper. "So you took the rifle along to shoot him just in case he had already fallen in. Hummmph!" The scorn in her voice destroyed my flimsy explanation. "O.K. If you won't tell me, it's evident you don't want me to know. So be it. But that horse goes *tomorrow!"*

She made no attempt at reconciliation as we lay in the darkness, and my feeble motions were met with an angry rebuff. She lay brooding and spiteful on her half of the bed. For the first time since we had purchased the farm, we went to sleep with a wedge of hostility between us.

Early the next morning I buried Sam. I checked the well to make certain that it was tightly sealed, and Barbs and I rode off to work, she thin-lipped and silent. Her farewell peck at the restaurant indicated that there would be no more war games in our back yard.

I spent a miserable day at the office reviewing insurance applications, and fending off my big-busted, sloe-eyed secretary. Before catching the bus for home, I stopped in at Meier & Frank, Portland's largest department store, and purchased an expensive desk pen set for Barbs. Perhaps the gift would take the edge off her disapproval.

She was waiting at the end of the line as usual. I approached the car, present held timorously behind me. She was frowning, but catching sight of my hesitant expression, broke into a delighted chuckle. "Cheer up, Joe. All is forgiven."

I grinned in relief, passed her the small box, and slid into the seat. She made the customary astonished squeals of appreciation, and kissed me vigorously, nearly running the car off the road.

As Barbs was preparing dinner, I walked across the fields to talk to Mr. Barrettson. He offered a fine price for the horse, I accepted, and he wrote me out a check. He promised to get his barn in shape, and to come after Champ the following day. I got back to the house just as Barbs plunked the sizzling steak on the table.

"Well?" She raised her eyebrows questioningly.

"He bought. He'll come after the animal tomorrow." I waved the check under her nose.

We had a slow, comfortable dinner, then Barbs donned Levis and shirt. She tackled the dishes while I made my way to the garden to test the grapes. I glanced at the well in passing, shook my head in resigned puzzlement, then determined to put it out of my mind for good.

We completed our farm chores at dusk, and returned to

the house, weary but content. Working with the earth is by far the most satisfying of avocations, particularly for white-collar people. I showered while Barbs soaked in a tub of steaming bubbles. Yawning healthily, we crawled into bed, and were asleep before we could get around to a good-night kiss.

I dreamed of my office secretary, the sloe-eyed, olive-skinned brunette. She had often given me the opportunity to make a pass, was always wanting me to pop out for a moment for a cup of coffee, and had in detail described her apartment where she lived alone. I, being a married man, still in love with my wife, made a practice of leering insinuatingly to hold my male status, and continuously assured the wench that sometime we would get together.

We were together in my dream. I'll skip the personal details, but we were in her apartment, she clad in a revealing diaphanous thing, trying to open a bottle of Scotch. The bottle was made of metal, and she was trying to unscrew the top with a pair of pliers. As the cap turned, metal screamed in torture. I winced, and tried to get her to stop. She eluded my grasping hands, and ran round and round the apartment, draperies trailing, wrenching at the cap. The sound of the tearing metal awoke me.

Barbs stood in the open doorway. I slid out of bed and joined her. "What's up?" I asked. "You have a bad dream too?"

She motioned me to silence, and, head cocked to one side, stood listening. And then it came again. A harsh, rasping, agonized tear, as if the threads on bolts were being stripped.

Bolts!

My thoughts flashed to the well. Did the thing have enough strength to bodily tear the plate from the well mouth? From the inside? Impossible. But even as I was trying to reassure myself, I heard a dull, blubbering exclamation, and the iron plate clanged as it rolled to one side.

Barbs moved down the steps. I leaped after her, grasping her shoulder in a grip of steel.

"Let go, silly," she said. "I want to see what's out there."

I shook my head grimly, picked her up, and carried her back into the house. "No, you don't," I replied. "I don't even know if I do."

She switched on the lights, but I was right behind her, and flicked them off again. I snapped the latch on the door, then stood listening in the darkness.

"Joe, what in heaven's name . . ." she began, but I interrupted her intended question. "Barbs, look. You say I've been acting strangely the last few days. Maybe I have. But with good reason."

I felt my way to the wall in the blackness, groping for the rifle. "Saturday, I took the top off the well," I continued. "Sunday morning we found Paul ripped to pieces. I told you that the horse stomped him, but actually he hadn't. Anyway, I don't think he did. It's something from the well, Barbs, something immense and deadly, something strong enough to tear metal . . ."

"What on earth are you talking about?"

"The thing from the well. Sunday morning I found his tracks, tracks big enough to belong to a bull gorilla. Or bigger."

"But I didn't see . . ."

No. I covered them so that you wouldn't become alarmed." I found the rifle, took it down, and moved to the bureau in search of the flashlight. "Sunday night he killed Sam. He . . ."

"He?"

"Yeah. The thing in the well. He killed Sam and covered his own tracks. He must have just gotten back into the well when you came home. That's why I wanted you to stay at Mary's. He was . . .''

"Joe, stop it!" She was beside me, and her hands caught my arm. "Stop it! I don't know what you're talking about." She pulled me away from the bureau, back toward the bed. She took the rifle out of my hands, and pushed me down. Then she sat on my lap, and taking my face in her hands, kissed me, long and fiercely.

"Now, then," she said, "evidently you are trying to tell me that a man lives in the well, coming out after dark and . . ."

"Not a man! A thing. A—monster!"

"I see." She smoothed my ruffled hair. "A monster who lives in the well comes out at night and kills things, then goes back to his well after carefully covering his tracks." She kissed me lightly. "Joe. Honestly. Possibly a five-year-old could swallow that, but we're adults, Joe." She snuggled up to me and her sharp teeth nibbled at my neck.

I listened apprehensively to the outside silence.

"I know what!" she exclaimed. "Why don't you take a vacation? Let someone else run the office for a while, and you sit out here on the farm and take it easy. Then, in a couple of weeks, you can go back to work without a care in the world." She sighed contentedly, and tried to push me back on the bed.

I resisted her efforts, and she sat up straight on my lap. "O.K.," she agreed resignedly. "Let's take your little gun and go out in the . . ."

Her words were cut off by a terrified neigh from Champ. I could hear him beating at the walls of his stall, hoofs pounding, body lunging. Along with his screams I heard the heavy, dull blubbering.

I tumbled Barbs to the floor, and reached for my rifle. In the darkness I could feel her growing terror. She scrambled to me, got both arms around my waist, and pulled herself up. "Joe," she whispered uncertainly, "you were—joking?"

I tore her arms free, and moved to the door. "No joke," I said unsteadily. "I wish it were. I don't think I'm going to like what I'll see."

She got to me again as I unsnapped the latch. Her arms were tight and restraining. "Don't go," she gulped. "If there's an animal out there, he might hurt you. You can't see. There's no moon. It's dark!"

The weight of her entire body was hanging on me, and I paused to shake her free. "Joe, don't leave me," she pleaded. "Don't go! Let it kill Champ, we don't care. Just don't leave me!" She lay huddled on the floor, sobbing.

I flicked the lights on to find the flashlight, found it on the bureau, then snapped the lights off again. I touched her shoulder gently as I passed. "Stay right here," I cautioned. "Keep the lights off. Keep the door locked. And don't come after me in any circumstances, not even if I shoot." As I closed the door behind me I heard the crackling of wood, and heard Champ give a frenzied wail of agony. Then there was silence except for the wind soughing in the pine trees.

I picked my way carefully through the darkness to the stable, rifle at the ready. I moved slowly, hoping to get a glimpse of the thing on its way back to the well. As I reached the barn door I stopped, unwilling to enter the inky blackness. My nostrils picked up a sour odor such as is found around a pool of stagnant water. I wrinkled my nose, and with a finger on the trigger of the rifle, pressed the switch of the flashlight with my left hand. The light beam swept through the barn.

Champ lay in a shambles of splintered planks, blood welling from a dozen terrible wounds on his neck and chest. Whatever it was that felled him was a creature of tremendous power; the heavy planks that had formed the stall were shattered far beyond the power of any domestic animal.

But this thing was not in the barn now. I turned the light to the floor, finding the earth too firm to show tracks. Almost. I bent closer and saw faint scratchings of claw marks. They led in, then out again.

Out? Where could he go except to the well? I hadn't passed him on the way. Into the fields? Unlikely. He had always returned to his hole after a nocturnal visit.

I turned and threw the light toward the well. The beam showed me nothing. I shrugged and walked that way, flashing the light from side to side into the bushes. Nearing the well, I slowed my pace, not wishing to run into him if he were hiding just below the rim.

Cautiously, I thrust the light into the opening. Nothing. I dropped to my knees, and examined the iron plate. The bolts were stripped, and the caps popped off the bolt stems. What a terrific amount of pressure that required!

The least I could do was to replace the cover. That way, if he should come out again before morning, we would be warned by the rattling of the iron plate. I lay my rifle and flash to the side, and struggled with the heavy covering.

As it clattered into place I resolved to notify the authorities. They wouldn't believe me, of course, but due to the killing of the two dogs and the horse, they might give me a few nights of police protection. A few nights would be enough. Should he climb out again, we'd get him. In the meantime, I'd see that Barbs spent her nights elsewhere.

The silence was split abruptly by the shattering crash of splintering wood, a crash from the front of the house. I heard Barbs scream. And again I heard the blubbering sound. The thing was at the front door!

I raced for the house, ignoring the clutching bushes in

the darkness. An unseen root sent me sprawling, and as I tumbled head over heels I remembered that I had no weapon. I scrambled to my feet, hesitated, and with Barbs' hysterical moans ringing in my ears, dashed back for the rifle and flashlight. I found them at first scrabble, lighted the flash, and ran for the house. Before I was ten feet from the well I heard Barbs scream my name in high-pitched plea. Then there was an audible crack, and a foreboding gurgle. A streak of white flashed out the front door.

I snapped a shot on the run, rounded the corner, and was up the few steps in one leap. My foot struck something soft on the doorstep, and I went flying headlong into the living room. I got to my feet, moved to the doorway, and switched on the light.

Barbs lay on the floor, her gown rumpled up around her waist. She was lying flat on her stomach, but her head was twisted around unnaturally so that her wide-open eyes stared at the ceiling. Her neck had been snapped, and even as I knelt beside her I saw blood slowly welling from the flaccid mouth.

As I raised her limp body, her head slewed around horribly to its natural position. Dripping blood trailed across the floor as I carried her to the bed.

I stood by the bed thinking, Barbs' lifeless form in my arms. Shock had not yet set in, and I felt only a listless apathy. Gently, I lowered her to the white sheets, then slowly and methodically, I gathered up the rifle and flashlight.

I would go to the well, I thought, and sit on the rim. I would sit there until morning, preventing the thing from getting back inside. If he attacked me, I would kill him. If not, the light of day would reveal his presence. Then I would kill him.

As I stumbled down the steps, my light caught a patch of glistening ichor. I raised the flash and saw that slimy marks led toward the front road. They were colorless, and were in huge globs, spaced every few feet. I had winged my monster!

Keeping my beam high, I followed the nauseous trail. The ichor stank, the same sour, meaty odor I had smelled in the barn and in the well. The gelatinous substance was softball-sized, and rather than being splashed cleanly over the ground, was congealed in ugly lumps.

My light reflected on our Olds in the drive. There, standing near the fender, maw gaping and shoulder dripping, was the thing!

It could be called a man. It stood upright, all seven naked feet of it, and it had the girth of a grizzly bear. It was a sickly white in color, had dark, dripping hair on the lower arms and legs, and from its shoulders protruded a waving pair of tentacles. The tentacles were more than four inches thick, and extended nearly five feet, ending in a multitude of tiny suction cups. The oily hands of the thing were clawed like a tiger, and the terrible feet had long claws at the toes, and rooster-like spurs at the ankle. But it was the face that stopped me.

One huge, opaque eye stared out from the center of the head. The eye was lashless, had no pupil, and was entirely expressionless. There was no nose discernable, nor were there any ears. Near the top, on each side of the head, were small gill-like openings, puffing in and out with the thing's breathing. The lower part of the face was nothing but jaw, cavernous and fang-studded like that of a dinosaur. The mouth gaped hungrily at me.

Observing that the thing could not see because of the light, I dropped to one knee and took careful aim at where the heart should be. Just as I squeezed the trigger, the thing moved toward me, mewing horribly.

The high-powered slug jarred him back against the car. I distinctly heard a tiny 'plup' as the bullet entered his body, a sound such as is made by dropping a small pebble into a pool of water. I also heard a second 'plup' as the slug tore out of his back and whined off into the darkness.

He pushed himself away from the car, his tremendous weight crumpling the fender. Again he started toward my blinding light, maw slavering, and again I fired, this time at his belly.

The bullet smashed its way into the naked abdomen and out his back with the same watery sound as before. He was not affected by the jar of the slug, and continued his ponderous advance toward the source of the light. I noticed transparent ichor leaking from the holes in his body, and fired again, trying for his mewling mouth. It was a bull's-eye! The slug, emerging from the back of his skull, nearly tore off the top of his head! Stinking, slimy fluid spewed with the impact.

Both writhing tentacles went to his head, the myriad suction cups holding the outer skin together. He emitted a heavy blubbering sound, turned abruptly, and went running off through the brush. I got one more shot in, directly between his shoulder blades.

I heard him crashing through the brush as I rose to my feet. I didn't believe him to be in any condition to do harm to anyone else, so rather than tracking him down, I returned to the house. I walked in the door, saw Barbs' bloody body on the bed, and collapsed into complete unconsciousness.

I wasn't out more than an hour. I crawled wearily to my feet, carefully avoiding a glimpse of the bed, and made for the liquor cabinet. About three straight shots would let me carry on until I could get the police out to view the evidence.

I took three quick ones, took a fourth for good measure, and turned to greet the first stabbing rays of the morning sun. As I reached for the phone, I heard the clang of the iron plate at the well. Heavily, I picked up the rifle, and moved to the door. As I walked around the corner of the building I saw the well, and more important, saw the thing sliding down into the opening.

He had the plate clutched in his hands and tentacles. I fired one shot, just as his head disappeared. The shell ricocheted off the iron lid as it clattered into place.

Furiously, I ran to the well and tugged at the plate. It slid, and I pulled it off the opening. He was gone. Gone into unthinkable nothingness. Screaming in frustration, I emptied the magazine into the depths, then threw the rifle in on top of it. I sank to the ground, panting.

The sun was high when I climbed to my feet. As I stumbled back toward the house I observed that the thing had again covered his tracks. This registered dully, but by the time I had reached the house, my mind was throbbing. He had cleaned up his venomous ichor. He had covered up his tracks. There was no evidence to show that he had ever been there. Just bodies. Two dogs, a horse, and a woman. Would the police believe my story? My nocturnal visitor?

How could I tell them that a monster lived in the well? Where was my proof? No. Being somewhat familiar with the process of law, I knew that they would look grimly at the bodies, glance at one another, and slide the handcuffs around my wrists. No, that wasn't the way to handle it.

I'm leaving this story on the table. Mr. Barrettson will be here soon to get his horse. After looking at the shambles in the barn, he'll come to the house. He'll find these papers. If he can take his eyes off Barbs.

Maybe the authorities will believe it. Probably not. It doesn't make much difference now, I have very little to lose.

Me? Oh, I'm doing the only rational thing. I've got

about two hundred feet of good, stout Manila rope, and a sack of blasting powder that I used to remove the stumps in the yard.

I'm going down after the thing. I don't think that I'll be back.

Flames

Jeffrey Lant

Dr. Jeffrey L. Lant has provided TALES BY MOONLIGHT *with one of its moodier, traditional yarns.* Flames *has a flavor similar to the classic ghost and horror stories of the Victorian era, without becoming stilted or feeling dated—an uncommon achievement. A period tale, it takes us back in time, to struggle alongside a couple of gentlemen investigating an occurence in* their *past, and its influence on their present.*

It was in the late summer of 189-, and I had only recently returned to London after the harrowing nightmare of the Castlemere case which has since gained such noteriety in the popular press. I had privately vowed not to quickly answer any further summons for help from those who are in need of nothing more than common sense and a certain detached and analytical coolness in observation. I was also anxious to pass some months of uninterrupted and leisurely study. But I found I could not gainsay the next request that arrived seeking my services.

One morning at breakfast I was brought a hand-delivered letter, which the bearer kindly though determinedly asked me to open and read at once. It was written in an educated hand on fine monogrammed paper.

Dear Sir,

Will you forgive the liberty of a few lines from a stranger?

Our mutual friend Jackson Lynchfield suggested I write on a matter of some concern to me. I am, however, a bad correspondent and am forever putting things off. However, I trust this note catches you in town, as I am now arrived here myself and hope I may have the honor of calling upon you at six this evening.

May I add that this cannot be entirely a social call, though I hope you'll forgive my not mentioning the nature of my business in this note.

Please indicate to the bearer whether this evening will be convenient for you.

Yours faithfully,
D'Lisle Traverne

Rather than simply indicate my verbal assent to Traverne's proposal, I myself wrote a brief note in response.

Dear Sir D'Lisle,

Having, as you may know, been rather engaged of late, I had forgotten Lynchfield's letter suggesting you might well contact me, though why he did not say.

Of course, I shall be glad to see you here this evening as you wish.

At six precisely, Sir D'Lisle Traverne rang the bell of my flat and was at once ushered into my study. As I rose to greet him, I took note of his general mien and appearance. He was a fair-haired and rather indeterminately young man. He might, indeed, have been any age from his early twenties to his late thirties, but he had an amiable, if possibly rather bland face, and was handsome and well-built.

He walked into the room too quickly, without considering whether his stride might be too long or his pace too fast. From that I gathered he was more at home walking in the country than entering salons. He took my hand warmly and seemed disposed to make up for what he evidently considered his inconsideration in calling upon such short notice by exhibiting an exceedingly good nature. In a moment, I was therefore quite disposed to admit that if he were perhaps not overly familiar with the niceties of making entrances to London drawing rooms (which is such a subject of intense study and consideration for some), he was nonetheless a charming fellow, candid and forthcoming.

"It is really most kind of you to see me," he began. "I was by no means certain you would wish to see anyone after that Castlemere business, which our friend Lynchfield briefly mentioned to me. And I'm more afraid to barge in, because I feel I may have come about a matter of such insignificance that it's frankly an embarrassment, although I admit my own concern."

I assured him that I was very glad to have him call and that I should be glad to consider his business.

"You may know," he said, "that my uncle, Sir Richard Traverne, was a substantial landholder in Devon. Although I have been his heir for some years, family circumstances were such that I was brought up abroad and recently came to Devon upon his death, when I inherited the property. I have only been in residence at Traverne House for about eighteen months.

"Because of the circumstances I mentioned, I have never spent any time in the country and little enough in England. Indeed, I have returned without much knowledge of the place and no acquaintances there. Moreover, it may take quite a while to settle in, not only because the natives are a terse, uncommunicative people, but because my uncle had the deserved reputation of being an eccentric recluse. In any event, he scarcely left the name of Traverne highly regarded.

"Nevertheless, I have been attempting to improve the situation and have done a good deal to become more knowledgeable about the property, the area, and the people."

Here he paused a moment.

"In the course of what I may call my reconnaissance, I have taken a good many walks in the vincinity. One day, while I was exploring my own property, I came across a sort of broad path which although heavily overgrown and evidently not recently traveled, had the appearance of having once been a major thoroughfare. I followed it as best I could until it ended at a sort of clearing. At the time I thought nothing particular about it, though it seemed a trifle curious that this rather oblong patch should be entirely bare, while the rest of the area was heavily overgrown.

"But as I say, this discovery did not particularly concern me. So much of my uncle's property is wild and overgrown that it will take me years to succeed in reclaiming it, and in any event the soil in that part of the estate seems too poor; it may be entirely uneconomical to do anything else but leave it scenic.

"One evening, however, as I was sitting in the library, I chanced to look up and notice a momentary blaze of fire in the same direction as the clearing I had noticed a few days before. The flames must have shot up a considerable distance, since that spot is fully a half mile from the house. Yet they were clearly visible from the library window. In a few seconds, however, they died down and could no longer be seen from where I stood.

"The next day, I walked out to the spot and to my consternation I found no trace of any fire, nothing at all to indicate that there had been a considerable spiral of flame

in the area only shortly before. I returned to make some
discrete inquiries of my steward, but his response was
most curious.

"The man was not merely uncommunicative as so many
of the local people are, but downright abrupt and suggested I should forget what I had seen. A preposterous
suggestion, of course! What could I think but that there
must be some underhand business in progress in which he
had a part. Poaching, perhaps, or even smuggling which is
still not unknown on this coast, the fire being some kind of
beacon. I don't think these possibilities can entirely be
dismissed yet, though I have no evidence of them. In any
event, I thereafter resolved to keep an eye on the man to
ascertain whether he would give me any indication towards
solving what I had by then come to regard as a mystery.
But he never has.

"All this took place at the beginning of last autumn. For
several weeks, nothing further occurred. Then again I saw
a quick flare-up in the same spot, though it lasted perhaps
less time than the previous fire. I thought surely this was
some kind of signal. If it was, I was not able to find out
who was involved, and there was again no residue of ashes
or other tell-tale signs. Nothing further occurred last year.

"Although I still have no notion of what the cause of
the flames may be, I now have some reason for thinking
that whatever has been causing them has been doing so a
long while. This letter I regard as evidence for my opinion."

Here Traverne stopped again and reached into his breast
pocket taking from it an envelope from which he took the
following letter which he asked me to read:

My dear nephew,
  *You will perhaps think me odd for not communicat-
ing with you long before now. And you will perhaps
curse me for letting so much of this fine property go to*

*rack and ruin. But you should know that my guilt
is somewhat mitigated by circumstances.*

*Some of the chaos, it is true, can be directly traced
to me. A substantial part of it, however, is a family
heirloom, handed on to me by my father and to him
by his father. Now you in your turn, as the head of
the house, must know something of the reason why we
left it uncorrected.*

*On my father's death, I found in his papers not
merely a request but a positive command to leave a
certain section of the northeast quadrant of this property untouched. This sector and a substantial part of
the land around it must be given up to cultivation, he
wrote, or any other use. And, so far as possible, no
one must ever go there, particularly in the autumn at
night.*

*Thinking this a peculiarity of my father's, I pondered,
as you will ponder, whether to obey the command or
no. For reasons which will become clear to you in
time, I have obeyed it and hope you will do so as
well.*

*Do not trifle with that piece of land. Do not ask
queries about it. Those who know anything of it at all
are very few indeed and are unlikely to be forthcoming with you, even though you own the property.*

*Perhaps you will think this no more than the pecu-
liarity of an old man. If so, you will not mind obeying
his last wish.*

Your fond uncle,
Richard Traverne

As I sat pondering this letter, Traverne continued.
"Although I cannot prove it, I suspect that my uncle saw
the flames. I suspect that his reclusiveness had something
to do with them, and that he separated himself from human

contact so that others would not come to know what he knew."

"But why have you come to me," I asked, "and what do you expect?"

"I realize you are an intellectual man, not a detective or a sleuth. But I have been informed, if you will permit me to say so, that you have a fine, deductive mind, useful in solving puzzles of an intractable kind.

"Besides, I have a more sanguine, less resigned temperament than my deceased uncle appears to have had. He was willing to impose a voluntary exile on himself from human society to guard some secret, which I suspect is involved with the autumnal fires. But I cannot do that. I do not intend to cut myself off. Neither do I intend to abandon my property.

"On the other hand, since there is a hint of danger and perhaps the likelihood of it, I cannot bring others to Traverne House until the mystery, if there really is one, has been solved.

"I have come to you because of your reputation not merely for intellect but for benevolence as well. I haven't friends in the county and do not trust my steward who seems to know something of the business. I need assistance, not because I'm afraid so much, but because I'm not foolhardy."

Having heard so many facts of the case and Traverne's sentiments, I believed he had done quite the right thing in coming. He was, indeed, a very sensible fellow, and I have always praised sense more than courage, which is after all so often no more than an animal response caused by fear.

"And do you know anything more about the northeast quadrant?" I asked. He did not. Having thought for a moment, I resolved to do some research concerning the corner of Devon where the Traverne property was located and follow him thither as soon as I could. The thought of refusing the case had never entered my mind.

As it turned out, I did not arrive at Traverne House for nearly a fortnight. The season had already changed by then from summer to autumn. There was the perceptible hint of decay in the air, of decay and changing weather. More ominously, D'Lisle Traverne had seen the strong fiery light once again. Again it passed without a trace.

While troubled that I had not been on hand for an observation, I knew that my days since seeing Traverne had not been wasted. I had spent my time in the British Museum attempting to discover anything about that portion of Devon facing the Bristol Channel.

There was a fair amount of information on the town of Lynton, which was the nearest place of any consequence to the Traverne property. It had once been a more considerable place than it was now, the site long before of not only a flourishing local market, but also of important judicial assizes. It was, in fact, from those assizes that it had gained a certain notoriety far beyond the area.

It was clear that these assizes in their time had often been bloody affairs, more than occasionally resulting in mass executions for sometimes trivial offenses. The population was rough and turbulent. The justice that was meted out was often correspondingly brutal and merciless. It was even hideously cruel.

Men, women, and children died on the gallows; hangings were commonplace. Then, as Traverne had told me, there had been pirates and when these were caught they were sometimes hung by chains in the town common to starve to death, their remains left to rot in the sun and rain. Sometimes they were stoned; sometimes buried on a beach at lowtide to await death by drowning. Occasionally, the accused were burned, especially in cases of suspected arson. All but the beach buryings took place on the town common which must have often resembled a sinister golgotha, with the bleached skeletons of the dead left hanging for years at a time.

So much I knew before I left London for north Devon. What I did not yet know was where the town common had been located during the time of the assizes and what it was used for today. I wrote to Traverne to find out this information for me.

Except that the fire had once again been seen, nothing else had happened by the time I arrived. Traverne told me that he experienced a fair amount of difficulty in answering my query only to learn that the old town common was his own property. More interestingly, it was part of the northeast sector of what he owned. Perhaps I should have been as surprised at this revelation as Traverne was, but I was not.

The property, it seems had come to the Traverne family in the eighteenth century. By a private Act of Parliament; they like so many landlords had received permission to enclose it. Unlike so many landlords, however, it does not seem that they ever made much use of the property.

We did not walk out to the place in question on the first day, but waited until I had rested somewhat. It was just as Traverne had described it, except that there were several overgrown paths about the site. None had recently been used. These, I decided, surely must have been the well-used foot paths and thoroughfares leading to the common.

Although Traverne and I searched the entire area as thoroughly as we could, we discovered nothing of any consequence, no sign of what could have caused the flames, certainly nothing that indicated men had been involved. There was not a footprint on the entire common save our own.

For three weeks I waited at Traverne House, but nothing transpired. Both Traverne and I were near concluding that word of my presence had leaked out into the village, and therefore nothing would occur. Each evening, nonetheless, we sat in the library and kept a loose watch into the distance. But we were continually disappointed. Then one night I, too, saw the flames rise up in the northeast. They lasted only a very short time and then were gone.

Although they had disappeared, Traverne and I resolved to set out towards the site. We were both armed, and we carried lanterns with low-burning flames. We moved stealthily the half mile to the northeast quadrant, sometimes simply creeping forward until at last we drew near the spot.

Pressing forward carefully to what we both agreed was the exact location where we had seen the flames shoot up, we yet found nothing; not the smouldering remains of a fire but simply darkness and an empty clearing. Having reconnoitered the ground to no avail, Traverne and I returned to the house.

As he and I discussed the situation that evening, it became clear that we could not wait until another fire started and then rush out possibly, indeed probably, unlikely to find anything there when we arrived. We decided instead to lay our own fire in the clearing, thereby hoping to keep the mysterious, emberless flames going far longer, until we should have time to reach the spot from the house. We thus covered the vacant oblong area with a thin layer of twigs, leaves, and small sticks; entirely covering it. But this was by no means all I planned to do.

It was obvious that even if a fire did begin, it would quickly consume this material; surely it would be virtually gone by the time Traverne and I had reached the area. It would not do to lay anything greater, however, for fear that the fire would spread to all the land nearby. Still, the problem was to keep the fire alive until we reached it, since I suspected that part of the mystery lay in the fact that it died so quickly. I thus persuaded Traverne that some logs should be soaked in paraffin and stacked near the edge of the oblong, but still entirely in the vacant and bare clearing, ready to be thrown into the fire if we needed them.

But I doubted whether even these preparations were enough. Much as I disliked the idea, therefore, I decided that Traverne and I should take up an outdoor watch near the site to see if anything would occur. I loathed the prospect of spending a considerable amount of time there, especially now that it was growing more autumnal, more dismal and cold. Unfortunately, there seemed no other possibility.

Traverne and I took up our station just off the common. We spent our days in the house, sleeping mostly, our nights on the edge of the common. We did this for several nights.

Our waiting was mechanical. We went to and fro without enthusiasm, without anticipation or expectation. The temperature turned quite cold in the days and plunged even lower after sunset. It might not have been so bad even so, except that a piercing wind blew over the ground in frigid gusts. Traverne and I were often quite numb by morning. Although neither of us said anything, the habit of conversation having waned in our odd circumstances, we were both beginning to doubt whether our self-appointed task would accomplish much. Still, night after night, we returned and for warmth sat back to back, parallel to the common but many feet removed from the oblong.

Thus we were sitting late one evening on the eighth night. The cold was bitter, the dew had settled thick and freezing, the wind blew fiercely whipping the leaves and twigs into the air. Traverne and I had been sitting heavily on the ground, our thoughts our own, when in an instant we were transfixed.

From nowhere, a small flame shot up near the center of the oblong and rapidly grew up into a spiral of fire nearly twenty feet tall. This happened with such speed that neither Traverne nor I had time to concentrate on the spectacle but moved back instantly, involuntarily, to avoid the searing heat. It was thus a moment before we were ready to concentrate our attention on the flames themselves. But when we did, it was obvious that these were no earthly flames and surely not fed by earthly materials.

More startling, in the midst of that fiery spiral there stood the curious apparition of a lady.

We perceived this lady quite clearly, though we were by now even farther away from the oblong than we had been while watching. The terrible thing about this apparition was that the woman seemed trapped by the flames, imprisoned in them. She was not being consumed. That was clear. But she was struggling to get out, though not fiercely, but rather as if she were resigned to failure, knowing she could not do so.

Most curious, in this entirely curious situation, were her expressions. At first, and while we thus stood watching, she seemed imploring, her visage piteous and heart-rending. I was not surprised that I should actually see tears glistening in Traverne's eyes as he regarded her. But that piteous look was not directed to us. Indeed the lady seemed never to notice that we were present.

There was, of course, an element of agitation and anxiety about the entire situation, but I do not remember these as being the predominant feelings I then experienced. No, it was not predominantly anxiety I felt, but curiosity and interest at the strange spectacle before us.

But this curiosity quickly changed to fear and terror as the woman's piteous expression became one of fear and pain as our ground covering caught fire and added its heat to the greater blaze burning without a source. In an instant the situation was transformed as for the first time sparks began leaping out of this combined inferno, being blown every way and quickly catching the pile of paraffined logs on fire, too. Our own situation became, for an instant, perilous. We shrank further back from the heat, losing sight for some moments of the apparition in the spiral. When we looked again the weird change had already begun to occur.

The expression of the lady was now one of frightening agitation and evident pain. She was shrinking inside the flames. Where before she had seemed suspended in the spiral, imprisoned, now she resembled a creature at the stake and was definitely afire, writhing in a frenzy. Her hair was a mass of glowing strands and her entire body began to be consumed.

Her skin reddened and then her entire body began to crack and split open in great sores. She was burning. And all the while her disfigured lips worked fearfully. She seemed to be screaming and shrieking, seemed to be, I say, though we were witnesses to the hideous spectacle, there was no sound except the crackling of the wood and the fire we had set.

Yet such was the obvious agony of the lady in the flames, I saw Traverne run for a shovel. He then began to dash at the fire and attempt to kick away the logs. But the heat was too great and his peril alarming. I ran for him, grabbing his arms and with all my strength (for he was a bigger man) pulled him back, holding him to the edge of the common with a strength I could not have predicted. Tears ran thickly down his face as the fearful scene continued.

After what must have been a considerable period, the great flames subsided and at last even the embers began to die. Traverne and I then went up to where the fire had burned most fiercely, the place where the apparition had first appeared. This time there was a residue—ashes and embers and dying bits of flame from the fire we had set. We began to turn over what remained, putting it out. In the process, Traverne happened upon a small gold band which had somehow survived the holocaust. For a few minutes we buried it in the earth to cool it, and then took it out.

On it we were able to make out most of the following letters from which we guessed the rest: "To my wife Jane with undying love. November, 1763."

In deep silence, Traverne and I concluded our task on the common and then returned to the house and to the library, where we sat quietly and abjectly for a long while. At last I said to him, "You will forgive me, I hope, for what I did to you tonight. I am no more cruel than you, but there was nothing you could have done to save that woman."

He scarcely nodded and did not look at me. I waited for an instant and continued.

"What I am about to say may seem strange to you, but the explanation to the hideous scene we witnessed this evening, may be in something I found in this very room."

I took down from one of the shelves a small folio volume and handed it to Traverne, whose interest, notwithstanding his shock, was awakened to what I had to say.

"You will notice," I continued, "that only a short section of this volume, which is a history of your ancestors, is much worn. That is the section dealing with a certain Jane Traverne, in which part there are a number of marginal notes as well in the hand of your late uncle, Sir Richard.

"From the entry and Sir Richard's marginalia, I have been able to reconstruct the following:

"Jane Traverne was the only daughter of the then owner of Traverne House. Although she loved another, she was told by her father in the spring of 1763 that she was to wed the heir to a neighboring property. She refused to do so, and her father chose to lock her away until she had changed her mind. She proved obstinate in her affections, however, and rather than relent she instead determined to escape and to elope with her lover. One evening she managed to do so and though intent upon fleeing paused long enough to set fire to the wing where she knew her father would be sleeping.

"The fire she set was not serious; she, on the other hand, did manage to make good her escape—for a short time. In the few days of freedom she had, she married, but then was tracked down and caught. Her lover—by then her husband—was killed as she was taken.

"Jane Traverne was brought back to the Traverne House to be sentenced to death by burning because of her arson attempt. Her father, a Justice of the Peace and local magistrate, concurred. Even in those cruel times, his decision was thought appalling. In the end, it was his colleagues on the bench rather than Traverne who decided she should not be burned at the stake but buried alive in what is now the northeast quadrant, a fire being set over the grave. And this was done.

"In time the girl's father died, raving on his deathbed about the flames. People at the time thought he was racked with remorse, but it may be that he had been the first to see the spiral of fire. In any event, he ordered his heir with his last breath to buy the common and prohibit its use. What is more, he forbade any autumn guests at Traverne House and moved the servants' quarters so that they could not see the northeast in the evening. Only the steward's rooms (as the senior servant) were allowed to remain where they were—facing the quadrant."

Through the telling of this tragic history, Traverne sat without much animation, still very much under the influence of what we had witnessed. When I concluded, however, he started up.

"But what of the girl in the flames?" he almost shouted. "Was she merely some apparition or was she something more, a creature alive all this time, killed tonight?" Alive or spectre? I thought.

"My dear Traverne, who is to say?"

An Egg for Ava

Richard Lee-Fulgham

I've a memory dating from a time before I was old enough to walk or communicate with grown people: There is a green country which goes on forever in all directions. From this green country a single tree rises into infinity and spreads its limbs overhead. From the limbs is draped a phantasmagorical tinsel, brushing the green world. Among this tinsel, tiny sprites of green, brown, and red move about. My tiny hands try to grasp these creatures, which are numerous about me. I've no memory of how I came to be here. I only know that I would like to capture the colorful sprites which hop along the green land and in the tree's tinsel. I cannot even crawl after them, and they evade my fingers easily. I never quite become frustrated. The sprites walk on me if I don't touch them.

For years I thought this was the memory of a childhood dream, for nothing about it suggests the real world. Yet I learned when I was a teenager that my mother had taken me to Florida shortly after I was born. My mother would place me on the back lawn beneath a huge tree from which spanish moss hung to the ground. The sprites were anole lizards, or American chameleons, living in great numbers around that tree.

Most of us lack memories of the fantastic world we lived in as infants: a world of giants where every incident and object was brand new and undefined. Richard Lee-Fulgham

in An Egg for Ava *captures that sense of differing perception between child and adult. He takes it a step further,
too, in assuming the child's reality is as valid or more
valid than our own definition-clouded rather than instinctual
views. In this story, Ava expands reality as she knows it,
evading the imposition of adults' interpretation.*

"Horses?" she asked in a whisper, twisting around and
gazing for an instant at her mother. But her mother was
busy and only nodded, not hearing, not thinking, not even
aware that her daughter was witnessing a strange battle in
the back yard. Just beneath the child's eyes, a column of
sixty tiny mounted soldiers marched at half-trot toward the
base of an old Elm.

Only inches tall, the horsemen carried heart-shaped
glass shields which caught the evening sun and sent it back
to her in dancing stars . . . sixty sparkling suns! She felt
like cheering as they smartly paraded by with their snow-
white helmets looking like mushrooms and their sharp
lances pointed menacingly toward the sky. Her eyes widened as she saw their bright blue crispy uniforms and
black leather tunics. And she wanted to faint when she saw
their leader on a perfect white stallion, carrying a long
saber and wearing red plumes on his golden helmet.
"Proud," she whispered back to her mother, "so proud!"

She was even more enthralled when a tiny bugler began
a call to battle and the soldiers dropped their lances to
ready and speeded as one to a full gallop toward the tree
roots. The column of little men sped along like an attack-
ing snake, twisting expertly around clumps of grass and
stones. Excited, she jumped up and ran to her mother,
pulling on her skirt and whispering, "Fight! Fight!"

But mother was used to her child's behavior. Though a
pretty little girl, if on the skinny side, she never talked in
sentences. And even when she did talk in those cryptic

single words, it was always about those things a shy child saw that others could not. So, logically enough, Ava was only tolerated when she came running and pulling on her skirts, whispering those nonsensical words about wars and colors and strange animals in the back yard.

"Not now, Ava," was the reaction; and too full of wonder to worry, she raced back to the window. Her pale pointed chin rested on the sill as she let two huge dark eyes focus again on the battle beneath her. The bugler cut into the air with several bird-like notes of fury as the column began galloping faster and faster across the grass. She could even hear little shouts and slogans in the air. "Death to the deadly!" they were crying out. "An end to the monster!"

"Monster!" she called back to her mother. "Death!" The lady smiled and nodded but didn't come, so Ava quieted herself as the column of horsemen and sixty suns broke ranks and furiously whipped their horses into a passion so great blood began to spurt from their nostrils and white foam from their mouths. Then, from its hidden lair, *it* came, all wings and beak and tearing claws.

No use to call mother again, she thought as the soldiers began pricking the strange bird with their long lances. Surrounding it, they showed no mercy, worrying it over and over again, causing it to spin in desperate gyrations trying to get at the tormentors.

Without a doubt it was the oddest bird she'd ever seen in her life, having bright golden eyes that seemed to spark with fear and anger, and shiny prismatic feathers that caught the sun in a thousand rainbows and sent them shooting toward her in a myriad of wild colors. Its beak was long and thin and curved like a scythe, snapping left and right, but never catching the quick horse swirling around and around in ordered chaos.

Then, in the confusion of suns and colors and sharp

lances and thumping hooves, she saw off to one side a nest, and in the nest a single mottled egg. And like the bird, it was strange enough, also glowing those many many swirling colors. With a start, Ava realized the bird was protecting its home! She's a mother bird, she thought to herself, whispering loudly, "Mama."

"Yes, dear?" she heard, but it was her time to ignore. She had to help the poor creature outside; she just *had* to. Calling "go play" over her shoulder, she jumped down and rushed outside, her young lungs filling with the scream she meant to use against the army. But it wasn't needed, for the horsemen took one look at the giant bearing down on them and reformed ranks and fled. Only the leader was left; but he was still determined and charged the bird a final time, sending his sword deep into the bird's heaving breast. It gave a final cry of surprise and anger and fell fluttering to its death. With a yell of triumph, the leader rushed away to rejoin his troops and lead them off the battlefield.

Sadly she picked up the lifeless bird and took it into the house, showing it to her mother, whispering, "War."

"What you got, honey? A robin?"

"Monster."

The mother laughed; she had such an unusual child! Though concerned about Ava's refusal to talk, she was secretly proud that her daughter was so "different" and fresh and imaginative. Imagine her thinking this dead robin a monster; she'll probably wind up an artist or great thinker. Looking at Ava affectionately, she noticed again how fine and regal her features were, how the wide eyes and narrow jaw gave her a pensive, well bred look, almost an aristocratic air. The only thing she couldn't really understand was why Ava was so shy: why she shunned her playmates and wandered around the yard alone for sometimes hours and hours. And more often than not, she would wake in the night and find little Ava at the window, peering wide-eyed into the night as if watching great incredible adventures out there. But fantasy is good for children, she knew, and was wise enough to not discourage it.

"No, Ava, it's not a monster; it's a poor robin. Maybe a cat got it."

"Soldiers."

She smiled at Ava and let it go. Let her dream; she only wished someone had let her dream when she was eight years old like Ava. Her daughter tried to tell her about the battle in the back yard, but she was already too lost in reverie to listen. Besides, how can someone describe a battle using only words instead of whole sentences? Ava knew the whole sentences all right; but she just couldn't force them out in proper order. She quickly gave up and excused herself by smiling and whispering, "Egg."

Outside it was getting dark, but she had no trouble finding the egg, for it was still glowing even though the sun had long disappeared. A gentle bluish light pulsated in and out of it, swirling on the surface like colored oils. It was almost alive the way it breathed that soft light . . . almost a living bit of tissue. Picking it up, she inspected it closely: it was making a sound, a humming noise like a gyroscope, all consistent and easy to her ears.

On one end was a strange thing: a peephole! Only a fraction of an inch across, it could hardly be seen until she held it right up to her eye. But then, she noticed, she could see into the egg itself: it was hollow, and inside there gleamed a light even softer than the morning skies, a bluish tranquil sky through which shimmered a far off and reddish sun round as a hen's yolk, but aflame and bathing the scene below with colors.

Even more amazing was the beautiful valley of ferns and mosses, cut through by a double stream of crystal waters, rapids and pools and waterfalls, scurrying along,

down the middle of the endless valley into an infinite
distance, blending into the blue expanses beyond. And
from within she could hear and see other things, tiny
animals with round glittering eyes and big ears that twitched;
they chattered and squeaked to each other, poking their
heads out of the mosses and gazing toward Ava thoughtfully,
then pulling their heads back into the ferns to hide. She
was delighted and thought to herself, "A egg . . . a egg
for Ava!"

She didn't even show it to her mother; it was far too
fragile to show around. Shells were thin and meant to be
broken, weren't they? No, it must be protected now its
mother was dead. The soldiers might even come in the
house after it! The thought frightened her: she had to hide
it carefully. But where? Where could she keep such a
magic egg?

With a child's simple logic, she realized that eggs spoil,
and so thought for a moment about the freezer. Would it
freeze in such a cold place, or was it protected by that
mysterious sun inside? She would try.

Using an alarm clock, she left the egg hidden in the
freezer first five minutes, then fifteen, then thirty, without
any sign of the land inside freezing too. Even after an
hour, when she picked it up off the nest of frozen French
fries and turnips, it was still warm to touch, glowing, and
still shone inside, all life still chattering away and glancing
furtively at her with curious amused eyes. It still hummed
away in the night.

And so it came that little Ava had a magic hollow egg in
her freezer that only she knew about. And as days passed,
then months, she came to live more and more for those
times she could take the egg out and hide under the covers
of her bed, watching the world inside for hours and hours,
ever fascinated by the infinite horizons and suns and bizarre creatures and clear streams. Sometimes in the air

over the streams she could see bright blue gulls swooping down for sparkling fish, raising them high into the air before dropping them back into the water with splashes even she could hear. The creatures inside eventually came to know her and would sometimes venture up to the edge of the little peephole and gaze wonderingly over the edge into her never blinking eye.

As happy as she was, it was quite a shock when the soldiers returned to finish their task. She was sleeping when they came clattering along the wooden floor and surrounding the bed with file after file of horsemen, sixty of them all with those clear glass shields and thin pointed lances. Stirring awake to the sound of cheers and taunts, she sat bolt upright, rubbing the sleep from her eyes, mumbling questions without answers, afraid at once of the miniature army shimmering in the nightlight. Trying to concentrate, she first heard a twang, then felt a tiny prick in her arm. Looking at the stung arm, she saw a sliver of glass sticking from the skin. And at the foot of the bed, a little uniformed archer was watching her expectantly . . .

With a sickening spinning sensation of falling, she thought she was fainting for the whole world was changing before her eyes: the covers were stretching to dozens of feet across; the pillow was expanding so fast it was looking like a huge soft mountain of cloth; the room shot out its walls in all directions; and worst of all the soldiers were growing up to her size. But then it hit her: the awful truth was that things weren't growing, she was shrinking, and fast.

By the time she realized it, she was down to only a few feet tall, still big enough to cow her tormentors, but too small to shout loud enough for her mother. Jumping out of bed was an exercise in terror and she hit with a painful thump that left her limping on the way to the kitchen. Just behind her she could hear the soldiers reforming ranks and slowly, patiently, trotting after her like a sure animal following its mortally wounded prey.

The bugler was playing a long drawn out taps for her, over and over, as if she were already dead, and this did nothing to allay her certainty that this was exactly the end they'd planned for her.

At the kitchen door, the bugler's tune changed to a strong determined marching song and she heard the horses change their gait to a faster, more threatening, gait. No longer was the column a slightly absurd spectacle, but a dangerous full-force trained cavalry unit intent on her destruction. They never relented, not for a second, and seemed to know every second what they were doing. Throwing a look behind her, she saw they had formed two long lines, staggered so that she was running from one uninterrupted row of cruelly tipped lances and flat shields, behind which gazed impassively the faces of sixty single-purposed soldiers. The leader, that little Napoleonic Captain in purple, strutted his horse stiff legged in front of them. The bugle became one long hysterical note.

Terror ran in her veins like acid and her eyes widened so they could widen no more, round as silver dollars. There was only one escape for her; but how to open the freezer in time? It would be next to impossible for a girl only a foot tall being chased like this. But with an instinctive uncanny knowledge, she managed to scale the chair to the table, then jump heavily to the handle of the freezer, which hesitated a moment, then popped open with a reluctant sigh. A blast of cold air like she had never known hit her as she swung deftly into the mountainous expanse of white and frost.

Nude, alone and afraid, she lay on the ice a moment with her eyes clamped shut, hoping desperately to wake up in bed where she belonged. But no, the sounds of shouting and impatient horses' hoofs wouldn't disappear; and open-

ing her eyes, she saw that several of the men had climbed
the freezer and were slowly, but infuriatingly and surely,
pushing the door shut.

"No, no, no!" she screamed, but too late. And to make
matters worse, just before the final snap of the latch, she
heard the unmistakable sound of someone jumping inside
with her. All was silent and dark at first, and very very
cold . . . she was trembling so that the first sound she
heard was her own knees knocking and her own teeth
chattering.

It was almost too much and she couldn't keep her head
from spinning and spinning. But, spinning or not, she had
to move and it didn't matter that she could hear someone
moving toward her. With a start, she heard a scratching
noise, then a light as a flame shot up in the near distance,
lighting up a foreboding purple figure carrying a torch in
one hand, a saber in the other. She watched in fascination
as the hard eyes peered out toward her. The light from the
torch licked her in red, the light glistening off the tiny
golden hairs on her thighs in sensuous evil delight. The
eyes of the captain caught hers and the chase was on.

In the far end of the frozen wasteland she made out a
familiar blue blow, and as her eyes grew more accustomed
to the darkness, she could make out the shapes of huge
packages like icebergs barring her way. Every steak became another mountain to climb; every chink between
foods a crevasse of the most dangerous depth. Slowly, in
great numbing pain, with breaths rattling her lungs like
paper, she made her way toward the blue horizon. Inch by
inch became mile by mile . . . and always just behind was
the scrambling sound of her otherwise silent pursuer.

The sounds began to intensify: the cracking of frozen
foil, the rustling of frosty paper, the clopping of thick
boots, the humming . . . Humming? Yes, and not electricity,
but the egg, becoming louder and louder, as if a siren was

going off within it. And other stranger sounds she hadn't caught at first, like cheering from somewhere, and the sound of a great wind from the distance, almost calling her, "AAAAAAAAAVVVVVVVVVVAAAAAAAAA . . . AAAAAAAAAVVVVVVVVVAAAAAAAAA. . . ."

It seemed to take hours, and all the time she kept shrinking and shrinking. She was so tired she could hardly continue, her breath coming in great gasps, the cold air burning her throat and lungs like wine, her muscles stiffening and cramping with every step. And just behind her, other steps, careful, unhurried, unconcerned but unrelenting, apparently in no hurry, sure that she must drop.

And drop she was about to do when she saw it, the huge blue-white curved wall, the rounded fortress from which there poured a warm wind and a thousand cheering voices and that strong wind calling her name "AAAAAAAAA-VVVVVVVVVAAAAAAAAA . . . AAAAAAAAAVVV-VVVVVVAAAAAAAAA. . . ."

She fell and could only crawl and was too tired to really care when the soldier appeared only a short distance behind her and quickened his pace with a tiny satisfied smile coming to his lips. Looking from those victorious eyes to the lip of the chasm towering above her, she saw dozens of the little creatures peering out toward her curiously. She couldn't be sure, but they seemed to be smiling; and their little strangled cries seemed to be joyous. And from somewhere deep within the egg came a harmony of voices, a mad chorus of ten thousand tongues and languages. Everything began to glow and swirl and pulsate; and everything that had seemed so hard and cruel, was now soft and flesh-like, warm and yielding as if alive.

But it's too late, she thought sadly, it's just too late. I'm freezing and I can't move and I'm caught. She did not even bother to look as the captain came up and stood triumphantly behind her. She hardly heard as he sliced his saber back into its scabbard and asked, "Ready now, Ava?"

Placing his jacket around her shivering shoulders, the captain stepped aside and began pushing a huge papered package, rocking it back and forth until it finally fell with a crash next to the round tower. He made no other sound as he returned to her. All he did was take her face in his hands and point it toward the rim. He didn't smile as she painfully began to pull herself toward the edge of escape.

As she neared, the warm winds took the chill from her flesh and she felt a strength rushing unexpectedly through her body. The lights became brighter and brighter, the cries and shouts reached a joyous crescendo, the chorus inside became louder and louder, calling and calling her. The gulls inside began to screech, the river could be heard lapping and lapping, the humming noise became a mighty hymn-like awesome song of infinite wonder. She got to her feet, no longer exhausted, and ran up the package, while behind her the soldier was beaming and waving. . . .

Laughing and shouting, she pulled herself inside.

See the Station Master

George Florance-Guthridge

George Guthridge lives in the Yupik Eskimo village of Gambell, Alaska, where he carries on shamelessly with a word processor. He has become a regular contributor to THE MAGAZINE OF FANTASY AND SCIENCE FICTION, *no mean trick, and has appeared in* ANALOG, GALILEO, *various small press and literary magazines, Terry Carr's* YEAR'S BEST SF, *and of special merit,* JACK AND JILL. *Usually a science fiction writer,* See the Station Master *may well be his first excursion into the realm of horror. A nasty little excursion it is, too, with a man of doubtful intentions behind the wheel of a vintage car.*

Indian Summer, Indianapolis. Humidity is high, tempers flaring, rapes and murders and larcenies up, my mill down for two-week inventory; I decide to take Crystal to Florida to see her mother. My darling Crystal, child of the modern age, born with a plastic spoon in her mouth. Too soon will she know too much about too much, without senselessly being exposed to a city in heat.

I pick her up after school, saving her a hot busride home and further needless mingling with strangers in a world grown feverish. She resists my suggestion concerning Florida—such a stubborn girl!—then starts to run away. I grab her shoulders and hold her neck so gently, oh so gently. Then we drive south, not speaking, down I-65.

The '55 T-Bird, opera windows and four-on-the-floor, is air-conditioned; Crystal reclines with her cheek against the passenger window, her head awkwardly crook'd, a slight moisture clinging to her neck as if to hide the fingermarks.

The world seems to bow as we push through shimmering heat, colorful trees standing against smog-dulled sky. "I know you might not want to see your mother, but this will be a long, long trip if you won't talk to me," I say as we near Edinburg. A smile appears to touch her lips, though she doesn't look my way. Dusk is coming on; passing fields reflect darkly in her eyes and along the windshield's interior. "You're a good girl, Crystal," patting her knee. "The very best." I straighten a pleat on her skirt, and smile. One of the few saving graces of a world gone mad: the starched, white blouses and blue skirts of parochial schools. Crystal thinks so too. I can tell by the glazed happiness in her eyes. I lean Crystal against my shoulder, her weight heavy and her right arm dangling, and I stroke her long soft hair as we drive past stables and white fences enclosing horses I might someday be able to afford for her. We are lovers of thoroughbreds, she and I. She of white stallions and carefree afternoons. Me of blond, ponytailed girls on white stallions. So much I wish to give her!

We swing onto I-64, stream past Lexington, bypass Knoxville, then leave the freeway at Chattanooga; the in-city wending and the brooding dawnlit presence of Lookout Mountain might bring on another of my migraines. Signs bloom along the two-lane. Collegeville, Graysville, Ringgold. Wreathed in fog, we stop at a roadside picnic table. I climb out and stretch; Crystal slumps down across the bucket seats, not awakening.

A passing headlight lances out and is gone, momentarily searing my soul, and in that moment, the skipbeat tableau, I see the fingermarks on Crystal's neck have darkened to blue-black weals. People won't understand if they discover us! I sit her up and slide back into the car.

Then another surprise, more terrible than those headlights. The Bird is nearly empty.

I should have known! Should have thought things through, and filled extra gas cans. Now we've got to chance stopping where people will see, and not understand.

Hands sweaty on the leather-enwrapped steering wheel, I roar back onto the road, spewing gravel. We pass through dawnmists and beneath sycamores heavy with shadow and Spanish moss. Finally—a populated area. BLAZE MOTEL: ROOMS BY NIGHT OR MONTH, says a sign resembling an uptilted carpenter's square; and in smaller cursive lettering. *No.* A hundred yards further, hunkered before a drive-in theatre and a row of boxy tract houses, is a service station. A winged red horse rides a teardrop sign atop a downward-tapering pole. Three old-fashioned bubble-headed gas pumps squat beneath a canopy that leans slightly sideways, like someone tipping a hat. I gear down. The T-Bird's muffler pops and rumbles. AC Sparkplugs, a sign informs me from a window streaked with dirt. A blue and white square clock above the office door says 5:15 and that Farmer's has Auto-Boat-Homeowner.

A blue-worksuited station attendant is standing in front of the pumps, waterhose in hand, washing oil and gasoline off the concrete pad. Not spraying the area, thumb against the hose end, but rather standing slumped, shoulders so thin they look pinched, the water arcing out feebly and splashing without pressure.

He doesn't move as I ease toward him.

I drum my fingers against the steering wheel. Then, impatient, I beep the horn.

The water continues to arc. He watches it solemnly through heavy-hooded eyes, his face pasty-white, cadaverous-looking except for deeply redded lips. Straight hair sticking from beneath his blue cap is slicked across his forehead. The Bird inches forward until the grill nearly touches him. Water cascades onto the hood; a hollow, metallic sound. I roll down the window. A blast of humid air hits me. "Hey!" I shout, again honk, really laying into it this time. Fear seizes me; I glance toward Crystal, then toward the row of tract houses.

No lights come on.

The attendant doesn't move.

Rock-and-roll suddenly jangles. I swivel, and am staring into the grinning, sallow-cheeked face of an attendant holding a transistor radio against his ear. Why is it that gas stations always seem to hire zombies? His eyes are protruding slightly, as if his thickly veined lids have to stretch to keep the eyeballs from falling out. "Fill it," I tell him. My hand finds Crystal's. The attendant nods more to the music than in answer and bop-stepping, heads for the pumps, snapping his fingers, his thick red lips going *ooh-wa-wa*, hitch of the shoulders, then again *ooh-wa-wa*. "It takes regular, not premium!" I yell as he lifts a hose.

He raises his index finger, points it down as if to acknowledge, *one for your side, buddy.*

> *I got my thr-ell,*
> *on Blueberry he-ll,*
> *on Blueberry he-ll*
> *where ah-a met you,*

Fats Domino tells me from twenty-five years ago as the attendant pulls the gas hose to its maximum length, the black cord straining, and rams the nozzle scraping into the tank.

"Hey. Take it easy!"

Again the acknowledging forefinger.

A grinding. The garage door lifts. What looks like tiny yellow and blue flames dance in the inner darkness, at floor level. Someone welding? A burly T-shirted man, belly wobbling, ducks beneath the door and ambles toward the car, wiping his hands on a red rag. The door cranks down, *whumping* against the concrete. The man bends and peers in, one hand on the cartop. Startled, I shift to block his view of Crystal. His eyes are cold. The fat beneath his chin appears to harden. "You ain't got call to go honking like that," he says, combing thinning hair back with his fingers. "It's enough to wake the dead."

"But he was blocking my way!" I point toward the attendant with the water hose.

Water suddenly splashes against my windshield.

"And now look!" I start to open the door and climb out. Spray mists against the side of my face and into the car.

"Now don't go getting your bowels in an uproar," the man says, holding the door so I can't climb out. "He's just a-washing the windows. Ain't no harm done." And then, gesturing, "Aaron, you stop with that hoo-raw!"

The splashing halts. The runoff comes down the windshield in droopy veils. I turn the key to ACC and work the wipers. The attendant stands facing the car, head down, staring at the ground, holding the hose straight up at his side, the water emerging and doubling back on itself, soaking his sleeve. His shoulders jerk and his chest heaves. He seems to be crying.

"You, Clarence. Git on up front there. Take a look-see at this man's earl."

The other attendant be-bops forward, transistor blaring as he passes, sets the radio on the fender, opens the hood, checks the oil by wiping the dipstick with his fingers, lifts the radio, slams the hood down.

Shoulders hitching, fingers snapping, Clarence starts back toward the hose. The T-shirted man grabs his arm. "You treat a car like this with respect," he says in a ugly low voice, his face darkening and his index finger sticking in front of Clarence's nose. "You hearing me?" Clarence's grin momentarily broadens, then fear enters his eyes and his face appears to collapse. Taking the transistor from his ear and lowering his head, he peers up, a dog expecting a beating, from the top of watery eyes.

The T-shirted man turns aside and, gripping the top of the window frame, leans back to inspect the Bird. Clarence carefully sidesteps around him. Radio against leg, the sound muffled, he makes for the hose. "Yep. Real collector's item," the T-shirted man says, grinning, showing crooked teeth. He moves around the car, stroking the fender, tapping the hood, admiring a headlight. "Just a bright little lady." Pausing by the passenger door, he raps a knuckle against the glass where I've placed Crystal with a pillow against the window, and then saunters on around back. "You ought to be real proud," he says, coming around again. His enormous head thrusts into the window and, folded arms against the door, he surveys the interior. I lean away from his stench. "Mint *con*-dition," he says. A pack of Camels—I can see the label through the cloth—is rolled up in his sleeve. "Yer little gal's just as asleep as she can be," he says, nodding. "Cuter'n a bug's ear." He winks.

"She's had a hard day. We're on our way to Florida." I force a smile, but my hands are trembling. I clutch the wheel.

"Tourist, huh?"

"Not really." Something in his voice troubles me. "Her mother—Phyllis—lives in Orlando." Immediately I'm angry with myself; where we're headed, and why, is no one else's business.

"Going to Disneyworld, I'll bet."

"Oh yes. Disneyworld." I manage a slight laugh. "But mainly to see her mother. Her mother lives in Orlando."

"Yes," he says. "Orlando. That's where she lives, all

right." He stands upright, again wiping his hands on the rag. "I'll tend to you later," he says to Clarence, then, whistling "Blueberry Hill," wanders toward the garage, the fat along the sides of his back shifting beneath his T-shirt. The door cranks open. Tiny blue flames flutter and leap inside the garage. I stick my head out the window for a better look. No flames. He enters shadows. The door comes down.

"Three-fifty."

I roll my hip up, reaching for my wallet. And then, *"What?"*

"Three-fifty," Clarence says. His hand is out, but he's not looking at me. He's staring toward the garage door. A nervous tic twitches beneath his left eye. He keeps the radio pressed against his side.

35.9, says the price gauge.

"Pumps so old they can't show dollars?" I laugh. "Haven't you people heard of the gas crunch?"

"Gas war?"—still looking toward the garage.

"You couldn't have filled this car for three-fifty!" I glance at the fuel gauge. It's at F.

"Make it five, then." His fingers make a crablike, impatient motion.

I smile triumphantly as I stuff a bill into his hand. "I should come here more often."

"Sure, man. Whatever you say." Water suddenly drums against my hood, the other attendant standing slump-shouldered, the hose cascading. But I don't let myself get angry; not at these prices! I back up before Clarence can change his mind.

"Hah!" I slap Crystal's leg with delight as we swing onto the two lane. "Five bucks!" I put my arm around her shoulders and pull her close, her flesh cold and clammy, and for the next few miles I drive one-handed, humming. What a glorious morning! A blue interstate sign comes up,

an arrow pointing south down a gravel road. I steer around
a dead cat, the car sliding slightly as if restless for the
freeway. Sunlight, breaking through the trees, is so brilliant it's almost spangling. Slatty shadows race past. "Next
stop, Orlando!" I tell Crystal, giving her another hug.

Half a mile later I see the figures.

Blue worksuited and blue capped, two lanky men are
hunched over something alongside the road. They gaze up
as I roar by, their eyes fear-strickened, the sunlight slanting like tape across pallid faces. Red-splashed mouths leer.
One of the men flicks his hand, sloughing off what looks
like soggy sausage, and quickly licks his fingers. Then
both men sprint for the woods, eyeing me over their
shoulders. I gear down. Too fast. The Bird shudders and
slides. A guardrail flashes along my right like an undulat-
ing ribbon.

Crystal falls forward as I'm pulling the Bird out of the
skid. I grab for her to keep her from hurting herself. Her
head hits my arm. A thud jolts the car, then metal screeches
against metal, and a guardpost lurches toward me. I wrench
the wheel to the left, my brakes squealing. Metal crunches.
The steering wheel leaps backward, slamming against my
chest, then a soft fuzzy darkness pulls down and I hear the
crying of metal and the hissing of a radiator as if in a
dream.

"Crystal?"

My voice enters my consciousness even before I open
my eyes. I blink. Sunlight swims within my vision, and I
wince. I lean back in the seat, trying to suck in air. My
chest feels like some great weight is pressing upon me.
There's a cottony, hung-over taste in my mouth. I touch
my forehead, feel wet warmth.

"Darling?" I probe my scalp. A small cut along my
forehead; very little blood.

Crystal doesn't answer. I jerk upright, anger and dread clenching my stomach. She's lying sideways, face up, arms around the gearshift. Her cheeks are ashen, her eyes rolled back. I slap her temples. "Speak to me!"

I'm all right, Uncle Jim.

"Thank Goodness!" I hug her and we rock to and fro, my eyes filled with tears and my pulse pounding. "Oh, baby, baby." I pull her onto my lap.

I've ruined your beautiful car, she whispers; *if only I hadn't hit your arm!*

"Just so you're all right. That's all that matters."

I climb out. The right fender is crumpled, the grill and radiator askew, the headlight hanging like an eyeball dangling by threads. I glance about the woods for the two figures, but the men aren't in sight. Squinting against the sunlight, my head throbbing, I walk across the road.

There in the dust is an opossum, eyes open and mouth closed and tiny claws curled down. Gouts of flesh have been ripped from its side. Pink and black entrails shine wetly. I retch and stagger back, hand over my mouth. Because I remember what I saw, or thought I'd seen; what made me gear down so suddenly. *Eating. The men had been eating.* I double over, again retching dryly, bile drooling between my fingers.

Uncle Jim?

I run, shaking my head.

She's lying across the seat, knees up, eyes rolled back, smiling. Struggling for air I lean with one hand against the wheel, the other clutching the seatback. My breaths come in shallow gasps. I shift position, blocking her line of vision from that terrible thing across the road, and touch her knee to calm her, assure her. Nothing evil or ugly will reach her, nothing will harm her, she'll know only good things, as long as I'm alive and we're together. Her legs are long, lovely, spindly; colt's legs. Babysoft down on her calves. *It's wonderful being with you,* she says. Sunlight is touching her face, her cheeks tawny and sleek. *I don't mind that you killed me. Really. It's about what I should have expected from you.*

"I didn't . . . You're just sleeping, that's all!" I angrily sit her upright and ease into the car, then sit gripping the wheel and glaring across the hood.

I remember you watching me from outside the school playground, clutching the wire as if you'd tear the fence down, and I'd be with my girlfriends, talking about boys and schoolwork and junk like that, but really I'd be watching you from the corner of my eye, and worrying, knowing how you are . . . A lech.

"Don't say that."

At home, when you and Mother made the bed squeak, I'd lie in my room, pretending to be asleep, and not knowing how to tell Mother that, you know, that you were constantly looking at me . . .

"Well, I *was* looking at you. But not the way you think. You and your dirty little mind! The whole time your mother and I would be together I'd be wanting you, not anything, well, anything *sexual*, just wanting to be near you, and feeling guilty for it. But I've never touched you, and never will. Our love is pure. You know that." I shake my finger at her.

There's more than one name for rape.

I glower and again grip the wheel. I'm not going to listen to any more of her asinine brattishness! I glance toward the opossum and, feeling nauseated, crank the key. The Bird spits, but starts—wheezing and jerking and the right wheel grinding against the inside of the crumpled fender as, jamming the gearshift forward, I send the Bird squealing in a circle. The two men were just looking at the thing, I tell myself, or maybe were highway department men or something, responsible for clearing the road. "Your

mother shouldn't have gone away and left us!'' I tell her.
''There we were—your mother run off to Florida, you and
your father suddenly thrown together, and me on the outside.
The three of us, in that sweltering Indiana heat. She
shouldn't have done that. Now shut up and buckle up.
We're going back to that station.'' We'll get the Bird
fixed, then we're headed to Florida as fast as speed limits
allow. I wonder what Phyllis will say when I tell her how I
feel about Crystal. Well, that's down the road.

Crystal doesn't touch her seatbelt. Just sits with her
head forward, chin against chest, pouting. I shake my head
in despair. Usually she's so mature, so very much older
than her twelve years. Then other times . . .

The front and back garage doors are open when we
return. A slight breeze has come up, and a cool feeling
hangs amid the humidity. Wrench in hand and cigarette in
mouth, Clarence is working beneath a dented-up Impala on
the rack.

I find the T-shirted man in the office, leaning back in a
swivel chair and smoking, his feet on a desk strewn with
papers as he watches a Chicano couple at the pay phone,
the wife jabbering and, cigarette in hand, pushing her hair
back, the husband, also smoking, staring sullenly at the
floor.

''They're trying to get a-holt of someone who's sposed
to get a-holt of someone else, someone with money, who's
sposed to get a-holt of Western Union, who's sposed to
wire money, so's they can pay me and get that goddamn
hunk of tin off'n my rack,'' the T-shirted man says.

''And if they can't pay?'' I ask.

''We keep the car till they do.'' He shrugs. ''That don't
work, we scrap the mother.'' Then, ''So what can I do for
you this time?'' He cranes to see over the desk, apparently
assuring himself the T-Bird has returned and he's speaking
to the right person.

"Had an accident. Hit gravel and slammed into a guardrail."

"Oh?" Again craning.

"Right side. It'll need some body work." Then I quickly add, "Nothing special. Just pound it out and I'll be on my way; I'll get it fixed when we reach Florida. And something's wrong with the engine. Carburetor, maybe. I thought I might have cracked the radiator, but it seems to be all right. At least, the car didn't overheat on the way back."

He nods absently, then his face suddenly goes white and he swings his legs down. "*She's* all right, ain't she?"

After a moment, "Oh, you mean Crystal. She's fine. Fine. Sleeping now."

"Sure do sleep a lot, that little gal." His eyes twinkle, and his broken-tooth grin hints of lechery.

"Well, what with the accident and all," my voice hard.

"Hey, Clarence?" the T-shirted man asks through the door adjoining office and garage. One eye closed, Clarence is squinting up toward the Impala through the little square hole in the back of a socket wrench. "Clarence!" The attendant doesn't turn. The T-shirted man's face clouds, and he glances around the desk. He grabs a small crescent wrench, pitches it into the garage. It hits ringing on the concrete, bounces, swacks the attendant on the calf. Clarence glances downward stupidly, eyes bulged. "See to that car yonder?" the T-shirted man asks, pointing toward the pumps. "Fella here had hisself an ac-ce-dent." Clarence points with the socket wrench handle toward the underside of the Impala. "That pile of shit ain't going nowhere," the T-shirted man says. "You get on out there." Then, to the Chicano couple, "And you grease-heads hurry and get off'n my telephone, you hearing me?"

The husband smiles and nods, obviously not understanding. I ignore him, follow Clarence to the car. I've left

the engine running, and for a few moments Clarence stands
beside the broken headlight, apparently listening, gazing at
the grill and rubbing his hand on the fender. Finally there's
a *screeek* as he opens the hood. The sputtering sounds
worse. His eyes are heavy-lidded and glistening as he
removes the top of the air filter. He wipes grime from the
engine block, licks his fingers as if wetting them to turn a
page, and peers into the carburetor. He takes a screwdriver
from his back pocket and prods the carburetor's butterfly.
Then he steps back, blows his nose in an oil-stained red
rag. "Try gunning 'er," he says, a rag-covered finger
exploring a nostril.

I climb inside. "What do you think it is?" I yell, my
head out the window. Clarence doesn't answer. He's leaning over the engine, tinkering. Something pops, then there's
a hiss as if I've blown a tire. Sparks fly. I lurch open the
door and start to climb out, but Clarence waves me back.
He eyes the engine grimly. Steam rises in lazy billows. He
motions: *turn the key.*

The engine doesn't turn over. Dead.

I jump out, slam the door and push him aside. He
doesn't protest—just looks downcast, screwdriver and crescent wrench in hand. "Look here!" I hold up the battery
cable. My blood's up, my face burning. "You bumped the
thing off the goddamn terminal!" Immediately my words
haunt me. *Bumped* the cable off? But I say nothing else; he
looks pitiful, and God knows where another station might
be. He doesn't resist when I grab his tools. I replace and
tighten the cable mount, climb back in the Bird. The other
attendant—Aaron—appears in the shadows alongside the
garage, holding a gas nozzle disconnected from its hose.
The thing seems to be dripping . . . dripping flame, tiny
blue and yellow firestars splashing against the pavement. I
stick my head out the window for a better look. Aaron
turns and walks away.

Get hold of yourself, Jim. For Crystal's sake. You'll have another migraine.

I turn the key.

The engine grinds, and grinds, and grinds down, a dying growl.

"Goddamn it!" I beat my fist against the dash. Again and again I try the key. The grinding grows lower. I sit cursing, my face aflame and temples pulsing, all the anger I've always felt for things that won't work, things that won't do as they're told, as they're asked, as they're pleaded with, cars and bad faucets and corroded screw heads that won't budge, girls who won't go to Florida and only laughing and insisting I'm a jerk when I tell her I'll get her drugs if she wants some, her goddamn schoolmates carrying coke vials in their training bras and snorting powder up their nostrils and throwing their heads back and laughing about a middle-aged man stupid enough to buy it for them just so they won't tell about him on the playground, *an accountant no less*, stupid enough to fall in love with tinkly laughter and spindly legs, and she not a user and not willing to go to Florida with you even if you were the last man in the world, or the wealthiest, or the most handsome, all of which you're not, just a creep Mother had sense enough to dump—that anger welling up, boiling, percolating my brain.

The key bends.

"No." I put my head against my hands, on the wheel. The word sounds distant. "Please, Crystal; no."

"Starter's out," Clarence says, standing beside the door. His voice is low and sympathetic, like that of a physician telling you you have cancer or clap.

"The hell." I don't look up. The damn pasty-faced clown! No wonder they're called grease monkeys! "It wouldn't just *grind* if it were the starter. It would make cranking noises, or something." I speak softly, questioningly, for I'm not sure he isn't right. I never did understand engines, friends back in high school talking about cams and gear ratios and synch, and me smiling, nodding, wondering about trig and bookkeeping III, wondering if my friends knew my head was what they with their cutdown, blocked-out, souped-up, smittied '57 Chevs called "empty-engined."

"Starter," Clarence insists. But those half-hooded eyes are pulled down further, betraying disbelief.

"The hell"—this time the words coming from behind me. The T-shirted man is standing with his forearm against the car roof, his other hand fisted against his hip. With his tongue he moves a toothpick to the other side of his mouth. "Just 'cause you got buzzard brains don't mean you can go telling a pack of lies," he says to Clarence, holding up the toothpick as if examining it. "Fuel pump, is what it is. Anyone can see that."

"Fuel pump?" I ask.

"Yep." He flicks the toothpick at Clarence and strides toward the office. Then suddenly turns. "Going to be a while 'fore we can get to it though. Wetbacks in here just got a-holt of some money." He pokes his thumb over his shoulder. "Two, maybe three hours, iff'n we can find a pump. Couple other helpers coming in 'round noon; I'll put them on it. Things'll start hopping here pretty soon, this being Saturday and all."

Saturday. And I picked up Crystal only yesterday, waiting for the weekend so the number of schooldays she'd miss would be minimized. It seemed so long ago!

Then he says, "Cafe 'round the corner from that movie house there." He points toward the drive-in. ROXY, the marquee says; Horror At Carnival Beach. I lift my hand in acknowledgement, and he goes in the office, plops in the chair, puts his feet up. Clarence, beside the pumps, takes a radio from his breast pocket and looks at it curiously as he works the circular on/off control. The plastic front's smashed and the back's missing, wires and battery hanging jumbled. No music's playing. He smiles sheepishly, slams down the hood and, snapping his fingers, ambles toward the garage, the radio against his ear.

For several moments I sit gripping the wheel, staring vacantly, fighting anger. My headache's a jackhammer. Need some sleep. In my rear-view I can see the motel's no-vacancy sign is off. I take my shaving kit and a blanket from the trunk and, wrapping up Crystal, steal away when the T-shirted man has his back turned, talking to the Chicanos. Crystal's sleeping soundly. I lie her amid tall bunchgrass growing among the wooden buttresses behind the drive-in screen. "Be right back," I whisper, and kiss her cheek.

The motel clerk, a blowsy redhead with sagging jowls and too much rouge, is putting on lipstick when I enter. She smacks her lips and drops the lipstick tube and her compact into her purse, snaps it shut and sticks it under the counter. "Help you?" She folds a curl behind her ear. I explain that my car's broken down and I need a room for a few hours. "Oh?" her voice lilting.

"For my daughter and I. She's at the station."

"Oh," her voice lower.

The room proves perfect—shielded from the motel office, yet with a view of the car. Two double beds: green bedspreads, the kind with little tufts arranged in chevrons. Some of the tufts have pulled out, and a yellow blanket peeks through the holes when I bring Crystal in. A black and white TV on a rickety Danish-modern bureau mirrors us. I kick the door shut with my heel and, kneeling awkwardly, pull back the covers. Then I help Crystal out of her skirt. She lies quietly, elbow akimbo, her left hand behind her head, on the pillow. Her right knee is turned against her left, legs together. Her smile is slight, but

sweet, as I close her eyelids. I go into the bathroom. For
Your Sanitary Convenience, the toilet tells me. I remove
the label carefully and wipe the seat with toilet paper
before using.

After a shave and shower I walk to Bea's Honeypot:
Good Food, Good Conversation. The cafe specializes in
pecan pie and blather about how bad business is, what
with them fastfood places down on Elvira. I return with
two paper plates folded like taco shells around charred
T-bones, two styrofoam cups of greasy coffee, plastic
knives and forks, a silver packet of ketchup with a dotted
line along one corner. In Florida we'll eat better, I promise
myself. No more of that junk food Crystal thinks she likes.

I eat hunched over on the bedside, the covers and sheet
pulled up to Crystal's chin. I offer her forkfuls of steak,
but even when I whisper her name she refuses to open her
eyes or mouth. The playful pup! My heart is thudding with
delight and desire. I can hardly eat, I'm trembling so.
Finally I can't control myself any longer. I wash off my
paper plate, put it in the bathroom trashcan, remove and
hang up my sports jacket and shirt. The hangers are wire
instead of broad-shouldered wood; I try hanging up my
undershirt, but the straps keep sliding off. I fold and place
the undershirt in the bureau. Leave my trousers on. I am
not large-genitaled—when my marriage was crumbling,
Jonaca, my ex, used to mock me—but the bulge might
show if I strip to my boxer shorts, and there's no sense
shocking her. I kneel beside her, draw the blanket back to
uncover her feet. "Crystal," I whisper. Her flesh feels
like ice. Poor thing must have gotten her toesies cold in
the car. I make a mental note not to keep the Bird's air
conditioning turned up so high. I put her toes in my
mouth, to warm them. Dust-moted sunlight, filtered by the
yellowed chiffon curtains, touches her cheek. After a moment she seems to smile, and I again cover her legs.

"At the office," I tell her, "were page after page of accounting sheets. Sometimes it felt like the grids were trying to put me into boxes. And the columns forever coming out wrong! Then I'd enter a 12, and think of you." 12: woman and swan; goddess and kneeling, bowing slave. How beautiful my Crystal! As pure as my own daughter. When I'd sleep with Phyllis—the first and only woman I was brave and foolish enough to bed with after my divorce—I'd awaken in a sweat, apulse with heat flashes, remembering how Jonaca and that squinty-eyed judge had taken Temple. Not even allowed visitation rights! Then I'd dream of Crystal in the next room, all innocence and intrigue, and calm would come. Crystal, my soothing drug.

"I worship you, my darling."

I know, Uncle Jim. Her eyes don't open. *But I'm afraid.*

Afraid to be alone, to sleep alone. I can understand that. Happiness washes over me. I slip under the covers beside her, and close my eyes. Her presence fills my spirit. My migraine stops throbbing. My heart quietens. Then I sleep, my dreams no longer only of her but of us together, our hands together and lives together, intertwined and pure.

Darkness has fallen when I awaken. Crystal continues to sleep; careful not to bother her, I slip from bed and quietly dress. Over at the station the two attendants are only now pushing the T-Bird into the garage. Strangely, I only feel joy at their sloth. Whistling, I walk toward the office for a paper. Rounding the corner I can see the drive-in screen. A bikinied girl with blond hair styled in a bubble, her back to the screen, is holding a beachball and running awkwardly after a dark-haired boy with a deep tan. In the background is a man-shaped shadow: hint of ominous portents. I shake my head in wonderment. Such mindlessness down into which our world's been funneled!

The news proves bad, as usual. Race riots in Houston, a

longshoreman strike in New York now affecting L.A., a torture cult discovered outside Omaha, interest rates up another point, nothing about girls smart enough to turn up missing in order to get out of Indianapolis. I read the paper while sitting in the lobby. Then I'll put the paper in the trash, where it belongs. No sense Crystal knowing of such things. Girls her age need to be protected.

"Car still ain't fixed?" Chanking gum, the motel clerk comes through the paisley curtain separating the lobby from what I assume are her quarters.

"Apparently not," and shrug.

"That ain't the swiftest bunch," she says, checking keys and sticking mail in the pigeon-holed boxes behind the counter. "Not by any sense of the word. There's goings-on over there that just don't set right, if you ask me. I swear he beats them boys."

"Oh, I'm sure he doesn't."

Her brow lifts, a confiding look. "I seen that Clarence kid once, with his shirt off. Had welts on his back the size of eggyolks. And them boys don't seem to have no homes, the way the four of them are always over there. So who else could have gave him them welts?"

Again I shrug. I turn back to the paper.

"Well, I'd keep a lookout of my car, if I was you. I wouldn't trust that bunch to turn off the water if the house was flooding, if you catch my drift. Fellow was there once, I bet there weren't nothing wrong with his car more'n needing gas or maybe something tightened. Took the rotor out of his distributor, them boys did, and told him it was the fuel pump. He found out about it and went to Deputy Cady."

I jerk the paper together so quickly it rumples to a wad. The blood has drained from my face.

"There was hell to pay around here when that happened,"

she says. And then, as I rush out the door, "Hey, ain't you going to take your paper?"

As I near my room I forget all about the car. The motel door's wide open. But the place was locked when I left! I know it was. Crystal? Crystal!

Gone. Went looking for me at the car, perhaps? I run down the alley, heels clocking against the blacktop, dread and despair and terror knotted in the pit of my stomach.

Halfway to the station I stop cold, seized by the image on the drive-in screen, and feel my soul shrivel. I stand whimpering, shaking my head in disbelief, wanting to beat my fists against my chest in anguish. On the screen the lanky blondhaired girl is lying on a pink coverlet, staring up in open-mouthed terror as a shadow slowly spreads over the beach, now over the blanket, now across her face. I can see clearly now, see it's Crystal up there as she raises her arms to fend off some offscreen, oncoming menace. Beyond the theater, past the bright-yellow fence, people are emerging from the tract houses, mothers and fathers and pigtailed girls and boys with Falcons sweatshirts, bringing out checkered green-and-white lawnchairs and chaise lounges printed with hyacinths and daffodils, setting up cedar tables, opening tassel-fringed umbrellas and boxes of Colonel Sanders' and Arby's double-deluxe with horseradish and Bea's oh-so-delicious pecan pie with her own special topping, relaxing now, laughing, delighting as on the screen long-fingered hands matted with dark fur find the girl's throat. Crystal's throat. And I run.

The garage doors yawn open, and the Bird slowly rises on the rack. The T-shirted man is in the driver's seat, his arm around Crystal in a fatherly embrace, she with her head tilted back, giggling and stuffing popcorn into her mouth, he leaning over to make some silly commentary on the show, both of them all innocence and intrigue, a scene out of the frontrow of a 1950's drive-in. "Crystal!" I shriek. "Please!"

Greenish fire erupts around the base of the rising pedestal, forcing me back, my arms upraised against the heat. Four attendants, blue worksuited and blue capped, emerge from the shadows of the office, carrying gas nozzles. White faces lifted, mouths bloodsplashed, eyes gleaming, they stand on opposite sides of the circle, watching the station master, their nozzles dripping blue and yellow flames. I can hear Crystal's bright laughter from above as on the screen a werewolf, eyes wild and froth dripping from his fangs, carries the limp girl towards the ferris wheel, a crowd of swimsuited spectators parting in a panic and then a close-up of the dark-haired youth inserting a silver bullet in the chamber of a rifle. He raises the weapon; camera angle of the werewolf seen through the crosshairs of a rifle scope. The trigger is squeezed, and above me Crystal's laughter suddenly rings louder, more cheerful, and somehow says *forever*. The laughter of the dead. I lower my arms and face the fire, my selfhood and hope crumpling like a bit of burning tissue. Is this, I wonder, some hell to which I'm to be relegated, forever to wear a blue cap and a blue worksuit, eternally youthful and beaten-down and crying as I watch the master accept a young girl's love, something I have never had and never will, while I must face what men fear most—a loved one enjoying another's embrace? Am I, like the other attendants, to rise each day to be run over by nightmare death, my eternity one of service and of cats and opossums on country roads?

If so, to be near Crystal, I shall endure the travail.

A Tulip for Eulie

Austelle Pool

For some readers, A Tulip for Eulie, *set during the Civil War, is a quaint period piece. For others, it will seem almost contemporary. There are places in the South today where the fall of the Confederacy is felt with the sting of this morning's news. Even though I was born in the Pacific Northwest, the Civil War yet impinged upon my life in an odd way. My great-grandmother on the maternal side once told me of the family's most dreaded secret (as she perceived it). Two of her uncles ran off and hid up in a tree to escape conscription in a passing Confederate troop. The South fell and those two boys had failed to fight for her. Their presumed cowardice so shamed the family that my great-grandmother could confess it only in a whisper, with tears in her eyes. I often suppose she was the last of my family to be affected by deeds (or lack of deeds) by men a century dead; but perhaps I've cousins somewhere in Dixie who know the same family secret and will die of mortification if they find out I told it here.*

Austelle Pool offers a tale of suspense detailing the lives of women powerfully independent in a way the South (I'm told) still breeds them.

Burying the gold, to Eulie, was hard work. She and Hiram, sneaking to the cotton house, had loaded the sacks onto a wheelbarrow, he pushing and she steadying, stubbing her toe and almost hollering, on their way to the orchard. Arriving, she rested against the crooked pear tree, amazed that Hiram could start digging at once. She thought also that he must have cat's eyes to see what he was doing under a moonless and cloud covered sky, though realizing that such a night was necessary for their work. It had been the same way getting it into the cotton house from the bank.

She was glad there was nothing more for her to do for the moment, so rested while he dug a hole big enough to hold the rust proof chest that lay atop the load. He inserted the chest and raised the lid, following which he communicated with her by prods and other soundless motions that she must start handing him the bags. Each bag was heavy in her hands, so soft and white that they almost gleamed in the dark. She lost count but there were enough bags to fill the chest.

He lowered the lid, locked the chest, and handed her the key. He then shoveled in dirt, packed it down, and flung the remainder, thinly, far and wide. On hands and knees she helped him rake twigs and leaves to cover signs of their work. No word was spoken until they were in their bedroom, behind closed doors. He brought a Bible and placed her hand upon it.

"Now you must swear to keep our secret until my return or until such time as is necessary to reveal it."

"Why must I swear? Don't you trust me?"

"Yes, but you are a woman you know."

The smarting of that remark she knew would seal her lips forever; but she swore to secrecy. "Why did it have to be in gold?"

She was sorry she asked when he replied, "Because, puddinhead, if we lose the war, Confederate scrip won't be worth a darn." He tilted her chin. "There are millions out there. Getting it broke the bank—mine and few other

withdrawals. Perkins, the banker, was powerfully mad.''
He shrugged off the edge of guilt. ''It would have gone
broke anyway.''

Hiram Jefferson spent a full hour, the following morning,
knee-trotting and peek-a-booing their year old daughter
Aurelia. Eulie clipped a blond lock from the child's head,
tied it with a tiny pink ribbon and placed it in a duffel bag,
along with a smiling picture of herself and child.

She and Hiram said their good-bye at the rose trellised
gate. He gave her a gusty hug, which they both knew was
to smother out the fear they felt. He mounted his horse
with one supple movement and looked down at her. She
managed a smile, saying a bit shakily that he would be the
best looking man in Lee's army. With a flourish, that
reminded her of a knight of old, he was gone to join Zeb
Matthews and other recruits. At a bend in the road he
waved a final farewell. She never saw him again. He died
at Mannassas.

She walked slowly to the orchard, hoping to seem casual,
meanwhile giving vent to tears. She leaned against the
pear tree, hoping its crooked trunk would never fail to be a
marker for the buried treasure. She lingered only briefly,
lest lingering give a clue to prying eyes.

She moved slowly to the house she had named Valhalla,
despite its Grecian appearance, because she loved Norse
mythology. Her figure looked small and lonely as she
passed between the great Ionic columns.

A resonant humming, coming from upstairs, filled her
with a fierce possessiveness, causing her to lift her skirts,
run upstairs, and seize her child from the arms of black
Aunt Kizzie. Finding another rocking chair, she proceeded
to continue the sleep wooing measure Aunt Kizzie had
initiated. Desolation settled upon her when the child
squirmed down and toddled back to Kizzie.

Julie Matthews came over in the afternoon and deposited her own little Ellen in the play pen with Aurelia. Julie's teeth were chattering. She sat down, heavily, and the two women eyed each other wordlessly, each seeking from the other an answer to the enigma of war.

After a moment Julie said, shakily, "Eulie, I'm scared. Let's go and stay with relatives until this thing is over," knowing that neither of them would desert their homes but wanting to discuss the matter anyway.

She was not at all disturbed when Eulie asserted she would not leave her home nor desert her Darkies. "I told my father, when he gave me Valhalla, that I would guard it like my marriage vows, and Hiram's father gave us Darkies whom we have sworn to care for."

Julie picked up her knitting, saying, "And I cannot desert you." The two had been friends from childhood. They had attended academy together, had met their future husbands at the same dance, and had celebrated a festive double wedding. Their plantations adjoined. Julie's house, though not as impressive as Valhalla, was yet a handsome place. On a clear day it could be seen from Valhalla sitting like a great white bird on a nest of shrubbery.

Julie thought of the new railroad that cut across the corners of both plantations, and brightened. "If worse comes to worst, we can always leave in a hurry on the train." She had never ridden on a train. Like the uninitiated the cabbage head engines, pulling three cars and puffing black smoke, were a magic carpet capable of delivering one from all slower moving dangers.

Days became weeks, weeks months, uneventfully. Eulie and Julie, whose training had leaned more toward the decorative than to the useful, showed surprising ability in managing large farms. Gentle firmness, the result of generations of the like, resulted in cooperativeness and even protectiveness from the Darkies. Aunt Kizzie, a natural matriarch, ruled over all. Always supreme in the household,

she was often seen riding the fields, voluminous skirts
flying, to see that the orders of her mistress were carried
out.

When exportation of cotton was halted by the coastal
embargo, bartering was resorted to successfully. Real hard-
ship was felt only after the fall of Atlanta. Both plantations
lay within the sixty mile wide swath made by Sherman's
dreadful march to the sea. Julie's house lay in ashes, but
Valhalla was miraculously spared. Aunt Kizzie said it was
spared because even the Yankees had too much heart to
destroy a thing so beautiful. After denuding the place of its
food supply, the enemy moved on, leaving peace and
desolation.

Eulie had not forgotten the buried gold. There were
numerous times she was tempted to dig it up. The first was
when Valhalla became a place of refuge for the hungry,
the sick, and the ragged soldier trying to find his way back
home. She found herself, spade in hand, going to the
orchard. Caution, however, checked her. The gold could
help to a limited extent. It would not cure the wound given
the south. Also times were lawless. If it were suspected
gold lay in the orchard, she shuddered to think of the
results. She, therefore, put her spade to good usage by
finding a moist spot of earth and digging for angle worms.
She found a goodly number and went fishing in a nearby
creek.

When Zeb Matthews returned, unscathed except for a
minie ball scalp scar that did not show, but with no house
to return to, Eulie opened her mouth to say she would pay
for a new one. Julie forestalled her by announcing that she
and Zeb had dug up a wagon load of gold and silver plate
and sold it to an Atlanta jeweler for a good price.

Laughing, she threw an arm around Eulie. "You're
lucky, Eulie, in not having to dig up something."

The third time, when temptation to dig came, concerned

her child's education. Post war schooling consisted of a one-room one-teacher three months session after crops were laid by. The Blueback Speller was learned forward and backward. Should a student wish to go higher, the teacher might supply the basics of arithmetic, history, and grammar. Eulie took the question to bed and wrestled with it most of the night.

Academies still existed. Should her daughter not have an education commensurate with her own? Yes, except that it seemed wrong to push her child beyond her less fortunate friends. The gold remained untouched with the compromise that Eulie, Julie, and the copious library of Valhalla possessed the potentials of education. Aurelia and Ellen were taught elocution and music to supplement the basics offered by the schools. With little prompting Aurelia turned to books and Ellen to music. Valhalla came alive with the strains of violin, organ, and piano.

Ellen grew into a beautiful young woman; was married to a young salesman of sewing machines, and went to Atlanta to live. Aurelia gave no promise of beauty, being freckled, stringy haired, and shy. At twenty she was referred to as Eulie's old maid daughter. Upon reaching thirty, still unwed, she had accepted the role of spinsterhood placidly.

Aurelia did not seem bereft. Skilled in needlecraft, her works of art took prizes at county fairs, and her book reviews were an endless delight for audiences. Economically, she and her mother fared on a level with their neighbors. Aunt Kizzie lived with them until her death, while the younger Darkies were eroded from the plantation by the spirit of adventure. The land yielded a livelihood from sharecroppers.

The general store at the crossroads served the double purpose of selling staples, such as flour, salt, tobacco, gingham, and calico, and providing a gathering place for the men of the countryside, after crops were laid by. On cold days they formed a circle around the big stove, sitting on wooden crates and split-bottom chairs. Discussions centered on crops, politics, and occasionally sneaky bits of masculine gossip.

Jim Perkins was the new drummer, replacing the old one who had retired to his farm near Macon. He appeared to be in his early thirties, was handsome, suave, and immediately disliked, although of some interest in bringing news from the outside world. He had a belligerence toward society, perhaps stemming from the fact that his father, an Atlanta banker had met bankruptcy during the war and died penniless. He blamed certain stockholders for lack of patriotism in withdrawing their holdings when the south most needed money.

"I understand one of these fellows lived in this community," he added. "He withdrew millions and demanded it in gold."

Old Mr. Withers, who lived with his son and liked whittling, looked up from his pine stick. "Must've been Hiram Jefferson. He was the richest man in these parts."

"Yes, yes! Go on," Perkins urged.

"He lived in a mansion. His widow and daughter have lived there ever since Hiram went to war and got killed. If he buried his money, it must still lie there, since Miss Eulie and her daughter have always seemed as poor as the rest of us."

Perkins spoke with self-assurance. "It's buried somewhere. I'll bet on that."

Zeb said he was mistaken.

"Well, what happened to it then?"

Zeb was silent. He and Julie had wondered, too. Most everyone bragged about the stuff they had hidden. All except Eulie.

Jim Perkins was in church the following Sunday and

created quite a stir among the women and girls, none of whom had seen him more than casually. There were peeps from behind prayer books, and blushes when eyes met his. The men, recognizing the drummer, gave glum looks. The minister greeted him with his usual warmth toward new-comers and invited him to join the picnic that followed.

Perkins, in his element among women, used his talent to good effect by mingling with mothers of pretty daughters, gravitating finally to Eulie and Aurelia. There he remained and insisted on hitching his hack to their surrey and driv-ing them home.

Zeb and Julie could not help hearing the disgruntled remarks that followed. "He's seen their house. Thinks they're rich," said a fat woman with a marriageable daughter. "He thinks he'll find that legendary gold," said a willowy blond, who despite her loveliness had not found a mate. "I heard his folks are Crackers," uttered a woman who had four unmarried daughters.

Poor womanhood! The war had depleted the male popu-lation to such an extent that the second generation of young men found themselves too burdened with the sup-port of female relatives to permit marriage.

Jim Perkins became a frequent visitor at Valhalla. He tactfully informed Eulie that in his work he had become a good judge of human nature. In women he admired beauty of mind more than beauty of form.

Eulie was skeptical, but held her peace. When she saw that Aurelia was in love with Jim, and Jim had declared his love for Aurelia, she set about making preparation for the wedding.

Hiram's brother from Savannah came to give the bride away. Aurelia, wearing her mother's wedding gown, looked beautiful as she came slowly down the broad stairs to the strains of Lohengren, as rendered by Ellen at the organ. There she was joined in wedlock with the very handsome

Mr. Perkins, whom everyone agreed acted as if he loved her.

After a week of honeymooning on the white sands and rainbow tinted waters of a Florida coast, Eulie made them a speech, holding a spade in either hand. "I suppose you have wondered why I haven't given you a wedding present. It is a very private gift, much too private to have presented at the wedding."

She handed each a spade, picked up a wheelbarrow and steered them to orchard. Under the crook of a pear tree she pointed to the ground and, with the air of a general, commanded them to dig. She was a bit surprised when Jim laughed, asked no question, and began digging. Aurelia, as was natural, hesitated, and asked questions.

"It's a big surprise, dear. Help him dig."

The chest, dug up, was carted to the summer dining room, where the mass of gold was dumped on the tiled floor when the mildewed bags spilled their contents. Jim picked up a coin from the dully gleaming heap, examined it even to biting it. Suddenly he let out a whoop, fell on the heap and rolled like a hog in a mud puddle.

Aurelia, throwing her arms around her mother, wept. "You saved all this for me!"

"You might say: 'The miserly Eulie Jefferson finally confessed.' Let's hope it won't make Atlanta headlines." She turned to Jim who had quit rolling and was back on his feet, although somewhat disheveled. "Now let's get it on the table and start counting."

Eulie was forced to produce Hiram's will to convince Jim Perkins that only half belonged to him and Aurelia. Aurelia's really. When the counting was completed and equally divided, and he saw that even half made him a rich man, he seemed satisfied.

Eulie rather grimly returned her share to the chest, locked it, and kept the key. Her share was soon invested in savings certificates, which would yield enough interest to meet her needs. In the meantime she wrestled with the fear that Jim Perkins created within her.

Jim was intoxicated with the fact that for the first time in his memory he might live like a gentleman. One of his first acts was the purchase of a brougham to replace the faded surrey. The next was hiring a gardener who also served as liveried coachman. He rode the fields in English riding breeches to inspect the work of hirelings. His clothing came not from Atlanta nor even New York, but from London tailors. He demanded that Aurelia dress according to his taste. He renovated Valhalla, and entertained lavishly.

He showed normal paternal pride when, a year later, a son was born; but, when a daughter appeared a year and a half later, he firmly stated there would be no more.

Little Jimmie and Fannie afforded Eulie the greatest happiness she had known since Hiram died. She cared for them lovingly when Jim and Aurelia toured Europe. Each night she prayed for them: her daughter, her grandchildren, and, most vehemently, for Jim Perkins.

Eulie grieved over the diminishing of Jim's and Aurelia's fortune. He had rebuffed any attempt made toward economy or investment. Even in the face of disaster he had put forth a bold front, refusing to acknowledge its presence. He, however, finally exploded at Eulie, hate in his eyes.

"How can you sit by so peacefully, hoarding all that money, and see your flesh and blood suffer?"

When Eulie was too surprised to speak, he tempered his speech. "All I need is a loan. You'll get it back—with interest." He could not avoid the contempt inflected in the last two words.

A bit subdued, she replied, "I may be selfish, as you say, and, if so, please forgive me, but my way of living is not your way. When I am gone, all will be yours."

He had said no more, but there were innuendoes that

made her uncomfortable. There was, for instance, the cold look he gave her, following the death of a friend, and his words: "She was younger than you, wasn't she?"

Apology for living was a new thought—a thought unpleasant enough to cause her to leave her pleasant room in the big house and take up residence in the guest house, formerly the overseer's cottage of antebellum days.

Her new abode, with some touching up with gay scrim curtains for the windows, was comfortable and even attractive. She enjoyed a new feeling of independence and more time for meditation.

She weighed her feelings toward Jim's financial problems. She had already begun helping with food and clothing, and she avowed she would never see her daughter and grandchildren become needy; but she could not see herself a partner to Jim's profligacy. Given free rein, he would make them all paupers. He must battle with his own pecunious weakness.

On the night she had settled the matter with her conscience, she went to bed and had a dream that set her mind topsy-turvy. She dreamed that she and the family were riding in a buckboard, which had replaced the brougham. Jim and Aurelia sat on the spring seat, and she sat just behind them on a cane bottomed chair. The children sat at the open back, hanging their legs out. Jimmie had his shoes off so he could pick up pebbles when going up hill.

The sky grew dark and ominous, accompanied by thunder and lightning. The children crept near, Fannie hugging Eulie's knees. Jim whipped the horses into a lope as the sky grew darker. He then rose to his feet and began whipping the animals unmercifully, ignoring the cries of the children and screams of Aurelia.

Miraculously the rig held together, and they reached

home in a torrential downpour of rain. Aurelia yelled for her to come to the big house, but Eulie went to her own.

Latching the door against the fury of the wind was difficult, but she finally managed it. She saw the man standing behind her when she turned.

"Who are you?" she cried. "I didn't see you come in."

He gave no answer but stood gazing at her with eyes that never blinked. "Well," she said, "if it's the rain you are dodging, you are welcome. Sit down while I light a fire."

He neither spoke nor obeyed, but continued to stare at her with eyes that looked like agate marbles. Unnerved, she started for the door, but he was there before her, flattening his back against it.

At last he spoke. "You will take the chair. Sit down."

His compelling eyes made her slowly obey. He then moved over to the far side of the fireplace to face her squarely. She noted his clothing was that of the conventional farmer. His head was large, his hair black and clinging to his head as if pasted. When he spoke, no muscle save his mouth moved.

"You are going to die soon. I came to tell you."

She waited for him to go on, but he was silent, staring with seemingly lidless eyes. She tried to rise, but the chair held her as if it, too, were under his spell. "I am getting along in years," she said, glad she had her voice, "but I'm healthy, so not planning on dying soon."

"You will be killed—soon."

Eulie was not one to cringe or be subdued easily. In her dream she remembered a panther she once met in the woods. She had screamed so lustily that, not only did the panther depart hurriedly, but Hiram, two miles away, heard and started for the rescue. She therefore summoned all of her strength toward screaming and wrenching herself from the chair. She succeeded with a desperate guttural sound that brought her into wakefulness.

Still disoriented, she yelled into the darkness. "Come out from there. I know you're there!"

She fumbled for matches on the bed table, breaking the first one but succeeding with the second in coaxing a flame on the tallow candle. Holding it high, she saw only the familiar objects of her room.

Getting out of bed, she threw a wrapper over her chemise, and managed to get a fire started in the fireplace. She sat and leaned her head against the crocheted headrest. Then she chuckled, knowing she had just had a nightmare.

Only children have nightmares, she told herself. There had been many in childhood, following Aunt Kizzie's ghost stories, but the effects had been erased by creeping into her mother's bed.

There was no mother's bed to creep into now, but she felt the need of human companionship, keenly. She thought of Aurelia in the big house but knew how silly it would be to go knocking on the door at this hour. She must wait till morning.

She busied herself tidying her room, knowing there would be no more sleep for her. She made her bed, plumping the pillows and placing them carefully behind starched pillow shams.

By the time she had finished the task, she had decided to say nothing to the family about her dream. Aurelia undoubtedly would say, "Mother, Mother, if all your dreams came true, we'd all be dead." Jim would also treat the matter lightly, or completely ignore it. The children would listen and be scared. She would tell her dream to Julie and Zeb. They would not treat her dream lightly, and she had a feeling they might help in some way.

Waiting for the dawn, Eulie kept telling herself that a

dream was but a dream, but it did not help. Perhaps her nerves needed doctoring. To her friends she must go.

She put another log on the fire when daylight shimmered through the windows, hung an iron kettle on a crane to heat water for coffee and cornmeal mush. For simple cooking she preferred the fireplace instead of the wood stove in the kitchen. It brought memories of childhood and mammies.

The mush, enriched with cream from yesterday's milking, was comforting. Later she donned her blue checked gingham frock, belted it with a lacy white apron, and tied on a bonnet that matched the apron. Throwing a shawl over her shoulders, she stepped out into the tangy morning air.

She saw Jim in the barnyard forking down hay, and remembered how he hated menial work. She called to say she was going to see Julie and would be home before night. He turned his head to let her know he had heard.

Her destination was more than two miles away, but she had walked it many times. The warming sun reminded her that spring was near. Robins were disporting themselves in preparation for their journey northward. A ragged blanket of forget-me-nots covered the red earth. She felt a tingle at the thought of dogtooth violets and wild irises.

She could hear the convicts before reaching the railroad; that is, she could hear the whip-popping and the cursing, and later, the chains. She concealed herself behind a young growth of sweetgum more from pity than from fear. After they were well beyond the crossing, she hurried across the track.

Julie greeted her with her usual kiss. She dried her hands on her apron, having just come from the spring where she had placed the morning milking. "Let's sit on the porch, if you don't mind, since the day is going to be warm." She brought out a lapful of dried peaches, sat, and began trimming the fruit for tarts. She motioned Eulie to a willow rocker, meanwhile giving her a keen look. "What's up, Eulie?"

Julie sat without relaxing. "I might as well tell you right off why I came."

Julie's eyes were popping after Eulie related the dream. "That was no dream. It was a message from the Lord." She turned to Zeb, who was sitting on the edge of the porch with his feet on the ground. "What do you think, Zeb?"

Zeb spat tobacco juice into a dry petunia bed. "Sounds a mite unusual, I admit, but I don't have any theory about dreams." He stretched his long arms in a yawn, saying, "I must leave you gals. Got to get a piece of land across the creek plowed before the rains start." He whistled to a large shaggy dog who was playing at stalking a toad. "Come, Shep." The dog bounded forward, his golden brown coat gleaming in the sun.

The day passed languorously. Julie brought pillows and blankets for the hammock Zeb had made from rope and barrel staves and suspended between two chinaberry trees. Eulie rested and dozed, feeling the security of friendship.

Zeb returned at four o'clock, leading Shep on a leash. Casting off his straw hat, he mopped his face with a blue bandana, slumping a little from fatigue.

"Eulie," he began, "how would you like to take Shep home for the night?"

Eulie regarded the dog's massive size with some doubts. The dog was looking her over, gravely. Zeb continued. "If you're afraid something might happen to you, I advise you to take him. If you are molested, he will protect you, but only if you command him."

She saw dignity and intelligence in the dog's eyes. "I'm sure he will, Zeb. Hiram once had a Newfoundland dog." She took the leash from Zeb. "You will never know how I cherish my good friends."

Zeb squinted down the road. "There's someone coming at a fast clip."

The newcomer was a sheriff's deputy. He carried a rifle across the pommel of his saddle in addition to the gun in his holster. He paused long enough to report the escape of two convicts from the chaingang, then was on his way to warn other farmers.

"Eulie, this might be the answer to your dream. Stay with us tonight. Please do." Julie was distraught over the possibility.

Eulie gave the matter some thought before replying. "I must go home. They will be looking for me. Will think a convict got me, if I don't show up as promised."

"Well, go if you must, but Zeb will take you in a buggy."

Eulie never wanted to burden anyone. Especially Zeb, tired from his toil. "I'll have Shep to protect me. Don't forget that."

There was another reason harder to explain. Eulie experienced a feeling of inevitability about her dream. If a convict were to be her nemesis, she wanted to face him squarely.

Seeing Eulie would not be dissuaded from walking home, Julie gave her a sack of cookies for the children. Eulie did not take the road but a cow trail through the woods that extended almost to her back door.

Courting danger, she reminded herself grimly. This danger was eclipsed by the risk of exposing Shep as her protector on the open road. Her would-be killer, whomever he might be, might merely postpone his evil deed, should he know about the dog.

Shep walked silently behind her, accommodating his tread to hers, only once pulling on the leash when a rabbit leaped across the path. A bower of yellow jessamine showered blossoms upon them, while a bluejay fussed with nestlings in a treetop.

Woman and dog reached their destination unobserved, and entered the back door. Shep moved about quietly as if he quite understood the role he was to play. Jim's watch dogs had however sniffed his presence, and started baying. Ignoring them, Shep busied himself with sniffing out Eulie's domain.

She saw through the window that the hounds had brought out Jimmie and Fannie. They were coming to her house. Telling Shep to lie down, she siezed the bag of cookies and hurried out to intercept them. With an arm around each, she ushered them back into the big house.

Her visit with the family was as brief as she could easily make it. Conversation centered about the chaingang escapees. Aurelia insisted her mother spend the night with them. While Eulie was trying to think of a reason for declining, Jim answered for her.

"I don't think she will be in any particular danger in her own quarters. The back door has a strong bar, and the front a good lock. Also there are the hounds. She'll be safe enough, for that matter."

"Besides," Eulie said, "I have Hiram's old shotgun." She laughed, then wondered at the hunch that made her refuse the greater safety of the big house when confronted with a bad dream and convicts.

Back in her own place, she pondered the matter further. Could there be reality in the belief that tonight an attempt on her life would be made? The idea would be preposterous had not Zeb and Julie reinforced it. Borrowing their dog was not a bad idea.

Shep devoured the leftover chop she offered him, following which he drank deeply from a pan of water. He then crouched and regarded her with brownish yellow eyes. When she was settled in her chair with her Bible, he came over and allowed her to stroke him. Later, resting on his paws, he gazed into the fire she had kindled to drive out the evening chill.

Eulie laid aside her Bible and wondered what a dog meditated about when gazing into the fire. She was beginning to doze when Shep lifted his head and gave her a look that seemed to ask when she was going to bed.

"All right, big boy, we'll go to bed." She proceeded to undress and put on her chemise. Turning back the covers, she climbed in. Patting the bed, she said, "Up, Shep." The dog leaped nimbly to the foot of the bed, turning himself until comfortable, and lay still.

She lay wide-eyed as the hours passed. She once heard Shep breathe as if asleep. Once she heard him whine softly as if dreaming. All sounds were magnified. Her ears missed nothing. The chirring of crickets, popping of floor boards, and the nervous sounds of the guineas in the barnyard took on ominous meanings.

Sometime after the clock on her mantel had struck midnight, she heard one of the hounds give a yap that dwindled into a note of apology to someone recognized. Propped on an elbow, she waited, holding this position even after her arm ached. Determined not to panic, she told herself she must be imagining someone turning a key in the lock of her front door. She tried to check her overwrought nerves by thinking she only fancied someone opening the door, holding it with a frim grip to prevent creaking. She then assured herself that there was utter silence when her senses tried to say someone was approaching her bed.

Imagination? Then why was Shep trembling? She sat upright. Shep's trembling had increased, and he was crouching. "Take him, Shep," she commanded in a low intense voice.

The dog leaped with a growl primordial. There was a

startled cry as two bodies hit the floor. The struggle, hideous beyond description, was mercifully brief. She could hear Shep pawing and sniffing something on the floor. He soon leaped back on the bed, and the only sounds were his panting and the beating of her heart.

She thought of the candles on the table but felt incapable of moving. Her eyes were kept on the window as she waited for dawn. After a seeming eternity, she saw the blackness become dark gray, then light gray. She could now see the spinning wheel in the corner, her chair, and the clock on the mantel. Still she would not move. When the upper rim of the sun became visible, Shep looked at her inquiringly. Thus prompted, she sat up and looked toward the floor to see what she must see. She saw the torn throat, the dark clotted blood, the staring, unseeing eyes, and the upper lip curled back from the teeth.

The day was bright now. She should no longer fail to see the dark curling hair, the chiseled nose, the familiar chin of Jim Perkins. His fingers, stiff and white, gripped a bowie knife.

She was not surprised. Not really. Fear of him had long dwelt in the recesses of her mind, culminating in the dream man who had come to warn her. It was easy to assume that Jim, having long planned his act, had chosen the time of escaping convicts as an escape for himself. The timing of her dream to coincide with his preparation for his deed was another matter.

Jim Perkins was given a Christian burial. His fingers had been pried from the knife, and a silk scarf had effectively concealed the ugly throat wound. The wails of his children, who had been spared the more gruesome details of his demise, aroused pity and some tears from bystanders.

Although Eulie and her friends believed that her escape from a horrible death was an act of Providence, there were others who doubted. There was, for instance, Dr. Samuel

Witherspoon, of Trinity College, who, having read of the incident in a newspaper, wrote a letter to Eulie, asking for an interview. He was gathering data for a thesis on extrasensory perception, a new field in which he was most interested.

He reached Valhalla when spring was in full bloom. Hitching his hack at the rose trellis, he felt less than middle aged as he walked the flagged path to the entrance. He even gave a little thought to springtime and a young man's fancy, and blushed.

When greeted at the door, not by his client but by her daughter, he was sure of experiencing a psychic shock. When he had met Eulie and the children, and had seated himself comfortably, he opened his notebook and scribbled; *empathy*.

The longer he talked with his clients the more interested he became. When at last his note taking was ended and his notebook closed, he showed a reluctance to depart. When Eulie invited him to see the plantation and to remain for dinner, his pleasure was noticeable. When he finally left Valhalla, he had invited the group to visit his own tobacco plantation in North Carolina. A week later he was back to escort them. Eulie, after having viewed his wealth, whispered to Aurelia: "He is not interested in gold."

He was, however, interested in Aurelia. Since he had had no experience in courting a woman, never having had time he explained, his approach was that of an awkward school boy. With some prompting from Eulie, and a show of receptiveness from Aurelia, he found himself engaged to be married.

No one blamed Aurelia for marrying the professor three months after the death of Jim Perkins. She would not have been greatly censured if she had made a grand affair of the wedding. She made it instead a quiet occasion, for she still ached with the memory of the man she had once loved.

Eulie clung to Valhalla, although everyone expected her to go with her family to North Carolina. She lived alone except for a black couple who occupied the guest house. At the turn of the century she bought herself a buggy automobile and drove it herself. Zeb bought one too, so there was much traveling to and fro.

On a dreary day in December she drove her noisy vehicle to Julie's to discuss plans for Christmas. The two sat cozily by the fire and basked in the happiness of their lifelong friendship. Valhalla would soon ring with the laughter of daughters, grandchildren, and friends. It must be the greatest homecoming ever.

Eulie fished a brier pipe from her reticule, filled it with tobacco, and lit it. Julie produced a silver snuff box, that Zeb gave her on their fortieth wedding anniversary, took a big dip, on the frazzled end of a blackgum twig, and transferred it to her lips.

"What would the professor think if he saw us using tobacco?" Julie said with a twinkle in her eyes.

"Nothing," Eulie replied. "I'm smoking his tobacco." She blew a smoke ring, a large one, a small one, and a middle sized one. She had become quite good at it.

Cobwebs

Jody Scott

Jody Scott is the author of PASSING FOR HUMAN *(DAW Books) and* I, VAMPIRE *forthcoming from Berkley. She was co-author of* CURE IT WITH HONEY *(Harper), a recipient of the Mystery Writers of America special award. Reverend Chumleigh, the astonishing modern-day vaudevillian, attributes his personal philosophy and burgeoning wealth to Jody's landmark short story* Go For Baroque, *originally in* FANTASY AND SCIENCE FICTION.

KISS THE WHIP, *Jody's most recent work, is purportedly the Great American Novel, but so controversial that it has been suppressed by New York publishers unable to cope with the world-shattering importance of this magnum opus. The rumor is that this novel rubs the noses of the oppressed in their own ca-ca. Whenever it sees publication, perhaps we'll all have our lives changed, just like the Reverend Chumleigh. It must be published, too, or we're doomed to an eternity of the same miserable lives we're living now.*

When I asked Jody for a short story for TALES BY MOONLIGHT, *I didn't think I'd be fortunate enough to get it. But I did. It's called* Cobwebs, *a sardonic, nightmarish story of young colonists.*

The Atkinsons got off the train at North Fork. They were heading wearily toward a creosoted shack to get their

passports stamped, when the thing happened. A gang of
beast-women, "shaggies," stark naked under ragged cloaks,
tried to jump Cort. Or maybe Cort and Stella both. He
couldn't be sure.

Of course they were just whores out to make a buck.
But they had double rows of tits; and the dumbshow they
put on was pitiable, but infinitely horrible. It all took place
in dead silence. They were mutes. The saliva drooled from
their jaws; and they wouldn't take no for an answer.

Then suddenly Cort went crazy in his pent-up fury. His
fist exploded into the nearest obscene mouth, and he shrieked
at the beasts to get the hell off, and stay off or he'd break
all of their filthy, goddamned, pustulous necks with the
greatest of pleasure.

The whores slunk away into the gloom beyond the
platform; and Cort felt swamped with emotions he couldn't
handle. He wiped his bloody knuckles, found his briefcase,
and lit a cigar with shaking hands. Then he stood brooding,
overcome with guilt because he'd smashed a beast-woman's
ugly face and perhaps broken a few of her rotten teeth.

And he wondered what to do now. The guards had gone
off duty. Nothing for it but to get their papers stamped;
then try to make sure the baggage was transferred safely
for once. Then with luck they could rest, and hope to
blazes the Express would be along in an hour or two.

As for Stella, she was too exhausted to complain or
even care much about what was going on. The worst of it
was how Stella was going to pieces before his eyes. They'd
had little sleep: had to sit up in a creaking, sub-zero coach,
and now Cort kept sensing a whirl of tilted buttes and their
shadows coming at him as they'd done all day yesterday.
And at night, nothing but blackness, eerie and hypnotic,
with the occasional kerosene lamp, where some lonely
squatter was probably enduring the most godawful non-life
imaginable.

And he'd thought Australia had been a barren country.

The wicket banged shut before they could present their papers. Bad luck, but the trooper in the booth shouted that it would be all right; they should go round and go into the shack and wait until they were given a number. Then as they turned to go, a flock of Gulfways skimmed overhead with necks out, wattles flapping, making a disgusting sound which was supposed to mean something, he didn't remember what. He pulled a face and said, "Bloody birds!" and the trooper gave him a suspicious look. Cort had what amounted to a pathological dread of the Gulfways, but he never spoke of it. Nor did he even think about it.

Aside from that, the sky here was really special. A fathomless and luminous pink shading into rose, with multi-colored bands unfolding over the steppes. The travel writers always raved about "breathtaking vistas; a rainbow heaven" and all such garbage. But Revelstoke wasn't a bad planet really. You got used to it. Things could be worse. Of course needless to say, it would be horrible to die and be buried in a place like this so far from home, but no need worrying about that at their tender age.

It was more cheerful when they stepped inside. The shack looked remodeled from a native homestead. A blazing peat-and-thorn fire crackled away; quite palmy, after the chilly night in transport. They went and had a wash, then found a coffee machine with real Instant steaming hot, costing an arm and a leg, but still a miracle, and they treated themselves to a couple of mugs and carried them to a bench; where they sat drinking slowly and gratefully and looking around at not much.

Stella began to perk up. After a bit she gave him a smile, bearing her pretty teeth and saying:

"You look handsome and refreshed, my darling. How do you manage after a night like that?"

And he gave the usual appropriate answer. Honeyed

words, calculated to cheer up a fellow traveler, but actually he'd seen his reflection in the coffee-machine mirror. The smudges under the eyes gave him a beaten and snivelly look like some little rat on a mountain or some wildfaced refugee bloke with his nerves all shot to pieces.

And having Stella humor him only made it worse. She treated him like a spoiled baby who needed to be handled all the time. That was false kindness. It was even a bit unethical; hardly worthy of her. And it filled him with unspeakable melancholy. Because the fact was, all that sweetness of hers didn't amount to a plugged nickel. The true state of affairs was that Stella wasn't in love with him any longer. They'd been on Revelstoke six months and she hadn't been in love with him for all that time. Cort was quite sure of it. She never reached for his hand the way she used to. Something had killed their love, and turned them into strangers. Something had sucked the life-force out of their marriage. He forgot how it all started; but Revelstoke had done it. This planet oppressed the heart.

They never should have come here. Never listened to the promises of a lot of lying, hot-air politicians. Never joined the horde of deluded newlyweds, to be sold a bill of goods by conniving thieves, telling them the streets up here were paved with bloody diamonds. Oh, yes; settling Revelstoke had made a lot of people a lot of money, but Cort wasn't one of them.

And Stella: he could feel her beside him, an appealing woman, even now quite composed, and fresh-faced, striking-looking, with a charming profile which he sat watching as she drowsed.

Six months earlier, they had asked each other:

"Are you sorry we came here, my darling?" all the time.

"Of course not," was always the reply.

Six months ago they asked, "What's wrong, my dearest,

my beloved?'' over and over; but as there seemed to be no sane answer, they began putting up barriers, hardly realizing what they were doing. Revelstoke had done it. Because back in Melbourne Stella had been so high-spirited, young, innocent, and a lot of fun to be with; and now look at her. Beaten and disillusioned, like he himself. Intimidation oozing from every pore. It was the bureaucracy of the colony, the alien conditions, and the homesickness. And he, just as troubled, too busy with his tenth-rate job to pay enough attention.

They'd had such hopes for the Great Beyond. ''Space, the last frontier'' would solve all human problems. Oh how the early tourists raved about this place. Oh yes, the perfect spot to open a law practice, start a family, buy a home, and bring up your kids to be decent people like in the old days. But what was it really? A lawless country. A lonely spot; beset with all the money-grubbing, and competition, and meanness, vanity, suffering, and pettiness, they'd tried so hard to escape.

So why not clear out? Ah, good question. They'd do it; as soon as they got the fare home. If Big Table worked out they could do it in a month. At the moment it was a matter of protecting their investment. At the moment, they were staying off welfare, they were squeezing by.

Cort unbuttoned his overcoat with a sigh, and unzipped his briefcase of much-cracked but genuine old cowhide leather that he kept polished to a mellow glow. It was good to buckle down to work, and dive into the arms of a contract or a trust deed, or an estate settlement, or a letter to a client. Property dealings were rum because of tri-valued ownership; and when you considered the rampant inflation, well, those bragged-about legal fees turned out to cover expenses, but only just. The truth of the matter was, the Atkinsons were quite frankly running out of money.

But things would go easier once they got settled in the

Capital. As Cort concentrated, a swink darted past his feet;
bold little animal a bit larger than a mouse. Stella didn't
like them but she didn't see this one. She just slumbered
on. When she next stirred, Cort was going to ask if she
would like to use his coat for a pillow, when suddenly a
window flew open behind a wicket, and a light went on.

Inside the booth stood a man in a white coat. He was
tall, and his head under a low-hanging bulb had the look of
a large melon. He seemed to be going through some
passport files. He slammed one drawer and opened another,
thumbing the metal tabs that were stuck to the tops of the
folders, then noticing Cort looking he smiled and said in a
hearty voice,

"I'm Doctor Fowler. It won't be long now."

"Will we be checked right on through?"

"That depends. If everything's in order, no problem."

"Do we need a number?"

"No; you're fine."

The doctor was rough in looks, but a soothing type,
with a good-natured face and a shaved head. His manner
made Cort feel relaxed enough to try and catch some sack
time. By now there was nobody else in the station except
for a woman with a baby, dozing at the end of the opposite
bench. Cort zipped his case and settled back on the frayed
plush for a bit of a snooze. Almost instantly, his head sank
like a weight; he fell into a dreamless sleep. But after what
seemed like only a minute he felt Stella nudge him.

"Look," she whispered.

She was staring at the woman on the opposite bench.
Cort raised his head to glance at this woman, who wore a
red velveteen dressing-gown and a pair of house slippers
with pink pompons on them. Against her robe, the baby's
hair was bright yellow. Cort scraped his feet and tried to
find a comfortable position as he whispered back,

"At what?"

Their murmurs caused the woman to give them a sudden, staring glance. Cort was struck at once by her powerful looks; a rather large woman, she resembled a stocky piece of sculpture, with a slightly undershot lower jaw. She was a type Cort always thought of as early Viking; husky, and with her hair in a thick yellow braid round her head.

He was impressed by her glowing, haunted eyes. He'd seen faces like that, on a cycling trip through Scandinavia the summer before he entered law school. But her eyes were dark, liquid brown; not the blue you'd expect of a nordic type; and she wore a fixed smile.

The baby clenched one small red fist and slept on. Cort saw a faint tracing of gossamer shimmer between mother and child for a moment and then disappear.

The woman dropped her eyes.

"Just keep watching," Stella whispered quietly in his ear.

"Are you folks going far?" the doctor called out suddenly.

"To Big Table," Cort told him.

"Really!"

"My firm is transferring me there."

The doctor said nothing, so Cort went on.

"Our title searches are being stalled, for reasons unknown. They felt it would help if one of us went in person, and handled the breakdown, if there is one."

There was no real reason to mention all this. But it could be a lonely trip, except for chance conversations with strangers. He knew Stella disapproved a little; she felt it was nobody's business but theirs. But the doctor merely remarked:

"Well, you'll be all right if you don't lose too much time. There'll be heavy storms up above, any day now."

He stood sifting and pawing the passport cards, then jerked one out and rolled it into an old-fashioned type-writer and began banging away at the keys. Cort settled back; he crossed his ankles, sticking his legs straight out in the aisle, but sleep was improbable after all the goings-on. He couldn't help sneaking glances at the Viking woman, trying to perceive what Stella had found so remarkable. But there was nothing out of the ordinary about her, so he rose and sauntered to the window.

The suns had crescented. They were two disks of intense light, marking opposite horizons. It would soon be burning day. Cort leaned against the wall and had a smoke while he stared through the dirty glass. Another depressing dawn. This was a great setting—for a creepy movie. For a person's real life it was confusing, in a strange, subtle way. Out there was a monotonous desert called the Steppes; all raddled with shadows, so that not even the bright coloring made it warm or inviting, in spite of the advertising blurbs. And it reached in after you. Until your soul felt as worn out and barren, and black-raddled as the plain itself.

He turned to study his wife's face instead of the view. She caught his eye and smiled . . . but for some reason it gave him a chill. Probably due to his own depressive thoughts caused by socking that poor drooling shaggy, as the beast-women were called. His hand still ached; it was odd, he'd never thought the day would come when Stella's smile or her soft, full, round breasts wouldn't exhilarate or comfort, or excite, sadden, or thrill him with ecstasy, worth a damn.

Here was the really ironic part. They'd left Melbourne because the city sickened them. It was crowded, they had a sense of not belonging; they cared nothing for groupsex, were madly in love with each other, couldn't stand the adultery, and despised all the softcore TV and all the conglomerate cheapness; in other words they just didn't fit in. It seemed childish now. Because after all they were plain, middleclass people and not pioneer types at all.

They weren't ruthless enough, or greedy enough, or even bright enough, when it came down to it, to compete here in the colony.

They'd been in love, and they'd had a fairytale romance. He remembered Stella sitting on a fence rail waiting for him to get off work, chewing a straw, green leaves rustling all about. But then: so much for time-softened memory, soft as cobwebs. If there was anything Cort couldn't stand it was self-pity.

He was pinching out his cigar when the Southbounder shot by on its blinking ray. They made the weirdest noise; hardly a roar, more like a mild, babbling chatter. A pure sound it was, soft and seductive as bees in a glade. He could never describe it except to call it "other wordly"; unnatural, you might say. But he was relieved these coaches were still running. The Express would be along soon and before you knew it they'd find a good hotel and have a decent meal and a really splendid sleep, and start getting back to normal.

He replaced the half-smoked cigar in its case and ambled restlessly about, keeping one eye on Stella as she watched the Viking. Stella had gone very pale. She stared openly, not hiding it, and with what seemed to be a growing uneasiness.

The Viking did look wraithlike. She'd gone all tallowy as if sick, and was gazing intently down at the infant. She was like a yellow candle in a red wrapper. Her face was very much like hard wax. Cort took his seat beside Stella, noticing that when he passed the woman and stirred the air, the filaments went puffing out. They were glossy, flapping languidly between the mother's mouth and the child's hand; then the Viking turned her head and more filaments appeared, this time attaching to her handbag. And there was an odor in the air. Stale dust. A musty smell Cort hadn't noticed before.

"Watch when she breathes," Stella urged.

It did seem that every time the woman exhaled, a thread would spin out sluggishly and attach itself to something. Either to her fingers, or her bag, or the plush bench; or to anything close.

"My God!" Cort muttered. "I see what you mean."

"But what *is* it?"

When he shrugged, his flesh recoiled in a kind of convulsive wrench so that he tasted the instant coffee again. Then while he stared at the Viking, fascinated, Doctor Fowler came out of the booth and sat beside them with a friendly and bustling air.

"No need to alarm yourselves," the doctor said quietly. "As you may expect, everything's been done that could possibly be done."

"But what *is* it?"

"Something new. No name as yet. But do me a favor and don't stare, will you? She's a shy one; you'll embarrass her."

Cort noticed that when the webbing got too thick the woman wiped it away, then wiped her fingers off on the underside of the bench. Each time, she wiped the sticky threads off carefully; and she did this with an air of the utmost sad resignation, until finally Cort stammered out in surprise,

"But it's getting worse by the minute!"

When he jumped up, Doctor Fowler put out a hand to stop him. "Easy, old boy. No use going round the twist—"

The doctor's tone was complacent, and a tiny strand blew out of his mouth, but he didn't seem to care or notice. Cort pushed the extended arm away and strode to the door.

"I've got to find the stationmaster," he half-shouted.

Outside, he walked round to where the ticket-taker had first told them to get a number; but his booth was closed and locked with a heavy padlock, and there was not a soul in sight. So Cort stormed back in, feeling a newly-forming urge to give the placid doctor a punch right square in his belly. He yelled,

"And just where the hell is the stationmaster? Where is the oh-so-cautious guardian of the inner door? Isn't anybody *alive* in this forsaken burg?"

The doctor, who up until now had regarded him with a benign expression, frowned and said quietly:

"Mr. Atkinson, will you please come here and sit down? I've got a question for you."

Cort sat angrily. "Well?"

"Do you know what the word 'phobophobia' means?"

"No, I do not, sir!"

"You wanted a name for the disease; all right, I give you one. Phobophobia, the fear of fear. So let's calm ourselves and not martyrize, and not scare the woman; everything's going to be fine."

And Cort felt soothed by the doctor's placid manner, in spite of himself. He asked,

"Just how fine is 'fine', then?"

"I mean that the disease doesn't bother its victim at all. There's no physical suffering; there's a relaxed, happy frame of mind and the best part is, it's all over in about an hour. What more can anyone ask?" He gave Cort's arm a bracing squeeze and stood up, laughing.

"Let's just say there are a lot worse things." Then he winked and spat into the fire. Then he walked into his office and shut the door but didn't turn the light on.

When they were alone, the Viking woman said in a breathy tone of controlled hysteria,

"I don't talk because it makes it happen twice as fast," and gave an embarrassed laugh.

She was right about that. A cloud of gauzy stuff literally flew out of her mouth and attached everywhere: to her

knees, to the bench and floor, and thickly all over the
baby's face, making it wake up and begin to cry. The
mother brushed the strands away, and passed her hand
under the bench to scrape off all the clinging filaments.
Then she raised one finger as if to hold their attention, and
slowly began,

"Well! I'm sorry it happened this way. You seem like a
nice couple, and I hope you don't blame me; but, it's a
matter of not starting a panic."

"What do you mean by that?" Stella asked in a stupe-
fied tone.

The woman raised her tragic eyes to them and said:

"Oh, Mrs. Atkinson, I'm sure if you give it some
thought. If you consider others. If you think of what might
happen."

Then her face broke into a smile, but the baby began to
scream; it was half-smothered in a layer of cobwebs. The
woman scraped this film away very serenely, and the baby
soon quieted down. Stella kept demanding to know what
the Viking woman had meant, but she gave them both an
amused look, and shook her head, dropped her eyes, and
wouldn't say any more.

Then Stella began to cry noiselessly. The tears ran down
her face.

"Oh, Cort. Oh, Cort," she sobbed after a bit.

"What the hell are you blubbering about?" Cort wanted
to shout; but there wasn't any point to arguing. His wife's
grief only made him feel all the more languid and bored.
At most it gave him a vague yearning for something, he
didn't know what.

"Oh, my darling," Stella moaned again. Her nostrils
were trembling and for some reason Cort thought this was
amusing. He certainly didn't intend being drawn into a
scene; really, why should he care? Stella could make a
fool of herself all she liked. It all came to nothing in the

end anyway. Didn't it always come to nothing in the end? But soon she perked up and dried her tears, and sat with a rapt look, just like that day she waited for him under the trees; what a happy expression she wore, with her lips parted, and the old glint of joy about her.

Cort yawned and unzipped his case, glad to escape into the sane world of legalese. He began working out a contractual fine point. "Purchaser agrees to assume every hazard of damage not excluding confiscation of property for the satisfaction of any and all claims of public demand—"

By now the Viking and her child were wrapped in a soft, shiny cocoon. Cort barely made out the woman's fingers brushing at the inside strands.

But then he couldn't help noticing a delicate thread that wafted in and out of Stella's nostril with every breath.

"Cort," she remarked once more in a flat, rather bored voice.

At this show of bravery, or whatever it was, Cort burst out laughing.

When he did, a glistening string drifted from his mouth and attached itself to the cracks in the polished leather of his briefcase.

The Toymaker and The Musicrafter

Phyllis Ann Karr

About 1973, Phyllis Ann Karr submitted a story to
MOONBROTH. *As it was not ghoulish enough to suit the
taste of Dale C. Donaldson, he kindly forwarded it to me,
since I had recently founded the magazine* FANTASY &
TERROR *with Dale's encouragement. I don't recall the
story anymore; I don't think it was about Torin the Toyman,
but it was probably something equally genteel. I do remember Dale's letter, which decried Phyllis' story as "too
literary" for the world's finest meathook horror magazine,
and just the thing for* FANTASY & TERROR. *Unless memory
fails, I didn't publish that particular story, but I eagerly
awaited another submission direct from Phyllis, and somewhere along the line the Toyman stories became a regular
feature of* FANTASY & TERROR. *A Torin story is also slated
for my Ace Books anthology* HEROIC VISIONS.

TALES BY MOONLIGHT *is a title which may imply, largely,
horror. But there's another type of moonlit tale: that of
Elsewhere or Eld; a gentle adventure encountered among
the butterflies and tiny mushrooms. Well, Torin the Toyman
is not exactly elfin—he's human like you or me (or at least
you)—but he's also of a further land than we can soon
visit: a land where culture is humane and peaceful. The
Toymaker and The Musicrafter is presented to you as a
resting place between tales of horror. So relax, and read!*

*   *   *

Torin had never before undergone a judgment, and he felt the blood in his cheeks even as he dipped a cup of spring water for the Judge whom Elvar had brought into his workshop. It was custom and courtesy that the receiver of judgment give the Judge milk or water before the decision, wine after. No custom forced the toymaker to extend his hospitality to the complainer, and he left Elvar the musicrafter to dip his own draft.

The Judge drank off his cup of water and turned the offending toy in his fingers. "Fine craftsmanship, Elvar," he remarked. "I see why it has frightened you."

The musicrafter snorted through his beak of a nose. "A quarter the size a five-string lyre should be, the bridge misshapen, the high strings gut like the low strings, instead of metal. And tuning pegs in the shape of owls!"

There was a rankle of truth in the musicrafter's words. Torin, trained as a toymaker, had no more than a layman's knowledge of music. Like all children, he had learned one instrument well enough to play a note-garland for his own First Name-Lengthening, and he still kept his old honeywood flute and beguiled an occasional quarter-hour with it, but he had fashioned this lyre with no model before him and with more imagination than cunning. However, faced with the musicrafter's scorn, the toymaker refused to admit any of this. "It was never meant," said Torin, "for anything but a child's toy."

An unmusical hiss came from Elvar's thin lips. "A toy!" he spat. "Next he'll be making small cooking pots and calling *them* toys!"

"I have never heard of such a toy," mused the Judge Mardanbur, rubbing his red and silver beard, "yet the poet Alberminar classes all musical instruments except the voice with life's non-essentials."

"And the poet Berandur, whose name would have had

five syllables had he died at sixty winters instead of thirty, classes them with the essential," protested Elvar.

"True," said the Judge, and covered his eyes with his hands to indicate his need for a space of silence.

While Mardanbur pondered, Elvar sat and stirred the small workshop with his gaze as if looking for some other toy about which to complain. Torin, unable to wait in idleness, rose and dipped water for himself, began to drink, coughed on one of his own brown hairs that had fallen into the cup, then glanced nervously to see if he had disturbed Mardanbur. He breathed more easily to find that the Judge appeared to have taken no notice. It was unwise to disturb the mindwork of any judge, even one with Mardanbur's name for fairness.

Indeed, Mardanbur's name for fairness argued against the receiver of judgment, since few complainers went to fair judges unless their complaints were firmly grounded.

After a short while, Mardanbur lowered his hands and looked up. "Had the poet Berander lived to earn five syllables," he remarked, "his thinking might have grown in other directions. But having only forty winters myself, I prefer not to give judgment on which poet has the right, but simply on which craftsman has it."

"Father," said Torin, "I admit that I had a new idea. I admit that no one until now has made a toy musical instrument. Until the time of Belsan, no one had made game boards. A craftsman must have some freedom. I don't tell Elvar what instruments he may fashion—how does he have a right to tell me what toys I may make?"

The musicrafter's thin nostrils flared. "And if I began making game boards?" he demanded. "What would you say to that?"

"Not a word!" Torin was a little ashamed to say this in the presence of Mardanbur, as he was far from sure of its truth; but he was not eating so lavishly that he could face an expensive judgment unmoved.

"Gently, gently," said the Judge. "Elvar, in fairness to Torin, repeat your reason for concern."

"Since you won't see it yourself, toymaker," said the musicrafter, "you can make and sell game boards, dolls, statues, useless decorations for home and body, bed charms, cake trinkets, and a hundred silly tricks to waste the time of children and foolish elders. I can make and sell nothing but musical instruments. If you make musical instruments, you take away my trade."

"I can't even sell it!" Torin burst out in frustation.

"You have sold it once," replied Elvar. "It did not remain sold, but not all people have as much sense as Brinda's mother."

The toymaker's lungs shrivelled. The musicrafter was closer to having the right, after all. The only custom Torin remembered at all fitting the problem was the fact that both toymakers and jewelcrafters fashioned body ornaments. But no, that did not truly apply. The wealthy persons who bought the high-priced gold and gems of the jewelcrafters did not wear the wood and commonstone pieces of the toymakers, made for folk who could not afford true jewelry, and so neither group of craftsmen took trade from the other.

There was no help, then. Torin would almost certainly bear the shame and, more important, the expense of Mardanbur's decison. The best he could hope was that it would be a soft judgment. Suppose he pointed out that he had been ready to take the toy lyre apart as a failure that could not be sold, and re-use the materials? No, some spirit whispered to him: to say this now would seem a lie and might only win him a harsher judgment. Still, he must make some protest.

"Father," he said, "Elvar has been an established craftsman for twenty winters and must take in more moneystones
in a single quarter-season than I've taken since the Fall
Festival. I haven't been here six seasons, and half my
nights my supper is too small to fill my stomach. And the
only child who bought my toy lyre brought it back saying
that because of it her mother had decided she should have
a real lyre instead, from Elvar's hand, as well as her
copper trumpet. How have I injured Elvar's trade?"

Mardanbur closed his eyes and slowly drew one forefinger across the toy's five strings. The fourth peg needed
tightening, but otherwise—to Torin's ear—the sound was
accurate, if foggy. However, Elvar said, "The tones themselves prove that toymakers have no right to meddle in
musicrafters' work."

"For that," said the Judge, "I must take your word, my
son. I have no ear for tones."

Torin began to say that by Elvar's own words, the toy
instrument could not take the place of a real one. But Elvar
spoke first. "All the more dangerous, father," said the old
craftsman. "If toymakers could sell such things as these,
how many children's ears would never learn to hear true
tones from false? Too many ears are dulled now by clumsy
musicrafters and musicians."

"You have stated your grounds firmly enough, Elvar,
and often enough," said the Judge, and again covered his
eyes with his hands.

Torin sat clenching his long fingers and glaring alter-
nately at Elvar's hooked nose and curling lips, and at the
small toy lyre. The musicrafter might have the right, but
what kindness was in his lungs, to make a hungry toymaker
such trouble over an idea that had failed? Hadn't it already
cost Torin enough? It had seemed a shining inspiration when
he made it, a toy musical instrument, something that had
never been thought of before. But when made, it had won

nothing but curious comments, giggles, and lopsided jokes from those who came into his workshop. The traders when they passed through on their way to Maethala had looked at it in puzzlement, given it cautious praise, and advised Torin that if a thing was too unheard-of it was not easy to sell. At last, four days ago, young Brinda had paid the three pebbles for it, only to bring it back yesterday and explain how her mother had told her: "If you want a lyre, we'll buy a real one from Elvar." By then Torin had used Brinda's pebbles to buy wine, bread, and a little yardfowl meat, so he had to give her their worth in other toys. There was the time lost in fashioning the lyre, the embarrassment of having it ill-understood, the three pebbles' worth of other toys, and now Elvar, who had learned of it from Brinda's mother, bringing its creator to judgment for it.

Mardanbur dropped his hands to the table, opened his eyes, and stood. At once the two craftsmen rose to their feet. "I regret," said the Judge, "that I must not think of one craftsman against another, but of the effect of such a judgment as this I must make now upon all craftsmen—not of a prosperous musicrafter and a struggling toymaker now, but of prosperous toymakers and struggling musicrafters in seasons to follow. Torin, you must destroy this lyre within ten days, and pay Elvar at once three pebbles, if that, as I understand, is the price you yourself set on it."

The young toymaker breathed deeply twice in order to control himself. "I have only two small stones in my box," he said. "Will Elvar accept my promise for the rest?"

"No," said the musicrafter, "but I'll accept the value in toys and allow you to redeem them, if you bow to your Judge and put your head under my hand according to the custom."

"Your pardon," Torin replied crisply. "I haven't had your experience with judgments." He went through the customary gestures, then put his two moneystones and toys worth the balance (chosen for their heaviness) into a carrying bag for the musicrafter.

"Don't forget the wine for your Judge," smirked Elvar before he left.

"Half a cup only, my son," said Mardanbur. He drank it off and lent the toymaker a few moneystones to live on. After the Judge was gone, the toymaker set to work on his revenge.

Ten days later they sat again in Torin's workshop. This time Elvar was scowling, the Judge laughing. Torin had spent his days cleverly. On the table stood a pinewood statue of a troll breaking a lyre. In each hand he held half of the splintered instrument, and he was chewing one of the strings. The troll was unusually ugly, but the hooked nose and thin lips were unmistakable. Likenesses were made every season, and no one had ever tried to bring a judgment even against the bitterest.

"Go about your own work in peace, my son," chuckled Mardanbur. "Torin's lyre is destroyed. You have no further complaint."

"You'll get no commendations from me, toymaker," growled Elvar as he stamped out.

"In that," remarked the Judge, "you'll be no different from any other craftsman. Elvar commends no one. Have you set a price on your new statue?"

"Five pebbles, father."

"A fair price," replied Mardanbur, bringing out his purse, "and a fair record of my decision."

"And you, father," said Torin, bowing more happily than he had ten days before, "well deserve your name for fair judgments."

Witches

Janet Fox

It's very difficult for writers who are not novelists to gain the sort of widespread acclaim they deserve for their work. In the recent decade, only James Tiptree, Jr. and Harlan Ellison leap to mind as famed primarily for their short stories. Janet Fox is well known to the horror aficionado; but she works exclusively in short stories and novelet lengths, so that that much deserved wider acclaim has not yet been hers. Perhaps time will rectify this.

A regular in YEAR'S BEST HORROR STORIES, *she has published in* AMAZONS!, FANTASTIC, MOONBROTH, SPACE & TIME, YEAR'S BEST FANTASY, *and many other magazines and anthologies. She teaches in Osage City, Kansas.*

If it weren't so damnably hard to sell a single-author short story collection nowadays, one of the best books of the year would be the Best of Janet Fox. The lead story might well be Witches.

He sat at the plastic counter and when his food came everything was in little plastic packets. A look out of the huge plate-glass window showed him the road he'd been driving all day, a featureless ribbon of blacktop rolled out indifferently through gutted hills showing strata of yellow rock. He opened a packet and put the white powder into his coffee, stirring it with a white plastic spoon. He watched the liquid swirl muddily, undissolved granules of imitation cream bobbing on the surface. It occurred to him that he was as close to being nowhere as you could get.

He left the turnpike just outside of Commercia, and the trees growing along both sides of the narrower highway engulfed the car in dancing patches of green-gold shadow, even more pronounced now that it was beginning to get dark. In the deceptive clarity of just dusk he saw something along the highway, a figure, slight, in jeans and a t-shirt, the shape seemingly distorted until one saw the canvas backpack. One thin arm was raised, the thumb extended. The same instinct which made him reject the plastic packets, put his foot on the brakes, tires gritting on gravel along the road's edge as he stopped. The figure, with an aptly feral movement, loped the few yards to the car, grasped the door handle. The light inside the car slid off very straight hair a color somewhere between red and gold. There were pale sun-freckles across the nose and cheeks and a mouth that seemed flexible to many expressions and now wore a furtive smile. The door slammed with an oddly inevitable sound.

"I'm going as far as Medicine Oaks," he said, hearing the grouchiness in his own voice with a kind of surprise.

"Thanks, mister."

He drove on, the car's interior now a capsule of darkness and silence except for the dim green glow of the dashlights. He'd seen the bud-tips of breasts under the thin cotton of the t-shirt and was filled with a vague unease. Only the nowhere feeling he was trying to outdistance had made him stop at night for a hitchhiker, a risky idea at best. She had put aside the backpack and was sprawled on the seat in apparent comfort. He'd been on the edge of delivering a lecture on the evils of hitchhiking for young girls until he realized he'd compounded the error by picking her up. It wasn't that she was in any danger from him.

He'd taught school, had children of his own. Still, he almost resented her posture of total relaxation.

"Are you going far?"

"I'm just seeing the country," she said in a rather sleepy voice.

"There isn't much country for tourists," he said hoping to insinuate that he suspected she had run away from some nearby home.

"It's interesting," she said. "Nobody bothers you."

Just as well she didn't seem to take his meaning, he reflected, since he might have to turn her over to the authorities at Medicine Oaks.

"Get many rides?"

"I didn't need one till now. I was traveling with someone."

"What happened? Or is it personal?"

"I don't know exactly. He was nice. He bought me these." She indicated the clothes and the knapsack. "But this morning I woke up in the hotel room alone; the motorcycle gone—Frankie too."

He was silent, with a last-of-the-dinosaurs feeling, wondering why it always surprised him, these girls putting on a casual sexuality with their training bras. But when he thought about it, he'd been left stranded, himself. Not that Cindy had run out on him; she'd done everything by the numbers. That was like her, managing the divorce like an elaborate dinner party—not to create publicity; that would be bad for her business, not to injure the children (they were like potted plants she moved so-delicately to avoid bruising the roots). "They're young," she said. "They'll adjust." He'd been awed by all of it, so that when the final papers came, he'd wanted to shake her hand, say "well done," but he'd left instead. He wondered why with all her careful building, he'd been able to see nothing but wreckage.

His headlights caught the doublestars of animal's eyes along the road, a blur of something small crouched in the border of weeds. Then, it was gone.

"What was that?" asked his hitchhiker, her voice a harsh whisper.

"Nothing. An animal along the road—a cat, maybe."

"I don't like cats." Her voice had an odd intensity. "Their eyes—they watch."

The lights of Medicine Oaks appeared, a starswarm on the side of the dark hills. It wasn't long before he was rounding the last wide turn and entering the main street, old fashioned buildings the color of dust lining it, overlaid with signs in garish neon. He knew where he was going to spend the night—a small dilapidated motel tucked away on a quiet side street. When he stopped in front of it he debated for a moment. He didn't exactly want to drop her off at the police station in the dead of night and it wasn't safe to leave her asleep in the car.

He got a double, not quite wanting to pay for two cabins. When he tried to waken her she rolled away from him so that he had to lift her, sleeping exhaustedly, and carry her inside. He'd been a little worried about the arrangements at first, but it was only like carrying a sleeping child to bed. Her face was curiously lax and empty of expression, as if the body were untenanted, the mind wandering some dreamscape.

When she showed no sign of wakening, he paused a moment, then undid the button and fly of her tight-fitting jeans, pulling them off the slim childish hips in cotton panties, then drawing the blankets quickly up to her chin. He prepared himself for sleep, liking the incongruity of having her there in the other bed. Her breathing was the last sound he heard before he fell asleep.

And then he was wandering in his own dream country.

The winds made a terrible racket moaning and whining around the angular contours of a strange distorted house. An immense oak tree grew by the door, its bulk seared white on one side by some long ago lightning bolt, and blood-red creepers grew rank along one wall of the structure, fluttering in the constant wind. As he watched, the door opened and three beings came out to stand in the shelter of the tree, their patched and ragged garments tossed in the wind. Their faces were dark and indistinct but he got the impression of age and a grotesqueness that surpassed human ugliness. They seemed to argue over something, skinny arms gesticulating. "You've stolen it, you hussy, and you will be made to give it back!"

He was awakened by a half-suppressed shriek and it was a moment before he remembered he wasn't alone in the room. The hitchhiker was sitting up, a hand over her mouth, the other held out as if to ward off some evil, her eyes large and dark with terror. He sat on the bed and put his arm around her. "Just dreams, honey," he said, as her half-shrieks subsided into sobs.

"They were going to bring me back there," she whispered, moving close to him. For a confused moment he thought she meant back to the strange house in his own dream. He became aware of her warm skin beneath the thin cotton shirt, the roundness of a breast against his wrist. It was one thing to tuck an inert sleeping body into bed—this was something else.

"I like it here," she said, looking up through the brassy-gold fringe of her bangs. "I like being close to you."

He moved away abruptly. "There now," he said, feeling stupid as he retreated from her warmth. He was possibly old enough to be her father, but he wasn't all that old. Christ, but he'd been a fool to even consider this arrangement. He felt vaguely as if he'd been caught molesting a student, but nothing for it but to grit his teeth till morning.

Then he could leave her here without worrying about the authorities. He wondered wryly if the motorcyclist had been such a moral sort as himself. She only wept a little longer, the sound deadened by the pillow.

He awoke and was confronted by the prosaic seediness of the motel decor. That weird place and those figures—only a dream and dreams for all their clarity, were nothing at all in the morning. In the next bed his hitchhiker was opening her gamine's eyes. Only a child and even if she were the teenaged queen of tramps, she had nothing to fear from him. He'd never been interested in jail-bait, after all. As a teacher and as a father, he should have learned something about children.

"How about some breakfast?"

"God, yes. How did you know I was starving?" she said, bounding barelegged from bed.

"Just a lucky guess. I'm Michael Payton. What's your name?"

"Rue."

"Ruth?"

"No. Rue."

He waited for a moment for a last name, but there was none coming. "You can get cleaned up and dressed in the bathroom. I'll buy you some breakfast, and maybe—well, let's just let the future take care of itself." He turned away and heard footsteps and then the sound of the shower.

Over breakfast in the cafe quaintly named "Mom's" he assumed his best teacherly manner, feeling now that he was in charge of the situation. "You won't prove anything by running away. Were they really so bad, your parents?"

She looked up stolidly. "I don't have any parents."

"Oh, I'm sorry. Well, who do you live with?"

"My sisters, but I can't go back there." She seemed to shudder a little.

"Were you mistreated? If you were, you wouldn't have to go home; there're places where you could finish school—"

"I do have a lot to learn about the world," she said with a mischievous smile.

"Sure, what if we went to the police station here, and—"

Her eyes wildly dilated and for a moment he thought she'd bolt from the booth, but she just crouched down against the window, making herself as small and unnoticeable as possible.

Outside on the raindamp pavement, two old ladies were them wore a bright flower-print dress on her sunken contours. They passed on by, their faces hidden by the umbrella.

By degrees Rue came out of her fearful, crouching stance.

"Did you know them?"

"Maybe—I'm not sure, but I've got to get out of here. You've got to take me with you—out of this town."

"You *are* on the run." He grasped her wrist, but a woman at the next table gave a shocked look and he let go. "You know I'll have to take you to the authorities."

Her mouth twisted into a smile, though her eyes had lost none of their terror. "Shall we inform them where I was last night?" she asked, her tone all innocence.

It was a moment before the anger came, before he realized just how neatly she had trapped him.

It was hot, the sun quickly drying the rain and creating a steam-bath atmosphere. Rue sat quietly, every so often turning to look out the back window as if she thought someone might be following. If she thought he'd forget the humiliation of this morning—

As he drove his anger cooled a little. He remembered her fear of those harmless old ladies, and how she'd cried out at night. He'd been thinking of stranding her along the road, but what if someone really dangerous picked her up? What she needed was help, maybe even the help of a psychologist. He resolved to keep her with him till he reached Salt City. Maybe he could reason with her, find someone to give her the help she needed.

The day was drawing to its sweltering close but he had every intention of reaching his destination before he slept even though it would probably take half the night. The road here overlooked a large state lake. Wind chopped the waves a little, and there was a cooling breeze through the car windows. "Can't we stop here, just for awhile?" she asked. He'd been thinking of the same thing. Grunting an ungracious assent he took the side road that would lead them down to the beach. As he turned off the motor, the noise of crickets scratched uneasy patterns on the silence. From here the highway was hidden and the narrow strip of sand beach was bordered with weeds.

Rue opened the door and slipped from the seat just as he told her to stop. She ran through the thigh-tall weeds until she reached the beach. Grudgingly he followed. The sun was clear amethyst seeping into a heatblanched sky, the wind brushing at the gritty feel of his skin. When he thought again of Rue, he saw her jeans and t-shirt lying empty on the damp sand. She was just shedding her panties and he saw her narrow buttocks just before she splashed into the dark water. He sat down in a dry place, loosening the collar of his shirt and laying aside his glasses. He sat with his head in his hands for some moments wondering if his concern for this stranger was because he wanted to ignore his own problems. Then he asked himself what problems, because it followed if you had no life, you had no problems.

When he looked up the shadow-webbed water was unbroken; no head bobbed there. With an awful feeling of loss he ran along the edge of the water. He saw nothing at first, then something that could be a body floating. He shucked his trousers, shrugged out of his shirt, and splashed toward the dark floating something, ripples casting back a thousand shards of broken moonlight. She was face down in the water, turning lazily. He struggled to turn her over, his feet seeking uncertain purchase in the mucky bottom. He thrashed in the water, pulling her toward shore. Her skin was waxy-white in the dim moonlight, her limbs lax, her face totally devoid of expression. Frightened he hugged her close for a moment and when he could detect no breathing, he opened her mouth and with a forefinger checked for obstructions. He put his mouth on hers, breathed gently in.

Her lips moved; one small hand clutched the back of his neck and her tongue darted delicately between his lips, so startlingly that he didn't move away. He felt her other hand, small and cold move down his stomach, insinuating itself under the waistband of his sodden briefs.

It was as if the world as he knew it had come apart. Cricket noise subsided into a burst of deafening silence. In his arms he held the delicate, almost sexless body of a doll . . . or a child, but when he looked into the face, something incredibly ancient and wise looked out at him, certain of a response. With all this, there was still an element of surprise in it when his hands, gritty with sand, found her breasts.

When he came back to reality, the droning insect song, the clammy gray sand, still holding the random sketchmarks their bodies had made, the brittle weed bending in the wind, he saw Rue sitting beside him, her face showing a drowsy satiety, her hands moving over the contours of her own body. "You won't have it back," she said, but not to him—to the darkness beyond the crazily waving shadows of dry weeds, as if someone were standing there listening. But no one was. "It's mine now. To use as I will. To enjoy as I wish."

When he looked at her, she fell silent, reached for the t-shirt, though the dampness made it translucent. He was half afraid to touch her, but he moved closer, staring into her face with a kind of horror. "Who are you?" he asked, not admitting that the question might as well have begun with a what.

"What do you think I am? Do you think I'm a witch? Maybe I am." She hugged herself. "I like this place. I do. And I like you and Frankie . . . and the others, so very many new others. So many, many new things to try." She rose and danced a little along the deserted beach, a moving white shape among the capering shadows that paced her.

He slept in the car, waking with damp and wrinkled clothing a crick in his neck, and an indelibly soiled conscience. He'd half hoped Rue had gone off somewhere on her own, but she came climbing up the bank to the car, smoothing down her coppery hair, if he hadn't known better, the child he'd accompanied down to the water the night before, except he knew better. She'd stopped to upend her sneakers, tapping the sand out of them. "It's not the end of the world, you know," she said as if sensing his mood.

"I just never quite thought of myself as a child molester," he said.

"Some things are real," she said, "and some things are only masks, hiding those things we don't know how to look at."

He didn't try to figure that one out; he just drove. There were only ten more miles to his destination when he felt too tired to go on. Leaving the highway for a small sleepy-looking town, he found a motel on the edge of it and pulled in.

"I'm dirty and tired," he said angrily.

Wind kicked up dust from the bare ground around the cabins. A lean and battered-looking orange tom-cat slunk from behind an untrimmed shrub and watched them for a moment with yellow-glass eyes, then withdrew. "I don't like this place. I think he recognized me."

"Go on alone then. Find some other sucker to pick you up."

"No, I want to stay with you."

His eyes burned and stung, a gauzy grey webwork appearing on his peripheral vision. He signed them in, remembering that he'd written Mr. and Mrs. Humbert Humbert. He showered, turning the water on as hard and hot as he could stand it, but that didn't seem to affect the lethargy that was claiming him. When he came from the bathroom, his skin was tingling, Rue was on the bed, her hair bright against the pillow, the curtains of the open window drifting flimsily onto and off her body with its duskily freckled fair skin.

"I was foolish to try and run from them," she said with a welcoming gesture. "The worlds lie close, as close as we are to each other now."

In her arms he dreamed. He was stifling in a small, dim, odorous room. In the odd perspective of dreams he saw a face, wizened as a dried apple, the jaw immense, the brow foreshortened with two green gleams where eyes should be beneath a bristling line where two eyebrows grew together over the bridge of the nose. Two other figures moved behind the first, and he thought that one of them wore a gaudy flower-print dress. A glass beaker filled with purplish liquid bubbled over a blue flame. He watched as a hand as skinny as a bird-claw brought something small and futilely writhing and dropped it into the beaker. He thought the figures clustered close together to enjoy its struggles as it was boiled alive. A casket broken, and encrusted with mould began to vibrate wildly, dark rotting fragments flaking off it. From it a skeleton, all discolored bone and dried sinew was struggling to rise.

"Sister-Cindy, bring the pot," said one of the entities in a hysterical half-shriek, and an amorphous blur, growing taller as it came gliding, resolved itself into a witch-shape. It poured the still-steaming contents over the skeleton's grinning skull, the stuff melting down the bones like candle-wax, clinging, and forming a human shape. A moment longer and he would recognize it.

He awoke with the curtains flapping above his head, the wind carrying the heavy, dusty smell of rain. Rue was gone, the door standing open. Thunder grumbled as he dressed, and when he left the cabin, the sky was full of sullen cloud. He saw no one. Behind the motel grew a scrub forest, thin trees already swaying in the storm wind. He called out for Rue but there was no answer. Thunder called again, with more authority, and the lightning cast an eerie glow over the trees. The further he went into the forest, the more sluggish his movements became, and at a certain moment he feared to turn and look at the motel because he had the sudden certainty that it wouldn't be there.

He caught a fleeting glimpse of two dark hunched figures in patchwork garments slipping through the trees carrying something that looked like a bundle of dry twigs wrapped in black rags. He tried to force his body forward but it was as if the atmosphere had grown thick and liquid and it was all he could do just to move his legs.

Then he saw Rue, standing in a small clearing. One moment her eyes met his, a kind of pleading in them, the next with eyes as blank as a doll's. Her skin gone translucently pale, she slumped to the forest floor. Then there were three clustering black shapes, sometimes appearing human, sometimes not, crying out with raucous voices as their black-nailed skinny hands fastened themselves into Rue's flesh.

"You're selfish!" Rue's inert body was jerked back and forth as they contested it, limbs bobbed lifelessly.

"Wanted to steal our persona when we all swore to share it."

"It's mine. Let me wear it!" Talon-like hands tore gashes in white skin. When he tried to shout, his jaw seemed frozen. The dark struggling bodies blocked his vision, still tearing and shouting, "Mine, mine!"

Time was distorted; the lightning when it hit was like a streak of gold melting down the tree beside him. There was a great concussion; a huge door slamming between worlds, and he toppled to the forest floor and lay there stunned.

When he awoke there was a charred smell in the air, and fire still smouldered at the base of the split tree. On the grass and soaked into the rocky soil everywhere were darkly glistening patches that stained his fingertips red when he touched them. "Who'd have thought she'd have so much blood in her," his thoughts giggled. And bits of yellowish muscle tissue and mottled lengths of viscera, here and there a shattered fragment of bone. "And who'd have thought she had the g—" The contents of his stomach burned up his throat and were expelled onto the grass.

He knew that somehow, he must have gotten himself together long enough to escape the motel and to reach the city. He must have talked to someone to rent this cheap room in a mouldering old building because he was here and the walls with their uncertain patterns of brown water-stains overlaying faded bouquets were the one reality he had. He rose and shuffled across the room, his foot kicking aside an empty whiskey bottle (he couldn't remember drinking that, either). He squinted through the slats of discolored venetian blinds and tried to estimate the time of day, but the sky was overcast, the wind pushing about grimy scraps of fallen leaves. Whatever the time, he was hungry, and he guessed he still had enough money left to buy a meal.

He went out into the semi-dark of the cramped hallway and began to descend the stairs. On the landing, where the stairs turned, he passed someone, perhaps another tenant, though he couldn't remember seeing her before—a very old lady in a shapeless black dress, her hand a brown-spotted moth hovering over the stair-rail. He could swear he didn't know her, but she looked at him lingeringly, and there was a gleam of green in each deep-set eye beneath a bristling thicket of eyebrow.

A Night Out

Nina Kiriki Hoffman

Artist Wendy Adrian Wees and I went to a small convention in Moscow, Idaho. As we aren't exactly getting rich off this business, it was not possible for us to afford a hotel room. Therefore a wrestling match was held between two Moscow feminists and the loser put us up for the weekend.

We stayed with Nina Hoffman, who played strange records by her brother, and also played piano (a hilarious and sacrilegious number written by her brother was particularly memorable), took us to the town's great coffeehouse, and otherwise made the trip more than averagely rewarding. During that weekend I read a vagrant manuscript called A Night Out and said to Wendy, "This is nice. This should sell to a good anthology." Wendy suggested I tell the author, who was in the other room pacing. So I told her, and many "shucks" and "gees" were passed around.

Later, I realized that someone had told me about this story before: author Eileen Gunn had mentioned that it was the one really good manuscript to crop up in a science fiction convention's short story workshop which she had coordinated. Unfortunately, Eileen didn't know where the writer lived, so it was only by coincidence that months later I happened upon the same yarn.

When Bob Garcia showed interest in doing this anthology, I was eager to include A Night Out in the book. It's a rare little gem.

*   *   *

They trusted me, they said, because their dog loved me. "Lionel has a real instinct for people," said Mrs. Henderson. "He's an animal and he don't get side-tracked by peoples' outer edges. The way he took to you—why, of course we'd rent a room to you any day."

Many animals take to me: we know how close our kinship is. Lionel knows that I'm just the kind of person he'd be if he had never been trained in the not-alloweds—not allowed to sleep in the flowerbed, sit on the couch, eat off the table; not allowed to tear the throats out of children who pester him. Lionel admires me for my freedom.
Heh.

So I unloaded my belongings from my VW bug and moved in—left room, second floor, overlooking the street, tree holding out a friendly arm close enough for me to make that after-dark leap from my windowsill, giving me a secret avenue to the ground. I don't want to arouse my landlady's suspicions by too many midnight trips down the staircase, which creaks.

I tried not to object too much to all the frills and chintz in my room. Her daughter's room, she told me, but now Lucy was away at college—imagine Lucy wanting to go to college in southern Idaho when there was a perfectly good university right here! I sympathized, stroked Lionel's spine, scratched between his upstanding German Shepherd ears. She was leaving me the bed, the vanity table, the curtains, and one bookshelf (full of Lucy's high school reading, Harlequin and Regency romances). I would have to find other furniture myself. Laundry cost a quarter each time I used the washer, dryer a dime, and she'd appreciate it if I got my own linen and bath towels.

"Fine, fine, thanks, Mrs. Henderson."

A hundred fifty a month and I got cereal for breakfast every morning and supper with the family every night.

"Great," I purred. "I think I'll love it here, ma'am. If it's all right with you I'd like to unpack now."

She took the hint and excused her way out. I opened the closet. Very few extra hangers. Lucy seemed to have left most of her frills behind. I'd have to live out of suitcases until I could buy some more hangers. Murmuring in my throat, I investigated the confines of my new space.

"Prostura—I can't pronounce that," says Mr. Henderson as I sit down to dinner. Imagine muffins, corn, potatoes, tubs of margarine, jello in quivering masses, meatloaf hiding under a slathering of ketchup, salad marinating in lo-cal dressing, beets exuding purple blood, little spindly slivers of leftover turkey, strawberries buried beneath an ashy layer of confectioner's sugar . . .

"Prosturanchek," I say, knowing his mid-American tongue would stumble over it. "Maybe you better call me Terry."

"Maybe I better," he agrees. Suddenly I begin to like him, in spite of the gun-rack on his truck. I'm not so sure about the two boys. One's immense, not a hard size to achieve with so many starches on the table; Tom: he's red-faced, taciturn, almost placid, and plays football, not well but hugely. The other one's small and quick and sneaky, with a strange sweet scent to him under the masking odors of dirt, ditch water, chalk dust, and boy. The tweaky kind, young Jim, a tail-grabber, a fly's-wing-puller, meaner than me, and anybody meaner than me frightens me.

I manage to eat something, then, pleading studies, retire upstairs to Lucy's uncomfortable frills. A short nap before moonrise. Downstairs they turn the TV on; but I can sleep through anything, anywhere.

*   *   *

My Mamka thinks I'm crazy. "*Krrristoverany*," she said to me, "why don't you stay here in the forest. *Miminko*, and hunt rabbits and mice and birds and squirrels like everybody else on your nights out, eh?"

"I want to get an education," I said. That's not really the reason, though.

"Why?" she asked. "I taught you your letters. You've been to town enough, eh, seen the people—you'll go crazy if you live there. None of us has an education, and we don't need one either. Life is good here."

"Even for Emelya?" I asked, which was mean. My brother Emelya was shot in the thick of his silvery winter coat; what's left of him probably lives in camphor and mothballs all summer in somebody's attic. They take packs of dogs after us sometimes, and if they tree us, we're dead.

I'm majoring in forestry.

Normally I can take music or leave it but when she turns on those screechy violins my hair stands on end: I can feel the prickle all the way down my spine. Intense rushes of desire seize and shake me; I long with every quivering whisker to go chew on the record player. My claws spring out with gorgeous curvy sharpness and in my overwhelming battle to control myself I find myself sharpening claws on the couch in lieu of assaulting that passionate record player, responding to its wild invitations to orgy.

Mrs. Henderson suspects me of harboring a cat. Luckily it is my own couch with the tattered upholstery, but she picks up the long silver hairs, sniffs them, and looks about, bird-eyed, for signs of a litterbox. But I have been in training for a long time and know how to use the bathroom, so she never catches my cat.

*   *   *

They took me to the movies the other night, an effort in intense concentration. My eyes kept trying to switch into dark mode, washing the colors off the screen and leaving only shadows. None of the smells there had anything to do with the shadows, either. I had a hard time sewing the pieces together. All couched in unreality, a cartoon, Cinderella: something about a girl who had a talking horse and a bunch of singing mice for friends (something wrong with their voices: I found my spine arching. I left clawmarks on the seatback in front of me) and she had sisters who had a cat named Lucifer. He didn't talk. There's an odd thing. If all the other animals can talk, why not the cat?

He wanted to eat the singing mice, but I shouldn't; they were wearing clothes. Besides, they smelled like popcorn.

My college advisor was not pleased. "No high school records?"

"No."

"No SAT scores."

"No."

"How did you qualify for college?"

"I went to the library a lot." I know all the smells in the forest: that's the animal in me. I learned all the names out of books, *Betula papyrifera, Alnus tenuifolia*. I don't think I pronounce them right though.

"How much math did you learn at the library?"

"Pardon me?"

"Arithmetic. Mathematics. Two plus two."

"Not very much."

He sighed and signed me up for remedial math.

I managed to survive registration. I understand several languages, including English, Czech, and Instruction. But I have trouble taking notes: the letters Mamka taught us take too long to write.

*   *   *

Loping the streets, dodging among darknesses, none of the shadows are solid, all of the colors are grey with silver edges. My pads whisp across the sidewalks, leaving pale echoes but no solid sounds. Odors assault me, the richness of rot, the wetness of water, powdery concrete smell, sun-softened asphalt, clean smooth steel, musky sweat, rank growy green smells, nose-nipping ammonia of others' territory markers, rich thin dangerous exhaust, tired car tires. The ticking, tickling heat of the town as it settles down rises, blurring the moon. Smells spiral upward on the exhaled warmth of day, cold creeping in to lull day-life to sleep.

I select my hunting ground with care. It must be far from my headquarters. The outer edge of town: hand-scattered ramshackle shacks—the people inside don't know, don't care, don't help, and won't report to the police. Down this dirt gash, children shooting craps against a warehouse wall in the bleaching wash of the watch-light, dice leaping, clicking, bouncing against the wall as though alive, as though they could control their next actions. I'm stalking, bobtail the merest twitch, lurking among the darks draped by the rubbish heap.

"Thirteen? How's it come up thirteen?"

"Aw, it's a speck a something. I'll wipe it off."

Young bodies radiate, alight with life. From inside another darkness, a deeper radiation, lower in the heat spectrum, throbbing life, its warmth a taste in my mouth, its scent strong and oily in my nose. I lick the backs of my carnassials; my eartufts vibrate, capturing sounds, heartbeat, breathing, shift of soft cloth against soft cloth, scrape of soles in the dust—life is a noisy business.

Suddenly he's out, claws/ knife drawn, pouncing, and I must admire—he moves almost as fast as I do, and smells not of rank fear but of joyous madness. The scent seems familiar—not the personal scent, the species scent. Jim smells like that.

I smell like that.

He is not one of the specific people I'm after, but he's a hunter, and I hunt hunters, remembering patching skins slung over barbed wire in the hot sun, empty reservoirs that used to hold streaming life, crisp clean flow of life weaving through the webs of dark and tangle, rock and river, snow and sand, bird and bush and brush and rushes . . . I reach him before he reaches them, and they run, too scared to scream, and I slash and crunch and claw and bring him down . . . then, gently, as if he were a kitten, I drag him by the neck into the shadows. Then I feed. The head first.

One of my new neighbors thanks me for returning her trash can lid, which blew into the Hendersons' yard on last night's wind. She doesn't just reach out, and grab it, thank me and close the door. She invites me in. She begs me in. She pulls me in.

She gives me a cup of tea, leaves the TV on, settles me on the couch where her poodle jumps up on my lap, and ignores the children, who are hyperacting among the toys scattered about. After her second child, she tells me, she almost died from internal bleeding, and they had to give her a hysterectomy. She believes she was meant to have more children. The soulbright, ghostly faces of four un-born children hover around her even as she speaks. Somehow, she says, she will have those children. I can almost smell their presence.

She is lonely this weekend. Her husband has put on his red hunting cap and loaded his guns into the camper and driven away, CB radio blasting. Elk season is open now. She's anxious for any company, even mine. She wants to tell me about these unborn children when she can't handle the ones she's got.

I'm not doing myself any good, sitting here and knowing her. It takes the fun out of it if you know the victim's wife and children. Not that he's an intended victim. He hunts for food, not for sport.

Or maybe, like me, for both.

Why do I do it? I try to pretend that I thirst for vengeance, that I'm getting back at them for Emelya. But that's not the type of creature I am. Actually, it's more of a hobby with me. I, having caught that rabid madness called humanity, I leave the forests of my ancestors and come to haunt the haunts of man.

I think I'm responding to the call of my human nature.

Jaborandi Jazz

Gordon Linzner

Voodoo. It has inspired tacky movies, racist doggerel, men's pulp adventure ("my best friend's head was shrunken by the voodoo devils as I escaped with the idol's eyes"), and, occasionally, a worthwhile, entertaining horror yarn.

Gordon Linzner edits and publishes the longest running small-press fantasy, science fiction and horror magazine in existence. Like the heroic Dale C. Donaldson, Gordon tends to specialize in giving new writers their first shot at publication. Unlike Dale, however, Gordon has managed to pursue his own writing with greater regularity. He was a familiar name to readers of FANTASY & TERROR *and, more recently, to* ROD SERLING'S THE TWILIGHT ZONE MAGAZINE *and* THE MAGAZINE OF FANTASY AND SCIENCE FICTION.

In Jaborandi Jazz *we follow a jazz buff into the lesser known dives to hear an unknown band whose drummer is, well, a little . . . weird.*

Drummers are weird.

That's not intended as a put-down, don't get me wrong. Drummers are pretty much like anybody else. They're kind to small animals, concerned about their families, frustrated by income tax forms. But the fact remains that drummers are stranger than your average person. The constant pounding noise their profession exposes them to must do something to their brains.

I first saw Carlos de Santos in a small jazz club on lower Tenth Avenue. I say jazz club, but it was really just a small bar trying to pass for a club on weekends. Its main attraction for me was that I could get a beer for under a dollar and nurse it undisturbed through maybe three sets of whoever was playing that night.

Carlos was doing drumwork for a quintet called The Slaughterhouse Five. It was an aptly named group, above and beyond any Vonnegutian implications. Of course, the bar couldn't afford any real headliners. Most of its attractions ranged from poor to competent, and even the half-decent ones had their off nights. At these prices, who could complain?

But never had I seen a group that had to work up towards mediocrity. I knew I was in for a unique evening when, halfway through the first number, the pianist forgot he was playing "Green Dolphin Street" and moved right into "Tin House Blues." You could tell it was not a conscious switch. The cornetist and sax man were obviously used to this shifting of gears, because they quickly picked up on the new beat and played right along to the end. When the cornet fell short of his final closing high note, a fast upbeat drumroll did what it could to cover the flub.

I'll say this for the Five—they had teamwork. They knew how to cover for each other, even if they didn't have much in the way of real talent.

Except for Carlos.

Twice more that evening the piano switched pieces, and once he stopped dead in the middle of a phrase, looking up as if the tune had ended. The cornet and sax missed notes—fortunately not at the same time. The bassist's hands grew stiff and palsied during the third and final set.

But Carlos kept on strong all night, never missing a stroke or cue, beating out some of the best drum solos Chelsea had ever known. If not for him, I'd have gulped down my beer and chalked up the night as a waste.

I told him as much when I suddenly realized the last set was over and I was the only person left at a table, watching Carlos pack up his equipment. The rest of the quintet had quickly split. For one moment we were eye to eye, and the silence was so uncomfortable I asked his name. He was easy to talk to, and we went on from there.

"With your kind of talent, Carlos, why waste your time with a nothing group like The Slaughterhouse Five?"

He looked at me as if I'd just recited a verse of Jabberwocky. Backwards.

"I'm not wasting time. I play my drums. It's what I like to do, what I do best."

"Yeah, but there are more together groups around who could really use a solid drummer."

"Oh, sure, I've had offers. Always for Latin groups. A Puerto Rican who plays anything but straight Latin? Unthinkable! So, with these guys I can play what I like."

I couldn't believe that jazz musicians were that narrow-minded, but refrained from saying so. After all, Carlos had been there. I was just a fan of the music. Probably the right people hadn't seen him.

I shrugged my shoulders.

"Don't think I'm completely without ambition, my friend," Carlos added. "One day I will play the greatest drum set in the world. If it's heard by only one appreciative ear, my whole life will have been worthwhile."

There was obviously no answer to that, so we dropped the topic. Not the conversation, though. Carlos was one of those rare individuals who could be open and friendly without being pushy about it. He ran off a list of his influences right up to Mel Lewis and Elvin Jones while I helped carry the drums to his Volkswagen. Then we were walking south along Tenth Avenue, exchanging life histories.

At West Fourth we turned left. The night was warm for late September, so there were still people on the streets at well past one a.m. Even some of the more esoteric shops on the block between Sixth and Seventh Avenues were still open.

I ignore these shops almost out of habit. They rarely contain anything to interest me and give the repellent impression of being tourist traps, albeit quaint ones. So I didn't notice until I'd walked several more paces that Carlos had pulled up short in front of one of them.

Its window was filled with the usual aggregation of clutter: candles, pendants, various sized jars and swatches of material, all lit with a soft purple light. On the door hung a plaque of dark-stained wood bearing the establishment's name in white ink.

It called itself A Magic Shop.

"Hold up a minute," Carlos said. "I have to pick up a few things."

I followed the musician up steep concrete steps and into the shop. Behind a showcase counter sat a heavy, middle-aged woman wearing a peasant blouse and ankle-length skirt. The latter resembled a tie-dyed army tent, and I almost choked to keep from laughing at the thought.

Carlos was asking her for some kind of powder, but he couldn't think of the equivalent word in English. He looked at me. I hadn't the slightest idea what he wanted, so I just shook my head. After more verbal fumbling, he came out with the Spanish expression.

She responded quickly and loudly and also in Spanish, accented by a great many gestures. The gist of the conversation was now totally lost to me. I turned my attention to a display case on an opposite wall, studying the workman-

ship of the more fantastic jewelry, pondering the alleged
uses of the vari-colored liquids lining the shelf above.

Carlos had quite a shopping bagful when we left the shop
at last. The streets were deserted now—at least, as deserted as they ever get in Greenwich Village. We sat down
in front of O. Henry's, the butcher shop turned steak
house, and Carlos pored over his treasures.

They consisted of a well-thumbed book with a loose
binding and faded Latin lettering, two dozen black candles
with curious designs embossed along their sides, and a
half-dozen jars of different sizes containing gray powders
and bits of bone and fur. In his shirt pocket Carlos had a
flat packet of wax paper folded around several long flat
leaves—jaborandi leaves, he called them.

"For the tea," he explained. I made no comment.

Carlos held up one long, thin canister of blackish
liquid. He swished it first, then held it up to the light of a
mercury streetlamp. The liquid left a reddish tint on the
sides of the canister.

"Bat's blood, from Mongolia," he said, as calmly as if
he were identifying a new flavor from Baskin-Robbins.
"I've been looking for this for over a month. The Asian
bats show properties lacking in New World species."

"Must be all the rice in their diet." I immediately
regretted the words. It was a stupid, condescending thing
to say. The hour was late, and I was tired, but I still
should've had enough sense to keep my mouth shut.

Carlos did not reply to my inanity, but he began replacing his paraphernalia in the shopping bag. He took great
care with each item, but replaced them as quickly as
possible.

"Hey, Carlos, I didn't mean anything. It was just a
joke. A dumb joke. C'mon, tell me more about this stuff."

But he refused to answer until he'd finished his task.
Then and only then did he turn to me with a solemn

but—fortunately for my latent paranoia—unmenacing demeanor.

"Look, you're good people. I like you. You understand my music. I can dig that. But I can also dig you don't understand this kind of thing, that you're not into it at all. That's cool. Don't try to bullshit me, okay?"

"Hey, Carlos, I wasn't . . . no, right. I know where you're coming from."

Carlos glanced up along the east side of Sixth Avenue at Prudential Bank's huge digital clock. "Hey, I gotta split. I got a gig in Morristown tonight, and I need some time to look this stuff over. Nice meeting you, man. See you around, right?"

I turned my head to see just how late it was. 2:58. "Wait up, Carlos," I said, raising myself slowly to my feet. "I'll walk you . . ."

But he'd already vanished into the maze of streets that make up the West Village. I thought of backtracking to the club where his car was parked, but decided against it. If he'd wanted company, he'd have waited for me. By the time I reached Tenth Avenue, he'd be long gone.

It was an interesting night, to be sure, but unless The Slaughterhouse Five played in Manhattan again—which seemed unlikely after the reputation they'd earned this time—I guessed I'd seen the last of Carlos de Santos.

I was wrong, of course.

The time was late December. Specifically, it was a bleak, half-hearted weekend marking time between Christmas and New Year's, both holidays inconsiderately falling in the middle of the week. It wouldn't even snow—just rain whenever the temperature became tolerably warm.

I had spent most of a cold Saturday in various states of non-wakefulness and was watching an extremely forgettable movie when the phone rang. It was Carlos.

"Tonight's the night," he informed me, after minimal phone introductions.

"For what?"

"For *it,* man. The pay-off. The greatest set ever played. And there's nothing but hicks out here in Pomona. They don't know shit. You gotta come down and listen. I gotta have someone who can appreciate what I'm doing."

"Okay. Where are you?"

"Place called The Roadhouse, about a quarter-mile south of Pomona limits. Get a pencil, I'll give you directions."

Fully half the small town bars in Jersey are called The Roadhouse, or something equally clever, so I made careful note of Carlos' instructions. At that, I got lost twice, and it was half past eleven before I finally found THE Roadhouse. I pulled up in front of the place, convinced that I was late. Carlos had not told me what time the Five hit, and towns like Pomona tend to roll up the sidewalks around eight.

But all was well. Reluctantly stepping in, I was greeted by the odor of stale beer and a high note on a cornet that just fell short of being musical. I noticed the moose-head over the bar didn't respond to its mating call.

I made for the bar first, thirsty after my trek through the New Jersey backwaters. "Heineken, please."

"Whassa matta, 'Merican beer ain't good enough for ya?" The bartender had a husky build and stood at least a foot taller than me. Part of his left ear was missing, probably bitten off by an irate customer.

"On second thought, make it a Bud." I received the bottle and change from my five with no further comment, although the bartender still eyed my beard and moustache with suspicion. After examining the glass he offered, I raised the bottle directly to my lips.

I worked my way through the indifferent crowd of underage drinkers until I could place myself in Carlos' line of sight. He was engaged in a discussion with the cornet and bass, who obviously wanted to call it a night. His face brightened when he saw me.

"See, I told you he'd get here. Okay, get ready—this is the last number. Honest." The others moved into their positions, grumbling but apparently satisfied. Carlos beckoned to me. I hesitated going up to him, but no one else in the darkened room was paying much attention to the group, so I swallowed my fears and joined my friend.

"Sorry I'm late," I began. "There was this weird turn-off on . . ."

"Don't sweat it," he said, cutting off my apology. He drained a cup of tea set on the floor beside him before continuing. "The important thing is you're here. I really appreciate this, man. And to show you how much, tonight you're gonna see a set you'll never forget."

Without warning, he handed me a dozen long, black candles similar to the ones he'd bought in the Village. These, however, bore images of grotesque anthropomorphic creatures in addition to the bizarre designs. "When the number hits," he said, "place these in a semi-circle in front of my drums and light them."

I stared at him blankly.

"It's the final step," he added.

Of course. That explained everything. For him, maybe.

"I, uh, I don't smoke."

He handed me a book of matches bearing the legend of The Roadside Inn in Carteret. "Look," he continued, "I know you don't dig this scene. Humor me. Pretend it's for atmosphere."

I shrugged. After a drive into these boondocks on short notice, this seemed a trivial enough favor. Carlos nodded to the cornet, who gave the downbeat to the rest of the quintet.

They started playing "When the Saints Come Marching In."

I felt pretty silly crawling around on the floor but, as I said, no one was really paying any attention. Most likely Carlos was the only one aware of my even being there. The candles kept falling over until I thought of melting a few drops of wax on the floor to support them. After that, it took only a couple of minutes to finish the task.

Sharing a nearby table didn't appeal to me, so I sat cross-legged on the floor a few feet from the candles, my beer between my knees, trying to figure out just what Carlos had planned. He'd told me previously that the group always ended a gig with "The Saints." It was an up number, easy to play, and about the only jazz standard most non-jazz buffs knew. Few true lovers of the music could sit through more than one stand of The Slaughterhouse Five.

I also knew, from prior exposure, how their particular arrangement ran. Carlos had maybe a four minute extended solo near the end, the likeliest spot for whatever he had in mind.

It didn't work that way. He did his four minutes and passed it to the cornet as usual. It was a brilliant piece of drumwork, but no more so than I'd remembered him doing back in September. The most spectacular thing about the number was that the other four members stayed in tune and carried the piece to its conclusion without mistake. Nothing to rave about, but they reached new pinnacles of adequacy. Fear does strange things to people. They were no doubt afraid that if they blew it Carlos would make them start over.

I was growing annoyed with Carlos myself, and intended to make my irritation known right after the final drum upbeat closing the number. It's flattering to be remembered by someone you admire, and it was nice to see Carlos' work again, but this hardly seemed worth the hassle of renting a car and entering the deeps of New Jersey on a freezing night like this.

The final upbeat wasn't. Final, that is. Carlos used it as the starting point for a whole new solo—to the surprise of the rest of the group, if I read their faces correctly. Sticks flashed from one drum to the other, to the cymbals and back again, with a hypnotic rhythm. He changed sticks several times, now using heavier ones, now using brushes, never missing a beat.

The playing lasted a long time. I felt my throat go dry, yet could not raise the beer to my lips. My sole raison d'etre was to act as audience to that Puerto Rican drummer. My eyes were glued to his sticks.

A sense of timelessness pervaded my being. After an incredibly protracted period of this incessant percussion work, Carlos seemed to be tiring. The beat slowed. The change was subtle, gradual, until waiting for the next stroke became an unbearable torment.

Carlos was keeping his promise. Never in my life had I seen such playing, nor am I likely to again.

In the same gradual manner in which it had slackened, the pace quickened again. Sweat poured down Carlos' face. He grinned with almost obscene ecstasy. Beads of perspiration, dripping onto the drumheads, vanished in short-lived clouds of steam. The sticks themselves were smoking. Carlos' hand blurred to invisibility, moving at superhuman speed. I felt my own blood racing, my temple pounding until I feared I would burst an artery. And still I sat transfixed to the spot.

The candlelight began to sputter and die. I realized for the first time that the club's electrical system had blown out. The flame of the last taper choked in its own melted wax, no longer able to support itself on a thoroughly used wick, surrendering the room to darkness—except for a faint, shimmering glow surrounding Carlos and his drums.

So numbed was my mind by the rhythmic beating that I did not realize until afterwards that the source of light was Carlos himself.

At that point his playing reached a new, frenetic intensity. His eyes glazed over, shining a vibrant, piercing copper. Individual beats were no longer distinguishable by the human ear, and still his pace increased. The aura exuding from the man grew brighter, until it hurt to look at it—though I could not tear my eyes from that burning, yellow-white outline.

And then the light vanished, and we were in pitch blackness. The echo lingered, but there was little doubt Carlos had stopped drumming at that same instant.

The blackness softened to a light gray as my eyes grew accustomed to the weak sunlight seeping into the room around the edges of heavily shaded windows. Someone threw open one of the shades, flooding the interior of The Roadhouse with brightness.

I looked around. Not one person had moved since the start of Carlos' solo. The handful of patrons still sat at their tables, half-finished drinks before them. The rest of The Slaughterhouse Five hadn't begun to pack their instruments. Even the surly bartender seemed dazed.

Only Carlos was missing.

The heads of the drums were scorched and blackened. I could not bring myself to touch them. A pair of drumsticks laid haphazardly across the center drum, charred almost beyond recognition, like used matchsticks. A loathsome stench permeated the immediate area, causing me to gag. I stepped away, back past the twelve globs of melted black wax staining the floor. Gulping the flat remainder of my beer, I left The Roadhouse as swiftly as my cramped leg muscles would permit.

The sun, mercifully filtered through clouds and pollution, was high as I climbed into my rental car. Carlos must have played at least ten hours, then, but I did not check the time. I drove home in silence rather than risk being informed by some obnoxious disc jockey. I didn't want to know. Not for sure.

I still go to that little club on Tenth Avenue on a semi-regular basis. Sometimes, if I'm impressed by a pianist, or a cornet, or some fine guitar work, I'll offer a complimentary word or two before I split. But should a drummer be the star of the group, he could combine the best moves of Gene Krupa, Buddy Rich and Elvin Jones—and I just can't bring myself to tell him so.

I'm not afraid of them, really. They're mostly good people, like anybody else.

But all that pounding does something to their brains. That must be it.

Because drummers are weird. . . .

A Wine of Heart's Desire

Ron Nance

The old WEIRD TALES, *the most famous of all horror magazines, was simultaneously a magazine of heroic fantasy. They seem often enough to go hand in hand. Therefore,* TALES BY MOONLIGHT *presents its token heroic fantasy yarn. . . . but one of a different mode than muscle-bound Conan. Indeed, Ron Nance's* A Wine of Heart's Desire *is antithesis to the usual characterization. Here we have two frail-appearing young men, one Edwin the thief, the other, Motley the jester. This is the story of their first meeting.*

I read my first Motley and Edwin story in 1973 and promptly purchased it for FANTASY AND TERROR. *In 1975, I co-authored with Ron, a novelet about Motley, which appeared in the final issue of that magazine. A story about Edwin appeared in the feminist fantasy and science fiction magazine,* WINDHAVEN. *The present story went several drafts before it was the best I thought Ron had in him; it's my personal favorite among all the Motley and Edwin stories to date.*

The original inspiration for the characters came from Bob Dylan's song All Along the Watchtower, *which years later provided Elizabeth A. Lynn similar inspiration for the Tarnor trilogy from Berkley Books. I'm surprised that nearly ten years later, Ron Nance is not well known. I fear he hasn't worked on it with quite the single-mindedness it takes. Yet he has penned a few excellent yarns for small press magazines and gained a reputation among writers and editors in that community. It's my hope that he'll get off his duff and finish a novel about this pair, and that the finished novel connects with the right editor in New York.*

Edwin lay in the bunk and let the cradle motions of the sea rock him back and forth between sleep and waking. He had no idea how he came to be aboard a ship; his last clear memory was of a gang of harbor cut-throats closing in on him to steal the—

Instantly he was awake, sitting up, groping around him in the dim light of the cabin until he found a large, heavy bundle stowed beneath the bunk. He dragged it out and undid the dark cloth, then let his eyes run covetously over an intricately carved chalice of gleaming electrum: the Great Cup.

The jewels that studded the huge goblet seemed to give off a light of their own as Edwin gently traced the maze of vines and serpents with a slender finger. A long sigh escaped as the young man released his pent-up breath. He reached into the Great Cup and was taking out a half-dozen musty books and yellowed scrolls when loud footsteps approached the cabin door. Edwin hastily stuffed the books and scrolls back into the Cup and rewrapped it, but there was no time to put it back under the bunk before the cabin door swung open.

There, outlined against an amethyst sunset, stood a large man who stepped aside to let a smaller one scurry into the cabin. This smaller figure carried a bowl and a lamp. He hung the lamp by chains from a hook in the cabin's low ceiling and left the large bowl on a table in the corner. About this nondescript man, Edwin could only tell that he was a seaman.

The broad-chested man who now entered and closed the door behind the departing sailor was another matter entirely.

It was certainly he who walked with those loud, confident footsteps. The golden light from the hanging lamp revealed the aquiline features of a swarthy face framed by a black beard and close-cropped hair above sturdy shoulders bearing an aquamarine cape. He was dressed for the most part in clothes like a common sailor wore, but made of silk, velvet, and fabrics that Edwin couldn't name. Many bracelets clasped his strong, bare arms, and rings glittered from his hands and ears. "I am Zarillian, called by many the Sailor-King."

"I am Edwin," answered the bearded young man.

Zarillian gestured to the bowl on the table. "Eat."

Edwin pulled a stool from beneath the table and sat in such a way that he could see the bundled Cup at all times. He found the stew in the bowl hot, with a strong, fishy taste. He gulped it down greedily while Zarillian watched, arms folded. "How long have I been here?" he asked around a spoonful.

"Two days since *Windsister,* my ship, left Guttra. Lucky for you that I stopped for water and victuals there, and luckier still that I let my men go ashore; they are a rough lot, but fair. They say you were set upon by six but still would not yield your bundle." Zarillian stood looking down at the dark mass on the bunk. He reached out a hand as if to touch or uncover it, and Edwin sprang up, his hand clenched on the spoon.

"Relax, friend," Zarillian laughed, "I will not rob you, but that spoon would be a poor weapon if I did."

"Sorry," said Edwin, letting the spoon clatter into the empty bowl. "I imagine you could have taken it several times while I lay unconscious."

Zarillian nodded. "But I am no thief," he said sternly. "I am an honest trader of the seas. Four score merchant vessels and warships acknowledge me as king and give me tribute. It is jealousy of kings of land and their paid admirals that makes them call me anything else." He finished with an angry voice.

Edwin sat unmoving, his face a mask. Zarillian eyed him sharply as the swinging lamp threw their shadows on the wall so that they seemed to spar with one another. Zarillian's bulky shadow advanced on Edwin's thin one, then fell back. The Sailor-King asked, "What is *your* trade, Edwin? By your rags I would guess you were a hermit, a beggar, or a storyteller, but none of these would possess a thing to die for or even take such wounds as you did."

Edwin abruptly asked, "Yes, how did you heal my wounds so quickly? I'd given myself up for dead when those wharf rats jumped me; now there's only a twinge in my left shoulder."

"That is salve from the Bormean Isles. It is miraculous; you will not even have a scar."

"My thanks," he said. "Where are we bound?"

Zarillian tensed. "Tomorrow morning we drop anchor in the harbor at Gedar. I am returning to fulfill a bargain King Zais struck thinking it impossible. In return for the priceless cargo we carry I will have the Princess Alianora for my wife and Queen." Now, the manly features of the king of sailors melted into the expression of a child who thinks of sugar candy. "She loves me well—she's told me many times—but her father has rejected my suit twice before simply because I have no land nor lineage. He shall not deny me this time."

"Or you will simply abduct the princess and sail away," finished Edwin, sitting cross-legged on the bunk with his arm draped casually across his bundle.

Zarillian turned an astonished, and guilty, face toward him. "How do you know that?"

"Why else stock provisions only three days from your destination unless you plan a sudden departure?" Edwin calmly addressed Zarillian's offended glare. "Besides, I am a Master Thief and recognize the look in your eyes when you speak of your love. You may be a peaceful merchant now, Zarillian, but you haven't always been; that look seems at home in your eyes." While the Sailor-King stood speechless, Edwin made his point. "You saved my life, healed my wounds and helped me keep the only thing I own. For that, I will help you steal your princess if the need arises."

Zarillian stood like a pillar, his face going from an angry glare to a smile then back again. "I am no pirate now, nor ever have been. I am as fair and honest as the man I deal with, but I will neither starve nor beg. True, when I had but the one ship and little to bargain with, perhaps I bullied and threatened, but I swear—"

"You needn't swear to me," said Edwin. "The only oath I need is your handshake." He held out his hands, clasping one of Zarillian's in both of his. "And to further seal the bargain I'd like to give you some fine rings."

"Thank you, Edwin, but I already—" The lamplight glittered in Zarillian's widening eyes as he stared at his bare fingers. "By all the gods my sailors swear by, you *are* a master thief!"

Edwin let the rings trickle from his palm into Zarillian's. "I don't steal from friends. I only wanted you to know I hadn't made an empty promise. If you need your princess stolen, I'm your man."

Zarillian stood for a moment then suddenly clasped the scruffy thief in an affectionate bear hug. Chuckling, he left the cabin.

When the cabin door had closed behind the Sailor-King, and enough time had passed to satisfy Edwin, he took the Great Cup to the table and spread out his books and scrolls. It had long been Edwin's passion to learn the secret of this enchanted goblet that in its design concealed the spell by which it could be made to yield the heart's desire.

Edwin had often wondered why he kept the Cup when he could steal virtually anything he wanted. But trying to solve the riddle of the Great Cup had become a habit, a matter of stubbornness really. He thought of giving up mostly when he was tired and the Cup seemed heavier than usual.

But he felt very close to success now. He had easily recognized in the jewels the constellations of the sky: the Hammer and Anvil, the Eagle, the Ship, and the Chariot. This had led to other clues in the ancient writings pilfered from various astrologers and magicians. Now, after so long a time, Edwin felt ready to test his spell. It was foolishly simple, but perhaps that was why it had been so difficult to discover.

Taking hold of the Cup so that he faced the Chariot, Edwin recited the spell, turning the Cup so that he faced the proper constellation as he named each element:

> *Earth, Water, Air, and Fire,*
> *Surrender now the Heart's Desire.*

There was a silence so sudden and supernal in the cabin that Edwin's ears popped. Then came a gurgle from deep within the Great Cup. Soon blood red wine was spilling over the rim of the huge chalice.

Edwin stood thunderstruck for a moment as the liquor sloshed onto the table and floor; then he snatched up a scroll and read from it the rune of cessation. A little more wine was spilled by the ship's roll, but the level in the Cup did not rise. The books and scrolls were ruined, so he dumped the sodden mass into a corner.

But I don't want wine, Edwin thought. Nevertheless, he tipped the Cup toward him and sampled the contents. He meant to take only a sip or two but ended draining the vessel. He immediately repeated his conjuring, this time stopping the Cup before it overflowed. Instead of filling him and quenching his thirst, this sorcerous vintage seemed to leave him empty and thirstier than before. In fact, he could not remember *not* wanting this wine.

While he was occupied with the Cup, Edwin did not notice the eye that peered through a tiny spy hole in the door, nor did he hear Zarillian's sharp gasp as he saw the magic workings of the Great Cup.

The light from the amethyst sunset streamed across the battlements of the High Castle of Gedar and struck shining highlights from the golden hair of Princess Alianora. She walked along sadly, accompanied by the court jester whose hair shone equally golden where it peeked from beneath a cap with seven points and bells. His jingling walk was erratic, interrupted by dance steps and sudden leaps to avoid stepping on the cracks in the stonework; the princess, however, was making a straight line for the parapet that faced the sea.

Once there, she took a deep breath of the tangy air and sighed, "Oh, Motley, do you think he will get here in time?"

The clown, who was no taller than the princess, came bounding up in his multi-colored suit of patches. "How can I know? I've never seen the fellow you're so in love with. But if he's got half a brain, he'll be here."

"Oh, Zarillian is very clever," Alianora said with great fervor, "and so noble and strong!" Her periwinkle eyes took on a luster not wholly attributable to the majestic sundown.

"And such a pirate," said Motley, a twinkle in his bright green eyes. As Alianora blushed with indigation, he quickly added, bowing to the ground, "I merely quote that font of all wisdom, your stepmother."

"*Oh, her,*" said Alianora with loathing.

"Yes, her." Motley's tone betrayed a similar opinion. "I've told many a story about a beautiful princess and a cruel stepmother, but none of my fictions could compare with your fact. Is it true you've had *two* cruel stepmothers?"

"Yes. I cannot remember my true mother."

"You should complain to your fairy godmother."

The princess made a show of exasperation. "Be serious for just a moment, Motley. What shall I do if they force me to marry that oafish Prince of Guttra just to get around some silly tax or tariff or something?" The princess stood wringing her hands at the prospect.

"It's a tariff," said Motley, his eyes on her hands.

"I know what I shall do," the princess suddenly announced. "I shall throw myself from this very wall. It is a long way down, but I would rather die than marry that pig of a prince!"

The harlequin blanched at her words, fearing she might follow her romantic impulses and actually do something rash. "If you jumped, King Zarillian would certainly never arrive in time. Think how much your death would hurt him."

"Oh, Motley," sighed the princess, "what could *you* know of *true love?*"

Perhaps for a brief moment the jester's smile was not as bright as usual, but if so, Alianora did not see. "Princesses and kings aren't the only people who fall in love," he said. "It might be that even I am more than a little in love with you myself." When Alianora looked at him in surprise, he laughingly added. "But then *I'm* a fool!"

Before she could speak, Motley leapt onto the top of a merlon and, striking a forlorn pose, recited:

Some lovers are not parted soon,
But hold each other an Immortal's time,
And share their love with stars and sun and moon,
While fools like me are left, alone, to rhyme.

Then he capered along the very edge of the wall until Alianora was beside herself with fear for him. She kept calling to him, "Come down from there, Motley! Come down this instant, I command you! Please?"

"You see, Princess, any fool can recite some maudlin words and play along the edge of death. Will you still throw yourself from this wall if King Zarillian is a little slow?" He swayed as if he were losing his balance, but with a dancer's grace.

Alianora cried out, "I promise not to. I promise. Do you hear?"

Motley smiled. "I hear." Just then a gust of wind whipped the cap from his golden curls and shoved him to the edge. Flailing his arms wildly, he virtually hurled himself toward the princess, but lit by her side with a little dance step so that she was never sure whether or not he'd really lost his balance. A moment later they heard a jangling sound as his cap struck the cobblestones at the foot of the castle wall.

"Motley, you frightened me terribly!" Alianora accused.

"Better a frightened princess than a dead fool," he answered.

Alianora spun and stamped off in a huff which Motley knew from experience could not last until they met again. The agile jester sprang into a crenel to look down after his cap, wincing as he saw the great expanse of wall that swept down from his makeshift stage and the certain death that had been his backdrop.

The last belch of the banquet was slipping from the greasy lips of King Philander XII of Guttra when a nervous messenger sped past him to drop to one knee before King Zais' seat at the head of the crescent shaped table.

"My King! The pirate Zarillian returns! His ship was seen in Guttra two days ago."

The banquet hall was thrown into an uproar which the bearer of ill tidings used to cover his retreat. Philander XIV, the porcine Prince of Guttra, squealed, "Two days? Why, he could be here tomorrow!"

His father, who ruled the kingdom of Guttra from a pastoral estate while letting his son gain experience by administering the city and Porte of Guttra, cast a reproachful look at him. He was equally aware of Zarillian's reputation for getting what he wanted, but such outbursts were unbecoming in a prince, especially when the object of terror is coming by way of your own Porte. He leaned to his left and asked his host and fellow king as casually as possible, "What about this pirate?"

Zais waved a confident hand. "No problem. True, I did promise him the Princess Alianora in marriage but set the price so exorbitantly high that he cannot possibly fulfill the bargain. You see," the sallow king chortled conspiratorially, "I stipulated that he pay in merchandise carried in only one ship. Impossible! And then, of course, there are certain tariffs to be deducted from the total. Tariffs are fine things for strangers and brigands, but hardly fitting for friends and relations, eh?" He winked at the balding King Philander.

From across the space between the two wings of the table, gray Queen Huldah spoke up in her strident voice. "And in any event the wedding between our houses would still take place within the week. We have no intention of diluting the blood royal with that of a freebooter."

Alianora, who sat on the queen's left, opened her mouth to speak but shut it at a sharp jab from her stepmother's bony elbow. The princess stared down at the plate of untouched food before her rather than risk meeting the obscene leer of Prince Philander who sat directly across from her and scratched at the patches of dingy beard that splotched his chins.

The visiting royalty seemed reassured by Queen Huldah's unyielding tone. King Zais clapped for entertainment.

Motley heard the call, as he had heard everything else, from the passage to the kitchens where he leaned, idly juggling five duck eggs. He tossed them to the scullery maids he'd been entertaining, picked up his lute and strode blithely into the banquet hall. He jingled past the tables of the lesser nobles and took a position at the open space between the two ends of the curved table. He gave Alianora an almost imperceptible wink with his right eye as his long, delicate fingers began to pluck a rippling melody from the strings of the lute.

When the music had become hypnotic, and even the rowdiest squire had fallen still, Motley began to sing in a pure countertenor. His song was of a prince of the sea who fell in love with a princess on land. Their fathers were at war with one another, but as the last ship sank and the last castle fell, the two lovers escaped on a floating island. When Motley finished there was no applause, only a tense silence and tears in Alianora's eyes.

Prince Philander mused aloud, "I never thought to hear so high a voice, even in a girl. Tell me King Zais, where does it sleep, with the ladies or the guards?"

If the jester's face changed at all, it was only that his eyes went from sea green to burning emerald. He set down his lute and took a bauble from his belt. He stepped forward, practically mincing, tossing the fool's scepter into the air and catching it without looking.

"Tell me, King Zais," he asked imitating the prince's nasal voice perfectly, "is it true Philander means 'a lover of men'?" Everyone looked very uncomfortable, but no one had a chance to speak as Motley turned to Alianora. "Careful, Princess, lest your fiance live up to his father's name doubly well."

Both Philanders were now beet red. Motley grinned and

addressed the younger. "Should you, Sir Prince, ever get
a wife and manage to keep her, I pray you teach our host
that art for he seems not to have got the hang of it yet."
The entire hall was bathed in stunned silence; Alianora
had never seen Motley go this far before and she was
afraid for him. "Of course, considering his tastes, a change
is usually welcome." He smiled winsomely at Queen Huldah.

She hissed, "At last you have grown too insolent for
your own good, Fool!"

"Insolence!" cried Motley. "It is the jester's insolence
    That makes the dullards take offense;
    These lack-wits find their sole defense
    Is to demand that jester's. . . ."

"Silence!" roared King Zais.

"An apt rhyme, my Liege," chirped Motley. "A trifle
obvious, but therein lies half its charm."

Zais was pounding on the table, upsetting goblets of
wine and screaming wildly, "Take him away! Fifty lashes!"

"A bargain, Lord!" Motley called over his shoulder as
two guards carried him off. "I promise never to have you
flogged if you will promise to stop playing the fool!"

The next afternoon, King Zais nervously settled himself
into his throne and summoned his steward. A lean man
with the smell of avarice about him promptly appeared,
followed by a helper carrying parchment and quills. Next
appeared King Philander who lifted a shaggy eyebrow as
he saw the sunlit hall ringed with heavily armed guards.

When he deemed everything ready, King Zais gestured
to a sergeant of the guards who threw open two huge
doors at the far end of the throne room. Through this
portal strode Zarillian, the Sailor-King, who had been
kept waiting since early morning. His azure cape swirled
as he stopped in the center of the throne room and bowed
slightly from the waist to the two kings on the dais,

greeting them as 'a fellow king. "I return to keep our bargain, King Zais. Do you remember it?"

"I do," answered Zais, "but first let me be sure you have violated none of its terms. Do you bring only one ship?"

"Yes," said Zarillian briskly.

"Is the price to be paid in trade goods only?"

"It is."

"And you have brought no men ashore with you, armed or otherwise?"

"My men are on my ship; your own servants have brought the cargo up the hill." Zarillian chewed on his lower lip, impatient to begin.

Just then a beady-eyed man entered the hall and whispered into King Zais' ear for a moment. That sovereign then said, "I am informed by my legal counselor that you have indeed complied with my terms. Let the tally begin!"

Zarillian beckoned the first wave of servants into the hall. "Fine fabrics!" he announced, taking a bolt of saffron gossamer and flinging it high through the air the length of the throne room. The sheer fabric caught the sunlight as it formed an arc then hung there, too light to fall.

When the steward, guards and kings could finally tear their eyes away from that gilded rainbow, Zarillian had already directed the arranging of cloths of every conceivable color, texture, and weave in a great fan-shaped display on the floor. Still the saffron veil hung there above them, quivering in the slight breeze.

"Precious metals!" Zarillian called, and another wave of servants advanced. They carried large coffers, six strong men straining under the weight of each. From the score or more of such massive chests, two were set down, one to each side of the Sailor-King. He opened one and proclaimed, "Gold!" Then with a roar he tipped the chest toward the throne so that a shining cascade of the yellow metal went rushing out across the precious fabrics all the way to the dais. Before the priceless tide could reach Zais' feet, however, Zarillian had cried out, "Silver!" and repeated the process with the other chest.

The double avalanche glittered and gleamed across the fabrics so that everyone was speechless for several heartbeats, as if time itself hung motionless like the saffron arc above them.

The steward rasped, "Trade goods only!"

Zarillian seized huge handfuls of nuggets, scattering them prodigally. "Not a single minted coin in any chest!"

A worried look was forming like a cloudbank on Zais' brow; Zarillian's eyes were fiery with pride and antici- pated success as he called out, "Jewels!"

As the next phalanx of porters advanced, the steward hissed to his scribe, "No! Only half that, and count only a quarter of that, and do not count *that* at all!"

There was a sound of tearing parchment, then Zarillian was spilling out torrents of rubies, emeralds, sapphires, and all other rare stones, finishing with a stream of dia- monds that shone so fiercely that Zais threw up a hand to shield his eyes.

Before he could recover from this latest onslaught of prodigal wealth, Zarillian cried, "Spices!" and soon the throne room was filled with such fragrances that the King of Guttra nearly drooled onto his tunic, and the steward and his scribe even stopped scratching on their parchment for a while. The tantalizing odors hung in the air like the saffron gossamer, defying and overwhelming the senses.

"Rare creatures!" In marched a procession of servants, each carrying a brilliantly colored bird. Some of the birds were making delicate music, each different but harmonious with all the rest, while other birds took turns reciting rare poetry. There were well over a hundred birds, but no two alike; they all fell silent at the approach of a loud, humming sound. Into the throne room flew a giant, bright blue dragonfly. Riding in a silver saddle on its back and holding silken reins was a little black child from the burning deserts of the north. This last, which Zais had first taken for a hallucination brought on by the spices, hovered over the rest, causing the saffron arc to ripple with the fanning of its wings.

A silence made only more silent by the whirr of the dragonfly's wings reigned for what seemed an eternity. Finally, King Zais wiped his sweaty brow, cleared his throat and asked weakly, "is that all?"

"Is it not enough?" Zarillian asked increduously.

The steward spoke up in his voice like a scratchy quill, "The total less import charges, harbor fees, tariffs—"

"Get to it!" snapped Zarillian.

"It is hardly half the amount required," said the steward dryly.

A half-dozen of the burlier guards had been edging toward the Sailor-King from behind, anticipating this very moment, but they found that notoriously violent individual smiling up at the little black child. "I see," he said at last. "Well, then I shall produce an item worth treble what is already here." As everyone looked perplexed, Zarillian called, "The Great Cup!"

Two servants promptly entered with the magical chalice, followed by a long line of others carrying basins, bowls, great tankards, and a host of other vessels. When the Cup reached the center of the throne room, Zarillian took it and declaimed the spell he had heard Edwin use:

> *Earth, Water, Air, and Fire,*
> *Surrender now the Heart's Desire.*

As he finished turning the huge goblet, a loud gurgle echoed in the depths of the Cup, and suddenly blood red wine was welling over the rim to be caught by the servants and carried to the royal taster, then on to the kings. As soon as he had quaffed a large beaker of the sorcerous vintage, Zais began whispering frenziedly with his legal counselor. While they conferred, servants from other parts of the castle appeared, each with a vessel of some kind. Some of the guards were using their helmets to sample the brew that flooded from the Great Cup.

The king finally waved his pettifogger away and asked, "Do you have an astrologer's permit or its equivalent?"

Zarillian stared. "A what?"

"There you have it!" cried Zais between slurps of wine. "Practicing sorcery without permission! I declare all your goods confiscate and herewith banish you forever!"

The six burly guards now found a use for their size and strength as they dragged a raving, cursing Zarillian from the throne room, where wine was starting to spill across the jewels, gold, silver, and delicate fabrics faster and faster, though no one seemed to care as long as they got their cup full.

The rising tide reached the ends of the gossamer arc, and two crescents of the crimson wine sprang into the air, meeting in the middle of the delicate veil. The saffron turned dark red, and the saturated cloth fell to the floor like a crushed and bloodied thing. The little black child sadly watched it fall, then tugged at the reins and flew away on the marvelous dragonfly as the last rays of the sun fell upon a scene of drunken revelry.

Edwin awoke for the second time aboard Zarillian's ship, but this time he did not enjoy that luxurious dalliance along the borders of the land of dream which had been so soothing the first time. Now, Edwin snapped into unpleasant self-awareness. The gentle roll of the ship had become a queasy lurch; his brain was swarming with fiery, red ants; the taste in his mouth was truly unspeakable. Edwin lay on the cabin floor and prayed to whatever gods might exist that he be allowed either to go back to sleep or to die.

After many hesitant attempts, the haggard young man finally sat up, soundly banging his head on the underside of the table, an accident which sent him back to the floor for a paroxysm of whimpering. Gradually he crawled out from under the table and across the sticky floor. The whole cabin reeked of soured wine, and Edwin thought he could live happily through all eternity if he never smelled it again. His initial plan was to crawl up into the bunk, but with movement came the awareness of an unbearable thirst. It was as if a stinging nettle were lodged in his throat. He dragged himself to the door and crawled up the wall into a standing position. He knew a moment of deep terror when his legs threatened to give way beneath him, but he eventually managed to open the door and wobble outside on trembling knees.

To Edwin the light was blinding even though it was only the fading glow of a red and gold sunset. It seemed to the bleary-eyed thief that the sky was a sickly mixture of chartreuse and a purple much too reminiscent of wine. He felt his way along the wall to his right, away from the painful glare and past the large door of Zarillian's cabin, his fingers clutching at the very grain of wood like the toes of some tree lizard.

In such a manner Edwin made his way to the foot of the steps leading to the poop. Sitting on the steps was an old sea-battered sailor mending a rope. Edwin's mouth worked soundlessly for a moment as the seaman watched with a twinkling eye. Edwin finally managed to croak, "Wa-ter!"

The man laid down the hemp and reached into his blouse, taking out a small flask. He handed it to the pathetic creature before him, saying, "This'll clear the barnacles off yer tongue. Careful! Just half a mouthful! It's mickle strong an' even rarer'n that."

Edwin took a modest swig of the bland liquid. He felt
nothing but a much-needed moistening of his tongue and
throat. The sailor kept eyeing the flask as if it held his very
soul, ready to snatch it back if Edwin moved to take
another sip.

"Twas brewed by an ol' hag in the Bormeans. She died
last year, takin' the secret to 'er grave, damn 'er black
heart!" The old salt spoke with true feeling. " 'At's likely
the last of it there'll e'er be," he mourned.

Abruptly, Edwin felt as if he had fallen his own height
straight down and landed on his feet; his eyes snapped into
focus, and the world resumed its true colors; a powerful
shudder accompanied by a warm, flushed feeling swept
over him from his head to his feet, and he was as good as
new. He stared at the flask, awed. "There's a king's
ransom here," he said as he handed it back to the sailor.
"I can't thank you enough."

"I know," agreed Edwin's savior.

"Is it always sunset in this damned place?" Edwin
muttered. He was now able to survey his surroundings for
the first time. *Windsister* was huge with three large, lateen-
rigged sails as well as a score of long oars along either
side. The crew all seemed to be fidgeting with little things
as if waiting for someone to signal a sudden departure. If
the tide was coming in, it would be a departure by rowing.

One sailor who was ostensibly mending something high
on the mizzenmast cried out and pointed toward the quay.
Edwin sprang to the poop, the old sailor on his heels. The
captain's boat was already halfway out to the ship, the oars
slapping the water angrily though two or three of them
seemed idle. The boat was soon alongside, and the crew
hauled up its cargo: a battered, bleeding Zarillian. The
Sailor-King fell to the deck before Edwin, unable to stand,
looking up from the one eye not yet swollen shut, trying to

speak through bloody, puffy lips. Edwin waved him silent. "I'll be back by dawn, if at all."

Before anyone knew what was happening Edwin had gone over the side; not in an heroic splashing dive, but down a rope, bare feet against the hull, slipping into the water with hardly a ripple and swimming silently toward shore.

Princess Alianora paced back and forth in her chambers working herself into an impatient fury at her own helplessness. Two of her father's soldiers stood outside her door by order of Queen Huldah who had confined Alianora to her rooms for her persistent snubbing of Prince Philander at the banquet. Alianora was not as angered by being punished—she had expected it—as by being punished like a child.

But there were still ways to get what she wanted in her lofty prison. A word to a trusted maid whose lover was a captain of the guards and the princess had her own kingdom within a kingdom. It was this shadowy chain of command that now affected the arrival of a very lumpy bag of jester's paraphernalia in her tower rooms.

When the two porters had gone and she untied the cord that held the bag shut, Motley raised his head and said weakly, "You're a wonderful huntress, y'know. Not many princesses ever bag a jester."

Alianora helped the unsteady harlequin to his feet, gasping as she saw his back torn open with the criss-cross marks of the whip and caked with dried blood. "Oh, Motley!" she cried. For a moment it seemed that tears would blind her, but she shook them out of her blue eyes and ran into the bedchamber, returning with a basin of water and a nightgown. While she was away, Motley had sagged to the floor where he lay sprawled, more unconscious than not. Alianora set the basin down beside him and tore the nightgown into pieces. At the sound of tearing cloth Motley's arms twitched, and at the first touch of the cool water to his raw back, his eyes opened. "Motley," sighed Alianora, "why did you do it? Why?"

Motley shrugged, wincing at the movement. "I don't know, Princess. I've been insulted worse by better men and better by worse men. Anyway, I just got started and couldn't stop." He grinned sheepishly.

"This must hurt terribly," said the princess as she cleaned his wounds. "How do you stand the pain?"

"You forget that I'm an actor as well as a fool. I'm simply acting like it doesn't hurt."

The water in the basin was a dull, reddish brown as Alianora improvised a bandage from the rest of the nightgown. "I thought they were going to kill you. I was so worried," she muttered, tying the cloth in place with the ribbons from her hair.

"I think that's what King Zais had in mind. You should've seen the giant they had whip me." He chuckled. "They didn't know that only two nights before he and I shared several mugs of ale—a veritable whale for ale, that one. He could've cut me in two, but he didn't. He used all my back instead of the same places over and over. And he counted badly. I was very lucky."

"Perhaps," said Alianora, her tears welling up again. "As a gesture of friendship to King Philander, father has banished you forever. You are to be out of the city by sunrise under the pain of death, but how can you travel like this?"

"Your father is generous to a fault," said the jester as he pushed himself up off the floor and swayed on his knees. He still wore the checkered tights from the banquet, but his tunic was gone.

As he knelt there beside her, Alianora suddenly realized that this clown, this talking house pet, this whimsical confidant of hers, was a young man about her own age.

His face, framed as it was by golden curls, had seemed more beautiful than handsome, but now she saw pain etching harder features. For the first time she saw his arms and shoulders bare and rippling with an acrobat's wiry muscles. It was a moment of revelation in which Alianora came face to face with the realization of how little she actually knew about Motley, the first time she had ever looked past his foolery. She was also made aware that the love he had professed, then mocked, upon the parapet might well be real.

The jingling of bells shattered her reflections. Motley pulled a jester's suit and cap out of the bag. "Ah, I knew I kept one in here someplace." He looked at Alianora in the glow from the many candles about the room, and his mood darkened. "The only thing I regret is that there is nothing I can do for you on my way out of the city." His face lost even more of its perpetual smile. "Fine words from a fool. I won't even get that far, and we both know it. There seems to be no way out for either of us."

"Perhaps there is, Motley." The harlequin cocked an eyebrow at the look that had come to Alianora's face. "But I fear it is too much to ask of any man."

"What have I got to lose? Ask."

"It is something I remember from a tale you told a fortnight ago," Alianora hinted.

"Oh la," laughed Motley. "I can't remember stories I told two days ago. I make 'em up as I go along, y'know." He gazed into that beautiful, determined face and added hesitantly, "I really should warn you, Princess, those things only work in stories."

"Later, as she emerged from her bedroom, jingling in Motley's spare costume, Alianora said, "I feel guilty asking this of you after what that swinish prince said. I mean . . . oh!" The princess stopped short at the sight of the jester.

"It's just another role," Motley said as he turned around letting the hem of Alianora's finest gown sweep the floor and its voluminous folds rustle in the air. He draped one of her lace scarves over his hair and wrapped it around the lower half of his face like a veil.

"Am I not a vision of beauty?" he twittered, pacing across the room in a perfect imitation of the princess.

"Oh, Motley, I don't walk like *that*!"

"Oh, Motley, I don't walk like *that*!" the jester parroted, his voice an echo of Alianora's. A true actor, once Motley began walking and talking like Alianora, he continued to do so, never slipping out of character.

"I'm having trouble with your cap," said the real princess, trying to speak in a baritone.

"The cap is fine; it's all this hair you're trying to stuff under it that's the problem," Motley lilted. "And stop trying to change your voice. Try not to talk at all." He deftly arranged Alianora's thick, golden hair beneath the jingling headgear, leaving a few curls outside for realism. "Let your shoulders sag and drag your feet," he instructed. "Remember, you have just been flogged to within a blink of your life, and your back burns like fire."

"And you?" asked the disguised princess.

"I must forget those very things." It was still bewildering to Alianora to carry on a conversation with herself. The veiled Motley stepped closer to adjust the sash around the harlequin's tunic. "You must not draw the tunic so tight, dear Motley."

"Why not?" Alianora asked.

Motley fidgeted with his makeshift veil and giggled naughtily, hoping to avoid having to tell the princess that her figure was far from boyish. He was spared any answer at all by the tramping of armed men and the abrupt opening of the door.

There stood Queen Huldah, flanked by two guards. Her

eyes glittered in the candlelight as they fell upon the jester. "I thought so," she crowed. "Take him away!" As the men advanced, Alianora sank to one knee and, taking Motley's hand, kissed it. Then the guards seized her by the arms and carried her out, leaving the "princess" standing with "her" head demurely bowed.

"I hope you have changed your mind by morning," the gray queen hissed.

"I have already changed more than that," said Motley-as-Alianora in a well-modulated soprano.

"Good," snapped the queen as she turned and stalked away, slamming the door behind her. Motley heaved a sigh of relief at having survived act one of a dangerous play. He snuffed candles until only one candelabra burned in either room. For this role he did not want a well-lighted stage. He could only hope to buy Alianora enough time to escape, then find some way to save himself. He fought the temptation to let his shoulders sag and his feet drag. He couldn't know when he might be forced to resume his role without warning.

Alianora-as-Motley was doing her best to sag as the guards carried her down the seemingly interminable flights of stairs. She had never realized how high her tower rooms were. From time to time she grunted or gasped as if in pain, but the guards seemed intent only on getting rid of her, so she gave up her efforts at acting for lack of an attentive audience.

Alianora became worried as they descended, fearing her father might have planned some gruesome fate beneath the castle. She practically sighed with relief when the guards stopped to unbar a heavy wooden door that opened to let in the smells of the city and the light of the full moon. Then she was dumped in the gutter, and the massive door slumped shut behind her.

The princess took her hand out of something she didn't

much like the smell of and looked around, searching for
the quickest way to the sea and Zarillian. She felt something shrivel up inside her as she realized she had never
seen this part of the city of her birth. She was lost outside
the door of her father's castle.

A muffled cough and the metallic slither of a blade
being drawn behind her made Alianora jump, bells jingling
at her movement. Footsteps approached from two other
directions to hem her in with her back to the implacable
door. As one of the men passed through a slanting beam of
moonlight, she saw he was a tall black man of the north
with a ruby set in the lobe of his right ear. He smiled
wickedly, another chuckled, and Alianora panicked. The
bells on her suit and cap jangled frantically as she flung
herself at the door, pounding on it and crying, "Open this
door! I'm Princess Alianora! Open up!" Her jester's cap
fell off, and her long, golden hair tumbled about her
shoulders. Her soft little fists made hardly a sound against
the thick planks of the door.

The men advanced, unhurried and smiling, knowing full
well that a princess' cries for help count for next to
nothing in an alley.

Motley pulled the scarf away from his nose and mouth a
bit. The lace smelled overpoweringly of lavender, and
Alianora's slippers were starting to pinch the jester's feet.
He crossed the outer chamber with the rustle of silk and
poked his head out the window, hoping to find some
escape route. His eyes slid down the tower wall without
finding any purchase except a few strands of lethargic ivy
and the cracks in the masonry. At full strength it would be
foolhardy but weak from pain and hunger it was suicide.

He gathered up his skirts and hobbled into the bedroom
only to be confronted with the same view from the window
in that room, too. He stiffened as he heard tramping in the

hallway, then stood puzzled as he realized that the guards were leaving. Motley was halfway out of the bedchamber door when the door to the hallway was eased open and the obese Prince Philander sidled in carrying a bottle of wine. From his movements Motley surmised that the prince contained more wine than the bottle. The prince peered about in the semi-darkness, crooning drunkenly, "Al-i-a-nooo-ra!"

Motley's skin crawled as the piggish eyes of the leering young man fell upon him. For a moment the clown thought the play had to end, but he thought of Alianora being forced to submit to this adolescent satyr; he thought back to the banquet and let a little pain from his back seep into his consciousness; he was filled with an icy determination to play his role to the last possible moment, to buy Alianora every bit of time he could before he was discovered.

"There you are!" The prince lurched across the room before Motley could get away from the bedroom door.

"Yes," the jester shyly tittered, "here I am."

"Queen Huldah said you would wait up for me, but I knew anyway," Philander said in a gust of garlic and wine. "You've been playing the good little virgin, but *I* know. You want me just like all the rest."

"I do?" Motley asked coyly.

Philander belched loudly. "Yes, you do. I can tell. I am an excellent judge of women." He proudly stuck out his flabby chest.

"Perhaps not so good as you think," ventured the false princess.

"An *excellent* judge of women," Philander repeated belligerently. He kept edging closer and closer, forcing Motley to retreat into the bedchamber. "And for all your fancy ways, you're the same as any other woman."

"Oh, I am not like any woman you have *ever* seen," said Motley, playing the coquette to the hilt.

"We'll soon see," said Philander. "You lead me in the right direction."

Motley took a quick glance over his shoulder at the bed, and in that instant Philander was on him, pawing and grabbing, trying to work a mephitic kiss through the veil. The jester squirmed about trying to keep the lecherous bridegroom from learning too much about the body he was so intent on fondling. "What about the wedding?" Motley finally managed to gasp.

"That's just for show," mumbled the prince as he nuzzled Motley's shoulder through the silk. The harlequin found himself wondering abstractedly what women saw in men that was worth this kind of treatment; he hoped Zarillian was a gentle lover. Motley's back was afire from Philander's pawing and spilled wine, but the prince took the gasps of pain as signs of aroused passion. Motley worked an arm free and slapped his assailant. "For my honor," he apologized.

Philander staggered back a step and shook his head to clear the ringing in his ear. "I like it when you struggle."

Motley rolled his eyes toward the ceiling. "You listen to too many storytellers, I fear."

Philander tossed the wine bottle into a corner and began taking off his clothes. Motley stood horrified, realizing things had gotten out of hand. He had given a good performance, too good in fact. Philander soon stood naked, his fat body in the candlelight like some obscene melon. Snatching off the veil, Motley squeaked, "But I'm not Alianora! See?"

"You'll do," said the prince as he advanced on the cowering Motley. He saw those frightened green eyes turn toward the window and fill with surprise. He turned just in time to see Edwin drop to the floor on soundless bare feet. That was the last he saw before the stranger snuffed the candles in one deft motion, plunging the room into a darkness broken only by a pale blue strip of moonlight from the window.

Edwin danced across the light, and Philander lunged after him. Motley sank onto the floor by the bed, hearing the scuff of Philander's heavy feet and heavier breathing, watching through a haze of pain and exhaustion as the two silhouettes flickered through the moonlight in their deadly *pas de deux*.

This stranger was too quick for Philander at first. Then it seemed to Motley that he became overconfident and stayed in the light too long, allowing Philander to locate him and charge like a maddened bull. Suddenly, the prince was toppling out the window, his upturned buttocks gleaming in the moonlight. His surprised screaming was terminated by two sickening thumps. The Prince of Guttra had bounced.

Edwin grabbed Motley by the hand and said, "Come with me!"

"Is there no end to this?" Motley wailed, nearly slipping into his own voice.

"Do you want to go to Zarillian or not?" demanded Edwin.

"Zarillian?" Motley tried to clear the cobwebs of fatigue from his mind. Philander dead, Alianora gone, and death at sunrise if he was found in the city: little choice here. "Lead on," he lilted, forcing himself to his feet, searching out his last traces of strength for one last, desperate act in this play.

The unlikely fugitives were slowed in their descent of the tower stairs by Motley's frequent stumbling. His hobbling steps finally became a limp, and he sat down on the stairs. Edwin, edgy from the absence of guards rushing to investigate Philander's fall, turned and impatiently whispered, "What's wrong?"

"It's these fuggering shoes!" hissed Motley, yanking off the offending footgear and wriggling his tortured toes.

Edwin had had few dealings with women of high birth, and none with princesses, but it seemed to him that Zarillian had chosen a rather coarse specimen for which to risk his life. The barefoot jester in princess' clothing stood up, and they proceeded downward to the main level of the castle without further incident, but with each wondering at the strangeness of the other.

At the foot of the stairs they came upon an unconscious guard with a purple chin. He was sitting slumped against the wall in a shallow tide of wine. Edwin made a face at the smell; Motley's eyes grew wide. "Where could so much wine have come from?" he asked, remembering to use Alianora's voice though the effort was wasted on Edwin.

"Only one place I know of. Come on." The master thief led the way, sliding his feet through the ankle-deep wine with hardly a sound, peering around corners and hugging the shadows in the great hallways. Motley was having less luck with his attempts at stealth due to the gown he was wearing. To Edwin's keen ears it seemed that the "princess" was following him in a boat. From time to time he turned to glare and gesture for silence, receiving an apologetic shrug in return. The lower half of the gown was purple with the wine it was absorbing like a sponge; it was becoming a burden to Motley, slowing them.

Slipping from shadow to shadow past the occasional guards who were either unconscious from the wine or too drunk to care, the two came to the portals of the throne room. After gazing at that scene of drunken debauchery for a moment, Edwin realized how lucky he had been to pass out *after* saying the rune of cessation, not before. He and "Alianora" were standing knee-deep in the swiftly flowing wine, but it was waist-deep and rising in the throne room, there being too much wine and too few ways for it to get out.

The Great Cup seemed to be gaining force and capacity the longer it worked. A blood red column shot into the air higher than a man. The wine was only around the calves of the drunken kings who leaned on one another, crowns askew, on the raised dais. The sea of wine was littered with exotic flotsam: the nude bodies of dancing girls overcome by the wine, brightly colored birds who were singing out of tune or reciting bawdy doggerel as they bobbed about on the surface. Most of the guards were still sober enough to stand, but a few of them were floating face down on the carmine sea.

As Motley watched with widening eyes, a page filled a tankard at the fountain of wine and started back toward the King of Guttra, but passed out with a loud splash before he could reach that royal personage. Philander XII, or "Philly" as he now insisted on being called, pushed his crown back from his eyes and quickly dispatched another cupbearer.

Meanwhile, Motley found a useful side effect of the winery flood as the fumes from the throne room cleared his head and gave him at least the illusion of renewed strength. He was stooping to sample the sorcerous brew when Edwin seized him by the hair and jerked his head up. "Your pardon, Princess Alianora, but if you start drinking this wine, you won't be able to stop 'til you've passed out! Let's get out of here!"

They were stealthily sloshing past the wide doors of the royal presence when, as fate would have it, King Zais caught sight of them. Though Motley no longer resembled Alianora as closely as before, having shed the veil, it was close enough to fool a drunken king. Zais saw blonde hair and a purple gown being led away by a dark, sinister figure. He lurched to his feet, belched raucously and yelled, "Guardsh! Heeshteeling m'daughter! Alianora!"

It was impossible to tell how much the guards understood, but they did recognize the name of their princess for it became their tipsy battle cry as they waded out of the room on the double. As they splashed out in wet pursuit, King Zais slumped back onto his throne and dipped his goblet down into the wine at his feet.

"Wha' was all 'at abou'?" asked King "Philly" XII.

"Alla wha'?"

Edwin heard the uproar of the guards behind him and quickened his pace, dragging the sodden "princess" along by the arm. The guards were picking up any weapon they could find and yelling, "Alianora!"

The two fugitives set out through the flooded halls, moving faster than the staggering guards who kept jostling each other and tripping over one another's feet. The distance between hunters and hunted, however, was still not enough to satisfy Edwin and Motley. They lengthened their lead considerably when Motley remembered a short-cut out a postern door into the streets of the city. The situation was simplified now; Gedar was built on a hill overlooking the harbor so that to reach their goal, the quay, all they had to do was run downhill.

They had paused for a moment to let Motley catch his breath, but the guards, augmented by other soldiers caught up in the frenzy of the chase without knowing the quarry, appeared around a corner running pell-mell over the wine-flooded cobblestones.

An arrow bounced off a wall to one side of the pair. Motley waved and called, "Don't shoot! I'm Princess Alianora!"

"Alianora!" bayed the drunken pack, and another arrow whizzed past Motley's head, brushing his hair with its feathers. With a burst of speed that even he did not suspect he still possessed, Motley shot off downhill with Edwin on his heels. The wine rushed downhill with them, growing shallower the farther they ran from the castle. Now they were splashing through a freshet of the brew that was not quite ankle-deep except where it paused to form puddles between the cobblestones.

Motley eventually gave up any attempt at thought, letting his body occupy itself with one thing only: running. Even the seemingly tireless Edwin was gasping for breath as he ran alongside the disguised jester, occasionally steering him around buildings that loomed before them forcing them to veer sharply as the streets wound sinuously to the sea. Loud crashes behind announced the guards' arrival at those buildings and their inability to avoid them.

Edwin had been keeping track of time in a corner of his mind: the setting of the moon, the false dawn, and now the lightening sky that meant morning. He recalled his words to Zarillian bitterly, "I'll be back by dawn, if at all." He could only hope Zarillian would tarry a little. Edwin hadn't expected the wine and a clumsy princess.

He judged their chances of escape by the sounds of the first guards being propelled through shop windows by the momentum of those behind. The guards were gaining on them. This was due to the "princess'" gown which had soaked up wine until it weighed as much as Motley, and kept tripping up "her" flying feet. More than once Edwin had to grab Motley's arm to keep him from sprawling headlong down the sloping street. Still they ran, their rasping breaths and splashing feet pursued by the baying and crashing of the guards through the slowly wakening city.

The fugitive pair gained much-needed ground when an archer trailing the pack fired a trifle low, bringing down the foremost guard with an arrow square in the back. The rest tripped over the prostrate body and sprang up crying,

"Ambush!" The archer cried loudest of all. When they saw no further sign of their mysterious assailants they continued the chase—all but two, the slain guard and one other who stayed behind on his belly to lap wine from puddles in the street.

By degrees Edwin became aware that they were running on dry pavement now, having outrun the flooding wine as well as the guards. This had hardly gained the thief's attention before they were at the top of the stone steps that led down to the quay. He grabbed the hurtling "princess" in a wiry bear hug to keep "her" from running into thin air. From the top of the steps Edwin saw *Windsister* leaving under full sail.

"A boat! A rowboat!" he hissed to the "princess" as he pointed out a boatman bending over to untie his small craft from the quay. The commotion behind him seemed not to have attracted his attention yet. The pair fairly flew down the steps and across the quay toward him. Edwin applied a well-aimed heel to the poor man's proffered buttocks to send him flailing down into the water with a startled "Whoop?"

Behind them the wine came splashing down the steps in scarlet cataracts that glistened in the ruby light of the rising sun. Behind the wine came the yammering mob of guards, even farther from their right minds than they were from their quarry. They ended up descending the steps in a human avalanche.

The fugitives leapt into the small boat, and Edwin seized the oars, summoning up his last desperate strength to row furiously after the rapidly departing *Windsister*. "Alianora" passed out in the bottom of the boat.

The foremost guards, true to form, were unable to stop at the edge of the quay and fell or were pushed into the harbor. The rest stood around bewildered until the rowboat had shrunk into too small a thing to occupy their attention, then started trying to fish their comrades out of the water. These resisted all rescue attempts, however, preferring to remain under the purple curtain of wine that came cascading over the edge of the quay.

Row as he might, Edwin knew he could never catch up to *Windsister*, but he could not return to shore either. So he threw all he had into the rowing. If it ended for him here, it would end with him doing his utmost. It infuriated him that he could not let Zarillian know that Princess Alianora lay insensate in the little boat that bobbed along behind his ship.

A loud bellow made Edwin look over his shoulder just in time to see a rope snaking through the air from the stern of the ship. He marvelled at the arm that threw it so far and yet managed to drape it across the little boat. Immediately Edwin threw down the oars and tied the line to the boat. It jerked taut, and soon the tiny boat was skimming across the water to the rhythmic chanting of the sailors. Edwin sagged wearily, nearly passing out like the "princess" now that he had quit rowing. He thought the sailors' voices made the finest music he had ever heard.

He was roused from his weary reverie by the thump of the rowboat against the ship's hull. Edwin reached out a hand and patted *Windsister's* hull as if it were the flank of some huge, friendly beast. Then voices called out, and a rope ladder clattered down the side. He splashed seawater into Motley's face until those green eyes opened dully, then commanded, "Climb!"

Edwin held his breath as the "princess" started up. The ship seemed higher than a castle wall from his vantage point, and if she slipped. . . .

Edwin began climbing after the "princess" but they were no sooner both on the ladder than he felt himself rising through the air and heard the rhythmic chant once more.

It seemed only a moment later that he was kneeling on the deck, too spent to stand or even voice his thanks. The sailors stood around him in a grinning ring, all talking, mostly about having never seen anyone row so fast. A familiar face detached itself in the haze of Edwin's vision, and a familiar flask was tilted to his lips. He waited for and soon felt the sharp drop and shuddering warmth. Then he stood up, stretching like a man who has just risen from a long night's sleep. He turned to the old sailor. "Thanks again."

The grizzled veteran of the sea was not looking at him, but holding the dark flask to his ear and shaking it. He looked at the bottle accusingly. "Barely enow t'see me through one more port, anyhow. Here." He thrust the flask into Edwin's hands. "Yer friend'll be needin' this last."

As a thief, Edwin had never dealt with anyone who was not prepared to fight or even kill to keep the most trivial gew-gaw; now this old sailor was freely giving away the last of his miraculous potion.

"G'wan!" growled the old man. "Don't stan' air wi'yer eyes lookin' like 'at!" The others roared with laughter at their shipmate's discomfort as well as Edwin's look of profound disbelief. They made way for the dark youth as he went to the pathetic creature for whom he had risked his life. He placed his hand under the golden locks and raised Motley's head, pouring the remainder of the miraculous fluid into the open mouth. Then he sat back on his heels to wait, but nothing happened.

Suddenly Zarillian appeared with a beautiful young woman at his side. She was dressed in flowing robes of multi-colored Alizarian silk. Zarillian beamed with pleasure from his rapidly healing face and said, "Edwin, now you may judge for yourself if this is not a princess worth stealing. Here is Princess Alianora!"

Edwin stood dumfounded for a moment, then burst out, "If that is Princess Alianora, then who have I brought you?" His voice had anger in it; his pride hurt by having stolen the wrong princess, he stood pale, hands clenched. He looked down at the impostor who had cost him so much just in time to see Motley's body jerk and shudder. The wan features of his face turned a glowing red, then subsided to a natural flesh color. The sparkling green eyes popped open.

Alianora, previously occupied with gazing at Zarillian adoringly, suddenly caught sight of the jester. "Motley your back!" she cried, her first impression from the wine-drenched gown being that the puckish young man was in danger of bleeding to death. As his green eyes focused on her, she cried again, "Your back!"

"So I am," Motley said calmly. "Though it's like I never left."

"Oh, Motley!" Alianora fretted. She promptly began ordering the sailors around, having them carry Motley to the poop and fetch him dry clothes and bring the Bormean ointment and. . . .

Zarillian took Edwin aside and explained how Alianora came to be aboard, pointing to three sailors lined up as if for punishment. One was the tall black man of the north who wore a ruby in the lobe of one ear. "I am trying to decide if I should punish them or not. They disobeyed my orders by going ashore to take vengeance for my beating, but on the other hand they stumbled across Alianora in the suit of the jester you found in her place."

"Reward them," said Edwin.

"Yes, I think I will, but let them worry a bit first. It's all very confusing; surely all the gods my sailors swear by joined together to bring these things to pass! You did more than I could have rightfully asked of you. Edwin, so do not feel bitter."

"The sting of it passes," mused the thief.

Zarillian ordered a passing sailor to bring Edwin the dry clothes he'd picked for him as a reward—if he returned. "One other thing, Edwin."

"Yes, I know. I forgive you for stealing the Cup."

The Sailor-King looked at him slyly. "But surely you have heard that to steal from a thief is not stealing?"

Edwin, enjoying the moment of making Zarillian admit his own larcenous tendencies, said, "That only applies to another thief, Zarillian," and climbed to the poop, leaving the Sailor-King to follow with a chastened but amused look on his face.

Edwin approached the cluster of sailors around Alianora and Motley, but stopped short when he caught sight of the jester's lacerated back. He knelt beside Alianora, taking the vial of ointment from her.

"That's right," chirped the refreshed Motley, "you have a husband now, Princess. No need to look after a second fool."

"Will you ever show respect for anyone?" Alianora asked.

"Not if I can help it."

When they had all compared their variant versions of the same story, and Zarillian had taken Alianora to the prow of the ship, Motley looked back at Edwin where the bearded young man stroked ointment onto the wounds. "Why the change of heart? I thought you didn't like impostors."

Edwin shrugged. "I've had a taste of the lash."

Sailors appeared from below bringing the jester's spare suit and a hooded cloak of a Barratrian charlatan for Edwin. The cloak was deepest black and full of hidden pockets; Edwin was forced to smile at Zarillian's thoughtfulness.

When they had donned the dry garments, they strolled

to the rail and looked back at the rapidly shrinking hill that was Gedar. "The Great Cup was all you had, yet you don't seem to grieve much about losing it," said Motley.

"Toward the end it came to possess me as much as I possessed it." Edwin waved a hand, dismissing the matter. "Possessions are clumsy for a thief, and besides, I *hate* wine."

The remark was not comical in itself, but both doubled up with laughter that, though it would make their ribs sore for days, was necessary if they were to release all the tension that had built up throughout their long, incredible escape. Even Zarillian and Alianora stopped their lovebird cooing for a while to look back and wonder at the strange pair laughing themselves out of breath and into tears for no apparent reason.

Spring Conditions

Eileen Gunn

Eileen Gunn is the only person besides myself who I know gets complimented at science fiction conventions for her wonderful costumes, when in reality these are the only clothes we have. As she manages to write only one short story a year, she isn't exactly cropping up in every anthology you find. Her last three years' output has appeared in AMAZING, Ace Books' PROTEUS, *and here. I consider it a coup, having acquired her major opus of the year for* TALES BY MOONLIGHT.

Despite the rarity of her tales, Eileen manages to make her living from writing . . . . .computer books and advertising copy. Originally from Boston, she is currently a minion of Seattle's Capitol Hill, and is one of the chief reasons the ''in crowd'' considers that part of Seattle to be Paradise (or is that Loonyville).

If you make it to the West Coast for a skiing vacation, keep the following story, Spring Conditions, *firmly in mind.*

Mia pushed herself slowly to the top of the rise on her long, narrow skis. She was still hung over and wrung out from last night, and though the hill was not steep, it required all the effort she wanted to give. When she got to the ridge, she waited there for Zeb.

The day was wet and too warm, the forest dripping, fog-muffled, monochromatic. The snow, heavy and granular beneath her skis, was still three or four feet deep. Dead sticks thrust out of it. Light rain fell with a distant murmur, like the sound of a silk shroud.

The top of the hill was only sparsely covered with trees, and she could see further ahead, where the trail sloped down to a small, snow-covered pond. It was darker down there, and a damp breeze was rising from the pond. Mia shivered. Warm air moves uphill; she had read that somewhere. Warm air moving uphill can be a storm signal in the Sierras. Or was that just at night?

They'd have to start back to the lodge soon, but maybe they'd have time to check out the pond. It would be a nice place to hike to later in the spring, but, like the woods along the trail, it was sad and decayed now. The death of winter is the first sign of spring in the Sierras, but winter here doesn't die easy.

Mia felt a small death in her, too: the first indication, perhaps, of a rebirth. Skiing, solitary, ahead of Zeb, she had come to a decision. Her anger of last night had dissipated, but like the alcohol that had fed it, it had left her feeling sick. They had fought so many times before, over such insignificant matters. It was time to put an end to it.

Zeb skied up beside her. Brown, bearded, not unfriendly in spite of their fight, he was a welcome sight, but Mia hardened her resolve.

"Porcupine tracks back there," he said, slightly out of breath. "Like someone dragged a broom across the snow."

"I've made a decision," said Mia. "I'm getting out of L.A. Maybe go to Oregon." She looked away from him, between two scraggly lodgepole pines, toward the pond.

Zeb stared at her warily. "It wasn't that bad a fight," he said. "I'm sure the staff at the lodge has forgotten all about it. There's no need to leave the state."

Mia smiled slightly, against her will. "I'm serious."

"We shouldn't throw away our time together so casually."

"You mean we should stick it out like a cat and dog tied tail-to-tail?" Mia didn't want to face him. Her eyes sought the distance, the dark woods beyond the far edge of the pond.

"We don't have to fight," said Zeb. He was still looking at her. "I don't even understand what we fought about last night."

Mia forced herself to turn to him, and the courage of honesty came to her. "I don't know, either. There's just something in me that lashes out at you. That's why I want to go. There's something in me that fears and hates and fights, and I have no control over it with you. It's happened before, too, with other people."

Now Zeb searched the forest, refused to meet her eyes. "This is no place to have a serious conversation. We've got to get going anyway, if we're going to make it back to the lodge before dark."

"I want to get a closer look at the pond," said Mia, relieved to drop the subject. She pushed forward on her skis. The corner of the pond that had been hidden by the pines came into view. The surface of the ice was broken, and there was a jagged circle of brown water, as though someone had fallen in. She called out to Zeb.

He came up beside her, and gave a puzzled grunt. "No footprints, no ski tracks. No sign of an animal. Kind of far from the trees for a limb to have fallen in."

The air coming up from the pond was wet and clinging. Mia shivered again. "Maybe something's breaking out," she said. Zeb looked at her blankly. She shook her head; that didn't make sense. "Let's go," she said. "It's getting cold and dark." As she turned to go down the slope the way they'd come, she thought she saw something move in the dark gap of the pond. "Wait." She swung back to see what it was. In the dark brown water, something was bobbing slowly, just under the surface. It was pale and bulky, like a badly wrapped package. A body?

"If it happened before the last snow, there'd be no tracks," said Zeb.

As they watched, the package broke the surface slowly and gently, like a bubble rising in oil. It bobbed uncertainly and rotated. A bare foot, white as chalk, appeared from underneath. The stench of rotting flesh drifted like mist up the slope. There was someone in there, past any help they could give.

"My god," whispered Mia. But Zeb was already heading down the hill to the pond. "What are you going to do?" she shouted. He didn't answer, and she pushed off after him, their argument already far in the past.

She caught up to him quickly. They stopped at the bottom of the hill, by the edge of the pond. They couldn't see the body any better than they had from the hill. Was it wearing a tan parka? The foot had sunk back down below the water: it wasn't visible. The smell of putrefaction was stronger now, almost overwhelming.

"We can't possibly drag it back to the lodge," Mia said.

"I know," said Zeb. "The shape it's in, it would fall apart anyway. But if we can get a look at the clothing, see if there's any identification on it, maybe the rangers will be able to figure out who it was."

"God, this is gruesome."

"Eh. Good an end as any. Bottom of a quiet pond in the Sierras." He was edging out onto the ice.

"Be careful. I couldn't drag you back, either." Now that she was down by the pond, the air felt even wetter, almost slimy. The hole was close to the edge of the pond, only about eight feet away. From close up, it looked larger and somehow hungry. Zeb's skis were leaving long, brown-soaked tracks.

"Give me the tip of your pole to hold on to," he said.

Mia did. "I don't like this," she said. "How can you go out there?"

"If you were in there, you'd want somebody to find out who you were." Zeb's voice was calm, the voice of a man who didn't believe he'd fall in. He was gingerly testing the ice. As he moved, the body bobbed. His weight was bouncing the ice on the water like a raft. Mia winced.

Zeb moved further out onto the ice, still holding onto Mia's pole, and she moved up behind him. Her skis were resting mostly on the land, with about two feet of the tips out on the ice. Zeb was all the way out, his weight distributed by his skis.

"I can almost reach it with my pole," he said. "Maybe I can pull it over and grab it."

"I don't like this, Zeb." Fear welled in her throat like vomit.

"There's something else in there!" Another light-colored mass was moving in the brown water, coming out from under the shelf of ice.

Mia pulled back, the hair bristling coldly at the nape of her neck.

"Don't do that!" shouted Zeb angrily.

Ashamed—they were dead bodies, after all—Mia moved out again onto the ice.

Zeb was redistributing his weight, extending his pole to snag the body on the top. There was a sudden splash, and something whipped out of the water and grabbed the pole, just above the round plastic basket at the end. Zeb let go of Mia's pole and without even a yell was pulled into the water.

Mia froze as Zeb disappeared under the surface. She could see more bodies below. Huge and pale, they rose like feeding fish from under the ice. The water began to ripple, then to boil furiously.

Mia yelled. She moved out onto the ice towards the hole, striking at the shapes in the churning water. A long thin hand reached like a tentacle out of the water and grabbed her pole. It was dead white, the skin wrinkled and sloughing off the wet bones. Mia pulled back, but it was too strong. She was losing her balance. She let her hand go limp, and her pole and glove were ripped away. Without thinking, Mia scrambled back for the bank, and landed heavily on her side. The hole in the pond was getting wider; brown patches appeared in the snow-covered ice and sank away into open water. There were more things trying to get out.

At the edge of the pond, she hesitated, stunned. It had happened so quickly. Zeb was still in there. Could he still be alive?

More holes opened in the ice and more claw-like hands grasped toward her. The water in the pond lapped at her skis. It was rising.

Faster than her brain, her body acted. When she snapped to, she was already half-way up the hillside, with no idea of how she'd gotten that far. She kept going, moving almost straight up the slope.

When she got to the top, she stopped, but didn't look back. Were there sounds behind her? She was paralyzed momentarily: her need to get away fought with a sense of duty. She should go back down to the pond and find Zeb.

The soft sounds behind her got louder. She didn't look back, but pushed off down the hill toward the lodge. Two sets of tracks went up the hill, only one was going back down. Mia forced herself to concentrate on her skiing.

After an interminably long time, pushing herself through the darkening forest, she swung onto the logging road that led toward the lodge. She pushed her way ahead with long skating strokes; it was a low, easy grade downhill. There were no more noises behind her. But was that a soft slithering in the trees to the right? Just the wind? She refused to listen.

What had really happened, she asked herself? Could she have helped Zeb? Was there anything she could have done? Would the rangers believe her if she told them, or should she make up a story that made more sense?

There couldn't have been live things in that pond. Maybe Zeb had caught his pole on some weeds, and the ice cracked and collapsed. She should have kept her head, and pulled him out. She had killed him by panicking.

The sound in the trees had passed her—just the wind after all. Mia knew she couldn't have helped Zeb. She pushed her body harder. A muscle throbbed in her thigh. She ignored it.

She came to a small meadow, with young pines freckling its edge in the fog, and Mia recognized the last steep grade before the lodge. It was almost dark and she was tiring. She wasn't good on steep hills, even when she was fresh, and with only one pole, she wasn't balanced properly. She pushed her heels down and dug in the edges of her skis going around the narrow curves. She didn't slow down.

She could see the lights up ahead now, hear the clanging of the yard-bell that helped skiers get their bearing in the fog. She dreaded arriving at the lodge. She dreaded having to tell anyone what had happened.

The logging road opened into the clearing, and Mia finally broke free of the forest. She was certain that nothing was following her: nothing had ever been following her. She stopped and looked back. There were no sounds behind or beside her, and she could see nothing moving.

Mia wanted to turn around and go back to the pond, to find Zeb and pull him out of the water, to breathe life back into him. She wanted to make right everything she had done wrong. It had been the anger inside her that had killed him, the force that lashed out at people close to her. Mia wasn't crying, but her face was wet with tears, and they kept coming, as if they belonged to someone else.

She faced back towards the lodge and pushed off, but there were no lights up ahead now. Power failure? It was almost too dark to see, but the trail was still a lighter tone than the forest.

Suddenly, the outside lights of the lodge came on again. She was very close, just a few hundred yards more. It had started to snow, and the lights illumined the heavy flakes as they fell slowly. But there were still no lights on inside the lodge.

She skied closer, staring at the dark picture windows that faced the beginners' slope. There was nobody outside, and it was very quiet. In the snow near the door, there were long brush marks, as though somebody had dragged a broom across it.

Mia peered into the windows. She had trouble focusing her eyes at first. Inside she could see huge, pale shapes bobbing slowly against the panes. Ragged bits of flesh and detritus swam in the air as in soup. Zeb floated there with the rest of them, his skin white and puckered, his eyes open and unseeing, his jaw slack. Aimlessly, as if on a current, he was drifting closer to the window.

These things wanted her. They were a part of her already—perhaps they had come from her. She would see this through to the end.

Mia skied over to the doorway and stopped. She tapped the toe clamps with her pole, and stepped out of the skis. Then she opened the door and went inside.

The Sky Came Down To Earth

Steve Rasnic Tem

Denver denizen Steve Rasnic Tem has appeared in an amazing number of major and small press anthologies and magazines in the past couple of years, which ought to qualify him for the title of Rising New Talent. He is also a poet, which shows in his style of spinning a yarn.

The Sky Came Down to Earth, like An Egg for Ava *elsewhere in this volume or the Aiken classic* Silent Snow, Secret Snow, *reveals a child's differing sense of reality. Russell, unlike Ava, is not gleeful about the wonders he observes in his finite universe. He is more aware that something is amiss, a threatening strangeness amplified by fear and insecurity. After reading this yarn, I'd ask you to consider whether Russell's inconceivable experience is something supernatural, dreadful and real, or something of not-so-simple madness. It could be both.*

The sky was like cotton candy, Russell thought at first. But then it changed somehow, and it was like cotton which had been in water a long time, until it had become fat and swollen, and each time you touched it cold milky water seeped out. Like the body of a dead white cat Russell had found in a ditch one time. It made the sky seem bigger somehow than it should be; the cotton was filling up everything, soaking up all the sounds, all the smells. Russell's head felt full of the sky.

He could not be sure, would not be sure how the Suttons felt about him. They'd told him to go out to play, to play in the back yard while they both talked. They said they needed some time to themselves.

They were busy. And he'd been in their way. He'd seen it in their faces. And seen something else too, the beginnings of something. He'd seen the same thing in other adults' faces just before they decided they couldn't keep him anymore. He wasn't sure, but he thought that was it.

It was cool outside, the sky a milky gray color. As Russell looked up above the porch, trying to find the sun, several ice crystals formed in the hair fallen over his left eye. He could feel another ice crystal on his nose, and one that fell into the corner of his mouth, but just as quickly disappeared. As if it had never existed at all.

The neighborhood was quiet this morning; Russell could hear little. He stood near the cedar fence and looked out over the back lot. The neighbors' cars were gone; there weren't the usual kids playing softball and tag. He thought he was going to have to be alone the whole weekend and it made him angry.

He'd miss the Sutton home: the big back yard, the swing under the mimosa tree that smelled so nicely in the spring, Marge Sutton's big flowerbeds—he wouldn't admit it to anyone, but he really liked flowers. It was the nicest place he had lived in yet.

The social worker had told him this would be permanent, that the Suttons had gone ahead and adopted him and that was that. But Russell knew better. Adults did pretty much what they wanted to; the rules were really just for kids. His birth mom had told him she loved him, then she'd left. After she'd made him feel so bad for lying. Well, she'd lied too, hadn't she?

He guessed he expected all this to happen; the first signs

were very familiar to him. He just wasn't sure why it was happening, and that bothered him a little.

There seemed to be something funny about the back lot. Usually it was so dusty, even in late spring, that you could see the little clouds of it lifting off in a brown haze with even the slightest breeze. That seemed to happen all day; the air always had a gritty feel, like you were swallowing some dirt.

But today the ground seemed still, almost fake. Russell wanted to walk over and look at it, feel it. He thought he wouldn't be surprised to find it was some kind of plastic, or painted concrete. But maybe the lot seemed that way because it was so cool today, cooler than he thought an early spring day should ever be.

Of course, he knew why the Suttons didn't like him anymore, Russell reminded himself. He did a lot of bad things. Marge Sutton had always told him people didn't like you when you acted bad like that. And he'd always believed her.

But sometimes it was really hard not to be bad. He would just do something, whatever it was he wanted to do, and for some reason most times it would turn out he had done something bad again. If he wanted something, or needed something, sometimes it was hard for him to remember it belonged to someone else.

His hands were getting cold. He held them up in front of his face and was surprised to see how white they were, and how stiff they felt. He didn't think he could bend his fingers at all.

Russell looked around anxiously. It didn't *look* that cold. He didn't understand. The mimosa and oak trees bordering the yard and back lot were a brilliant green, glowing except Russell couldn't understand how since there really wasn't that much sun out. The trees looked like it was a bright summer day.

Except that they were so still. Just like a photograph. Even the individual leaves on the trees were still, not moving the slightest. Everything so quiet. Like it could be this way forever.

"Hello!" Russell shouted. He was suddenly afraid he'd lost all his hearing, it had been so quiet, so he'd had to test it. Now he was embarrassed, and a little scared about having broken the silence.

He could not smell the flowers, or the trees. He could not smell or hear anything. He wondered if he were to go get one of the oranges from the kitchen counter and start to eat it out in the back yard, if it would have any taste, any taste at all.

Sam, Marge's husband and Russell's father for now, thought Russell was a thief, and a liar. "And no one likes liars and thieves," Sam had told him.

The day before Russell had used one of Sam's shirts without asking. Sam seemed to hate that worse than the time Russell had taken some money from Marge's purse. He'd yelled at him a long time.

Russell knew he shouldn't have taken the money but he had bet a friend that he was brave enough to ride his bike through Mr. Watson's front yard. But he just couldn't; Mr. Watson had been sitting on the porch and would have called the police or something. So he just had to have that money to pay back the bet; the boy would've stopped being friends with him if he hadn't. And he needed friends; he didn't have many friends.

Then there was the time he had taken one of his friend's toys, a small model car. He knew it was wrong, but he didn't have one like that and he suddenly felt he just *had* to have it. It had scared him real bad—what if his friend had caught him? Then he wouldn't be his friend anymore.

When Sam accused him of taking the money, saying

that no one else could have taken it, Russell had lied about
it for hours. He had to! There was no telling what Sam
would have done! But he found out that Sam knew for sure
he had done it anyway—Sam had said it so many times it
just *had* to be true—although Russell couldn't understand
at all how Sam had figured it out.

So Russell had finally admitted it, crying, and Sam had
put his arm around him telling him he knew how hard it
was for Russell to tell the truth sometimes and that he
knew Russell was real scared sometimes, and that had
been nice. . . . And Russell had to do some work to pay
Marge back the money.

But they didn't trust him. They were going to give him
back to the social workers; he knew it. No matter how
much Sam and Marge said how much they still cared about
him, that they loved him no matter *what* he did. . . .

Russell could see in their faces that they were lying. He
could see it in their faces more and more every day.
Something had gone away from their faces when they
looked at him.

There were more ice crystals in the air. Russell stared
up into the sky in wonder. He didn't know it ever snowed
this time of year! He suddenly felt very excited; he could
almost jump up and down. He couldn't control himself!
He always seemed to feel this way when unexpected things
happened.

The sky seemed closer to the ground now, and Russell
had noticed this before about the sky just before it snowed.
But not like this . . . it seemed closer to the ground now
than Russell could remember it.

But he soon felt very afraid, and he didn't know why. It
wasn't going to snow, he somehow knew. The sky seemed
closer and closer to him, but it wasn't going to snow.

Sometimes he felt nervous because the sky seemed like

fog, so close to the ground. It didn't break up and get all misty like fog, but for some reason the trees and Mr. Watson's house seemed a little harder to see, even though there was nothing in the way that should have made these things hard to see. It was like the sky was so cottony it made you look at it, like it wanted you to come into it, so that you didn't notice other things like the trees and Mr. Watson's house as much. It was funny. Russell had felt something like this before, but he couldn't remember when.

He was scared. He ran back into the house, slamming the door behind him. He had to see Marge and Sam, be sure they were there. He was suddenly afraid they weren't there, that somehow they had gone off past where the sky had lowered itself toward the ground, their bodies absorbed. Maybe he was the only one left. . . .

Marge and Sam looked up when Russell ran into the living room. Sam had a scowl on his face. "I thought I told you. . . ."

"I thought you'd gone. . . ." Russell said breathlessly. "I'm sorry."

"Well, never mind," Sam said. "We were going to call you anyway, Russell. Your babysitter can't make it tonight and we're supposed to go to a party. I think you're old enough now, though, that we can trust you by yourself. We'll be leaving in a half-hour."

"You're gonna leave me alone?" Russell said, his voice quivering.

"We couldn't find anyone this late. . . ." Marge began, pulling at her black curls nervously.

"You're old enough to stay by yourself a little while, Russell. Why, you'll be a teenager soon," Sam said, and then smiled.

Russell looked out the window. The sky was so white! It seemed to have pressed itself against the glass. Somehow he knew that if he went over and touched the pane it would be ice cold.

A half-hour later Sam and Marge were back downstairs, all dressed up. "Here's a number to call us, just in case," Marge said, scribbling it on the pad by the telephone.

"You're going now?" Russell said.

"You'll be fine," Sam patted his shoulder.

Russell looked around in desperation. He knew he was old enough; he'd been left alone before. But for some reason he couldn't bear the thought of being left here. "But . . . the weather, the sky! It's all white and it's come to the window!"

Sam looked down at him with a puzzled expression. "It's dark out, Russell. That's just a little snow."

"No, no it isn't!"

Russell ran to the window and looked out. It was dark outside, pitch dark, and it looked like there were glistening patches in the dark. It seemed as if they were shiny places in different dark pockets in the air, then suddenly brilliant white ice crystals would explode out of those dark pockets. So white, they hurt his eyes.

"What if you can't get back . . . because of the weather?" Russell asked. He turned to Marge.

Marge stooped down and hugged him to her. "It's not supposed to be that bad a night. We'll leave if it storms. You'll be okay." Russell could tell she was looking at her husband with that nervous expression of hers. Out of the corner of his eye Russell could tell that Sam was nodding. "I'm sure you'll be fine," Marge said.

Sam started toward the door.

Russell screamed and ran in front of him. "Don't open the door! Don't open the door!"

"Why, Russell, what's wrong?" Sam crouched and held Russell by the shoulders.

"You'll let it in! You'll let it in!"

"What, for heaven's sake?"

"The sky . . . it'll push in. Make us cold, all cold!"

Sam stood deliberately and pulled open the front door. A few stray ice crystals whirled in and landed on the carpet. They melted immediately, while Russell stared at them. As if they had never been there. As if he had merely dreamed them.

"There . . . just a little snow," Sam said. Russell looked up at Sam and saw the disappointment in the adult's face, the same look he had seen on the Reynolds', the Carters', and the Wades'. They were going to give him back to the social workers soon, he just knew it.

"Maybe we should stay, Sam. He's so upset."

"No, Marge. Russell is a big boy now." Sam looked down at Russell deliberately. "It's not good for him for us to give into all his fears."

And then they were gone. A pat on the shoulder, a quick kiss, then the door shut behind them. The little night air which had entered the house when they opened the door seemed to stay around Russell in a little cloud, making him colder than he could ever remember. He began to shake violently.

He rushed to the window. He was just in time to see the twin headlights of the Sutton family car turn onto the main street. It was too dark to see the rest of the car.

Russell watched with mounting fear as the headlights pulled behind another pair of headlights, and then another, and another, until there were hundreds, thousands of head-lights making one long snake of light drifting off into the darkness. Away from Russell.

They were all going away from Russell.

The sky was lowering. The glistening white fog whirled down, filling the depressions and irregularities in the lawn, covering the flat areas, covering everything with white. Russell thought about the cold, white sky that afternoon. It was as if streamers of that sky were falling to the ground, covering the ground and leaving the blackest of blacks where that white sky once had been.

The sky had come down to earth, and the whole world was smothered in it.

Russell watched as the last set of headlights disappeared into the darkness. Then he realized none of the houses on his block were lit up, and all the street lights had gone out too. They'd broken away and joined the headlights. The entire lit-up snake had disappeard into the dark.

Russell began to cry again. He couldn't see beyond the front yard now. He couldn't see the other houses. There was black and whirling fog, falling cold where the front yard ended.

Russell watched as faces formed in the drifting fog. The sky drifting into hollows and rises, eye holes and long noses. The sky curled up around a stone in the lawn and suddenly a wide, thin-lipped mouth was there, grinning its cold smile at Russell.

An arm curled out of the cloud-filled street and drifted up over the front porch steps, fingers breaking off and blowing with the cold wind toward the window with Russell's head in it.

Russell had stopped crying. The lights in the house had gone out. He felt very, very cold.

The tree limbs bent down, the black hair of the trees raking the fog arm, the cold sky body stretched out on the Sutton lawn.

Russell breathed the cold house air deeply into himself, drawing it down forcefully, feeling it enter his fingertips, the ends of his feet.

He watched as the white fog wiggled and jumped, hungry for him.

Russell didn't care that they had gone, the Suttons. He

no longer cared about any of them. He was glad they had all gone away.

Russell watched the white clouds forming before his lips and nose. He laughed, but there was no sound.

He wasn't to go out after dark; he knew that was the rule. But the Suttons were gone and would not be coming back.

Russell touched the doorknob and it seemed to turn silver under his grasp. It seemed very cold.

Russell opened the door and felt the cold sky's embrace. The indifferent sky swirled higher and higher; a wisp of fog drifted through the door.

Joan

Mary Ann Allen

*Mary Ann Allen is the nom de plume of Rosemary
Pardoe, expert in the writings of M.R. James, and editor
of the British magazine* GHOSTS AND SCHOLARS. *With the
help of her husband Darroll, Rosemary has been working
with unpublished James manuscripts, attempting to deci-
pher his nearly unreadable handwriting.*

*Not too surprisingly, the Mary Ann Allen stories are
patterned on the ghostly tales of M.R. James, with humor
as well as eeriness. A non-obtrusive but definite feminist
perspective, and actual knowledge of old English churches,
brings more of a personal, original flavor to these stories
than a straight Jamesian pastiche could achieve. Ultimately,
we have an old-fashioned ghost story suited to our new era
in the following tale called, simply,* Joan.

> *Here am I*
> *Little Jumping Joan*
> *When no one is with me*
> *I am all alone.*

In the spring of 1978, my work as a restorer of ecclesias-
tical furnishings took me to Norton Hills, a quiet village in
southern Essex, rather too close for comfort to Basildon.
My task was to restore an unusually beautiful turn-of-the-
century reredos; a painted triptych in Pre-Raphaelite style,

which was one of the treasures of St. Peter's church. The
rector of Norton, the Reverend Jonathan Pride, was a High
Church man—unlike his predecessor—and since he had
only taken over the living a year previously, the villagers
still treated him with extreme wariness. For this reason, I
think, he was especially pleased to welcome me to the
rectory. I was someone with whom he could relax and talk
easily, for the first time in months. Luckily, we hit it off
from the start.

Jonathan (as he quickly insisted I call him) was in his
early thirties, only a few years my senior; so it is not too
surprising that we found many interests in common. During the first evening of my stay, our conversation ranged
over subjects too numerous to mention, from the Beatles to
the books (at length) to Burne Jones (whom Jonathan liked
but I confessed to find insipid). The topic of architecture
soon arose, and prompted a guided tour of the rectory: a
splendid red-brick Jacobean edifice, with highly decorated
chimneys as its most distinctive external feature; and some
fine strapwork plaster molding in several of its rooms.
Although not overwhelmingly large, it boasted four
bedrooms, a comfortable library cum study and a pretty
dining room. Since the rector was unmarried and had no
living-in help, much of the space was unused, but by no
means neglected. The approval which I expressed, as we
walked around, was sincerely felt.

Further conversation followed and we completely lost
track of time, so it came as quite a shock to realize that I
was very tired indeed. As we took our leave of each other,
shortly afterwards, a look of concern suddenly clouded
Jonathan's face, and he said, "Promise me, Jane, that
if you hear any noises in the night you won't leave your
room."

I must have assumed he was joking, or perhaps I was so
tired that it didn't sink in fully, but whatever the reason,

I'm rather surprised now that I promised so willingly and without question.

As so often the case when one is over-tired, I simply could not get to sleep: an hour later I was still tossing and turning. Thus when I heard pattering footsteps outside my door, in the short corridor which led to the stairs, I knew at once that I was not dreaming. The steps seemed to belong to a small child who was skipping and running along in an erratic fashion. They could not be the steps of the rector, and he did not own any pets whose nocturnal wanderings could produce such sounds. "I promised that I wouldn't leave my room," I said to myself, "but I can still open the door and look out, can't I?"

Unfortunately, by the time I reached the door, the footsteps had started down the stairs, and although the corridor was well lit by the bright moon which was shining in through the landing window, I saw nothing unexpected. Then a soft crying began in the hallway below me. I think I would have gone to investigate but at that moment, Jonathan came out of his bedroom, midway between me and the staircase.

"You heard it, did you?" he said. "I wondered if you would."

"What is it?" I asked predictably. "Shouldn't we go down and see?"

"No!" he almost shouted. "There's no need. I'll tell you all about it tomorrow, but please go back to sleep now. The crying will stop in a few minutes." Feeling slightly disgruntled, I climbed back into bed, and listened to the child-like wailing as it reached a mournful and heart-rendering crescendo before fading away to nothing, as Jonathan had assured me it would.

Next morning, I came down early, having slept well for the remaining few hours of the night. Jonathan was already eating breakfast, and as he helped me to some homemade muesli, I waited expectantly for his explanation. "I'm sorry I didn't prepare you for it yesterday," he began. "But I honestly hoped you wouldn't be affected. This house is haunted, of course, you don't need me to tell you that." I agreed, spluttering through a mouthful of cereal that it was not the first ghost I had encountered.

"The reason I didn't want you to see it last night—as you would have done if you'd gone downstairs—was that I saw it once myself, and it isn't something I'd wish on anyone else." He paused to butter some toast before resuming. "Ever since moving in, I've heard the ghost regularly each evening, although the timing varies—it's always an hour or two after I've gone to bed. Naturally I very quickly determined to get to the bottom of the thing and, if I remember rightly, it was during my second night here that I followed the noises down to the hallway.

"The culprit was standing near the front door: a tiny figure in a loose white garment of some sort. She seemed very solid, but she was—to put it bluntly—no more than a cadaver. I could see the bones of her arms through the dried-up skin, and her head was a stark skull." Jonathan shuddered, "I'm ashamed to say that my faith failed me then. I turned tail, and spent the rest of the night cowering under the bedclothes!

"Afterwards, I briefly considered exorcism, but didn't feel that it would be right. Despite her appearance, she is not an evil ghost; I'm convinced of that. If she wishes to haunt my house, I must allow her to do so. She has never harmed me, and I find I'm starting to get used to her."

"I'm sure you've made the right decision," I said. "Although I don't envy you having to live with it. Why, by the way, do you call the spectre, 'she'? Judging from your description it might be of either sex."

"Ah," my friend smiled slightly. "After a good deal of effort I finally managed to extract a little information about her from one of the more garrulous villagers. Apparently, she has been known for hundreds of years, and her name, traditionally, is Joan. That aside, her identity is a mystery to the parishioners, although there are vague tales of her being the victim of a hideous murder. Some say a former rector was the killer.

"I treated these stories with a pinch of salt," he added. "But a few months ago I had a spot of luck when sorting through the parish chest: I discovered a set of Overseer's Poor Records, complete for the seventeenth century. Being keen to learn all I could about the history of my parish, I read them through . . . and I think I found our Joan.

"Look, why don't you come over to the church and I'll show you, before you start this morning? There's a graffito I'd like you to see as well." I willingly acquiesed and within ten minutes, we were ensconced in the cramped vestry, with the Poor Records open before us. Jonathan pointed out the relevent passages, which I studied carefully. They related to one Ruth Lange and her six-year-old daughter Joan, who both received Parish Relief in 1653. The payments had ceased in October when Ruth died by her own hand, carrying her daughter with her when she jumped into the River Crouch just outside Norton and drowned. Labourers on a nearby farm witnessed the event, but were too far away to prevent it. By the time they reached the scene, they could only pull the bodies from the water.

Because of the unusual nature of the case, the Overseers had included some useful background notes: the father of Joan Lange was a Royalist soldier who was killed while fighting in Colchester in the Civil War, when the child was hardly more than a babe in arms. Ruth Lange seems to have reacted to her early widowhood by becoming slightly deranged; but the rector kindly took her in as an assistant housekeeper. This was in 1648. In 1653, the old rector died, and was replaced by a staunch Puritan who immediately turned the Langes out as Royalist sympathizers. It was then that they began receiving Poor Relief.

Reading between the lines I deduced that such help as they got from the Parish was begrudged by the now largely Puritan villagers, who were not too sorry to see them go. (Ironically, those same villagers were eager enough to pledge allegiance to Charles II at his Restoration seven years later. A large Royal Coat of Arms still in the church is dated "1660" and festooned with such loyal inscriptions as, "Fear God, Honour the King, and Meddle Not With Them That Are Given To Change.") When I had finished, Jonathan moved the Overseers' Records to one side and opened up the Parish Registers for the relevent period. Under the deaths listed for 1653 were Joan and Ruth Lange, with a brief note in the margin to the effect that Ruth, being a suicide and a murderess, was buried outside the churchyard in unconsecrated ground.

"A tragic story," I commented finally. "The poor woman must have been quite desperate. And I suppose little Joan haunts the rectory because it was the Puritan rector who contributed so greatly to the tragedy. Now what about the graffito you mentioned? Is it connected in some way?"

"Oh yes," said my friend, getting up and putting the records away. "I nearly forgot about it, but it really is very intriguing and quite relevant."

I followed him out into the body of the church, where he knelt down and pointed to a spot hidden behind the pulpit. Some words were crudely incised into the plaster of the wall, and with difficulty I made them out to be:

> Joan Lange
> All Alone
> God Forgyve Me
> T. Cotter

I looked at Jonathan for elucidation. "Thomas Cotter was the name of the Puritan rector," he said. "It seems that he came to regret his actions."

That night I did not expect to sleep well, at least not until Joan Lange had completed her rounds; but I dropped off very quickly, and slept soundly. Just before waking I had a short but vivid dream: I was standing in St. Peter's churchyard, by the high stone wall which seperated it from the rectory garden. In front of me was an enchanting little girl; even though her face was puffy and stained with tears she was still one of the prettiest creatures I have ever seen. She was jumping up repeatedly and trying to reach for someone or something on the other side of the wall, but each time she fell back, crying sadly to herself.

I heard a small voice saying, "Please try again; I will help you," and then, suddenly, I realised that I could see, or at least sense, what was behind the wall. It was a young woman, so haggard and worn that she was painful to look upon. Her hysterical attempts to get a grip and clamber over the barrier were being continuously frustrated by what appeared to be slime or mud on her hands, making them slide over the stones and leaving rows of greenish brown marks.

This was all I saw before the vision ended. My first thought on waking was, "We must pull down the wall," and it was two or three minutes before I remembered that only a low privet hedge now separated the churchyard from the rectory.

As I expected, Jonathan was thoroughly sympathetic when told about my dream. "Perhaps, we can bring the poor little soul and her mother back together again," he remarked. "It's strictly unorthodox, and I would have to make sure that the archdeacon didn't get to know, but I'd be quite willing to re-inter Ruth Lange's bones in conse-crated ground if only we could find them."

"We could try," I said enthusiastically. "And I believe

we ought to start searching at the spot where I saw the figure of the woman in my dream.''

It was just after one o'clock on the following morning that we ventured forth with our spades; thankful that the rectory garden was not overlooked, and that heavy clouds covered the moon.

The bones were exactly where we had hoped, although it required several hours of hard work to reach them and remove them all from the earth. We took the remains to a secluded area of the churchyard, where we made a small grave for them, and Jonathan said a few words of blessing. I was touched by the impromptu ceremony although, at any moment, I expected to be set upon by irate villagers and accused of bodysnatching or desecration. Fortunately nothing of that sort occurred, and to our delight the rectory ghost did not return in the ensuing days. It seems that we had accomplished what Joan Lange had been wanting for over three hundred years; to be reunited with the mother she still loved in spite of everything.

After some of the initial relief and pleasure had worn off, our single remaining worry was that someone would find out about our scandalous behaviour. We had disguised the disturbed ground as best we could, but when the old fellow who helped to tend the garden arrived a few days later he soon noticed the change.

"Been busy gardening then, parson?'' he said.

Turning an embarrassed pink, Jonathan managed to stammer out a reply: "Er . . . well . . . yes, actually I was making a start on building a rockery. I thought it would look nice down there by the hedge.''

The old man took him at his word, and insisted on taking charge of the proceedings. When I revisited the village recently, to have an informal dinner with my clerical friend, I'm pleased to say that the rockery was ablaze with colour in the summer sun, and a credit to all concerned.

The Night of the Red, Red Moon

Elinor Busby

Elinor Busby is one of the first women to win a Hugo Award, or a third of one at least, while she was part of the triad editing the legended fanzine CRY OF THE NAMELESS. *She is still an active member of the semi-organization (perhaps disorganization) of the Nameless Ones, who have met once a month in Seattle pretty much consistently since 1949. Its lack of formality is probably the key ingredient insuring the Nameless its long life. Elinor must also be credited with originating the word "wahf," fan jargon signalling that list of names which appears at the end of many a letter column in fanzines today, meaning "we also heard from." She and husband, Buz, were the first people I met in the f/sf community, after Dale C. Donaldson that is, and remain among the few people in this community who I'd feel comfortable calling in a moment of need.*

Elinor is a serious writer, too, with stories in AMAZING *and the Canadian literary magazine* A ROOM OF ONES OWN. *The present tale nearly defies categorization, but might be termed Weird Science Fiction. If you're in a particularly evil mood sometime, you might consider reading* The Night of the Red, Red Moon *to a small child as a bedtime story . . .*

If Jonah were a girl, in the right clothes, he'd be Little Red Riding Hood. He is carrying food through the woods to near relatives, and he is afraid of wolves.

No, not wolves, and he is not afraid. On the planet Wulfkill, the natives are called Wulfs. They resemble wolves only quite generally. They are not dangerous and Jonah is not afraid. He is no more than wary.

(Jonah is terribly afraid.)

Earlier that evening, Jonah's parents went to the Frontier Ball. The colonists on Wulfkill like to dress in costume and pretend to belong to the American Wild West. Jonah's mother wore a peasant blouse and long pink, flounced skirt over ruffled petticoats. She looked very young and pretty, with her short, curly light brown hair and big round blue eyes.

(Jonah is proud of his mother's youth and good looks.)

Jonah's father, tall, thin and dark, wore a brown tunic and pants, fringed imitation buckskin.

(Jonah admires his father's look of distinction.)

Through the window Jonah saw a reddish light and looked out of the front door. The moon, just barely on the horizon, was a brilliant red.

"Oh, no!" he cried out. "You mustn't go off and leave me alone tonight. The moon is red!"

His mother was do-se-doing around a kitchen chair, to his father's whistled accompaniment. They did not listen.

"Please!" said Jonah. "Please don't leave me tonight. It was on a night like this that the Wulfs took Lenny."

"Wulfs are perfectly friendly. They don't harm children," said Jonah's father. His mother continued dancing, happily picking up her long pink skirts and shaking her layered ruffles.

"I'm afraid! Don't go! Please, please don't go!" Jonah was in tears.

His father looked at him sternly. "You're a big boy now. You're quite old enough to be left alone at night. Your mother and I have looked forward to this ball, and we certainly won't give it up because of any childish foolishness!''

"But the moon is red!''

"The moon can't hurt you.''

"Wulfs steal children when the moon is red. They eat them!''

"Ridiculous.''

Jonah's tears were wasted. His parents were interested only in their party. How handsome they were! How attractive, with their look of vitality and high spirits. Jonah admired his parents so much.

(He couldn't wish for staid, middle-aged, unselfish parents. Could he?)

Then Jonah was all alone, and the moon on the horizon a brilliant red.

Wulfkill is strange even in the daytime. It is like Earth out of focus. The leaves and grasses are the wrong shades of green, too yellow or too blue—wrong. It is stranger in the light of its enormous orange moon, and strangest of all when the moon glows red.

The natives are like Terran wolves seen out of focus. They are uncanny. They have large furry ears and slanted golden eyes and run on all fours like animals. But their hip joints are such that they can stand erect when they choose, and they often do. No one knows why. They do not use tools and their forepaws are not dexterous. There seems no reason for them to stand on their hind legs, and often when they do, they laugh.

(Do they copulate standing up? Is sex funny?)

So far as is known, they have no language but ours, which they speak very poorly. The structure of their jaws limits the formation of consonants. Their level of intelligence is not known, although they seem friendly, they have not agreed to tests of any kind. They are enigmatic, incalculable, and remote.

With Jonah all alone in the house, the Wulfs were very close. He could hear their weird, shuddering, sobbing cries. He went into his parents' room, got into their bed, buried his head beneath their pillows. He longed for their presence. Then he went to sleep.

He was awakened by a call on the famfone. The ball was over. His parents were at the tharrel shearing shed. Jonah's mother spoke. "We're going to have a picnic, darling. You bring the food. The moon on the river is so beautiful, like a stream of phosphorescent blood. The three of us will enjoy it together."

"I'm afraid."

The joy left her voice. "Not that again. I don't want to be ashamed of you."

Jonah didn't want her to be ashamed, either. He wanted his parents to love and admire him. He felt the threat in her voice.

"What shall I bring?"

"Whatever you like, plus a bottle of wine."

Jonah packed some peanut butter and jelly sandwiches, and after careful thought, chose a bottle of rose wine. Then he set forth.

How strange it is, to be outdoors on such a night! The light from the moon is so brilliantly crimson that the shadows are a rich blue.

Jonah was outdoors on the night of the last red moon, three years ago, when he and his family were newcomers on the planet. He was on a Boys' Club campout. The children, horrified, saw the red moon rise; none had seen it before, all had heard of it from earlier colonists. They huddled close together around the campfire and listened to the Wulf's pulsing cries.

When Jonah got home, his little brother was missing.

There weren't any answers as to where or why Lenny was gone. Almost worse, there were no questions.

"Where's Lenny?" cried Jonah.

"He's around somewhere."

"He's not!"

"He'll be back when he feels like it."

"He's only five years old! He can't take care of himself!"

"Oh—"

Jonah looked everywhere for Lenny, and his friends helped him. No adults looked, and they seemed vaguely embarrassed by the children's search.

Jonah missed Lenny. One night he dreamt his brother had come back. The next morning he told his mother the dream, and he cried.

"Lenny!" she said. "That was his name. I remember him; he was cute and cuddly, and I liked the way the hair grew at the back of his neck—" and then she cried too.

(What happened to Lenny? Did he fall in the river and drown? Did the Wulfs eat him?)

Jonah follows the blue shadowed trail, through the shadowy blue woods, under the red, red moon. At first he does not turn his light on, partly to enjoy the mysterious night, mostly to escape being seen. When he realizes that to keener night vision he could be seen without his knowledge, he switches on his light.

Leaning against a tree stands a large blue grey Wulf, his eyes glinting golden in Jonah's light. "Come with me," he says.

Jonah has never seen a Wulf so close before. The native is less wolf-like than he had realized, the brain pan deeper, the jaw differently hinged. His fear changes, becomes tinged with nonrecognition, disorientation.

"No," he says.

"With me! With me! With me be safe!"

"No!"

Suddenly, Jonah wants to go with the Wulf. He seems to feel waves of good will and protectiveness coming from the creature. The glittering eyes seem warm and friendly; the shrill, whiny voice sounds kind.

So now he knows why the Wulfs are so dangerous! On a night of the red moon they can make human children trust them!

"Come with me, me keep safe," says the Wulf.

Jonah thinks of the Pied Piper, who lured the children of Hamelin away to who knows where. He won't be caught that way. He puts his hands to his ears and runs. The Wulf drops to all fours, chases, surrounds, tries to herd him off the path.

(But does not bite. No, the Wulf does not bite.)

Jonah brushes past him and runs quickly, quickly to the shed. Outside the door he pauses, to catch his breath, to appear mature, to make his parents proud. He hears them talking.

His mother's voice. "I am so excited," she says. "I can hardly wait. It is better than sex, better than anything—"

"Hush," says his father.

The sound of their loved voices breaks his attempted calm. He opens the door. "Oh, Mama, Daddy!" he cries. "I've been so afraid, but you'll keep me safe!"

His parents look at each other and laugh—high-pitched shuddering laughter. Their faces shine with a mirth that seems to mask an underlying horror. As his father speaks, his teeth gleam sharp and white.

"Oh, yes," he says. "We'll take care of our boy. Our lovely, delicate, tender young boy."

Bliss vanishes, renewed terror courses Jonah's veins. He turns, slams the door, darts away.

His father comes out and chases him, but Jonah is small and quick. He runs under a tree limb which catches his father and knocks him out. So Jonah gets away.

And there the Wulf is again. The Wulf sees him, and speaks to the moon with his weird sobbing cry.

"Wulf!" cries Jonah. "I'm here! You promised you'd keep me safe!"

And the Wulf says, "I lied."

Toyman's Name

Phyllis Ann Karr

Phyllis' many novels include FROSTFLOWER AND THORN
(Berkley) and its sequel FROSTFLOWER AND WINDBOURNE,
WILDRAITH'S LAST BATTLE *(Ace), and an Arthurian fantasy mystery, also from Ace. As she happens to be among
my favorite writers in the whole world, I feel compelled to
bestow upon her the honor of being the first author I've
ever featured twice in the same anthology. I somehow
doubt anyone will find cause to complain about it!*

*If you're reading these yarns in the order I arranged
them (and not reading my introductory natter before sampling the tales themselves), you should by now find yourself ready for another breather between the likes of ghosts
and killer dogs. Again, Phyllis Ann Karr provides that
resting point between tales of terror and the supernatural.
Herewith, a second glimpse of prettier moonlight, upon
the world of Torin who makes toys.*

"So that's the piece of work that's going to win you a
three-syllable name tonight, is it?" said Yarkon.

"What?" Torin looked up from his quartz throstlebird
to find the old Master Toymaker standing at the cottage
window.

"You've done better things," Yarkon went on, studying
the statue of Thyrna, "but she's not bad. For something
you chopped out in odd scraps of time. The way you've

219

kept your showtable full for the buyers, you couldn't have had much time or energy left over. Were you planning to paint her?''

Torin smiled and pushed back a few light brown hairs that the autumn breeze had blown in front of his eyes. ''You don't remember, uncle? This is the statue I made during my second or third year as your prentice. You told me to burn it and give my attention to the skills you were trying to drive into my fingers.''

''I did, eh? Why didn't you burn her, then? You'd have saved Vermek an addled stomach this fall.'' Yarkon turned and shouted to the young prentices, who were running-free in the garden, ''Time's done. Inside and wash if you're going to the Name-Lengthening.'' As the boys and girls kicked their way back through the crackling leaves toward the main building, the old master explained to the young toymaker, ''Some of those saplings told Vermek about your statue, and he got it into his prune of a mind that you were going to win Elimdorath's prize away from him.''

''But I never meant to enter!'' exclaimed Torin. ''Besides, I'm still too young for a third—''

Yarkon snorted. ''Chicken scales! What does this new breed of craftsmen want, cluttering up their lives with three-syllable names?''

Torin dropped his eyes back to his throstlebird. There was a part of him that cherished fancies, sometimes, about a longer name for himself. ''One of the poets,'' he remarked, ''said that extra syllables are only another kind of toy. Irvathel, I think it was.''

''Ah?'' said Yarkon. ''Well, as long as they're giving out syllables for the taking, why don't you enter her?''

The young toymaker glanced into the old one's face. Yes, Yarkon seemed in earnest. ''The work of a second-year apprentice?'' Torin faltered.

''There'll be worse, and from older hands. You'll make

yourself no more ridiculous than anyone else." Yarkon
had often enough voiced his opinion of some of the craftsmen who would try for the extra syllable to be won at a
Mage's Fourth Name-Lengthening. "If she wins," he went
on, winking one grey eye, "that'll show us what these
contests are worth."

"But Vermek?" asked Torin, arguing against that foolish fancy-weaving part of himself.

"If you don't beat him, somebody else will, and the
prize would be better in your name. You're a good steady
lad. You could handle the weight. Vermek would only puff
himself up too big for my doors." The old craftsman
patted the statue's curly head with one forefinger. "Don't
paint her," he said, and returned to the main buildings.

Left alone, Torin turned the statue over and over in his
slender fingers, trying unsuccessfully to find the place he
had not quite finished ten years ago, when Yarkon caught
him at his forbidden carving. He had been trying to capture his youthful idealization of the Spirit of the West
Wind, full of wisdom and grandeur and solemnity, but
Yarkon's harsh words had reduced the statue in its maker's
eyes to a crude and clumsy mistake. Still, he had not been
able to burn her; he had hidden her instead, and eventually
forgotten about her. By what process she had travelled to a
little-used cupboard in the garden work cottage he was
now using as Yarkon's guest craftsman, he could only
surmise, but here he had found her again, among old tools
and rags and dusty odd-sized chips of wood. By now he
had grown more tolerant of his own early efforts, so he
had wiped her clean and set her on his window ledge to
preside over his quarter-season's work. The likeness did
not have those grand qualities his untrained hand had tried
to capture; but the real Thyrna was a kindly spirit, who
clothed the leaves in bright harvest colors before gathering
them to herself, and she would not be offended by the

quaint body and mischievous face unintentionally given her by an awkward prentice who might almost have been someone else.

And now Yarkon had called this little statue "she" instead of "it," and thus raised her again to a respectable work. True, her whimsical charm had come through accident, not design. It had taken ten years of the old Master Craftsman's strict discipline before Torin was equipped to produce quality work with little need of pure luck; that was why no prentice was allowed to spend any energy on uncommanded pieces before his fifth year of training, and that was why Yarkon had ordered this statue burnt without hinting that in herself, and if she were not the fruit of disobedience, she deserved a better fate. Was she, as Yarkon hinted, as worthy to stand in Elimdorath's contest as the piece Vermek had been laboring upon behind a closed door?

Torin deliberately returned to the white quartz throstlebird, finished hollowing it out and coated the inside with bluish-green dye, sealed a firespeck-stone base to it with clear resin glue, nodded as he held it up to the light, and finally cut his symbol on the bottom. He owed it to Yarkon to finish this last toy for the showtable, and he also owed it to himself, since if it caught the moneystones of some lingering visitor, a share of the price would come to the guest craftsman.

Twenty-five days ago, at the Fall Festival, when he had proudly accepted Yarkon's invitation to return for a quarter-season as guest craftsman, Torin had given up all fancies about making a statue for Elimdorath's contest. There were too many toys to be made for the unusual crowd gathering in Horodek Town in honor of the Elder Mage's Fourth Name-Lengthening. But even left to his own work in his own small shop, the young toymaker might not have carved anything for the contest. He was too busy carving the pieces that were his livelihood; for although he seldom went hungry now, he indulged in costly foods even more seldom, and the straw still tickled through his coarse bedclothes. Honor was pleasant, but a little redspice would prove its usefulness day by day, and softweave sheets their value night by night.

Still, it might be ten years before another chance came for a toymaker to win a three-syllable name. Torin picked up his little statue and looked at her again. "Thyrna," he whispered, half to the likeness and half to the real Spirit of the West Wind, "would it be fair? Would you mind?" Then he thought, "What would Talmar say if I won a third syllable before him?" And he winked back at the peachwood statue.

A few hours later, washed and clad in his festival attire, the young toymaker stood in a corner of the town's new Gathering Hall. Here there was a cool draft, which made his short blue cape welcome. (It should have been russet in color, but he could not yet afford a different holiday cape for every season.)

Legendary people painted on the walls and carved into the rafters gleamed richly in the combined light of magic globes and thick wax candles set in clusters of five. Ropes of freshly gathered autumn leaves garlanded the eastern platform, the contest table, and everything else that would support a garland. For once, magic-mongers, judges, and sky-readers outnumbered common workers who could spend less time in travel, so that plain white tunics, dark breeches, and short russet capes were swallowed up in the press of green, blue, silver, crimson, and purple robes. Wealthy laymen, too, mixed in the crowd, their tunics and capes so heavily embroidered that the cloth beneath was all but invisible. Small children in pale green smocks chased each other amongst their elders' legs and skirts, while old people wearing bright harvest colors moved about cheerfully

or looked on from the benches along the far wall. There
was almost too much to catch the eye, yet Torin's glance
returned again and again to the single long table with the
contest figures awaiting judgment, and from time to time
he furtively drew up his left sleeve for a moment to read
the number "4" brushed in blue dye above his inner wrist.

A young girl in the light green robe of a conjurer had
marked his wrist and his unopened carrying bag, as she
numbered the wrist and wrapped statue of each craftsman
in turn. Two sky-readers then carried the wrapped statues
across the hall to the contest table, where the youngest and
the oldest judges present unwrapped them, carefully transferring the number on every bag or box to the bottom of
the statue within. The Elder Mage's choice would be as
free as possible from knowledge of the statues' makers,
but the number on his wrist would identify the winning
craftsman.

"Is this my clear-thinking older brother?" said a voice
at Torin's shoulder. "Who puts less value on the length of
his name than on a straw water jar?"

Blushing, Torin pulled his sleeve back over the number.
"I never went that far," said he.

"You did," said Talmar, who could store up the chance
overstatement used no more than once, and bring it back
years later. "Shortly before you left us. I won't insult
Elimdorath's contest by asking which is yours, brother,
unless it's the tall one of silverwood and brushed giltdust?"

"It's not. I didn't have that much time."

"Or skill? Unfortunate for you. That piece will almost
surely take it. Not that you have years enough for a third
syllable."

"I have two years more than you," replied Torin.

"But then, you haven't followed your family's calling,"
said Talmar, who, as a magic-monger, was assured of a
second name-lengthening before his fortieth autumn, and

would likely earn a third name-lengthening and perhaps even, like Elimdorath, a fourth, though these were rare enough that not even a Supreme Mage was assured of one.

Torin turned from his brother and looked again at the silverwood likeness of Thyrna. Her face was solemn to the point of sorrow, her eyes gazing downward with unhurried compassion, the fingers of her right hand gently plucking two leaves as if from the air, her left hand holding the folds of her cloak to form a kind of net against her own swelling west wind. Every line indicated long seasons of living behind the hand that had carved it, and even across the years Torin felt a twinge of envy, for this was what he had attempted, at the age of seventeen, to give his own little Thyrna.

Aztomlyn, the musician of Lyn Forest, played five notes on the ceremonial golden flute, and the gathering eagerly fell silent. Elimdorath parted the curtains and stood for a moment in the west doorway, then walked quietly to the eastern platform, the folds of his azure-lined silver robe melting into each other, his long white beard swaying a little on his breast. He mounted the steps unaided, and easily enough for his eighty-odd winters.

When the Elder Mage had taken his place, the Supreme Mage himself, the seldom-seen Parthenderak, appeared at the back of the platform and came forward in his golden robes. Elimdorath knelt before him. The Supreme Mage placed a wreath of red oak leaves upon the Elder Mage's white head and nodded five times. The golden flute played again, this time in a weaving of five times five notes. Torin mused discontentedly that he might be better able to enjoy this ceremony if his mind were not continually picturing himself in Elimdorath's place an hour from now, with the Elder Mage placing the oak leaves on his head and the flute weaving three times three notes.

Parthenderak struck his palms together five times and

quit the platform. Elimdorath rose, faced the people, and pronounced his name as it would be henceforward: Elimvandorath. All the company raised their voices in the time-hallowed hail to a mage, the hymn to the Twin Spirits of Fire and Water.

Close to the platform, a baby suddenly squalled. The mother, a young carver of moneystones who lived in Horodek, tried to slip away with it, but before she could press through the crowd the Elder Mage, smiling, had come down the platform to her side. He took the child and bounced it softly, whispering to it until it was smiling back at him. Only then did he return it and move to the long contest table with its half-hundred statues.

Now that the Fourth Name-Lengthening was done, interest in the actual judging of the contest ran high only near the table. In other parts of the room, where the view was blocked, knots formed and murmured conversations began to rise. Torin glimpsed Yarkon's neighbor steal out with her baby, but most of the assemblage waited for the evening's second climax, waited to honor the craftsman whose skill was to earn him a name of three syllables.

Slowly Elimvandorath walked from the west end of the table to the east, searching every statue in turn for a few moments. Before half a dozen he paused a longer time. One of these was the tall sad silverwood lady. Another was Torin's mischievous sprite.

When the Elder Mage had moved on past his work, Torin drew a deep breath and looked around. He became aware of Vermek standing ten or fifteen paces from him. The older craftsman's profile was pinched and tight as he kept his squint fixed on Elimvandorath's progress.

A giggling boy of seven or eight summers burst between Torin and Talmar, saw that he was within a dozen paces of the table, and turned to dodge back between the brothers, only to collide with a second boy who had been chasing him. Talmar grumbled an opinion that saplings like these were the rightful property of Gorzor the demon, but Elimvandorath turned his head with a smile at the commotion. Then he started back along the table from east to west, stopping for painfully close looks at the likeliest half dozen.

At an alabaster one carved with the simple flow of a cat's tail Elimvandorath gazed his fill, and at one whose stark lines were softened with a wealth of many-colored wood inlays. Then he came to Torin's small offering, and stood, and gazed, and picked her up in his brown hands, and turned her about, and studied her, and set her down, and continued to gaze.

Torin felt a tightness at the bottom of his head, and a sort of large cocklestone that wedged itself somewhere between his lungs. He looked again at Vermek, and as quickly looked away, away from the grey hairs clinging thickly to the hired craftsman's head while the rust-colored strands had thinned, the wrinkles come into his cheeks and forehead, the dark places beneath his eyes and lack of laugh-lines at their corners . . . Torin thought of his own little workshop waiting for him among the trees, and he thought of Vermek, growing old and bitter in another man's service and laboring alone in a cramped private workroom for hours into the night and hours before the working day began.

"Talmar," whispered Torin, "that's mine he's looking at. No, I'm not lying," he added as his sorcerer brother gave him a glance of weary indulgence. "Send him a mind-message not to choose it."

"What?" said Talmar.

"It *is* mine, I tell you, and I've decided I don't want to win. I'd send the mind-message myself, but I'm not sure I remember how."

"Your brain is tied up in knots," said Talmar. "You want me to interfere in an Elder Mage's contest?"

"I was wrong to enter. It wasn't even made for this contest. Are you going to send the mind-message, or do I have to try it?"

"I'll send the message," muttered Talmar, "but you'll come and explain matters to the Elder Mage."

The young sorcerer closed his eyes and pressed his fingers to the back of his neck. For a few seconds his face flushed a dark red and the veins in his neck and temples bulged. The white magic-monger's star on his left cheek seemed to pulse a little.

Elimvandorath replaced Torin's statue on the table, brushed its head a last time with his fingertips, and walked on to the silverwood and giltdust Thyrna. Talmar sighed as his blood flowed back to its normal channels. "I take you to the Elder Mage at evening's end," he said, "and then, Cel willing, you can explain and I can leave and be out of it."

Torin leaned back against the wall. He found he was trembling, and he gave little attention to the rest of the contest. At length the Elder Mage took the wreath of oak leaves from his head and slipped it over the silverwood statue. Torin closed his eyes and, hardly thinking, joined his voice in the song of Derwynthal the Stonecutter.

When he looked again, the maker of the silverwood Thyrna had come forward. It was a small stooped woman with a few traces of red lingering in her neatly braided hair. It was not Vermek. Torin could not see Vermek anywhere in the hall.

Another half-hour, and it was done at last. The small woman's name was no longer Birlyn, but Birtelyn; the flute's tripled chain of notes was played; Elimvandorath's words of praise to all the craftsmen were spoken, and Birtelyn's thanks to them for increasing her honor by making his a hard decision; the last hails were sung; the Elder Mage was gone from the hall, and one by one the assemblage were going—the craftsmen, contest helpers, and buyers waiting until all who wished had looked their fill and the statues could be cleared from the table. "Now," said Talmar, and plucked Torin by the sleeve.

Outside the door they almost stumbled over a man sitting hunched on the steps. He looked up, and by the light coming from the hall Torin recognized Vermek. "So, you young sapling," said Vermek, "I didn't win, but neither did you, Gorzor take you."

"I'm sorry," Torin replied, wondering if Vermek would believe it. "Which was yours?"

"The inlaid one. The one he almost chose. But it's trumpery wins these contests, not skill." Vermek spat at the lower step. Talmar snorted.

Vermek got to his feet and went on belligerently, "Well, there's a sky-reader in there who knows skill when she sees it. She's paying me fifty pebbles for my statue, and that means wine enough to heal the sore for a while."

"And that," muttered Talmar as he pulled his brother on in the direction of Elimvandorath's silver tent, "is why Vermek will never be anything but a hired craftsman."

The Elder Mage's door curtain was stiff and hard, but when Talmar traced his name on it with his wand the stiffness melted. The sorcerer drew it aside and half-pushed Torin through. The toymaker felt his brother's arm shake a little.

Elimvandorath sat facing the door. His blue eyes appeared watery and gentle, and he had changed his silver mage's robe for one of bright harvest colors, such as anyone might wear who had seen more than sixty winters.

Talmar touched his left hand to his right shoulder and rolled his palm up in the less advanced magic-monger's gesture of submission to the higher. "Father," he said, "I have brought him, as you commanded, and I pray your forgiveness for my part in this scandal.''

Torin put both hands behind his back, as befit a layman. ''The blame is entirely mine, father,'' he said, no longer much caring how it would end, if only it ended quickly.

The Elder Mage nodded. ''Talmar, son of Laterindal, sleep in peace. None of this shall be held against you, nor go beyond us three.''

Talmar knelt, touched the Mage's foot, then rose and took his departure.

''Nor will I press it against you, Torin son of Laterindal,'' Elimvandorath went on, ''but try not to chance such a trick against a less tolerant mage. Why did you withdraw her?''

''I withdrew for someone I thought more deserving,'' replied Torin, ''but he didn't win, either.''

''You're tired,'' said the Mage. ''Sit, and remind an old man of the trials of the young.''

When Elimvandorath had heard a fuller account, he mused in silence for a moment, then said, ''So it was the work of an even younger hand than I had thought. No, Birtelyn's Thyrna is a masterwork to stand in my room of quiet thoughts, but yours, Torin, is the charm I have hoped to find to cheer my dying bed. I would like to give you a hundred pebbles for her loan.''

''Take her as a gift, father,'' stammered the toymaker. ''I. . . .''

''Allow an old man to be generous at the end of a wearying day,'' replied the Mage, laying a small green silk bag of pebbles on the study table before him. ''I will arrange to have her carried back to you in a few years, when I have no more need of her.''

Torin rose and took the bag. ''I'll bring her to you at once,'' he said.

''One thing more, my son,'' said Elimvandorath. ''All this ceremony and added weight of honor must be endured

for the sake of my calling and of the people, but had it
been my own choice, I would have shortened my name
instead, in silence, and waited for Thyrna with more
simplicity. Know your own soul well before you go chasing honors again.''

Torin nodded and went out again into the field. ''You
came off well enough, I see,'' remarked Talmar, who was
waiting near the tent.

''Listener at doorways,'' said Torin.

''It was easier than finding you again in the morning,''
shrugged the magic-monger, and slanted away from Torin's
side to enter his own tent.

The night air was crisp, and a few thin clouds idled
across the stars. Torin kneaded the moneypebbles through
the silk for a moment before tying the bagstrings to his
belt. There was no sign of Vermek, either outside or in the
hall. Nor was there any sign of the inlaid statue. Craftsmen
and buyers were gathering up their pieces. Torin lifted his
statue and showed the number on its base and that on his
wrist to one of the young conjurers standing watch.

''Is this yours, then? I think you ran me a very close
race, nephew.'' The craftswoman Birtelyn had come up,
trailed by happy well-wishers, probably friends and relatives.
She still wore the oakleaf wreath on her silvering hair, and
her round face beamed up at Torin. ''Let me buy it from
you,'' she said. ''You see, I can't seem to carve anything
but sad statues, myself, and I do like to see happy ones
here and there about my workshop.''

''I'm very sorry, aunt,'' replied Torin. ''Let me carve
you something happy when I go back to my workshop.
But this one is already spoken for by . . . someone else.''

Dog Killer

William H. Green

*The seemingly contradictory feelings in most of us are:
we fear large dogs and the threat they potentially embody,
but we despise the criminal intellect which would set out to
destroy the very thing we fear. William H. Green of Geor-
gia brings off this psychological horror well, giving us a
character we hate to see win but also a monster we agree
should be stopped: killer dogs. There's more than psychological horror to the story, however, as we learn from a
derelict of a special supernatural kind of dog which a man
must especially fear if he happens to be a* Dog Killer.

It was black morning in the eroding suburb where I
lived with my wife. Sam Tifton and I had been out hunting
with a flashlight, and he dropped me two blocks from the
house. A bag of rabbits hung over my shoulder, a vinyl-
wrapped shotgun in the crook of my arm. I listened to
far-off birdsongs and the sandy crunch of my shoes against
the blacktop. Then there was another sound, a faint moving *tick*.

It was a dog trotting along the gray line of the opposite
curb—a long-nosed, dome-chested mongrel with spots.
When he sat in front of the Bakers' house and scratched
his ear, I walked faster. But he followed. Having disturbed
his fleas, he ran along the curb beside me. Filthy dog!

My right hand began to move, walking like a spider

along the vinyl guncase. Now the shotgun seemed awkward
on my right arm, so I shifted it across, holding the game
bag and the encased barrel in my left hand. Near the
trigger my fingers walked. There were holes in the guncase,
torn by a decade of fishing lures and burned by campfire
sparks. The spider found a hole and entered.

I am not sure what I was conscious of. Did I remember
that the gun was loaded? That, dangerously, I had released
the safety? I think I realized that the barrel, bouncing as I
walked, was pointed toward the dog. But I did not reason,
nor feel the trigger. It was the spider, not I, that pulled.

The gun exploded out of my hand. Echoes cracked
against the sleeping houses. Out of the park behind the
Faircloughs' house, a cloud of birds came screaming,
swirled vaguely, and vanished into black treetops. My
victim lay on summer pavement, blue entrails hanging out
of his side and a pool of blood growing.

I snatched up the smoking guncase and sprinted down
the Johnsons' driveway, staying on thick grass as I crossed
their back yard. When I heard distant sirens, I was already
in my own bathroom, cutting up the guncase and flushing
it down the toilet. Then I cleaned the shotgun, put away
the cleaning kit, and woke my wife.

"Good morning," I said.

Be assured, the wife is *not* the last to know. She suspected instantly, and each lie only confirmed her suspicions.
But she loved me. All she said was, "My god, Dave,"
and all she did was leave me, leave me free to pursue my
deadly craft. Alone, I was able to plan new attacks, devise
new tools. I became a professional.

I added a metal lathe and a heavy-duty drill press to my
basement shop; and every day after work I spent my time
there underground—cutting, filing, polishing, drinking beer,
and thinking, endlessly thinking about dogs. During these
months my life reassembled itself into a new shape.

I remembered how, thirteen years before, I was drinking underage in a bar south of Egas when an old man with hair like steel wool bought me a rum toddy, which he claimed was very good. Incoherently, he recounted twenty years in the merchant marines, all the time drinking straight gin from a shot glass. Finally, the bartender said he was sorry and began turning out the lights.

Remembering this, I knew I had been foolish to go home with the old derelict, but not for the most obvious reason. Some would say a much graver reason, implying that with the old man my ruination began. In his disheveled room, surrounded by broken furniture and leak-stained wallpaper, the ex-sailor whispered to me in a grainy voice:

"I kill dogs."

"What?" I said.

"You heard me," and he punctuated this remark with a belch. "Doggies!"

Not knowing what to say, I sipped the sherry he had given me and tried to look nonchalant.

"You don't mind?" he said. "You don't mind drinking wine with a dog-killing bastard?"

"Really," I said, "I think there are strong arguments for the extermination of dogs." The sound of my voice gave me courage. I doubt that I believed what I was saying (surely I had never said it before), but I identified with the old man and wanted to please him. "You see, the police have to wait until they're sure the dog is a killer, but then it's usually too late. Figures show that. We need people to do what the police can't. Right?"

He was staring at me as though he neither heard nor cared about my words. He was reading something else, something in the darkness behind my eyes. "I'll be damned," he said.

"Won't we all?" I answered, trying for a joke. But he reacted strangely.

"There's ways this old boy won't be damned," he shouted, drawing a revolver from his baggy pants, "not if he can help it, by hell!" He started to laugh, but it turned into retching, and he stumbled into the bathroom, where his vomiting echoed off the bare walls.

I tried to look at the room instead of listening, but its splotchy contents repelled my vision. Endlessly he vomited, shouting and coughing. I was about to stand and leave when he suddenly reappeared at the bathroom door with a sherry bottle in his hand and a gleam in his cloudy eyes.

"I'm gonna show you something nobody seen before."

Then he sat close beside me and whispered, his breath like week-old garbage. "You see that fat old couch?"

I nodded.

"Well, sit on it."

"What?"

"Sit on it! Son-of-a-bitch."

I sat. The springs gave like warm marshmallow, but they bottomed out hard.

"That's soft, ain't it?"

"Yes, sir."

"That's what you think," he said with a twitch of his mouth. "That's what you think. Get up and let me show you."

I was happy to stand while he fumbled under the front of the sofa, as though untying an old sea knot. Then he lifted, pouring empty bottles and wrinkled clothes (I remember a gargantuan pair of black, lace panties) onto the floor and window sill. Underneath, built into the sofa so carefully that no seam showed, was a velvet-lined chest containing a shotpistol, poison, a hatchet, and three short-barreled rifles, each in its own neat compartment.

He seemed offended when I refused to touch them. Offended or not, though, he had every reason to confide in me now, for I knew his most dangerous secret. That night

I learned a thousand unrepeatable details about his life: his dogs, his women, his betrayals—everything. Most of it is vague now; but one scrap of conversation read itself over and over again in my head as aluminum curled off the bar I was machining into a silencer in the beer-cozy damp of my basement.

"Killing is easy if you got tools. Getting away is the trick."

"I heard they doubled the number of police in—"

I paused because he was staring at me with an amused, pitying grin, his head bobbing.

"Bull!" he said.

"Sir?"

"It's the Vengers. Don't a lot of amateurs know this, but there's two kinds of dogs—them that kills people and them that kills dog-killers. Vengers, I call them. Thick-necked, knob-nosed, big-toothed Vengers. That's why."

"I read there was an increase in harmless packs—"

"Vengers!" the old man said, his eyes wide. "Vengers. Now you know why I carry this .38."

"To kill them?"

He grinned. "Myself," he said. "To kill myself. Them Vengers ain't gonna eat this old boy. Not alive, they ain't!"

I was thinking about the sailor, thinking and wondering as I screwed the aluminum-alloy silencer onto the dog-rifle I had spent the last two months making. It was a .22 rifle with the barrel cut to twelve inches and the sear modified so that it fired automatically. I had replaced the wooden stock with a folding steel one and installed a forty-shot magazine, a telescopic sight, and a large, homemade silencer. Taken down, the tiny machine gun filled a slim briefcase; but I could assemble it in twenty seconds and, softly purring, it killed anything its crosshairs touched.

The next evening, just before sundown, I parked my

slate-blue sedan (I sold my orange-and-black GTO because it was too traceable) in a slum neighborhood where dogs were known to abound and lay down in some overgrown hedge by a condemned apartment building. Soon an old boxer came trotting in front of a used clothing store across the street.

I crossed his ribs with the fine, black hairs and squeezed. *Blurrrr!* The gun whispered and the dog squealed. Suddenly, a hand-sized part of his flank became chopped meat. The disadvantage of small-caliber machine guns, however, is that they lack knock-down power. The boxer remained standing for several seconds—then he stumbled and began to crawl, howling enough to wake the dead.

Blurp! I aimed a quick burst at his head. It was foolish, I know. It quadrupled chances that I might be caught, and I never did it again. I disassembled the weapon and walked to my car. Twelve minutes later I was safely on the freeway, lost in the anonymous flow of suburban traffic.

Most of my hits were that easy, so uneventful that they evade recollection. My thoughts always turned forward, toward the next dog, and if I had not kept count in a small notebook, I doubt if I could even estimate how many I killed. But one job, the sixteenth, was particularly memorable because it nearly got me arrested.

I shot a dalmation from my parked car on a quiet, tree-lined street. No sooner had I unscrewed the silencer than a police car nosed out of a side street near the dog, who was dying very noisily about half a block from my car. At first I sat very still with the rifle out of sight, but when they took out a shotgun and started toward me, I knew my bluff had been called.

Roaring away from the curb, I watched them in the rear view mirror, standing still, then running toward their car. I always splashed my plates with mud before a job to obscure the number, and with a head start I was sure I could outrun them.

Several turns and five minutes later, I slowed down and headed toward the freeway, through more of the shady residential streets typical of the northwest quarter of the city. There, on a long, straight boulevard lined with century old mansions, I heard a chilling whine and saw the police car closing like an arrow.

Parking, holding the dog-rifle in both hands, I crouched low in the front seat. *Waheeh! Waheeeh!* The siren grew louder and louder until, when the car was scarcely a hundred feet away, I leaned out my window and aimed at the center of the approaching windshield.

Without a silencer, the .22 crackled harshly in the quiet boulevard, frightening songbirds and rattling off white facades. The windshield dissolved. The driver swerved. The car sprang over the curb and struck a trellis, but I still held back the trigger, perforating the fenders and trunk until the rifle emptied. The black car overturned a wrought-iron table, climbed it, rolled over, and crashed into a wall overgrown with wysteria.

But most of my hits were uneventful, and until the last (the book indicates my forty-third) I saw no evidence of the "Vengers" about whom the old sailor spoke. To be sure, sometimes packs of dogs approached as I drove away from a kill, but groups of people often approached as well, and the dogs never pursued me. Of course, I always escaped by car and never struck when more than one dog was visible.

For my last job, the forty-third, I did not use a car. Carrying the rifle in a briefcase no longer seemed hazardous as long as I dressed conservatively and never lingered around the scene of a killing, and I carried the weapon almost absent-mindedly with me on a subway trip downtown one Saturday when my car had transmission trouble. The theater posters did not look as good as the newspaper

ads, so I had a beer and went for a moonlight walk
instead, a walk which led me east of downtown into a
district of car dealerships, night clubs, and office supply
stores. I got a liverwurst sandwich (on pumpernickel) at
Fatti's and was walking through a deserted side street,
between signless, three-story brick walls when I saw a
pregnant hound in the streetlight at the next corner. Lick-
ing a piece of garbage on the sidewalk, she seemed indifferent to everything around her in the dark, thrumming
city.

On an impulse—like a shadow in a dream—I leaned in a
gloomy doorway, assembled the rifle, and killed her. Her
life-force was weak; she did not cry long. But no sooner
was she silent than a liquid baying welled out of the night
and I saw a pack—it must have been ten dogs at least—
trot up and sniff at her dark little corpse.

Even before I saw them turn as one and howl at me,
before I saw a second pack clamor in behind them, already
I was looking for a refuge, or at least a firebase from
which to hit them. Twenty yards away I saw a drainpipe
that started within seven feet of the sidewalk and reached
up three stories past a grate-covered window.

The two spare magazines of ammunition in my pocket, I
dropped my briefcase (no identifying marks, I hoped) and
began to walk back toward the drainpipe, slowly, not
encouraging pursuit. But they came anyway, surging toward me like a furry mudslide, like howling death.

At the drainpipe I stood and delivered a long fusillade—
blurrrrrrrrrr—thirty slugs into the thick of them, and the
yelping was tremendous. About half in the front of the
pack were hit, several dead, but the little rifle, as I said,
lacks knock-down power; so I barely had time to insert
another magazine before they were loping toward me again,
a bloody-flanked mastiff as their leader.

I aimed a long burst straight at him, dangerously long,

and again I gave thirty bullets to his companions—as evenly divided as possible. This time I saw some effect. Over half of my pursuers lay dead or dying by the time my rifle clicked empty, and the rest were dispirited, snuffling and howling in a wide circle around me.

I leaped up and grabbed the drainpipe bracket with both hands, the empty rifle slung over my back. Terrified, I climbed easily up the rough brick wall while my trembling hands gripped the pipe like steel clamps. The window ledge on the third floor was wide, a slab of imitation granite, and made a fair shooting stand after I hooked my arm through the window bars. Here I fitted the last magazine into my rifle, which stank of hot machine oil. First I would finish off the main survivors, sniping carefully in quick bursts. Then I would climb to the roof and cross to another street, where I could commandeer a car.

Several dogs were under the drainpipe now, sniffing the pavement and whining up at me. I framed a scroungy half-collie in the sights and touched the trigger gently. *Blurp!* The dog went down and, drunken with numbers, I realized that I had killed at least fifteen tonight. That would be sixty in all—sixty dogs! Only four remained (sixty-four that would be) close enough to be cut down in one smoking flourish.

Blurrrrp! Two dogs crumpled, yelping, and the others cowered, staring up with wild eyes. Then I realized that I was squeezing the trigger of a silent rifle—a rifle that was not yet empty. I pulled on the bolt, and the steel handle burned me. For the first time, I realized that the trigger guard was painfully hot. *The gun,* a quiet voice said in my head, *was not designed to fire a hundred rounds in less than a minute*. Wrapping a handkerchief around my hand, I pulled, but it was true: the bolt was fused to the receiver. The gun was hopelessly jammed.

Four new dogs had gathered beneath the drainpipe, six

in all. The only way out was up, up the drainpipe to where the roof's concrete rim cut off the field of stars. I unhooked my right arm from the bars and was wriggling into climbing position when a light flared behind the dusty windowpane, dazzling straight into my face.

"Just hold it there," a dark voice said. "Let go of the gun."

The machine gun clattered against the sidewalk.

"I'll open the window now and unlock the bars. You think you can get yourself inside?"

"Don't know," I said, squinting into the light.

"Well, you manage," the voice declared, more petulant, it seemed, than commanding. "And remember, I'm armed."

I slid along the ledge, holding unsurely to the drainpipe, until I was clear of the opening bars. Maybe I could climb the drainpipe now, escape to the roof, escape as I had intended. But something in the voice, its cloudy intonation, told me that my chances were better inside. Ten yards below on the dark sidewalk, the dogs circled my broken machine gun, circled and sniffed. If the man was armed, I needed his weapon.

I worked my feet through the window and climbed into the room—possibly a cavernous office once, but now a long, high-ceilinged storeroom, glimpsed in the overwash of the flashlight beam. Then he turned on the light.

"Close the window," he said.

He was an old man in a starched nightwatchman's uniform, and he stood in front of an open door, the only exit from the room—except, of course, for the window. I turned and closed the window, first the bars, then the heavy wooden frame. Outside, dogs howled softly when they saw me, softly and horribly.

I turned back to the watchman. "I give up," I told him, holding out my hands awkwardly.

"Just stay there," he said.

He was thin, thin and old, I told myself. The big, nickel-plated revolver and its bulky holster seemed almost too much for his frame to support. He would not shoot unless frightened, and then he would not shoot very well. I leaned against a stack of soft-drink cases, the end of a long row which ran the length of the room.

"I'm not moving," I said.

"Rex," he said sharply, oddly.

The dogs were still moaning outside, keening and crying, but over their cries I could hear the old man breathing. And there was another sound, a canine moaning and a dry scratching which seemed to come from far beyond the doorway, as though conducted by carpetless stairwells and carpetless halls.

Grabbing a twelve-ounce bottle by the neck, I rolled to the floor behind the stack of cases. Glass exploded from the case just over my knees when the gun fired. Foaming liquid gushed from the stack. Then, still gripping the bottle, I scrambled a few feet farther. He fired again, this time coming closer. My neck was drenched with warm cola and stung by a needle-like spray of glass.

"Rex," he repeated. And, hideously, he whistled.

I stood and flung the bottle. He was looking away, and I caught him by surprise. The projectile bounced off his temple and his knees buckled. A third shot exploded harmlessly into the floor. Then he was on his hands and knees, shaking his head and gasping. I kicked the pistol away from his hand and lifted him by his lapels, shoving him hard against the wall. The wall boomed like a timpani, and he slumped unconscious to the floor.

The fight took several seconds, during which I was understandably preoccupied. I must have been preoccupied or I would have heard another sound, the scratching-ticking-thudding of feet on the stairway beyond the open door—and a gray, inhuman gurgling. I listened for a moment in timeless terror. Then I moved toward the pistol which gleamed on the dark threshold.

Too late. Ghostlike and tall, a German shepherd materialized beside the weapon. He was sleek and wore a leather harness—a trained guard-dog. I studied his eyes, his gray expressionless face. I stood very still.

"Rex?" I said.

His ears lay back. Dark lips rippled over his fangs. He took a step toward me, into the light, and a cold reflection lay upon his eyes. Then I understood why he had been downstairs.

"You thought I was outside. You're one of them," I said. "Damn you."

He snarled and leapt toward my throat. But guard-dogs, I knew, were trained to go, not for the throat, but for the upraised (and padded) arm of a trainer. So I raised my left arm. Better to lose that—

He struck and I fell under him, thrusting my right arm out as far as I could, out toward the threshold. Ignoring the flamelike pain in my arm, the nauseous impact of teeth on bone, I crawled spiderlike, on my back, reaching always toward the gleaming pistol.

Then he let go of my arm and, suddenly, almost before I could react, struck again—this time imbedding his fangs into my shoulder. But I had time, barely time, to lunge a few more inches toward the door. I felt, first, the smooth wooden threshold, and then the oily roundness of the pistol. Shaking, I pressed the barrel into his side and squeezed twice.

The beast stiffened and went limp. His side was blown open, and his blood and mine were commingled in the flow which soaked my torn jacket and spread on the floor beneath. I pushed the furry corpse aside and stood. My left arm hung limp, a dull flap of pain. Blood dripped from the fingertips.

After the explosions, it felt for a while as though the room were swollen with cotton. Then, with a soft whining, the sounds of the world returned—vague, then gradually more distinguishable. The dogs were still outside, crying in the night for my destruction.

Maddened by the sound, I moved like a bloody revenant across the floor, laid the pistol on the sill, and opened the window. Outside in the night, a vague pack of dogs raised a baleful howl. Streetlight glinted from their bare, innumerable fangs.

"Die," I said, and emptied the revolver at them.

They did not move or cease their howling, but now their lips formed words.

"Die!" they answered. "Die!"

A dark feeling possessed me. "Die! Die!" I shouted, and my words echoed from the buildings across the street. "Die!" I howled.

And they answered, "Die! Die! Die!"

Then a white light touched them and the pack dissolved. A blue spot moved across the face of the opposite building. Two policemen stood at the doors of their car by the curb, and the dogs melted into darkness, down sidewalks and alleyways, as the blue light moved and moved and moved. . . .

"Hey up there. . . ." a policeman shouted, but I did not hear the rest.

I heard instead two stragglers on the sidewalk below, a doberman and a big mongrel, who howled words to me almost as clearly as a man might. Or more clearly.

"Next time," they said in unison. "Next time. We have your scent. We know you."

The Mourning After

Bruce McDonald

I recall the old Alfred Hitchcock television series with a definite nostalgia. The thrill of unexpected death or murder planted the first insidious seed of criminality in my mind; and I've since slaughtered something on the order of nineteen small children. Or, at least I'm told that studies prove the enjoyment of television viciousness makes for a vicious populace, so I must have killed at least nineteen small children. Actually, I threw my television on the floor (bam!) and broke it about twelve years ago and haven't owned one since. I despise the little buggers. But far from inducing violence, I suspect the penal system would work a lot better by sending those guilty of violent crimes home with a $5000 projection-screen television set. There'd be no violence (nor friendships either) because everyone would stay home and become a vegetable.

Despite my dislike of that Evil Eye kept in triplicate in most American homes, I'll still watch an old Hitchcock rerun given the chance. Most of the episodes don't hold up over the years, but a few do, particularly those with the touch of the supernatural. Connecting with my childhood viewing experience, I can only say the best episodes are effectively, thrillingly YUCKY.

Bruce McDonald's The Mourning After *evoked for me that old Hitchcock Show dread and fascination for the unknown. I think it'll do the same for you.*

245

*   *   *

"Stop! Do not touch her," demanded Madame Duvrai.

An uneasy groan whispered through the black crepe curtain.

"But . . . she's so real. Please," begged Jacqueline Saxton. "Couldn't I just—"

"No! You must not! Monsieur Saxton, please restrain your wife."

A gaunt Christopher Saxton III responded gently, placing a large inhibiting hand on his wife's tense arm.

"Merci, Monsieur." Madame Duvrai relaxed as she spoke. She had warned them repeatedly that any attempt to touch the materialization of their daughter would be disastrous. Great pain and discomfort could befall the medium seated behind the curtain, and any future materializations could be severely endangered. Yet, she had known Jacqueline Saxton would try. Indeed, she had counted on it.

The materialization of Victoria Saxton had been disturbed by Madame Duvrai's first command to Mrs. Saxton. It had begun to dissociate almost immediately, gaining the quality of a fine, floating mist and finally dispersing in the direction of the black curtain.

"It is over for today," declared Madame Duvrai.

"Oh, my baby . . . my darling Vicki. If only . . ." Jacqueline Saxton began crying softly.

Crying did not become her. Nor did the black mourning she habitually wore. Her face was thin and pale, delicate enough without the painful longing it revealed. But Madame Duvrai recognized a driving passion beneath such frailty. Jacqueline Saxton would give anything to see her daughter again, to touch her child once more. And she would give even more to have her back again.

Christopher Saxton eased his wife to her feet and toward the closed door of the chamber. It was evident that he was the strength of the family. "Enough of this," he determined. "We shall not return."

Stopping, his wife peered up at him with hurt and pleading eyes. "I *must* see Victoria again," she whispered. "Please!"

In the silence Madame Duvrai allowed her crooked lips to smile. She knew what would happen next. Christopher Saxton's strength was not enough to resist the passion of his wife. Had she demanded or become hysterical, he might have been resolute enough to deny her. However, her weakness was too much for him to combat. Just as Jacqueline Saxton would give anything to see her daughter again, Madame Duvrai recognized that Christopher Saxton would gladly give all that he had to lift his wife out of anguish. That knowledge satisfied Madame Duvrai. The Saxtons were ready.

Christopher Saxton turned to Madame Duvrai. She understood his look. Nodding her head slowly, she said, "If you will wait in the drawing room, I shall join you momentarily."

As the chamber door sealed with a hollow click behind the lonely couple, the old woman turned her attention to the dark room. She rehung the black crepe covering the windows and raised two of the window shades. Late afternoon light seeped into the chamber, spilling across the single oval table. Near the curve of the table furthest from the door sat the special wooden cabinet, its sable curtain still stretched across the front. With withering hands the aging woman parted the crepe and peered inside.

Seated within on a high, cushioned chair was a young girl-woman. She remained quite still, though her closed eyes reacted slightly to the increased light.

"Christie," beckoned Madame Duvrai quietly.

The figure stirred, taking a deep breath.

"Christie?"

"Yes, Mother. I'm all right." Her forehead glistened in the dim light, and wisps of raven hair hung limp and lifeless about her face.

"Fine, child. Rest where you are. I have some business to conclude. I shall return shortly."

"Mother?" asked Christine. The plaintiveness of her girlish voice warned the old woman.

"What is it, child?" sighed Madame Duvrai.

But the girl hesitated. For a long moment she sat motionless in the jaundiced shaft of window light as if unable to put words to her feelings. Finally she managed to say, "Mother, I'm afraid."

"I know, child."

The girl rushed on. "I'm so afraid. I feel so empty, so alone. It was terrible, worse than any of the others. I don't think I can do it again."

"I know, Christine. But you must."

"Why must I?" she asked desperately. "Why can't I stop now? I'm afraid to come into this room anymore. It's so lonely sitting in this . . . this . . . upright coffin." She shivered suddenly, then tried to continue. "When you close the curtain on me, I feel like . . . like . . ."

"I know, child, I know," soothed the old woman. She needed no reminder of what it was like. It was not something easily forgotten. Recoiling from the memory, she shivered also. "Do not be afraid. All will be well. Remember what I told you about our family and the gift."

"I remember, Mother, but . . ."

"Be still, Christine," admonished her mother softly. "You are nearly at the age when the gift passes. Soon you shall not have to fear ever again. So quiet your worries for now. I think the next will be last."

The daughter clung to the words hopefully. "Only one more? Are you sure, Mother?"

Madame Duvrai shook her head tiredly. "One can never

be positive. Yet, I feel only one more session will be necessary.''

"Oh, Mother! Promise me there will be only one more!"

The old woman sighed, finally conceding, "I will try, child. I will try."

Jacqueline Saxton huddled before the drawing room fire, her shoulders shuddering occasionally. Out of earshot by an unshaded window, Madame Duvrai whispered with Christopher Saxton III.

"One more session, Monsieur. That is all, I assure you."

Mr. Saxton glanced at his wife briefly. Almost inaudibly he said, "I sincerely hope so."

"It is settled, then?" asked Madame Durvai. "You understand what to expect from me and what I expect from you?"

"Yes, yes, I understand," replied Mr. Saxton, looking at his wife. "Anything to still her. She cannot go on like this."

"You will bring it then?"

"I said I would, didn't I!" His voice rose impatiently, but his temper was subdued by his surroundings. He peered furtively around the room as if his tone would awaken the dead. "Pardon me, Madame. Yes, I shall bring it."

"Good. Five o'clock tomorrow?"

"I believe I can manage it."

Madame Duvrai smiled as he gathered up his grieving wife. Then she escorted them to the door and watched them leave. When she turned, Christine was standing in the door of the seance chamber.

"Come, child," she said gently. "Sit by the fire."

They settled before the dancing orange warmth of the fire, the old one holding the young one's hand. After they were comfortable Madame Durvai spoke again.

"It is settled. One more session and it will be over.

After that, no more worry, no more fear. They will return at five o'clock tomorrow.''

"Tomorrow?" Rising hope melted from the girl's features. "Must it be so soon?"

"Yes, it must. But it will be the last. Soon it will be done.''

The fire brightened at her words. Logs cracked and weak showers of cinders spewed against the fire screen. "Soon it will be done," the girl repeated to the flames.

The next day at five o'clock precisely the Saxtons returned. In the wane light of winter dusk Jacqueline Saxton seemed composed yet impatient, while haggard lines tracked her husband's face. In his right hand he clutched a small black suitcase as if it contained all the cares of the world. Madame Duvrai bowed in silent greeting and motioned them toward the drawing room where Christine was seated before the fire.

"Daughter, it is time," said the old woman.

Christine rose obediently. She gave no sign of recognizing anyone as she left the room in her mother's wake. When Madame Duvrai rejoined the Saxtons a moment later, a smile touched her crooked lips.

"Everything is ready.''

"She looked ill. Is anything wrong?" questioned Mr. Saxton suspiciously.

"The girl is a bit tired, Monsieur," admitted Madame Duvrai. "But she is quite well. Come. She is waiting.''

Before she could lead them from the drawing room, Christopher Saxton stopped her. "What about this?" He thrust the black case toward her, impatient to be rid of it.

Bowing shallowly, the old woman accepted it without a word and turned toward the seance chamber. The couple followed her through the door and took seats at the oval table while Madame Duvrai stooped to set the suitcase against a wall. When she closed the chamber door, the room sank into darkened limbo. Black curtains draped the windows, barring any direct light so thoroughly that only an eerie, evanescent trace lent body to the chamber.

Madame Duvrai took a seat opposite the Saxtons. On the table between them lay the usual tools of her seances—a tambourine, a small toy trumpet and a pencil and pad. These would be unnecessary.

At the curve of the table between Madame Duvrai and Jacqueline Saxton sat the wooden closet. The sable curtain was already drawn across its front. Gently it swayed to the rhythmic sound of Christine's easy breathing.

"We are ready, Christine," whispered Madame Duvrai.

The breathing gradually grew more labored, and the curtain swayed more perceptibly. Then suddenly it ceased moving altogether. The breathing stilled. The pencil rolled across the table, falling to the floor, but nothing else moved. There was a rustling from the wooden cabinet, then a groan. Silence reclaimed the chamber.

A fine, diffuse mist crept from behind the curtain. It began to condense as it had so many times before, though it was faster and more thorough this time. Madame Duvrai knew instantly that it was a perfect materialization. She knew immediately that she had been right. It was so complete that it seemed quite solid enough to touch, substantial enough to be flesh and blood.

Another crooked smile revealed her satisfaction as she peered across the table for the reactions of Christopher and Jacqueline Saxton. Mr. Saxton's face announced that this materialization was more than he had ever expected or believed possible. Mrs. Saxton, pale and thin, had not reacted at all. Instead, she had closed her eyes tightly so she would not have to watch the materialization form.

"Call your daughter, Madame," whispered the old woman.

Jacqueline Saxton's eyes opened and her voice croaked involuntarily, "Vicki! Oh, my baby!"

"Mother," responded a weak, plaintive voice. The figure raised her arms pleadingly.

"Oh, Victoria," sobbed Mrs. Saxton, raising her own arms. But the girl could not move toward her.

Just then the sable curtain shuddered as a low moan issued from the cabinet, stopping Mrs. Saxton. She and her husband turned nervously to Madame Duvrai who nodded her head once decisively.

"Oh, Vicki, darling Vicki," mumbled Mrs. Saxton hoarsely as she lurched from her chair to sweep up her daughter. Her husband was at her side immediately, crushing both of them in his arms.

Again the curtain shuddered. A piercing shriek shook the chamber, stunning the Saxtons, tearing at their hearts. Afraid to release their grip, the three figures hugged each other tightly while they stumbled toward the chamber door. Christopher Saxton swung it open frantically, and the reunited family plunged through in a frightened mass. The door returned violently, slamming shut with a splintering crash. With that, the shattering scream died.

Madame Duvrai looked at the quiet curtain of the pine closet where her daughter sat. She sighed, remembering the pain and the loneliness, remembering also that it was over.

She moved as a tired woman moves, as an old woman moves. With withered hands she parted the black curtain. The darkness within matched the still blackened room. She moved slowly around the chamber, hanging the black drapes for the last time and raising the shades on two windows to let in the otherworld light of the streetlamps. But she did not look at the wooden closet where her daughter sat. She already knew what she would find there.

Instead, Madame Duvrai crossed the room to the wall by the door. There she found the small suitcase where she had left it. Picking it up expectantly, she carried it to the table. The tambourine, the trumpet and the pad of paper were scattered across the floor with one sweep of her arm. She set the suitcase in the center of the table.

Madame Duvrai already knew what she would find inside the suitcase, too. Christopher Saxton III would not break his word. He was afraid of her. Just the same, she wanted to see it anyway.

Delicately, slowly, she unlatched the stays, lifted the lid and smiled. She pushed the case toward the closet as if seeking her daughter's approval, though she expected none.

Slumped in the ashen light of the streetlamp, head rolled back in the cushioned chair, was the spent, lifeless figure of Christine. Her skin and hair were a cold, bleached white, startling in their brittle, frozen appearance. Her mouth, stretched in silent scream, and her shadowed eye sockets were voids of blackness. Across one cheek glittered the dead track of a single, fleeting tear frozen before it had fallen.

"I know, child," said Madame Duvrai with tired sympathy. "I know. But be still for now, my daughter. Rest yourself. You shall have nothing to fear. Look. We have enough money here to live forever." She cackled to herself. "Yes, forever. Soon I will find a good medium, and I will call you back, my child. Just as Jacqueline Saxton has called her dead Victoria back. Just as my own mother called me back."

And she smiled as crooked fingers fondled the money in the small black suitcase.

The Hill Is No Longer There

John D. Berry

John D. Berry shares abode and commode with the infamous Eileen Gunn, but his personal fame does not stop there. He reviewed fanzines for AMAZING in the days of the Ted White regime; he edited the PACIFIC NORTHWEST REVIEW OF BOOKS during its short life; and he comes from good East Coast stock. Who could ask for more?

The Hill Is No Longer There is John's first fiction sale. It hinges on a bit of Seattle lore and history, but I'll leave it up to the reader to figure out how much of the story is absolutely authentic and how much of it is fancy.

"—Did you know"—the old drunk's breath was foul—"that this here's the Denny Regrade? This whole neighborhood! And you know why it's called that? It's because it all used to be a hill. You follow me? They knocked it down. Wasn't a very big hill, but it was a steep one—too steep for a horse to get up if it was dragging a wagon behind it. So they dug it out and they hosed it down and they dumped all the dirt and all the rocks into the bay."

A young man named Alan Haggerty was sitting at the bar of a tavern on First Avenue in Seattle, not listening to the drunk whose voice droned beside him. Alan was finishing his beer and staring at the mask on the wall at the end of the bar. It was a Coast Indian mask, an old one, carved of wood to look like a bird, and it had little tufts of feathers—the stumps of feathers, really, that must have been worn off years ago—and faded paint that may once have been bright. The beak stuck out in front, sharp, and its underside looked as though it could have moved. Alan kept feeling that he had seen the mask before, but he couldn't place it. It hadn't been on the wall of the tavern the last time he had stopped in, and the young woman tending bar was new to the job and didn't know where the mask had come from. Maybe he had seen one like it in a book of Indian masks. He didn't know. But he kept thinking about it.

"There used to be a hill here—right here where we're standing, from here right on up from the waterfront. Used to be a good forty feet higher here than it is now. But there isn't any hill here now."

The drunk released Alan's shoulders, and Alan quickly downed the last of his beer and stood up. He was still staring at the Indian mask.

"It's not right," said the drunk to Alan. "There ought to be a hill here now. It's just not right."

Then the drunken old man teetered and tried to walk back to his table. Grabbing a chair for support, he fell over it and sprawled flat on the floor. As the bartender hurried around the other end of the bar to see to him, Alan grabbed the mask off the wall and walked out the door.

With the stolen mask tucked under his arm, Alan hurried across the street and up a sidestreet. The night was dark and foggy, with pools of water underfoot.

He cut through an alley and started across an open lot of dirt and grass. The fog clung coldly to his face and hands, and as he stepped across the ditch in the middle of the open lot he heard the fog horn of a boat on the water: once, and then nothing. No other sound. It was odd, he thought, for a horn to sound once and then not again.

He pushed through bushes toward the street, with the

mask getting wetter under his arm, but the bushes didn't
end, and over his head in the fog swayed the dark limb of
a huge Douglas fir, its needles dripping with condensation.
He stopped, his shoes silent on the ground beneath his
feet. He could hear nothing. He could smell damp earth
and the scents of trees and bushes—no city smells, no city
sounds. The street wasn't there. All he could see was the
black trunk of the Douglas fir and its one swaying branch.

The chill cut through his thin pants, and the fog crept in
the collar of his jacket. He started moving, walking forward,
slowly. As he walked under the big trees, the ground
began to rise.

It was dead dark. His shoes slipped on mud, and he
stumbled into cold running water. It was a tiny stream,
barely a runnel, draining quickly down a trough between
two steeper slopes. The black trees arched overhead, but
didn't quite touch; the fog clung about the stream bed, but
it seemed to be less dark there. As he squelched forward,
upstream, trying to keep his feet on the mud and not in the
water, he thought he could see a faint glow ahead of him.

Ferns crowded thickly about the stream, and he had to
push through their clinging branches. The mask kept catching on fronds and leaves. His feet were wet and cold; his
hands were scratched and his fingers chilled. The fog
loomed ahead of him and the faint glow had disappeared.

He stopped. Water trickled at his feet. He could hear the
wind rustling leaves somewhere far off. Trees closed him
in on all sides. There was no sign of home, nothing
familiar. He didn't know where he was. He was scared.
He turned around, to try and follow the stream back down
the hill.

A woman stood in the stream. He froze. She was pale,
dead white, but she was dressed in a cloak that looked
woven of grass. She was barefoot, and the cloak hung in
wet tatters. The fog obscured her face.

Alan shivered and couldn't move. His mouth opened as though he had no control over it.

The ghostly figure raised its arms toward him. The fog dissolved in front of its face, and Alan saw that it wore a fantastic mask. It was carved wood, the geometric designs of the Coast Indian carvers, like the one he held in his hands, but it was a woman's face. Feathers waved gently around it where hair should have been. The figure moved toward him.

He broke and ran. Clutching the bird mask, he crashed through the brush to his right and stumbled up the slope beneath the trees. He could hear nothing behind him over the pounding of his own ears and the raw wheezings of his breath. He climbed higher.

Abruptly Alan reached the top of the ridge. The trees were thinner, but they thickened again on the other side, where the hill sloped down again into the fog. He stopped running, clinging to the wet trunk of a Douglas fir, trying to catch his breath. He had to force himself to turn and look behind him. Nothing was following him.

There were no stars above, only a low, dark sky and the overhanging branches. The night air was damp, and fog roiled below him on either side. The ridge rose slowly to his right, and to his left sloped gently down into the fog. He could see a little way up the ridge between the sparser trees. There was long, wet grass in clear patches.

The young fir he was leaning against grew up between the halves of a small boulder that had been split in two. Moss grew around the base of the rock, and its face was mottled with lichen. Needles covered the open ground. Alan slowly sank down onto the rock, his right hand sliding down the slick bark of the tree.

His fingers slid down onto something soft and moist. He yanked his hand away and sprang off the rock, only to trip on tangled tree roots and slide partway down the needled slope. His ankle twisted, and pain throbbed up his leg.

Eyes wide open, he turned and crawled back up toward the boulder and the tree. He saw nothing but stone, tree, moss, and lichen. As he pulled himself opposite the cleft in the rock, he saw a wide fungus that was growing on the tree. It was only tree fungus. That was all he had touched.

Alan sighed and leaned back against the boulder. His ankle hurt, his hip was bruised, he was cold and chilled through. But he laughed. Afraid of a mushroom! He laughed harder.

He heard his laughter echoed. He stopped, but the other laughter didn't. It wasn't an echo. It came from the fog in front of him.

He heard the sound of someone trudging up the slope. He crawled behind the boulder, hidden by the narrow trunk of the tree, and peered around it.

A shape appeared in the fog, moving toward him. As it climbed, it laughed. The laughter chilled like a deeper, colder fog. The shape was that of an old man walking up a steep hillside, wearing dirty old clothes, no shoes, and a wide straw hat with a conical top, like the old rain hats woven by the Coast Indians. But the man had a bushy beard under the Indian hat, and he looked like the old drunk that Alan had left in the tavern.

Alan felt relief. Whatever he might be doing, an old drunk wasn't going to hurt him. At least he was familiar. Alan pulled himself up over the boulder and waved to the old man.

The figure stopped, and his laughter stopped. He raised his head, and beneath the brim of his hat Alan saw the mask.

This mask was old, weathered wood with no decoration. It was carved like the face of a man, but simplified, stylized. Thick moss grew around its cheeks and chin, and it was that that had looked like a beard. There were no eyeholes.

Alan found his voice. "Who are you?" he cried. "What do you want?" He dropped the bird mask to the wet ground. The figure made no sound, and Alan cried again, hysterically, "What do you want? Who are you? Who are you?"

The figure raised its hands to its face and pulled its mask off. Alan clapped his own hands to his face and squeezed his eyes shut, digging the heels of his hands into his eyes. He saw red bursts of light in the blackness.

Alan turned and lurched away from the boulder, up the crest of the ridge. He opened his eyes, but he could barely see. His ankle hurt terribly, but he ran, scraping his arms on the trees, banging his head on a low-swinging branch. He scrambled as fast as he could push his tired body up toward the top of the hill.

He ran from the shape below, and as he ran he heard more of them running through the fog around him. He saw ghostly faces in the treetrunks, each one impossibly carved, but looking hauntingly familiar. He dodged around them as best he could and ran on.

He reached a clearing at the top of the hill. There was a shallow depression in the ground there, next to a large, rough rock. Alan plunged into the depression, barely longer than his body, and rolled against the rock. There was long grass all around it, but no bushes to hide him. The fog swirled on every side. The sounds of feet running seemed all around him. The fog began to close in. Alan dug his fingers into the rock and pressed his whole body against the ground. He jammed his eyes shut and pressed his face against the rough, cold surface of the rock. He shivered, and he ground his cheek against the stone, scraping and hurting himself but unable to stop. The fog closed wetly around him.

And then it was gone. The sounds were gone. He saw
bright light through his eyelids: sunlight, beaming warmly
on his sodden back and hands. He smelled wild grass,
though his half-open mouth tasted of stone and dirt. He
heard birds chittering in the distance.

Alan pulled his raw-cheeked face away from the rock.
His fingernails were broken and sore. He was bruised. His
ankle throbbed. He tasted blood. But when he opened his
eyes, he had to blink in the daylight.

The noonday sun shone down on him in the field. It was
the same clearing he had stumbled into in the night. He
rolled away from the rock and lay on his back in the
shallow depression he had dived into only moments before.
The sky was blue above him, without clouds. The ghosts
of the night were gone.

From where he lay, Alan could just see the tops of the
trees all around. He looked at the sky, and the bright sun,
and he breathed raggedly through his open mouth.

He heard the raucous caw of a raven, and in a flapping
of wings a big black bird flew down and landed on the
rock beside him. He flinched away. It was a raven bigger
than any he had seen in the city. It looked at him steadily.

"Hello, bird," Alan said, in a hoarse voice. "Where
am I? Is it over now?" He sighed. He tried to sit up, but
his ankle shot a swift pain up his leg and he dropped onto
his back again. He laughed weakly and smiled up at the
bird.

As he looked into the eye of the raven with its steady
gaze, he thought he saw expressions flicker across the
raven's face. He couldn't look away. Features formed and
disappeared, human features, familiar but on the edge of
his memory, each one there but a moment and succeeded
by another. The raven's black, round eye stared from a
series of nearly recognizable faces—just suggestions of
features under the shiny feathers, and then they were gone.

Alan felt the ground soften under his back. It felt like dry mud, oozing slowly around him as he sank into it. All he could see was the raven's eye. Suddenly the eye closed, and the raven's dark form shifted, changing before his eyes into something else. The beak lengthened, the head swelled; the wings and body disappeared. Feathers grew in tufts from the sides of the face, the features took on the geometric shapes of an Indian carving, the hard beak turned to painted wood. For one moment there hung above his head the stolen raven's mask. Then it dove toward him.

He yelled and jammed his eyes tight shut in his face, flailing his arms in front of him to ward off a blow. His hands closed on the wooden mask, his fingers curling around the edges. The inside was wet. He tried to push it away and let go, but his rigid fingers wouldn't loosen their grip. He felt the hillside under him dissolve, and he fell.

At the corner of Second and Bell in the Denny Regrade, on a foggy morning, Alan Haggerty was found dead in the street. His neck was broken from a fall. There was no blood on his body, though it was bruised and broken and his clothes were torn. The police aid unit that took him away ignored an old broken Indian mask that lay in the alley behind him. On the smooth inner surface of the bird mask was the shine of blood, slowly soaking into the wood. A hill had once risen over that spot far above the present street level. But the hill is no longer there.

The Inhabitant of the Pond

Linda Thornton

Linda Thornton is a Texan presently living in Jamaica. She has provided TALES BY MOONLIGHT *with a horror yarn of such classic feel and dimension that I felt it belonged at the anthology's end, to leave every reader sated, no matter how ghoulish your reading requirements. There are not many authors as capable of capturing a mood as dark, as foreboding, as perfectly tense as* The Inhabitant of the Pond.

It may not be kosher for an editor to admit to having a favorite yarn in a given anthology. And it must be said that favorites change like emotions and weather, each story having something about it that puts it first *for one reason or another, at one time or another. The process of selecting stories is, for an editor, so intensely personal, that choosing a* favorite *is a harrowing experience best left untried. Yet I will relent enough to confess that, at this point in time at least, my favorite yarn is this one.*

I used to sit for hours at the window of my second story room and watch Edward down below at his strange play in front of the crumbling cherub. His angular blond head would bob contentedly in the shadow of the smiling statue, and his pale, slender hands would lose themselves in the verdant recesses of the ivy that coiled like serpents about the figure. Edward loved the ivy, and he would not hear of my offer to pull it, although I tried without success to warn him that the vines would in time disintegrate his beloved cherub into fragments.

This dismal spot had once been a picturesque little marble-bottomed pond, with an abundance of lily pads and fish—a cool and refreshing bower over which the cherub had reigned as a benevolent shade. But the neglect and disuse of fifteen years had seen it transformed into a choked, moss-covered sanctuary for fat, torpid insects, while the guardian statue had assumed the aspect of an eroded tombstone.

It would seem an unlikely playground for most children, but Edward had little in common with other children. Although I realized it too late, I see now that its very wildness and desolation was a comfort to him. Because it held so little allure for other members of our household, it was the one place where he was able to find peace and happiness. There he could forget his own ugliness, as well as the viciousness of his tormentor.

I must confess now that when I watched Edward I did not do so out of sisterly solicitude. While I never actually felt hostile toward him, I could never overcome my sense of revulsion at his strange appearance. His face made me uncomfortable, and I avoided looking at it when he spoke to me. And yet, concealed behind the curtain at my window, I spent hours watching him, enthralled by a morbid fascination with his queer looks and behavior. The overly large, bullet-shaped head, with its sparse furrow of limp, blond hair; the high, browless forehead that threw cavernous shadows over his pale, weak blue eyes; the nearly lipless mouth that hung open idiotically as he played. All held me spellbound in revulsion.

It is perhaps no surprise that Edward's and my father was not overly fond of this grotesque changeling. I do not think he loved me, but I know for a fact that Father hated Edward—hated having spawned something ugly and repulsive. And while he was indifferent and cold to me, he turned the full force of his hatred and vicious loathing on his unfortunate second son.

Our mother had died shortly after Edward's birth. Although I was twenty at the time, ten years later I remember her as nothing more than a rather insipid, neutral presence. She lived and died with no visible effect on our lives—an invalid who was content to stay confined in her room so long as her maid was at hand to fetch things, to console her, and to listen to her complaints. As far as my father's feelings toward her, he considered the only useful thing she had ever accomplished had been to bear Thomas, our dead brother.

Thomas was perhaps the only bright spot that ever shone in our dismal household. While he loved all of us, he was particularly fond of Edward. It was as if Edward's unfortunate appearance made him all the more endearing in Thomas' eyes. Thomas, on whom my father doted, was the benign intervener for Edward. He could turn Father's unprovoked and sometimes maniacal rages against the child into harmless and forgiving smiles.

I do think he was the only living being Edward ever loved, and when he died, Edward seemed to turn all the frustrated love that welled in his poor small soul on to the cracked cherub in the garden.

A sudden illness took Thomas away from us, and with him went all the sunlight our house had ever known. With Thomas went the only tempering influence on Father's depression, as well as the only real friend Edward had ever known. The effect on the three remaining members of the family was swift and prostrating: Father retreated to his study to release his frustration and sorrow in his frightening rages. I retreated to my room to avoid him, and Edward disappeared.

So heart-broken were we all upon Thomas' death that we at first paid no heed to the daily disappearance of Edward. No one said so in words, but I believe we were all rather glad to be relieved of seeing him, particularly Father. His rages seemed to abate in proportion to the infrequency with which he saw Edward, and thus the servants and I gave our tacit approbation to his absences.

I do not recall ever wondering where Edward passed his days at first. When I did discover it, it was quite by accident, and not from curiosity or alarm.

Within a few months of Thomas' death, Father's fits of temper became more frequent, regardless of whether Edward were there or not. So impassioned were these fits that I suspect Father, had he lived, would have grown insane. The seed of madness had been germinating for a long time. But at the time these storms were virulent enough to send me up to my room to spend the greatest part of the day. Father's former indifference to me had changed. I was now a convenient presence on which he might vent his violence.

It happened that on one of those days when I was driven to my room, I was sitting by my window and attempting to lose myself in a sort of distracted daydream. I had been there for a long while, gazing into space, when I happened to look down on the garden below and see Edward engaged in some busy occupation. There he was, kneeling in front of the dilapidated cherub, waving his arms about in a strange, animated sort of play. Although I could see only the back of his odd little head from my vantage point, I could sense from his movements that he was as happy as on those occasions when his brother had played with him.

I felt a mild sense of surprise to have discovered his hiding place so near. His daily disappearances had taken him no further than the rundown pond in the garden. The pond was in a tiny clearing surrounded on all sides by an overgrowth of vegetation, and thus Edward, or anyone who wished to secrete himself there, would be hidden from all views save mine from the window.

This particular mode of playing struck me as so unusual that I watched it curiously for some time. At first I could not imagine what sort of peculiar game he was playing. His odd, jerky movements seemed more the aimless antics of an idiot than the actions of a playing child. Then it came to me. He was pretending to talk to the cherub, perhaps making believe that it was a playfellow.

I cannot deny that I was eager to know what he was saying. I felt the same urge that drives people to gaze surreptitiously at passing cripples. I raised the window noiselessly.

Although I was certain I had made no sound, Edward froze. He became as still as the statue. I strained my ears for a sound, but I heard nothing. I began to feel faintly uncomfortable lest he should turn around and catch me spying on him.

I held my breath, hoping that he would resume his former play, but he did not stir. Nor did he look up at the window. I began to entertain the peculiar sensation that I was an intruder, and that if he did not actually know it was I watching him, he was at least aware that he was not alone.

Regretfully, I closed the window as quietly as I had opened it, and drew back behind the veil of the drapes. Sure enough, he resumed his weird rituals as if the disturbance had never occurred.

I watched him for the rest of the afternoon, and for many afternoons after that. I saw very little of him except during my activity as a spy. Sometimes I would pass him in the midst of his passages to and from the garden, and I would say good morning or good afternoon to him. He always responded politely, but would pass on quickly if nothing more was expected of him, as if some urgent business lay in front of him. I knew he did not like bothering people with the sight of himself, but this preoccupied rushing away was new with him. It made me wonder.

Neither my father nor any of the servants concerned themselves about him. He would rise in the morning, dress himself, and go in the kitchen where the cook would have left his breakfast on the table. After hurriedly wolfing down his food, he would bolt out of the house to retreat to his sanctuary, hopefully after having avoided contact with our father, who kept to himself in the study except for odd moments. His other meals were the same. He would creep furtively into the kitchen to eat hastily, and then vanish, either to the pond or to his room for the night.

Thus Edward's childhood progressed. He was left without interference to eat what he chose, to wash himself when and if he pleased; in short, to spend his days in whatever manner his imagination suggested to him. His delicate and sensitive mind was directed by no sympathetic person to learn books or to appreciate moral and cultural values. His character was left to grow as wildly and as freely as the ivy in the garden.

I was the sole observer of this little scene, and I did not observe from a sense of concern. It is an admission which I do not like to make, for it shows my character to have been unforgivably disgusting. I was moved by an insidious and loathsome curiosity. I suddenly had something in my dreary existence to amuse me. Strangely, the little boy whom I had always sought to avoid in conversation took on new interest for me as an object to nourish my bored sensibilities.

As the weeks passed, the need to watch Edward secretly grew to an obsession. My sick fixation drove me to outrageous lengths to learn what transpired between Edward and the statue. I had tried the open window incident numerous times in order to hear what he said, but without success. One morning, I even got up before Edward so that I could raise the window before he arrived. But it did no good. He seemed to have an uncanny awareness that someone was listening to him, and he would keep perfectly still for as long as the window was open.

Finally, I felt I must speak to him about the matter. I resolved to make an offer to help him pull the ivy in the hope that he would take me into his confidence and allow me to know what he was doing. I was certain that he knew I had been watching him anyway, so I decided it would do no harm for me to present myself as a sympathetic third party to his play.

One day I stopped him as he was sneaking out of the house after lunch.

"Edward," I began, trying to sound like a helpful sister. "I have noticed that the ivy growing around the cherub is becoming rather unmanageable. Would you like for me to help you pull it? I'm afraid such an old statue as that one will fall apart if something is not done soon."

If I had any hopes of being invited to his playground, I was soon disappointed. His little slash-mouth gaped open wider than ever, and his eyes receded further back into his head, narrow with suspicion. I cursed myself for my ill-timed overture. I feared I would cause him to cease playing altogether on my account.

He stammered a reply to the effect that he thanked me very much, but he was very fond of the ivy and everything would probably be all right. He was as polite and self-effacing as ever, but I read something new in his face. Some hard, adult emotion lurked behind those hooded eyes—eyes which glittered with a potent awareness of deception.

He scuttled away quickly then, and I climbed the stairs

to my room with heavy steps. I feared I had lost my only amusement through my own carelessness.

I was wrong. He was there in the garden just as on previous days, kneeling in front of the cherub and going through his weird play ritual. At first I approached the window with caution, and I hid behind the curtain, ready to dodge out of view should he look up. But all that was unnecessary, for he seemed as blithely unaware of my presence as ever.

A few days passed thus and I was ready to settle back once more in the routine. So intent had I been on my stealthy preoccupation that I failed to notice certain ominous signs that were brewing in the study below.

I suppose I should have seen it coming and done something to warn Edward. I should have known that the day would come when Father's murderous temper would not be content with merely having Edward out of his sight. A hatred as deep and vicious as Father's needed the presence of the hated person. It was a hungry, voracious emotion that had to be fed.

One afternoon as I was sitting by my window, engaged in my usual occupation, I heard Father scream. The sheer, insane pitch of the outburst was something new even in that house accustomed to his ravings. I began to tremble in confusion and fear, because I recognized in those mad, staccato shrieks a call for Edward. Father was no longer satisfied with coldly rebuffing those around him. He needed someone to attack.

As Father's screams grew louder, I looked down to see if Edward had heard. He appeared as serene and untroubled as the idiotically smiling cherub he worshipped. I could bear it no longer. The thought of Father bursting out on the grounds to search for Edward, and discovering his secret hiding place, filled me with horror. Even I had compassion on the poor child when I thought of his only refuge violated and denied him.

Quickly and quietly I opened the window. I spoke to him in a loud, hoarse whisper that got his attention immediately. The bullet head spun around to confront me, and the narrow gash of a mouth hung open limply.

"Edward," I called, hoping Father could not hear, "Father is calling for you. You must go to him, or he'll search for you."

There is perhaps no more perfect expression of terror than a frightened child's face. Edward looked up at me so pitiably, with a face so eloquent with helpless, terrified confusion, that for the first time in his life, I forgot his ugliness and my heart went out to him.

"You must go, Edward. If he has to look for you, he—" I did not finish. Edward understood. With a look of helpless resignation that would have more befitted a man walking a gangplank, he turned and began to crawl through the small underpath he had carved out for himself through the vegetation.

I left the window to stand beside the door of my room. I opened it slightly. My father was still raging when I heard the muffled sound of the kitchen door opening. Tears sprang to my eyes when I thought of the poor child facing Father, and I hated myself because I was too cowardly to help him.

I emerged slightly from the security of my room to peep over the banister, where I could just see the doorway to the study. I heard Father cursing and beating the top of his desk. I could picture him in there, tearing at his hair and pounding out his maddened fury in a fierce tattoo on his desk. Then I saw the top of Edward's odd blond head as he crossed to the study.

For a moment all was expectantly still. And then I heard

Edward shriek and I raced back to my room and closed the door tightly.

Even fortified in my room I could not shut out the terrifying sounds that issued from below. I walked to the window and pressed my fingers to my throbbing temples in a vain attempt to block out the cries from the study. I glanced down at the abandoned sanctuary, where only moments before my small brother had played peacefully without thought of the dreadful storm that was to break. Never had the place looked so forlorn or sad. The cherub smiled imbecilely into space, its recent companion already forgotten.

As I looked down at that wild knot of ivy and cracked marble, I was suddenly seized with an impulse. I wanted to quit that horrid house with its unhappiness and sorrows, and seek protection in the shadow of the cherub. The tendrils of ivy seemed to wave beckoningly at me from below, and I was irresistibly drawn to come down. Perhaps I was moved by another impulse—the desire to see for myself the place where my strange little brother played.

I crept downstairs past the study, refusing to hear the pitiful cries of the oppressed child and the harsh curses of the father. I walked as if in a dream, oblivious to all else save the irresistible pull of the ruined pond.

Once out of the kitchen I made for the wall of shrubbery that concealed Edward's hiding place. I looked down and saw that I would have difficulty tunneling through the entrance that his small body had fashioned. But I knelt down on my hands and knees and saw that although the opening was small, the tangled mass of vegetable growth was more of vines and leaves than woody stems. I began to crawl through.

In a few seconds I was in Edward's sanctuary. Before me were the broken pond, with great gaping cracks in its floor that had rendered it useless, and the despoiled cherub, one of its plump, moss-laden arms already broken off and mouldering in the stagnant pond.

It was terribly still in this spot; I began to realize how Edward had remained oblivious to the business of the household. The wall of shrubbery provided a natural cushion from sound. It would have taken an exceptionally strong gust of wind to even ruffle the leaves. A more perfect hideaway could perhaps not be found.

I must say that I by no means felt comfortable in this isolated spot. It appealed to me in its wilderness state as little as it had years ago when it was still in use. What appealed so much to Edward, I asked myself as I sank to my knees in front of the grinning cherub? I regarded the figure with a critical eye.

The cherub returned my gaze noncommittally.

Although vines had grown around much of its body, the head was still free from entanglement. I thought back to the statue and the pond in its heyday. A vague memory stirred in my mind, of something which I had thought unpleasant about the statue. What was it?

Then I noticed something I had forgotten. There was an opening in the mouth. It was one of those ridiculous pieces of ceramic from which water is meant to spew. Suddenly I remembered. In the winter, when the water was not flowing through the fountain, the cherub's mouth was used as a home by numerous fat insects. I drew my head nearer to the mouth for closer inspection.

From out of the black crevice there came a sudden movement. I tumbled back with a small cry and landed on my backside in the festering pond bottom. I clambered up quickly, to see the largest black beetle I had ever experienced staring placidly down at me from its perch inside the cherub's mouth. With a shudder of revulsion I warily surveyed my skirt to see if any other of the loathsome inhabitants of the pond had invaded my person during my fall.

Fighting back my urge to flee, I forced myself to take a closer look at the bug. It was an awesome specimen, big as a field mouse, with a brace of bristling antennae which it waved menacingly at me.

My reason told me it was silly to be frightened of an insect, so I instinctively made a quick swipe at the statue's head, hoping to scare the bug away. The next moment I was again on my backside in the pond, brushing moss and mud from my dress.

What had sent me reeling back into the pond was a quick and unexpected movement by the insect. I looked up at the cherub's head to see that the entire body of the creature was now revealed. I could not restrain an audible gasp of amazement when I saw how truly large the thing was. I felt distinctly uneasy now, for instead of scuttering away like insects are prone to do in the face of a human attack, the thing had lunged at *me*—attacked me, in fact.

I now felt a very real sense of danger, being alone and cut off from other humans with that placid, staring insect confronting me. Its glistening body was too plump and well-fed, too shiny-moist with sickening healthiness. I began to edge away slowly and carefully, for fear those short, hairy legs would hurtle that body tarantula-fashion at my face.

During those awful moments when the creature held me at bay, I felt the enormity of its power. The antennae waved hypnotically and I dared not look away. I glanced up for a hurried second to see the uncertain blue of the sky giving way to the encroaching darkness. I was terrified at the thought of having the dark enclose me with the black beetle nearby.

It seems as if I were held for an eternity by the thing. I am certain that within those awful moments it learned what it needed to know about me. It was not physical fear that rooted me to that spot, but the same dreadful power by which certain serpents captivate their prey and then move in for the kill.

And then, just when I was forming panic-stricken plans to rush by the cherub and dive into the underbrush, the insect was gone. It vanished inside the cherub's mouth as quickly as it had appeared. I did not hesitate, but clawed my way through the brush and into the open.

The reviving chill of the enveloping evening outside the pond site jolted me back to reality. Only then did I remember Edward and Father. How long had I been with the inhabitant of the pond? I do not know, but it was as if the rest of the world had not existed while I was imprisoned there.

I hurried back to the house, and paused at the back door before I entered. Not a sound issued from inside. The silence struck me as somehow abnormal. Although all the servants had left at noon that day, something still seemed out of joint. I opened the door and quickly entered.

I crossed through the darkened kitchen where Edward's uneaten dinner lay on the table. I made my way noiselessly into the hall outside the study and paused before ascending the stairs. There were no lights on, nor was there the sound of human movement inside. I assumed that Father had finished with Edward and gone to his room to collapse in the nervous exhaustion that always overtook him after his fits. I hurried quickly up the stairs.

When I reached the landing I paused and looked down the hall toward Edward's room. There was no shaft of light under his door. I padded down the hall and stood in front of his room, listening. After a few moments I discerned muffled, choking gasps as if he were sobbing and expending great effort at making himself unheard. I opened the door carefully and went inside.

There was only a feeble glow of light coming from the window, but I could discern a vague shape huddled in the corner. Edward had wrenched himself between the bed and the wall in order to hide.

I crossed the room quickly to the cramped recess. The sobbing ceased abruptly.

"Edward," I called softly, "Edward, did he hurt you?"

There was no response, so I edged closer until I could reach out and touch him. I groped for his hand and held it in my own.

"Please, Edward, are you all right?"

The sound that came from him startled me so that I jerked my hand away instinctively. He spoke in an unnatural, guttural voice, like an animal.

"He won't ever do it again. He'll be sorry, the old bastard!"

I was glad I could not see his face, for repulsive as it was, I had never seen his features marred with the kind of vicious emotion his voice expressed.

"Don't say such things, Edward!" I cried. "Father's very ill. He isn't capable of knowing what he does."

"He's a bastard. That's what he is. And by God, he'll pay for it," sniveled the animal voice.

"Where in the world did you learn such language? What are you talking about?" A sudden fear overtook me. "Edward, you haven't done anything, have you?"

"I don't have to. Someone else is going to fix him." I heard Edward suck in his breath quickly as if he were excited by some idea.

"Someone? Who? Have you been imagining a friend?" I asked anxiously, remembering my recent meeting with the ugly beetle.

"Just don't you worry about it, and I'll see you get off." The little boy's voice laughed hoarsely in a tone that chilled me. "Keep out of this, understand?"

I had begun to tremble slightly. It must be nonsense, I told myself. The imagination of a lonely child left to work out terrible fantasies in such a desolate spot as the pond. Even I had fallen under its influence.

"Edward, you haven't been carrying on some absurd fantasy about that beetle in the pond, have you?"

"Huh?" He sounded surprised. "Oh, you met him, didn't you?" I heard him snicker softly.

"I saw a bug, Edward. A black beetle and nothing more. Come now. There's nothing to be embarrassed about. I know children often make up friends and tell them secrets. They even imagine their friends tell them things."

"What are you driveling about?" Edward sneered impatiently. "Go away and quit spying on me. We won't tell you anything."

"There is no 'we'," I told him sharply. "It's nothing but a stupid bug."

"He's not a bug," he insisted sullenly, "and you'll see."

"All right, Edward. Just what is there going to be to see?" I tried to keep my voice calm and even, but I was ruffled at Edward's nasty tone, and I felt uneasy.

"Father's going to get ripped."

My mind would not accept the lip-smacking satisfaction with which Edward uttered these words.

"By a bug?" I said mockingly.

"He ain't a bug."

"Then what is he?" I demanded.

"You won't be able to see him," said Edward impatiently. "He'll crash through the bushes and beat down the door, and then he'll tear Father's head off!" he whispered mirthfully.

"You must stop this dreadful fantasizing! It's wicked to wish things like that to happen to your father, no matter what he's done to you. The bug is simply a large black beetle and nothing more!"

I felt the attack coming, but not in time to avert it. Two hands were thrust savagely into my face, and as I retreated, they caught in the flesh just below my ears. I struck out fiercely with my fists, landing several blows to Edward's face. He released my face with a howl of pain and fell back into his corner to whimper angrily. I put my hand up to my stinging cheeks and felt the telltale ooze of blood.

"You're acting like an animal," I hissed at him, backing out of the recess. "What has happened to you?"

"You'd better shut up and leave me alone! I hate you now and he hates you, too. I know you've been watching me. He told me every time you were there. We laughed at you because you're a stupid old maid that nobody wants to marry. He wanted to rip you, too, only I told him to leave off. Now I just might tell him. All I have to do is tell him and he'll tear your head off."

I could scarcely believe the vehement glee with which the child spat out his tirade. He no longer resembled the meek little boy that I had known.

"You ugly little monster!" I cried as I rubbed my smarting cheeks. "Your mind is as ugly as your face."

"Now you've done it," he hissed. I felt him draw closer, and I backed further away. "You old hag! You witch! Okay, come on then!"

I did not have time to wonder at this non sequitur, for at that moment there came a dreadful roaring and crashing sound from below. I dashed out of the room and leaned over the top of the staircase, trying to penetrate the gloomy region at the bottom of the stairs. My first thought was that it must be Father, but I could not imagine even him having created such a noise. The sound that had traveled up the stairs had shaken the whole house like an explosion.

Edward was soon beside me, his mouth agape in an odd

manner. His eyes were unnaturally large with fear, and he clung to my skirt like a child, all traces of the demon vanished.

"He's here," he whispered to me. "He's come 'cause I called for him. Oh, I am sorry." The frightened child was close to tears.

"Nonsense," I said brusquely, although at that point I was not very certain of myself. "It's only Father. Come on."

Tugging the quaking little boy behind me, I set out timidly down the stairs. At each step I paused and strained my nervous senses for a sound or a sight of what had created the uproar.

I had nearly reached the bottom of the staircase when something arrested my attention. A faint thumping noise issued from somewhere near the kitchen. I held my breath and squeezed Edward's hand hard.

The thumping drew closer. It might have been a person walking, but there was never a human gait that sounded like that. Too heavy, too awkward, too fast. Too many legs, I realized.

Nearer it came, until I heard a shuffle at the very bottom of the stairs, followed by a pregnant silence. My heart was in my mouth, and sweat oozed from the pressure between Edward's hand and my own.

At the moment's peak of terror, I thought I saw a vague shape in the darkness. It was probably only the rustling of the drapes or my imagination at work creating monsters in the dark. Of course, it really didn't matter what it looked like, for my mind had already imbued the thing stalking the halls with a distinct shape.

Then silence. It had crossed into the study, but what was it doing?

The searing, ripping sound of the drapes being torn into shreds came almost as a relief in that suspended void.

Through the wall to the spot where we sat huddled on the stairs came the most frightful uproar—sounds of destruction and chaos that traveled like vast shock waves through the rafters of the house. It was as if some crazed animal of supernatural strength had been loosed upon that room. It trampled and tore, splintered and shattered, clawed and crashed in a senseless, destructive frenzy. But I knew as I sat there trembling, with my hands to my ears to block out those awful sounds, that the orgy of destruction going on in the study was no senseless rampage. The thing was looking for someone. Someone whom it had not yet found, but soon would.

And then, the whole room seemed to explode with one final violent cadence, and it was quiet again.

For a strained eternity I sat cowering on the stairs with the boy, not daring to move lest it come for us. When I was at last satisfied that it had taken its search to other parts of the house, I rose numbly and closed the short distance between the stairs and the study door. Edward followed close behind.

I switched on the lights and was struck dumb by the incredible scene before me. All the unleashed powers of hell could not have manufactured a more complete destruction.

"Look," said a small voice by my side.

I followed the boy's finger to the opposite side of the room. There, where the only other door to the study had been, was a nightmare tangle of splinters and loose wood. The massive oaken door had been shredded like a piece of cabbage. I think at that moment I must have been near hysteria for suddenly the analogy of the formerly imposing door with the lowly vegetable struck me as extremely humorous. I began to chuckle to myself, and was just turning to share the joke with Edward when something on his face made me stop smiling.

He was not aware of me. Calm and preoccupied, he seemed intent on studying the ravaged door.

I watched his face as the transformation took place and became complete. I saw the innocence of childhood drained away in an instant—drained away to be replaced by an abominable, hard glitter in his dull eyes. He looked up at me and smiled, childish fear gone. I could not refrain from recoiling when he turned those hard, pale eyes upon me, so full of a new, fearless knowledge of evil.

"He is here. He's going to rip Father now. Soon as he finds him."

My legs began to buckle but I somehow managed to remain standing. I began to back away toward the fireplace, away from the boy who had been my brother.

"Aren't you afraid of him any longer?" I asked.

"No," he smiled. "I didn't understand then. Now he's made me see."

"Edward," I said tremulously, "you must stop him. Where is he?"

Edward listened for a moment, his ear cocked as if receiving some silent signal.

He looked at me and gave a reassuring smile.

"He's at Father's door. He found him. It won't be long."

Although he smiled ingratiatingly at me, I saw the animal cunning that lurked behind it. The eyes were too bold and knowledgeable for a child.

"Don't you worry. He'll be here soon. But you can't see him. Nobody can but me." He smiled to himself. "And he'll rip whoever I say."

I was as terrified of the small monster in front of me as I was of the unseen thing that even now was lurking in front of my father's room. Poor Father! I could picture him, lying across his bed in a state of unconscious exhaustion from the terrible mental anguish that tormented him. Then, without warning, the door would open; he would awaken in surprise; and his son's hideous ally would be upon him. But I could not move to help him, for I was paralyzed with fear, just as I had been when Edward needed my help.

Thankfully, Edward was paying little attention to me. He was intent on listening for something. His eyes were riveted on the ceiling above the study, where Father's room was.

I watched him closely, and then I saw a tight-lipped smile spread on his face. A muffled thud penetrated the ceiling, and my gaze followed Edward's. Directly above us was Father's room. I waited expectantly.

For the third time that night the violent report of a door shattered by an unseen force rocked the walls of the house. I had scarcely formed the frozen scream of warning in my throat before the thing was done. The faintest scuttling of several heavy legs on the floor; the confused stirring of someone aroused from sleep; and then it was over. I heard the faint jangle of bed springs as they sagged under the enormous weight, and then the bed went crashing to the floor. I covered my ears with my hands to block out that dreadful scream—the scream which had never been uttered by my father, but which now clanged and echoed in my head like the peal of a bell imprisoned in the belfry.

Edward stood immobile in the middle of the room. The changeling glanced at me with a face full of unrestrained glee. He had enjoyed it.

"Edward," I rasped, my mouth dry, "you must send it away now. Father's dead."

"Can't." His lips were twisted in a cruel curve. He looked at me with a kind of breathless expectancy.

Some idea was forming beneath the abnormally bright eyes. His face was suffused with unnatural color, contrasting oddly with his usual pallor. His breath came in spasmodic gasps.

"Tell your friend to go away."

"Can't. You'll tell. He says you've got to be ripped, too. He's coming now. I hear him."

I was about to reply when I heard a slight movement from above. A series of uneven thumps rolled through the ceiling and out of hearing, down the carpeted hall. I glanced nervously through the doorway of the study to the bottom of the staircase.

"Send it away, Edward."

"Can't." Edward smiled. He sauntered lazily over to an armchair and plopped into it. He folded his thin white hands across his stomach and regarded me with an amused expression.

"You all hated to look at me. You won't have to any more because you'll all be dead."

My pretensions to remaining calm were rapidly dissipating. I began to look frantically about the room for a weapon—anything with which I might fight.

"Don't bother with that. You won't see him. You can't even touch him. But he can get you." Edward chuckled. "Oh, here he comes."

I did not need Edward's report, for I, too, had heard the slithering, sliding thump down the staircase, as if some giant six-legged bull were descending. I was nearly hysterical. More out of reflex than actual plan I grabbed the poker from the fireplace. Thus armed with this puny protection, I awaited anxiously the inevitable thud at the bottom of the stairs. Almost at the exact second that I had tensed my muscles for battle, and raised the poker aloft, the dull clatter resounded, followed by a quick shuffle as the thing approached the doorway.

Edward was in the meantime lounging comfortably across the room with an expression of sadistic amusement on his face. He looked first at me, and then at the doorway, smiling as if at an old friend. He did not speak a word, but seemed to be giving silent encouragement with his eyes.

I am not sure what moved me to edge over to Edward's chair and stand behind him—perhaps it was only the self-protective instinct to use him as a shield. But as I moved toward him with my raised poker, I was aware of some fleeting change of expression which at the time puzzled me.

It was not as if I was capable of logical reasoning during those frightening moments, for my mental state had been reduced to that of a caveman stalked by a predator. But perhaps those same instincts which lead wild animals to escape from death served me. My subconscious mind interpreted Edward's facial expression, and connected it with the cessation of the thing's progress. I moved quickly and stealthily behind Edward's chair, with no conscious will of my own.

I could hear the thing coming then, describing a wide circle around Edward's chair, so that he would not be hurt when the attack came.

So that Edward would not be hurt. The words raced through my mind like high-charged electricity. Edward. He was the key. Without him . . .

There was no more time to think. Edward had turned in the chair and was looking at me suspiciously. I think he must have guessed at that moment that I knew his secret. He gave an anxious glance over to the left, but the unseen creature had temporarily halted.

The poor child had not even time to cry out, so quickly did I smash the poker down into his skull. I hit with such force and determination that I think he must have died immediately. I glanced at his face as he fell to the floor, and saw that it still bore that look of faint astonishment with which he regarded me. He tumbled out of the chair and on to the floor, where he rolled slightly and then landed face up. Blood began to ooze from the wound in his scalp and form a brilliant puddle on the carpet.

At that moment I was still not quite sure that I had saved myself. I waited for the sound of the thing's retreat. Nothing. It did not complete the attack, nor did I hear it run away.

But somehow I knew that by the stillness which enclosed me in the study I was indeed alone. Whatever it was that Edward's mind had summoned to work his vengeance had disappeared the moment his brain had ceased to function.

I know very little about the queer workings of the psyche, but I think that that night I must have been granted some extra sense to deal with the horror that confronted me. Perhaps just as adrenaline will make our muscles work faster and more effectively in emergencies, there is a kind of spiritual adrenaline that is activated when we deal with the extraordinary.

Somehow, I sensed that even after killing Edward my task was not complete. I was not compelled to go out alone to that dark, desolate spot out of a sense of ridding humanity of a horror; I had to go to save myself.

I ran to the kitchen and searched frantically for a flashlight. I was still armed with my poker, which bore the feeble stain of Edward's blood. But I did not think of Edward, nor even of my murdered father; the dead had no interest for me. It was the living presence in the garden I had to deal with.

With no sense of fear I raced through the kitchen door and out into the garden. I walked steadily on to the shrubbery that shielded the pond and shone my light there. No need to crawl on my hands and knees to the pond this time. The shrubs and vines that had grown there had been torn up by the roots and trampled down into an unsubstantial vegetable mat. The pond and the statue were in plain view. The cherub glowed eerily in the pale light of my torch, and its usually idiotic smile was transfigured into a certain spectral impudence.

I drew closer, searching the ground carefully for a movement. I began to feel rather desperate. With all that trampled vegetation, it would be easy for the thing to hide where I might never find it. I turned the stems and vines gingerly with my poker, shining the light in every hiding place. I grew impatient, and began beating the ground wildly.

I did not at first notice a shadowy object eject itself from the web of branches at my feet. But for a sudden glimmer of light which its inky back reflected as it shot up the statue's body, I might not have seen it. I sprang to the pond in an instant and swung a wild blow at the swiftly fleeing insect. The mouldering statue caught the brunt of the blow and crashed to my feet in a thousand dusty fragments.

Only the head escaped shattering. It rolled a few feet from me into the farthermost corner of the pond. Quickly I shone my light through the black hole of its neck, where I saw two stubby antennae, bristling and waving furiously at me. The bug was curled back into the recess of the head as far from me as possible. With even more effort than I had exerted to bash in poor Edward's brains, I smashed the head of the statue. The pieces flew apart like an overripe fruit. At first I could not see the insect, and I began to fear that he had escaped me after all. I turned the fragments of the head over with the poker until at last I uncovered him—stunned but not yet dead. Quickly I recovered my blow and began beating the black beetle madly. He burst at my first indirect hit, and all his venomous life juices splurted out, staining the pond floor a murky green. I continued to beat at him until there was nothing left of his vile life—only a sickening brownish pulp that would wash away with the rains and in time be obscured by the renascence of the plant life about the dead pond.

I left that desolate spot that night and have never set foot there since. From my old room I can see that once again the shrubs have sprouted up rampantly about the pond, concealing it from any chance passers-by. Beneath the unharnessed growth of several years lie the fragments of the broken cherub, as well as other secrets of this house. With no one to play there, the spot has grown so wildly that I expect by next spring I shall not even be able to see it from my window.